HEART OF THE NILE

Also by Will Thomas

HEART OF THE NILE

THE NILE

WILL THOMAS

MINOTAUR BOOKS
NEW YORK

Published in the United States by Minotaur Books, an imprint of St. Martin's Publishing Group

HEART OF THE NILE. Copyright © 2023 by Will Thomas. All rights reserved. Printed in the United States of America. For information, address St. Martin's Publishing Group, 120 Broadway, New York, NY 10271.

www.minotaurbooks.com

The Library of Congress has cataloged the hardcover edition as follows:

Names: Thomas, Will, 1958– author.
Title: Heart of the Nile / Will Thomas.
Description: First edition. | New York : Minotaur Books, 2023. |
    Series: [A Barker & Llewelyn novel] ; [15]
Identifiers: LCCN 2022052661 | ISBN 9781250864901 (hardcover) |
    ISBN 9781250864918 (ebook)
Subjects: LCGFT: Detective and mystery fiction. | Novels.
Classification: LCC PS3620.H644 H43 2023 |
    DDC 813/.6—dc23/eng/20221104
LC record available at https://lccn.loc.gov/2022052661

ISBN 978-1-250-29202-5 (trade paperback)

Our books may be purchased in bulk for promotional, educational, or business use. Please contact your local bookseller or the Macmillan Corporate and Premium Sales Department at 1-800-221-7945, extension 5442, or by email at MacmillanSpecialMarkets@macmillan.com.

First Minotaur Books Trade Paperback Edition: 2024

10 9 8 7 6 5 4 3 2 1

HEART OF THE NILE

PROLOGUE

Boxing Day 1893

The British Museum has always had a reputation for possessing the rarest of ancient relics in its Egyptian collection. A few years earlier, in 1887, they added several new items to their archives, including a successful bid upon six mummies in a lot of antiquities at Christie's. One was of consequence, an architect from the rule of Ptolemy VII, which was in excellent condition and the specific reason for the purchase. This left the other five of indeterminate value to be catalogued and examined by a junior staff member or volunteer at a later date. The five anonymous citizens of ancient Thebes, Luxor, or Memphis had to wait in queue, however. There was a glut of mummies, which were stacked like cordwood in the bowels of the building.

There were several reasons for the overabundance. English travelers to the back streets of Cairo were often waylaid by merchants and suddenly found themselves in possession of a bagful of bones and ancient wrappings, their pockets suitably lightened. Others, in the excitement of being on the Nile, fancied themselves adventurers in search of treasures and came to their senses only when they reached British soil again. Young rakes away from home for the first time made their purchase as a lark or to impress their friends, but when being fitted for the matrimonial collar a year or two later, were forced to rid themselves of their purchase as a condition of the union. Then there were the so-called mummy parties, in which a group of gentlemen got sozzled and tried to vivisect a third-century B.C. official with no medical skills whatever. Afterward, it was off to a museum to get some money out of it. In short, it was raining mummies that season, and the only thing to do was to assign a storage room in the basement of the British Museum as the "mummy vault" and see if they could fob off the work of examining and cataloguing them onto the shoulders of an eager volunteer. Someone like Phillip Addison, for instance.

Addison was more than willing to do the work. A young man with a degree in Ancient Studies from Oxford and a teacher at St. Olave's Grammar School, Addison was blessed, or perhaps cursed, with a font of personal energy combined with drive and not a little intelligence. He suggested to the director, Clive Hennings, that he could come in during the late evenings and work to the wee hours cataloguing the mummies. In the process, he created a new and more efficient method of recording the specimens. This was a bargain the museum could not refuse. Addison was an enthusiast, literally willing to work for nothing to be a part of the famous museum. Hennings considered this a reasonable salary and let him loose in the vault, happy as a clam.

Addison's current interest was a mummy's weight after two millennia. He conjectured he might devise a formula to calculate a mummy's original weight. Most of the specimens in the collection were no heavier than a large spaniel. There was an old scale in the room, originally from the Smithfield Meat

Market, and Addison carried each mummy from its shelf to the scale and back again, as lovingly as if they were sleeping infants.

"Excuse me, Your Majesty," he said to one of his charges. "Forgive the informality."

Addison had designated mummies by location on the shelves, so that "Mummy 12/5/6" was the sixth mummy from the top in the fifth section of the twelfth row. The old pharaohs and their courtiers were resting on common shelves. Most were wrapped in canvas, or placed in sacks, but no other attempt had been made to preserve them. Someday, but not yet, Addison hoped to change that.

The young man, thirty-one last year, lifted the mummy from the lowest shelf in the sixteenth row. The canvas was covered in dust. Her card read:

Sex: Female Identification: unknown Purchased: Cairo Origin: unknown Date: 04/08/1889 Dealer: Ibn Adir Age: mature Filing location: 8/16/12 Weight: ?

He carried the canvas-wrapped specimen to the scales, and as he did so, he talked to it.

"All right, dearie," he said. "Up you go. My, we have put on a pound or two. Too many pork pies I expect, you naughty girl. However do you hope to attract a pharaoh that way?"

The mummy was almost half a stone heavier than the female before her, 2,278 grams, to be exact. He carried it to the examination table and set it down gently on the slab, the slender neck resting on a wooden block. The woman had been small. Measuring the head and torso along with the lower limbs, which had become detached at the head of the femur, he judged her to have been just under five foot tall in life. One arm had become detached as well. With some excitement, he saw that it was bent, which was a very promising sign. Not just anyone was interred with one hand upon its breast and the other at its side.

She was a horror to look at, but then put a demimondaine in sand for two thousand years and see how she fares. Her skin was brown as an old saddle, her nose and cheekbones sharp. The rats had nibbled at her ears and her eyes had shriveled in their sockets. Still, Addison had seen worse. Much worse, in fact.

He heard a far-off tolling and fished out his watch. It was midnight exactly, time for good husbands to be abed. He thought of his wife, Elizabeth, asleep and alone, while here he was mucking about with another woman in the middle of the night. That weight, however, he thought. It wasn't right.

"What's your secret, darling?" he murmured. "You can tell me."

He lifted her off the table again. Inspired, he jumped up and down once. Sometimes the simplest method is the most logical, but nothing happened. He tried again. There was a hollow thump inside the mummy. A final jump. Yes, he heard a definite knock.

"Ah," he said. "You've swallowed something, you little minx."

Setting down the mummy again, he reached for a lens and began inspecting the torso inch by inch. There was a plaster cartouche attached to the navel, but it was too faint for him to read by the feeble gas lamps in the room. Addison persevered, looking for an opening. There had to be one in order to both remove the organs and insert an object inside. But what could it be? A small burial urn, perhaps.

Addison pushed on the ancient corpse's abdomen. He heard a crunch, and a vertical crease appeared in the stiff skin. He found a fissure at the top, just under the sternum, which had been covered by old wrappings and coated in bitumen. It followed the natural line of the rib cage and was just wide enough to slip a few fingers into.

"Hold still, old girl," he murmured. "This might hurt."

Addison lifted a large pair of forceps and pushed the tips

inside the chest cavity. He was doing this all wrong, he knew. There needed to be a supervisor or assistant in attendance in case anything of consequence was found. Proper notes should be taken, but he was too curious. There was also the danger he could cut himself on something sharp and unleash an ancient plague on unsuspecting London. Still, he was eager and ambitious, not just for himself. Poor Elizabeth hadn't had a new frock in the two years they had been married. Women needed things, he'd discovered.

Impatient, he tossed the forceps aside and pushed his fingertips under the resinous wrappings. There was more stiff material inside. Then his fingertip grazed something hard. That was strange, he thought. The cavity should be empty. The organs would have been removed and put into jars during the mummification process. He knew that according to ancient Egyptian custom, the heart should be in place for the god Ra to weigh it against the feather of the goddess Maat, so her spirit would be given entrance into the afterlife. Humble as his life was now, he'd have a better eternity than this wretched woman, relegated to a bottom shelf in a faraway land for all eternity.

He took up the forceps and opened them as wide as they would go, but it was not far enough. Frustrated, he threw them on the floor with a clatter in the dusty stillness of the vault.

"What's your secret?" he demanded. "You can tell me."

It was back to the fingers, then. Momentarily he thought of the plague again, but plague be damned. This was important. He seized the crusty cloth and began to tug at the stiff fabric wrapped around the object. His hand finally closed around it just enough to get a purchase, but it wouldn't budge. He felt like the boy in the Aesop fable with his hand full of filberts stuck in a jar. The mummy refused to give up its prize.

"Let go, I say," Addison muttered. He pulled with greater force and there was a muffled crack. Hennings, the head of the department, would have something to say about his mummy.

Or rather, the British Museum's mummy, that hallowed institution he wanted so desperately to impress.

Finally, the lump came out with a sound like a matchbox being opened, and a sigh escaped the long-dead woman. He carried it to a second table and lit a lamp nearby, looking at the wrapped item, which was oblong and roughly the size of a grapefruit. Eagerly, he began ripping at the bandages, like a package on Christmas morning. Like yesterday morning, in fact.

At last, he uncovered his prize. It was a brick, a common-looking brick: ruddy, scraped, and broken. He wanted to throw it after the forceps. He gave a sigh, just as the mummy had given when she'd parted with it, and then patted the ancient shoulder joint, fragile as glass.

"It's not your fault," he told her. "Obviously, you didn't put it there yourself."

He turned his attention to the brick again and saw that it had yellowish veins running through it. Addison paused, frowning. Egyptian bricks weren't red. He lifted the object to the lamp. Immediately the chamber was bathed in a scarlet glow. He turned it over, wondering if it was glass, but no dynasty he could recall made glass objects this large.

Then he gasped, and his chest began to hammer. It wasn't a brick at all. The shape seemed familiar, but for a moment he couldn't work out what it was. Then he clapped his hands to his forehead. It was the shape of a human heart. What else would one expect to find in a chest cavity?

His legs nearly went out from under him. He seized a chair by the desk and fell into it just in time, barking his shin. Turning the stone over in his hands, he cursed, and the sound echoed in the chamber.

Addison pushed himself to his feet. This could be a major discovery. Hennings had to be notified immediately. Of course, he'd be angry at being disturbed after midnight, but that would change soon enough. It would be the making of both their careers and another addition to the museum's outstanding collection.

"Sorry, my dear," he called over his shoulder. "Stay here! I'll be back soon."

He jammed a disreputable trilby on his head and stuffed the object into the pocket of his coat, then hurried down the hall and out the back door, which shut behind him with a finality. It was bitterly cold, but he'd pawned his greatcoat. There were loiterers in the street, talking and laughing raucously as he clutched the stone in his pocket. Who knew how much it was worth? Suddenly every man in Russell Square seemed to have a sinister aspect. Perhaps he should turn 'round and take it back. Then he realized he had no key and the night janitor was notoriously hard of hearing. He didn't want to be accused of theft, but then one couldn't be accused of stealing something the museum didn't know it had. Or could one?

To Addison's credit, he didn't think of selling it on the black market or to a private collector like Lord Grayle, a prominent member of Parliament who, though a member of the museum board, had an unscrupulous reputation. His Lordship would buy an illegal antiquity and never tell a soul. However, this wasn't just any antiquity. Who could even determine how much this was worth?

Phillip Addison felt exposed. It had been an act of lunacy to take the stone beyond the safety of the museum's walls. He could be beaten and the object stolen. Or he could be arrested, his feeble reputation ruined. Should he take it to Hennings or would his superior consider it an act of outright theft? In half an hour he could be a hero, or he could be headed for a cell at Scotland Yard. He had an urge to run, but where? He could throw the stone through one of the windows, but Hennings knew where he lived and worked.

Addison blinked and stepped back as a hansom cab bowled past. The streets were nearly empty now, due to the cold, but it only made the danger more palpable. He cursed himself for getting locked out of the museum. *Bad decision, Phillip! What were you thinking?*

Then it came to him. There was one person he could trust who had a perfect place to keep the treasure safe and sound. His stomach relaxed and he took a deep breath. Grasping the heavy object in his pocket but trying not to hurry, he crossed the street.

In the quiet of the vault the Nile Queen lay exposed yet somehow still regal on the marble table, her nest of tawny braids resting on the wooden block. She'd waited two millennia for this time. Another day or two wouldn't matter.

CHAPTER 1

A shiny new Royal Warrant issued by Queen Victoria herself was attached to the hoarding above our door. That door was freshly painted a deep yellow, and there was never so enticing an enquiry agency in all Craig's Court as ours. We were prosperous and successful. Cyrus Barker's name and even my own were bandied about the great city of London. All that and our chambers were empty. Keenly empty, achingly empty, profoundly empty, and had been for two days. At that moment, we were without client and there was no certainty that one would appear that day, or that week. No one had requested an appointment. No one from Scotland Yard had stopped by. The Wheels of Commerce, as far as our occupation was concerned, had ground to a halt.

I blamed the weather. It had been a frigid Christmas and every house was temporarily well-stocked with food and treats and things to do. No one thought of poor enquiry agents scratching out a meager existence. Very well; it wasn't meager. It only felt that way.

"Have you got those case notes for the Emberley business typed?" my partner growled from his green castored chair.

"Typed and filed," I replied.

"Mmmph."

Barker tends to brood when there are no cases at the door, though perhaps brooding is too romantic a term. He was irritable, and when he is irritable it is like being locked in a cage with an old lion. He paces. He stares out the window. He sits and a moment later stands again. I looked at our clerk for sympathy but Jeremy Jenkins was sitting behind a newspaper dozing. I dug into my pocket for my watch and flipped it open. It was almost nine o'clock.

"Go, then," the Guv barked.

"What? I was just sitting here!"

Very well, perhaps I was irritable as well, but it was his fault. I was an innocent victim.

"You opened your watch and looked relieved. The bookstores in Charing Cross will open in a few minutes and you were hoping to sneak out the door when my back was turned."

"As a matter of fact," I said, "I no longer have to sneak anywhere since I have become a partner."

"A junior partner," he clarified.

"Senior enough to nip out to a bookstore when I wish," I replied. "I'll be back in half an hour."

His eyes would have burnt a hole in my suit were they not covered by his black-lensed spectacles. I walked out serenely, an act that would have gotten me sacked five years before.

If I have one weakness, it would be a love for collecting books. If you like a book, it will become an old friend. If you don't, it can warm you in the grate. I have dozens in my rooms in Newington, more in the library on the ground floor, which my partner and I share, and still more at the house my wife inherited, which we visit a few times a week. There are more than I will ever read, but like every other book collector, I tell myself it will be for my old age, as if I would stop collecting even then. On my last day on earth, I expect to stop into a bookshop at least once, probably there in Charing Cross. There's something sacrosanct about the area.

The tables in Charing Cross Road had been carried outside and were filled when I arrived, though the street was dusted with snow. I would allow myself one book only, knowing the sight of any more would only poke the lion further. I was looking for a collection of Ben Jonson's plays in one volume, a hole in my education I hoped to darn, and as luck would have it I found a copy in fine condition published in 1825. I much prefer an old copy to a new one, if the boards are sound and the inner hinge uncracked. I paid the owner a few coins but left a little disappointed. It had been too easy. It was like traveling to the country to go grouse shooting and having a beater flush one right off and you shooting reflexively. The deed is done before you have the chance to savor it. Or so I would imagine. I've never shot a grouse in my life.

When I returned I stamped my feet on the mat, both to shake the snow from my boots and to get the circulation going in my limbs.

"It's brass monkeys out there!" I complained to our clerk.

Jenkins smiled but held a finger to his lips. He nodded toward our chambers. *O frabjous day,* I thought. A visitor at last.

I stepped through the door and found a prospective client sitting in our visitor's chair. However, Barker was having a time of it and I almost felt sorry for him. A young woman was wringing a handkerchief in her hands and he was all nerves, afraid she would cry. He cannot abide strong emotion. Bawling women, children, and even high opera sets him on edge. When he saw me, he jumped to his feet with relief.

"I'm Thomas Llewelyn, ma'am, at your service," I said, coming forward. "How may we help you?"

"My name is Elizabeth Addison, and my husband has gone missing," she said in a ragged voice. "He went to work last night and has not returned."

"Mr. Addison volunteers at the British Museum at night in the Egyptology Department," Barker stated.

"Just disappeared, then, without a trace?" I asked. "Has he ever done that before?"

"No!" she replied. "Not once. He's home the minute he can get away. This is completely unlike him."

She was a good-looking young woman, a petite blonde whose dress was attractive enough but far from new, her boots the same. It appeared the couple had fallen on hard times. I've known poverty well in my life and recognize it at once.

"He volunteers?" I asked. "What is your husband's occupation, if I may ask?"

"He is a schoolmaster at St. Olave's School," she replied. "He teaches history."

"Mr. Addison has a strong interest in Egyptology," Barker explained. "He works at the British Museum three nights a week."

"Phillip hopes to earn a position there soon," the woman said. "He'll do anything anyone asks. He loves the work. I tease him that he loves it more than me. More than anything, he'd like to go to Egypt and participate in an excavation. I'm afraid he lets his enthusiasm get the better of him."

Barker and I glanced at each other. If what she said was true, Phillip Addison was unlikely to have a mistress or anything of the sort, and if something had occurred, he would have sent word to her as soon as he possibly could. We had a sense of foreboding, but neither of us would voice it.

Barker handed me a pocket photograph of Mr. Addison. He was in his early thirties, as I was, a genial-looking, slender fellow with a short beard and a tight collar. He needed a haircut. They looked suited to each other, a matched pair.

"Mrs. Addison," Barker rumbled. "Was there anything unusual in your husband's behavior before he left for the museum yesterday evening?"

"No, sir," she replied. "He was in an excellent mood. He told me about a drawing one of the boys had made on the chalkboard in his classroom. I had to convince him that he did not look like Mr. Darwin's missing link. We talked of going for a skate in Battersea Park on Sunday."

"Is there anyone with whom your husband is on bad terms?" I asked. "A family member, perhaps?"

Mrs. Addison put her handkerchief in a reticule and snapped it shut.

"He is cut off from his family, unfortunately," she said. "I have no family, either, save a sister in Southend-on-Sea, so you see, we feel quite alone in the world. Phillip has no enemies. He's very kind and amiable."

It's easy to think the worst of people in our profession. One sees such evil at times. I wondered if he were as good-natured when he was away from her. It takes a good deal to be shunned by one's family.

That being said, I understood her meaning. Though my wife and I each had family, we felt alone in the world as well. If I had been prevented from returning to her, I would be frantic to send word. Likewise, Rebecca would do anything to find me, including hunting for me herself, no matter the danger or damage to her reputation.

"Who is his superior at the museum?" Barker asked in his deep basso voice.

"Dr. Hennings," she replied. "He is the head of the Egyptology Department."

I scribbled the name in my notebook.

"Did you communicate with him?" the Guv continued.

"I left messages, but was told he is busy or out of town. The secretary I spoke to was not helpful. I assume it was because of my sex. Scotland Yard was the same. I came here because I thought a gentleman might be more likely to be able to speak to Mr. Hennings."

Barker nodded. "Has your husband any friends at the museum, anyone to discuss Egyptology with, perhaps?"

She shook her head. "No, sir. As far as I know he's alone there in the evening. He works from eight to midnight. He and the janitor have the establishment to themselves."

"That is unusual, is it not?" Barker asked. "Your husband, a mere volunteer, working at night?"

"It is," I spoke up. "The museum closes at nine, and they herd the public out the door efficiently and without any nonsense."

"Phillip enjoys the quiet," Elizabeth Addison explained. "He spends all morning with rambunctious students and finds his work at the museum soothing. 'Just me and the mummies,' he says. 'And they don't talk much.'"

Dried cadavers, more like, I said to myself. I'm not the type to crawl about in tombs looking for forgotten kings. If they stayed buried, it would be no loss to me.

"You say he hopes to work at the museum permanently?" Barker asked.

"Yes," Mrs. Addison answered. "The few positions are highly sought after, and unlike some, we don't have a personal fortune to help support the museum."

That last remark was rather arch, I thought. No doubt Addison had been passed over in favor of an earl's son or two. Even an earl's son might covet the prestige of working in the British Museum, one of the greatest institutions in the world. I thought if we found and restored Addison to his wife, we might be in a position to help him. The British Museum is one of the institutions to which Barker donates. I know because I write the cheques for him.

Elizabeth Addison cleared her throat and looked down at her

reticule, playing with the clasp. She was embarrassed but would see it through for her husband's sake. She steeled herself and spoke.

"Is hiring an enquiry agent terribly expensive?" she asked. "Of course, I'm willing to sell all we own to find him if necessary."

Her cheeks flushed, and to some degree, so did the Guv's. Barker is uncomfortable discussing money, perhaps because he has so much of it. As a ship's captain in China, he'd found a sunken ship whose proceeds allowed him to move to London and open our agency. He was wealthy but had endured privation for much of his life. We all had.

"I would not charge you a fee to talk to the museum director, ma'am," he answered. "Allow me to speak to him and we can discuss the best course of action afterward."

She rose, clutching her bag as if it were a shield against the world's ills. She put out her hand awkwardly and Barker took it in like manner. He bowed like a courtier, and she bobbed a curtsy. Then I saw her out.

Barker walked to the window and watched her leave.

"Poor woman," he said.

"You think the man dead?" I asked.

"Don't you?" he responded. "Would you not move heaven and earth to return to Mrs. Llewelyn's side?"

"You know I would. I was thinking of that myself."

"That is all that need be said. However, Mrs. Addison is right to be concerned, and it costs us nothing to look for him."

"And we have no other client at present," I noted.

"Precisely." There was a drop of acid in his tone.

"The museum it is, then," I said, reaching for my bowler and scarf.

I love the British Museum. When I first came to London, I was able to use a recommendation from a gentleman in my town in Wales to avail myself of the Reading Room. I spent many an hour there, not only in study but as an escape from my cold, drafty room. It is the greatest museum in the world, and if I spent every minute of my life studying there and examining the exhibits I would barely scratch the service. Lord knows, I tried. I was fresh from prison and on my own and I needed something to hold me together. It was a second womb to me.

Bloomsbury became popular a century ago and still has not lost its regal charm. The present building replaced a mansion, Montagu House, in 1759, and has been enlarged ever since, first one wing, then another. As I recalled, it all began when a crafty devil named Sloane, rather than seeing his private collection of curiosities plundered by relatives, donated it all to George II. George thus felt obliged to put the collection somewhere. Hence the museum.

The building itself is large and intimidating. Every time I step through the stately front doors I feel as if some official will seize me by the scruff of the neck and toss me out again. Not Barker, of course. He strolled in as if he owned the place and was paying for its upkeep. But then, as I said, he was. That might work in our favor.

"Your shoes are squeaking," Barker remarked after we crossed the lobby.

"I don't carry another pair," I retorted. "I've never heard a building echo so much. Where do we begin? Shall I ask for the Egyptology Department at the front desk?"

"No, I prefer to ramble, I think."

We did so for a quarter hour at least, playing at tourists. Barker was impressed by the Reading Room, having seen it only once before. When we reached a staircase, we climbed it on the assumption that powerful men do not dwell in basements. Eventually we found ourselves at the director's office.

"How can I help you, gentlemen?" the man's secretary asked.

"We'd like to speak to the director," Barker stated.

The man smiled politely. We knew not what we asked, apparently. I could see him looking us over, pricing our boots, waistcoats, and ties, and weighing them against the fact that Barker looked like a ruffian. A well-dressed one, of course, but a ruffian nonetheless.

"I can schedule an appointment for you next Tuesday," he replied. "I'm afraid it's the best I can do."

It was Barker's turn to smile. "I'm sure you'll find my name on your list of donors."

I pulled a business card from my pocket and pitched it across his desk. He seized and studied it, knowing it would be rude to make us sit while he looked for Barker's name among the contributors, and tried to triangulate how large a quarterly donation would allow him to break in upon the director. He looked worried. He couldn't see Barker's eyes, so he looked in mine. I gave him an impatient look.

Finally, the secretary cleared his throat and excused himself, stepping into the office behind him. A plaque on the wall informed us that the director's name was Edward Maund Thompson. When one attains a certain level in society one is obliged to dig about in the family archives for a third name.

"The director will see you now," the secretary stated as if bestowing upon us a great honor.

We bowed and entered as the director came around his desk. If I were to cast a play featuring a museum director, I would hire him on the spot. Thompson was tall, thin, and stately looking, with a graying beard and formal day apparel. He was a hybrid of scholar and businessman, moving freely between both fields of endeavor. I'll grant that at first appearance he seemed highly capable of doing both.

"Gentlemen!" Thompson said, putting out a hand, as if he came that day hoping we would appear at his door. Barker took the hand but as before with Mrs. Addison, the exchange was awkward. I knew why, however. I recognized a Masonic handshake, subtle as it was. Thompson harrumphed and the three of us sat.

"How may I help you, gentlemen?" he asked.

Barker cleared his throat. "Last night, a volunteer in this building stepped out the door around midnight and disappeared. His wife visited our chambers this morning quite concerned. We have agreed to look for her husband."

"His name, please?"

"Phillip Addison," the Guv replied.

The director looked to the ceiling, running through names in his memory. I took the time to look about the room, which was well furnished but not opulent. I thought another director would have stuffed an extra thousand pounds' worth of furniture into the room without effort.

"He left around midnight, you say?" he asked after a moment. "We close our doors at nine. Employees are encouraged to leave within half an hour."

"Mrs. Addison intimated that her husband had an arrangement with the man for whom he was volunteering," I supplied.

"Who was that man?" Thompson asked.

"A Dr. Hennings."

"Clive, yes," he replied. "His department is one of the busiest. Sometimes he uses volunteers. I have not overseen what he does since he is so capable, but perhaps it is time that I should. We can't have volunteers just disappearing. Has she gone to the Metropolitan Police Department?"

"She came to us first, sir."

"For everyone's sake, we'd like this matter resolved with as little publicity as possible. Dr. Hennings should be in the building now, but I'm afraid I have a meeting in a few minutes. The Egyptology Department is just below the ground floor in the East Wing."

My partner rose immediately, so I did as well.

He bowed. "Thank you for seeing us without an appointment."

"I hope you find the fellow," Thompson said.

"Oh, we shall, sir," Barker said. "You may count on that."

I nodded at the director's puzzled look and tipped my hat. Then I hurried out the door. The Guv, like Time and Tide, waiteth for no man.

We wandered for a while again, descending into the bowels of the building where there was no marble, only corridors with walls dented by carts and rooms with no obvious purpose. The lower levels seemed deserted in the middle of the day. No one questioned our right to be there or showed the slightest interest in us until we came to one corridor where a crowd had gathered. I hazarded a guess that this was where everyone had gone.

Like bees in an apiary, workers dipped into and out of an unmarked room. We sauntered down the hall until we came to the open door and peered in. A half dozen men were huddled around a table that looked like a makeshift operating theater. The patient, I realized, was a mummy. Two of the men held lamps aloft, and a third had the largest lens I'd ever seen, over a foot in diameter. There was a sense of suppressed excitement I hadn't felt since my university days. Perhaps it was my professional instincts, but I got the feeling they were hiding their activities from Director Thompson. Barker came to the same conclusion. There was a slight smile under the shelf of a mustache he wore.

Our presence was noted then. Everyone shuffled to hide the still figure on the examination table, and the fellow holding the magnifying lens came toward us. He stepped out the door, closed it behind him, and leaned against it.

"This is a private area, gentlemen, restricted to employees only," he said. "You must be lost."

"There is that possibility, sir," the Guv said. "Unless your name is Hennings. If so, my partner and I are where we should be."

"Gentlemen, I don't have the time for riddles. Pray state your business."

"Very well," Barker replied. "We are enquiry agents investigating the disappearance of Phillip Addison. I believe he works for you."

Hennings's back went stiff, so that he nearly knocked the back of his skull against the door. "Do you work for Scotland Yard?"

"No," the Guv admitted. "However, we frequently work with them and are well known there."

Yes, I thought. *Well-known for causing trouble.*

"I understand Mr. Addison worked last night," the Guv continued.

"He did, but let us not gossip in the hall. Come to my office." He stepped back into the room to tell his colleagues he'd return shortly. Then he closed the door again.

"Step this way, please," he said.

If Hennings expected to shake my partner's hand, he would be disappointed. Barker had exceeded his limit for the day and Hennings was but a humble department head. If Mrs. Addison's statements were correct, it was a position some might kill to attain. Or to keep, I suppose.

CHAPTER 2

Clive Hennings led us to his office. Over the fireplace was a large and impressive painting of an archeological dig, in which the central character held aloft a crown from a tomb that had just been unearthed by the North African workers who surrounded him. They looked up with wonder at the Englishman, who just happened to look like Hennings. Perhaps it was him, but the cynic in me wondered if one could get ahead in the business of archeology by hiring a painter to re-create one's own likeness on an established painting: *Man with Crown, Pose #7.*

There were bookcases surrounding the room and I stepped closer to take a look. I had not realized that there were so many books written about Ancient Egypt. It was a dry and dusty subject.

"Have a seat, gentleman," Hennings said. "I'm concerned about Phillip, I don't mind telling you. He's a serious young man, not the sort to disappear like this. I can't imagine where he's gone."

Hennings was a man of average height with a bluff manner and a clean-shaven cherubic face. His skin was bronzed the color of a walnut. He was about forty-five years of age, sturdily built but not heavy. I could easily picture him ordering native workmen about and ducking into tombs. I supposed it was a powerful position, being head of the Egyptian collection of the British Museum. His whole manner seemed to say, "This is where a man can go if he applies himself."

"Has there been any word?" he continued. "I'd consider looking for him myself, but we are quite busy. I'm glad his wife had the presence of mind to hire someone."

"You will be the second person we've spoken to about Mr. Addison," the Guv said. "And of course a wife tends to be biased toward her husband. As a more objective observer and an employer, what impressions have you gathered about him?"

"Since he first arrived, I have been highly impressed," Hennings stated. "In fact, I thought him a gift from the gods. He is intelligent, but I don't believe he realizes his own abilities. A young man like that shouldn't work for nothing. He is full of new ideas and the ways of implementing them. In fact, I have been asking our director for the funds to hire a permanent assistant. He'd be helpful."

"If he is as gifted as you say, why was he not employed fully already?"

Hennings smiled but there was a tinge of sadness to it. "So far Egyptology is a wealthy man's hobby, with digs often paid for by families or sponsors. Phillip dresses like a church mouse. His knowledge is excellent but sometimes it is obvious that it was learned in books. He's is out of his depth when more experienced men discuss what is necessary to accomplish a task. In other words, it is a closed society, and he is excluded. He asked to work at night partly because some of the fellows you just saw are not particularly friendly. I hoped that as my assistant he could gain some polish and gather the knowledge and connections necessary to be competitive here."

"When did you last see Mr. Addison?" Barker asked.

"This morning," he replied.

"Today?"

"Yes, very early. Around one o'clock in the morning, I think. He arrived at my door and woke me from a sound sleep. I'd never seen him so elated. He claimed he'd made a great discovery, and that I needed to dress and come with him to the museum immediately. It concerned a mummy that had been in our collection for years."

"What did you do?" Barker asked.

"What could I do but send him home with a flea in his ear?" Hennings replied. "He was green, gentlemen, and didn't know that all of us make a discovery now and again that we think will shake the pillars of Egyptology and make us famous men. That almost never happens, however, and like as not, most of the discoveries come to naught. I said I'd investigate what he found in the morning, and the moment he finished his school day he should come and see me and we'd discuss it."

"And did he?" I asked. "Make a discovery, I mean?"

"Oh, yes! Rather. I feel churlish now for how I treated him. I assume he'd left in a fit of pique at my rudeness, then had gone off and got drunk or something, which would have been perfectly appropriate. I called his school, but they said he hadn't come to work this morning. His wife has no telephone set, and there was the discovery to consider."

Our patience was wearing thin.

"What discovery?" Barker growled.

"I'm afraid that is museum business, except to say that it appears to be a large discovery indeed. Either it is chance, or Phillip really has a fine career ahead of him. I choose to think the latter."

I thought we were at an impasse, but Barker did not. He stared at Hennings; that is, he presented two mirrored disks in the form of his darkened spectacles until the Egyptologist looked away.

"Not good enough, Mr. Hennings," the Guv said. "You must tell us what Phillip Addison was doing shortly after midnight on the twenty-sixth of December or we will pass such facts as we possess to Scotland Yard. In fact, they must be notified; it is simply a matter of when. What are you doing so secretively that even Mr. Thompson has not been informed?"

Hennings sat up to defend himself. "It is not a secret. I must present a report to Thompson properly researched and with citations or I'd be like Phillip, appearing with large pronouncements but very little evidence. This is the British Museum. We owe it to the public not to be slapdash or hasty in our pronouncements, especially over a matter of this importance."

"What importance, sir?" Barker purred like a cat about to devour a mouse between its claws.

"It is private museum business."

Barker frowned. "Is it really? We've just come from the director's office. Mr. Thompson claims to know nothing about it or even about Addison. Perhaps we should return there if we seek clearer answers."

The man gave a sigh. Cyrus Barker was not going to let this alone.

"Yes, sir," I said. "Didn't Mr. Thompson mention having a closer hand in the Egyptology Department?"

"He did."

"Very well, gentlemen," Hennings said. "Let us visit the mummy vault."

We followed him down the hall to the anonymous door again. He stepped inside and spoke for a moment or two with his assistants. They filed out the door in a petulant manner. A few cast resentful glances in our direction.

"Come in, gentlemen!"

The room consisted of rows of shelving, an operating theater table, and a large scale. A mummy was lain on the table,
partially in pieces. It was brown as tobacco after aging for two
thousand years, and it was female. It hadn't occurred to me that
women were also mummified. She lay stiffly, one arm across her
breastbone, the other at her side. Due to desiccation, she was rail
thin, her features taut, the skin stretched across her face so that
the lips were drawn back almost to her ears. Her cheekbones
were prominent, the skin nearly broken by the sharpness of the
bone. Her eyes had collapsed from the lack of moisture, her lids
mostly closed. Her nose was aquiline and so fragile it looked like
it could break from being touched. The most remarkable thing,
however, was her hair. It was braided in long, thin plaits, dozens
of them, and had been wrapped in a loose circle with her head
resting atop it. The hair was a rusty reddish color.

"Apparently, this mummy has been here for several years
without drawing attention," Hennings explained. "It was purchased in a lot and considered of little account in comparison
with the others. Once a mummy is broken like this it loses its
appeal for some archeologists. It's also missing any sort of sarcophagus or coffin, so it would be difficult to identify. She was
an important person, that is obvious from how she was mummified, but any jewels, headdress, or identifying items have
either been thieved long ago or more recently when she was
unearthed, wherever or whenever that was. She is a mystery."

"More likely she is a conundrum," Barker replied, "or you
would not have gathered a team to examine her."

I looked at them, perplexed. When one got down to it, this
was just a corpse, ancient though it was. It had surrendered its
gender and become a thing, mere bones and dried sinews. Yet
they called it "she" like it was a living thing.

"A conundrum," Hennings repeated. "Yes, decidedly, and for
more than one reason. Do you notice this fissure here below the
breastbone? It was probably made last night by Phillip Addison.

He was instructed not to do anything but weigh and catalogue the mummies, because he is not qualified to perform any examination. I'll have some words for him when he returns. You note an opening here? We believe something was in the hollow cavity where the organs once lay."

He inserted his fingers an inch under the mummy's breastbone to show where it was.

"What was it?" I asked.

"We haven't the slightest idea. The cavity should contain a heart. All other organs are removed from a mummy during the embalming process and put in jars, but nothing is added. Certainly not inserted. Also, whatever it was, it's large, at least the size of a fist. You see the diameter of the opening? Phillip was careful. He would not make an incision any wider than was necessary to remove the object."

"What became of it?" Barker asked.

"We don't know that, either," Hennings admitted. We've searched the vault inch by inch. There was nothing placed on my desk, and Phillip's locker is empty. He told me he had come to my house directly from the museum, so his wife would not have it. I would assume it was on his person, but it would have bulged enough to be obvious to me. It might even have been heavy. I feel justified in believing that they disappeared together, though that seems unlike Phillip."

"But you just said he didn't have it with him when he came to your house," I reminded him.

The department director crossed his arms, which I considered a defensive posture. "Yes, but he could have hidden it in the bushes or employed an accomplice."

"An accomplice?" I asked. "So you do consider it theft."

Hennings nodded. "What else are we to think? Whatever he found is now gone, as is he. The object could be quite valuable. In fact, we are positive it is. Phillip was a poor man. Now look, gentlemen, there could be some other explanation, and I am willing to give him the benefit of the doubt, but his behavior is against him. At some point it will be out of my hands. I'll have to inform Thompson. Phillip has placed me in a position where I shall be blamed for giving him the run of the place. It's possible the boy walked off with a priceless treasure."

"Why do you consider the possibility that the object may be priceless?" Barker demanded.

Again, Hennings demurred, not wanting to give away British Museum secrets. The Guv looked menacing, which he does very well. Reluctantly, Hennings continued. He leaned over the ghastly spectacle on the table.

"Look carefully, gentlemen. Do you see the faint hieroglyphs across this piece of plaster? That is called a cartouche. It represents the name or title of a particular person. If you had studied history at Oxford, you'd recognize the cartouche immediately."

"I did," I told him.

He handed me the outsized lens and I studied it carefully. As he said, it was very faint, and the course I had taken had been ten years earlier. That cartouche did look familiar, though. I stopped and stared at him.

"It isn't," I said.

"It might be," he responded.

"That's impossible."

"No, it isn't, merely unlikely. Certainly, it is important enough to consider."

Cyrus Barker frowned.

"What are the two of you blathering about?" he demanded.

"He thinks it's Cleopatra," I said.

Hennings held up a finger. "It is Cleopatra, according to the cartouche," he said. "However, there were several Cleopatras in the Ptolemaic line. The famous one, the one who seduced Julius Caesar and Mark Antony, was Cleopatra VII."

"William Shakespeare," Barker murmured. "*Antony and Cleopatra,* correct?"

"'Age cannot wither, nor custom stale her infinite variety,'" Hennings quoted.

"'Other women cloy the appetites they feed, but she makes hungry where most she satisfies,'" I added. "Act two, scene two."

Perhaps feeling he had revealed too much, Hennings began to dissemble. "Of course, there are dozens of hurdles that must be jumped before daring to suggest that this mummy is she. I have promised myself I would not be rash. There are too many other possibilities."

"Such as?" I asked.

"Such as the chance that the mummy was used to smuggle something out of Egypt. It's not unheard of. Near Eastern traders will employ any dodge. They are thieves and rascals all."

"If one were trying to smuggle an artifact out of Egypt, the last thing one would do is put a famous cartouche on it to attract attention," Barker countered.

"But still," I said. "Cleopatra. The most famous woman in history. You're saying they just happened to use her body to smuggle something to Europe?"

"That would be extraordinary," Hennings admitted. "But it's only one of a half dozen theories my lads have been voicing today."

"Gentlemen," Hennings continued. "I fear I have given you the wrong impression about Phillip. I don't want to see him punished. Far from it! If this proves to be Cleopatra's mummy, he will become famous and his future will be assured. He'll finally get the opportunity to attend a dig in Egypt, and his church-mouse days will be behind him. Phillip would get the credit for the discovery. That is, we both would. My name would be paired with his. It's standard procedure. There is more at stake here than you realize, gentlemen. If the mummy were proved to be Cleopatra, there would be an announcement made to the international press. The museum would launch a major exhibition. Egyptologists from all over the world would be forced to admit that the British Museum's resources are the greatest. I don't know if Phillip is feeling low or nursing a sore head in a public house somewhere, but you must find him. His time is now and his place here. You must find him!"

"We shall," Barker stated, as if it were a foregone conclusion. "Come, Thomas."

We went our way. Barker and I climbed the stair to the ground floor and when we reached the lobby again went to the Reading Room. There Barker spoke to the librarians, who provided him with three different books about Cleopatra and a fourth on Egyptian mummification. He took the first three and sat, while I took the last to the old chair I'd been visiting for a decade, with its cracked, turquoise-colored leather back and the "CD" carved on one leg, which I knew had not been carved by a bored Charles Dickens but still secretly hoped and believed it was.

The book in my hands was gruesome. I believe the Egyptians were an amazingly advanced civilization for their time, but I'll take the modern age, thank you very much. When I die, put me in a box, drop it in the earth, say a few words, and have done with it. Don't try to remove my brain through my nose and have me desiccated so that an ignoramus in the nineteenth century can decide I am medicinal and grind my bones for a tisane or to put me in pills.

A thought occurred to me, and I looked about. An acquaintance of mine haunted the Reading Room and might have some answers for us. I didn't see him there that day. That was highly unusual, since to my knowledge he'd never missed a day of work, or even an hour. One could set a watch by his movements. I noted that Barker was still in his chair not far away, reading. It made me pause. I'd purchased a book that morning during business hours and now Barker was reading in the middle of the day. Just when you think you have the world worked out, they change the rules.

"Excuse me," I said to a librarian at the desk. "Is Liam Grant here today?"

"No, sir," the young man said. "He isn't. We've been expecting him all morning."

"Has anyone gone to his rooms?"

The young man shrugged. "I don't know, sir."

"It is your job to know things," I told him. "You are a librarian. I can get a shrug from a bootblack."

"I'm sorry, sir," he said.

Now there were two men missing and one of them a friend. Barker set the books on the counter beside me, nodded to the librarian, and left. I gave the man a final look of disapproval and followed after.

CHAPTER 3

We lunched at a tavern across the street. When we entered, I surveyed the room. It was noon precisely.

"For whom are you looking?" the Guv demanded. "I also saw you searching for someone in the Reading Room not half an hour ago."

"I have a friend who inhabits the museum," I answered. "He was nowhere to be found this morning. His name is Liam Grant."

Barker took a swallow of stout from his pint glass and set it down again.

"Grant," he said. "You've spoken of him before. He is your first Watcher, is he not?"

"He is."

The term was Barker's, which he uses to describe a person he could rely upon to provide information or help during a case. An enquiry agent cannot be expected to know everything, so he must rely upon men in various fields who have expertise, even if that expertise involves nobbling someone's knee. Grant had once been instrumental in solving a case, thereby becoming my first Watcher, at least in Barker's eyes. To me, Liam was simply a friend.

"Are you concerned about him?" the Guv asked.

"I am," I admitted. "He practically lives there."

"Does he reside nearby?"

"Just down the street, actually. His flat faces the museum."

"How convenient," he stated. "I imagine that must cost a wee bit."

"He's not a librarian as such. He is a gentleman," I replied. "He has the funds, the freedom, and the time to indulge himself. I gather that was not always the case. He was a Grub Street hack until he was bequeathed a tidy sum by a maiden aunt. Now his life revolves around the British Museum."

"He sounds eccentric," Barker said, biting into his bacon sandwich. The bacon is very fatty there, I've found, which Barker enjoys, generally accompanied by pickled onions. I cannot abide either. I ordered shepherd's pie. As we ate, a thousand remarks came into my head regarding eccentricities, but I wasn't going to be foolish enough to say any of them.

"Yes, decidedly."

"I would like to meet this fellow."

"I would appreciate it," I admitted. "I'm concerned."

Barker finished his sandwich, took a final pull of his stout, and brushed his mustache with a serviette. "Let us pay him a visit, then, shall we?"

I paid for our meal and we left. Outside, we turned up our collars. It was but a few days before the New Year. There was snow on the ground. I'd call it a fine time to dawdle in a museum if there weren't a man missing and a distraught wife to help.

The elegant flats in Russell Square are not for those without the benefit of a bequest. At Grant's building, we stopped and brushed the snow from our boots and stepped inside. When I knocked at his door, Liam did not answer.

"Allow me," Barker said.

My partner rattles doors when he's merely knocking. I watched him raise his ham-sized fist as if it were a hammer. Mercilessly, he brought it down on the door. He smote it five times, paused, and then delivered five more. By then, other tenants had come to see what was causing this disruption to their day. I shrugged my shoulders.

"It is too much of a coincidence that two denizens of the museum should disappear in a single day," he said. "I do not believe in coincidence."

Barker's hand went to his waistcoat pocket where he kept a skeleton key that would open any door. Even now both men could be lying dead on the other side.

"Wait," I said, stopping him. "I have an idea."

I went down on one knee and spoke into the keyhole. "Liam, it's Thomas Llewelyn. Let me in!"

There was a silent pause, long enough to make me think my idea had failed. Then I heard a voice from the other side of the door.

"Thomas, is that you?" he asked.

"It is," I replied. "What's going on? Why aren't you at the museum?"

I heard the door open tentatively and then a pale, haggard face looked out at me.

"Oh, thank heavens. I've been barricaded in here for hours." He stared at the looming figure behind me.

"Liam, this is Cyrus Barker," I said.

Grant answered. "My nerves are on edge. Come in, gentlemen."

He tried to smile but he was nervous as a cat. As soon as we squeezed inside the entrance, he turned a stout lock and threw a heavy bolt. Then he bowed to the Guv.

"Sir, I have long wished to make your acquaintance," Grant said. "I'm sorry it is under these circumstances."

"What circumstances are those exactly, Mr. Grant?" Barker rumbled.

"Where are my manners?" he replied. "Come in and take some tea and we shall discuss it like civilized men. You didn't notice anyone loitering about the building, did you?"

"No, sir," the Guv assured him. "And I am circumspect."

When one enters Grant's door one faces a row of tall filing cabinets no more than five feet away. They form a narrow corridor leading to the front windows and a roaring fire. Then the room opens into an impressive library, not only lining the walls, but projecting into the center of the room like the spokes of a wheel. It was the British Museum Reading Room in miniature.

I visit Grant every couple of months and not merely for informational purposes. When I arrive I always like to see what he has acquired since my last visit. He is omnivorous but tends toward collecting esoterica. The first book I saw was called *Daemonologie,* commissioned by King James. The second was on the secrets of Tibetan Lamaism, and the third a worn black volume tall enough to scrape the top of the shelf. I could not read the title, but the author had the flamboyant name "Alhazared." In front of the books on the inch or two of available space on each shelf was a curio, generally antique and always exotic.

Barker said nothing but looked about the room as I did. A stuffed alligator was suspended horizontally above our heads and a live owl sat on a perch, regarding us as gravely as his master.

"Sit, gentlemen, sit, by all means," Grant said. "I so rarely have visitors. Tea . . ."

He pushed a few beakers to the side and found a disreputable-looking iron teapot.

"I only have Assam, I'm afraid," he said. "Thomas, how is Mrs. Llewelyn?"

"She is well," I said.

He lit a burner and set the kettle on a metal ring over it. Then he spooned tea into it as we watched. Grant was over fifty. He had gray hair, with a tonsured bald spot at the back. He wore pince-nez spectacles that always seemed in danger of falling off his nose yet somehow never did. He wore a crooked tie and over it a jumper with the elbows going out. Generally, Grant was natty, but at home he dressed as if he'd donned his clothing in a hurry.

I met him years before when I mistook him for a member of staff at the museum. It was something he enjoyed, impersonating a librarian. He knew more about the collections than anyone, having read all of it that interested him. He also provided himself with felt-bottomed shoes that made him nearly silent as he glided about the Reading Room. He wore white gloves to protect the old and rare books in the collection. He seemed to know everyone and everything. Six out of seven days a week he entered the building at nine in the morning and left at nine in the evening, dining afterward in the tavern where we had just lunched. He was proud of the fact that he had not left this street in ten years. I gathered he thought the museum would fall to pieces if he ever left. Perhaps it would.

"It's always nice to have visitors," Grant said as the kettle began to shriek.

"But not today," Barker growled.

"No, sir," my friend agreed. "Not today."

"Tell us, is Phillip Addison here at the moment?"

"He isn't, I'm afraid."

"Where is he?" Barker demanded.

"I don't know, sir."

"But he was here!"

Grant spilled some of the tea, missing the first cup entirely. I could see his nerves were frayed to the breaking point. He took a rag and began mopping the spilled tea.

"Yes, sir, he was, shortly after midnight."

Barker looked at me as if to say "Now we're getting somewhere," and visibly relaxed. Now that he knew he was in the right place, he was willing to let Grant tell it as he saw fit. In doing so, Grant relaxed as well. Belatedly, our host brought us the tea.

"I'm sorry," Grant said. "I'm out of cream. Do you like shortbread?"

"Very much," Barker replied.

Grant retrieved a round tin painted in a garish red tartan and offered it to us. Barker took one, but I was dubious. I doubted it had been purchased that year, but with shortbread one can never tell.

"Inverness born, are you?" Barker asked.

"Nearby, yes," Grant replied. "Let's see. Barker is a sept of the Stirling clan, is it not? That would be near Perth."

It hadn't even occurred to me that Grant was Scottish, but Barker knew.

"What did Addison want?" I asked.

Barker gave me a look of disapproval at my lack of patience. Of course, he always forgives his own.

"I should have realized the two of you would be aware of his disappearance. He has disappeared, hasn't he? I'm sure his wife must be frantic."

"She is," I admitted.

"I've never met the woman, but Phillip speaks highly of her."

"He came to your door last night?" Barker prompted.

Grant nodded. "He did, sir, just after midnight. He claimed he'd made an historic discovery, but he wouldn't say what it was. He was going to speak to Mr. Hennings even if it meant waking him in the middle of the night. He had a problem, however. He'd come out with an object to show his superior but was concerned that it would look as if he had stolen it. He couldn't return to the museum, because as a volunteer he had no key. Then he thought of me. I'd vouch for him, you see. We'd spoken often around closing time, and he had even come here once or twice for a chat."

"Are you still in possession of the object?" Barker asked.

"I am, sir."

"May we see it?"

"Of course." Grant stood and walked to one of the bookcases. Reaching behind a row of books, he retrieved a small object wrapped in rags. There was an empty chess table in a corner and Grant pulled it forward, setting the package upon it.

"Have you opened it?" Barker rumbled.

"No, I haven't the nerve." Grant admitted.

"Did Addison say what it was?"

"No," Liam answered. "He can be maddeningly coy some-times. Other than that, however, he is a fine fellow. I hope he is safe somewhere, and this is all a misunderstanding."

"But you don't believe it is," Barker said

"No, sir, I'm afraid I do not," he replied. "I'm very worried about him."

"Professionally speaking, you have reason to be. May I open this?"

"You may do more than that, Mr. Barker," he said. "You may spirit it away. It has given me a sleepless night. If Phillip comes to my door again, I can tell him it is in safe hands."

Barker took the object in his palm, weighing it.

"It is heavy," he noted. "I'm going to unwrap it now.'

He did so, too slowly, I thought. But then, we'd handled bombs and poisons before, so his caution was understandable. When the object finally lay on the table, I was disappointed.

"It's a bit of brick," I said. "A red lump. Is this what Addison pulled out of the mummy's chest?"

"Mummy?" Grant asked. He jumped to his feet as if it was an adder and backed away. He was superstitious, I presumed. The object, whatever it was, unsettled me as well, I just didn't want to react in front of the Guv.

"Do you know what it is, sir?" I asked. "Perhaps Addison was merely excitable."

"He had every reason to be excited, and to want to hide it," Barker replied. "This is a jewel, an uncut ruby of unusual size."

"Are you sure?" I demanded, dubious.

"I know jewels, Thomas. You may take my word for it."

There was little light in the room save for the fire. Barker stood, crossed to the table, and relit the burner. Then he held the jewel up to it. It glowed like a coal fire. Grant and I stared at it, our faces lit with a sanguinary light.

"If we take it," I asked. "What will we do with it?"

"See who comes for it," Barker replied. "Mr. Grant, did Phillip Addison seem frightened when he visited? Above and beyond the fear of being sacked, I mean."

"He said he'd never been around anything worth so much in his life, and out in the street it seemed as if everyone he saw meant him mischief."

"Was he afraid of anyone in particular?"

"I'm not certain, but Phillip does not have a high opinion of a board member named Lord Grayle. He specifically said he wants to keep this out of the man's hands. I fully agree. I was upset when Grayle bought his way onto the board of directors. Everyone knows he's only there as a collector."

I smiled. "So sayeth the man with a flat furnished with treasures from the museum."

I knew my man. Grant didn't take offense at the gibe. He appreciated the irony.

"All I have is the offscourings, what the museum considers surplus," he replied. "Nothing here is worth a great deal financially. However, most of it is ancient. I collect what interests me. Some pieces I have purchased believing it was fool-headed of the museum director to get rid of them, and I would keep them until he come to his senses. You'll take it then, Mr. Barker?"

"I will, sir. Now, you must understand that every word Addison spoke might have some significance. Can you give us a more precise version of the conversation you had with him?"

Grant nodded. "Certainly. He knocked at my door about a quarter past twelve. I was shocked, to say the least. I am the last person to whom such an event would occur. I have a small circle of friends and prefer it that way. Most of them are people who work in the museum. Phillip apologized profusely for interrupting my sleep."

"Was he agitated?" I asked.

"Decidedly," Grant replied. "Then he brushed past me and came inside without being asked. I was surprised again. Normally his manners are impeccable. He hurried down the hall and dropped a wrapped object on the table and stepped back, as if he wanted nothing to do with it. Then he said he found it while doing the inventory. He wouldn't say what it was, except that it was a major discovery and that he'd intended to take it to Mr. Hennings. When the museum door closed behind him, he realized he'd inadvertently stolen the object in the eyes of the law. Also, he said he thought several of the individuals in the street appeared suspicious but that it might have been his imagination."

Barker looked about the room. "But so far no one knew about the item in his possession, or that it even existed, is that correct?"

"Yes, it is. I don't believe he found it more than a quarter hour before he reached my door."

"This is fascinating, Mr. Grant. Pray continue your narrative, sir."

"I remonstrated with him," Grant replied. "You must understand, gentlemen, that I am on sufferance of a sort. I'm merely a patron, but I've been given access to the museum others have not. A museum is like an iceberg, gentlemen. The public sees less than a tenth of what it owns. Such a privilege can be taken away if I am involved in anything against British Museum policy. As much as I like Phillip, and I do like him, he is a delightful fellow, helping him to hide an object that belongs to the museum was not something I wished to do."

"How did he convince you to take it?" the Guv continued.

Grant shifted in his chair. It was obvious that even speaking about the matter made him uncomfortable.

"He didn't," he answered. "I tried to refuse, but all he did was pat me on the shoulder and laugh as if my refusal was a joke, and then he fled. The last I saw of him, he was standing in Russell Square hailing a hansom cab."

Barker scratched the underside of his chin. It was a good sign. He was connecting bits of information that other people would assume were unrelated.

"Very impressive, Mr. Grant," he said at last. "A capital story. Do you stand by it? Nothing added, nothing left unspoken?"

"I do, sir, as God is my witness."

Barker sat back. It was time for me to step in.

"Tell me, Liam, are you positive that Addison said 'a mummy,'" I asked. "He did not identify it?"

"He said it was a random mummy that had been there for years. He wouldn't have noticed it if it wasn't for the fact that it seemed unusually heavy. I knew he was cataloguing the collection, and I supposed weighing them was part of the process."

"Has anyone called or visited you to see if you are well?" my partner asked.

Liam shook his head. "I do not own a telephone set, Mr. Barker. A few have come to the door and knocked but I did not answer."

"Mr. Grant, before yesterday how often have you missed days at the museum?"

Liam sat with his hands clasped between his knees as if stopping himself from running about the room in a panic.

"Sir, I have gone to the museum every day since I purchased this property," he said.

"Your sense of duty does you credit."

Grant smiled. He'd long heard of Barker, who was known for

being a rough fellow. That he should praise him exceedingly was more than he expected.

"Go back to the museum tomorrow morning and act as if nothing happened," the Guv instructed. "If asked, say you were feeling ill."

"Yes, sir."

"Thank you for seeing us, Mr. Grant," Barker said, standing. "It has been a pleasure to meet you."

"And you, sir," Grant replied. "Will you take the ruby? I fear it will be the death of me."

Barker glanced at it as if it were an object of little concern to him, this stone whose worth probably eclipsed his own several times over.

"Very well," he said, stuffing it into his coat pocket without ceremony. "Let us be off, Thomas."

We stepped out into the cold. Barker readjusted his woolen scarf, which was the same sober color as his coat.

"An interesting fellow," he pronounced. "I like interesting people."

CHAPTER 4

Barker and I found a cab in Russell Square. The cabman was kind enough to provide us with a lap blanket, which we both made use of.

"Brisk," the Guv remarked.

"Stiffish," I agreed.

It is considered bad form in British society to admit to being cold, as if it were a criticism of the country and Her Majesty's government. A boy hopped up onto the board of the moving cab in front of me, receiving a few choice words from the cabman.

"Is you Mr. Barker, sir?" the boy asked.

"I am," he replied. "Thomas, a shilling."

I traded the coin for a slip of paper in the boy's hand. He jumped off again and was gone like a will-o'-the-wisp. Barker frowned at the note as if it vexed him.

"Driver," he growled. "Take us to Wapping Old Stairs!"

Our driver was not overjoyed at the prospect of going to

Wapping, but then, no one ever is. The Thames Police had been headquartered there long before Great Scotland Yard first housed "A" Division, and though the former was now only a branch of the latter, rivalry still ran high. The station is down-at-heel and underfunded, its old, squat building overlooking the stinking river through a bristle of tall pilings like cattails.

When we arrived, setting aside the warm blanket was like tearing plaster from a wound.

We stepped down the worn Old Stairs and made our way through the back door into a warehouse. Among the rowboats stacked there was a table with a body laying atop it. I recognized the corpse at once from the photograph I'd seen. It was Phillip Addison.

"Oi!" an officer called as he entered from the depths of the building. I hadn't met him before. He had a gray mustache, and all his features were packed down in the lower half of his face, leaving a bare expanse of forehead below a peaked cap.

"Barker and Llewelyn, enquiry agents," the Guv stated. "And this poor soul belongs to our client."

The officer nodded. "I'm Inspector Lamont, Thames Police. Just brought him in a few hours ago. Floating along, minding his own business, I heard."

"How did he die?" I asked.

"He was stabbed, poor blighter. Not a normal end for a corpse so clean. At first I thought he was a jumper."

For once Nature had been kind. I've seen many a contorted corpse in my day, and too much mutilation. Mr. Addison looked as if he was sleeping. He might have been Shelley on the sandbar at Viareggio, at least the artist's version. He looked placid, brine dripping from a curl on his forehead. He was pale, eyes half open. Like Cleopatra's, in fact.

Barker leaned over the corpse. He seized a wrist and lifted it, and it slapped onto the table when it was released. Rigor mortis had set in and then dissipated again, which meant he must have been dead at least fifteen hours. I wondered whether having floated in freezing water for so long might affect determining the time of death. The Guv began examining the wound, a small purple mark on the gray chest. By my reckoning, Phillip Addison had been stabbed between the fifth and sixth rib on the left side. The knife must have been long enough to pierce the heart.

"Pockets?" the Guv asked.

"Empty," the inspector replied. "And before you ask, we are honest here."

Barker bowed his head, showing that he never thought otherwise. "What time was he found?"

"He was brought in around six this morning. We early-shifters hadn't even had our tea."

"You did not find the body yourself, then?" Barker asked. "Who did?"

"Coffee John, he calls himself. I never heard a last name. He finds floaters and transports people along the river. That's him over there."

We looked at the far end of the dock where a man was seated among vertical pilings, some nearly ten feet high. He was so heavy that his girth hung over the shorter piling he sat upon. He was an African with a thick gray beard and long, matted hair. There were tribal scars on his face from a lifetime ago. He wore a shirt that looked as if it were cut from duck canvas and a wide, unbuttoned waistcoat. His pants and boots were faded and grimy.

Barker crossed to him and lowered himself onto the dock so that his boots dangled over the edge. He removed a sealskin pouch from his pocket, took out a meerschaum pipe, and then pitched the pouch into Coffee John's prodigious lap. The latter took it up eagerly, produced a short clay pipe from his pocket, and stuffed it until it runneth over before tossing the pouch back. It was probably the best tobacco he'd ever had. The two men lit a vesta and sat back, momentarily content.

"Barker," Coffee John said. "We meet again."

"On the same dock, in the same way," the Guv added.

The sailor pointed toward the warehouse. "Was dat another assistant?"

"No, my client hired us to find her husband." Barker turned toward me. "Thomas, Coffee John found Quong."

It had been before my time. Quong was his former assistant who had been found in Limehouse Reach with a bullet in his head. He had been about to marry the Guv's ward, Bok Fu Ying. It had been a tragedy, but then murder always is, for someone, at least.

Smoke plumed in the cold air. I could smell Barker's private blend. Coffee John took our business card and studied it for a moment. Then he scratched his chin in thought, and gave it back.

"Pretty," he said. "Can't read."

"How do you know what the signs along the river say?" the Guv asked.

"I learn the words, I just don' read them."

"Let us discuss business, John," Barker said. "How much to row us out to where the body was found?"

"Five pounds," John stated. "Gentleman's discount."

"You'll take two," I countered. "And be glad for that!"

He grinned, showing a wide gap between his teeth.

"Dat's the discount," he said. "You the gentlemen."

"Five it is," Barker stated, overriding me. "Is it far?"

"Not far at all," Coffee John replied. "Millwall."

"Isle of Dogs, then," Barker grunted. "Again."

The sailor grinned, looking like a pirate as he did so.

"Never saw a dog on the Isle of Dogs before," he said. "Why is dat?"

"Sheer contrariness, I expect," I answered.

His boat was tied to one of the pilings. It was fourteen feet long and whatever color it had once been had faded away long ago. He descended the dock ladder with a protest of the old wood. Inside his boat, his castle, he sat down on a heap of ropes and nets in the stern and made himself comfortable. We climbed aboard and sat in the bow.

"Payment firs'," Coffee John demanded.

"Why?" I asked.

"You could get stabbed like that fellow," he replied. "Den I wouldn't get paid."

"Of course you would, and to spare," I insisted. "You'd just pick my pockets."

"Spoils of the sea," he answered. "No harm 'n dat. Dead men need no money."

"We're on a river," I reminded him.

Coffee John shrugged. "Spoils of the river, den."

"What did you find in the victim's pockets?" Barker asked, still puffing on his pipe.

"Not much," the man replied. "A key to his house, I'm think-ing. A comb. Wallet wit' a single pound in it. Two and sixpence, no more. Nice-looking fellow, but poor."

"He had a pound note," I pointed out.

"Yeah, but it was folded many times and stuffed in a corner of the wallet. The folds are worn. He saved it for emergencies."

"His watch," Barker boomed. "Give it here."

"Spoils of the—"

"For his widow," my partner said. "He was a poor man, if you will recall."

Coffee John looked downcast. "So am I."

"John," the Guv rumbled. It was a request, and it wasn't.

"All right, Push." Reluctantly, he pulled a watch from his pocket and extended it to the Guv. He received a cold smile in return.

"You remember him after ten years?" I asked.

"Everyone on de river knows Push."

Push was Barker's nickname in the East End. It is Cockney rhyming slang, a patois the locals use to confound foreigners like us. Push-comes-to-shove. Guv.

Barker held the watch in his hand. It was faded gold. Addison must have fought like the devil to retain it while the wolf was at the door.

I'd wanted to deliver Mrs. Addison's husband to her safe and sound, to see her with a smile on her haggard face. I know what it's like to lose someone. So does Barker.

"Bad business," I murmured.

Millwall is below Limehouse Reach. The Thames, having snaked due south suddenly reverses itself north again, then turns east, leaving behind a peninsula or bump that is the Isle of Dogs.

Millwall is the west side of that isle, fronting the East India Docks. The east is called Cubitt Town.

I defy anyone to find a more inhospitable spot to end one's days than Millwall, especially after whatever passed for a Yule holiday in Dockland is done, and the world becomes a little darker and grimmer about the mouth.

Millwall is a sailor town. There are public houses, ship's chandleries, and other places that cater to the seafaring trade. Like every sailor town, many of its shops were empty and had boarded windows. I imagine that midwinter must be a difficult time for this area, with ships in dry dock and no steady pay coming in. It had been a lean Christmas for most. The only thing that can be said about Millwall in December is that it doesn't reek of fish and sewage as much as it does in July. That is not the highest recommendation for the prospective merchant considering a lease here. I've heard someone say, "At least it isn't Whitechapel." This is high praise indeed, I'm sure.

"Right here," Coffee John said. We were hard by Millwall Dock. The walls on both sides of the river were coated in ice.

There was two feet of it circling each piling. It was no wonder Addison's body looked dewy. It was probably thawing.

I was reminded of stories my grandfather told when I was a child of the Frost Fairs nearly a century ago, when the entire Thames would freeze solid and merchants would move out onto the river with their carts and makeshift booths and stay there for weeks. A carnival atmosphere was achieved despite the cold, with merchants and publicans making a brisk trade. Souvenirs with the Frost Fair's name were printed on cups, plates, and figurines. My grandfather had a ticket that was given him as a tot, calling him "Sir Owen of Gwent." The freeze had gone on for centuries but stopped unaccountably in 1816, the devil knows why. No merchant since has trusted the ice enough to carry his merchandise onto it.

"We might as well be in Spitzbergen or Oslo," I said, shrinking into my coat collar.

"If we were in Rome, you would complain of the heat," Barker remarked.

"It is beastly hot there," I admitted.

"He could have come from anywhere," Coffee John said, meaning Phillip Addison. "Upriver, downriver. Flow tide, ebb tide. Der is ice afloat, so he could have been pushed under the surface. I doubt there is anything worth finding."

"And yet we must look," the Guv replied. "Steer us over to the ladder there."

We climbed onto the dock and walked along the edge looking for any sign of human existence: a spot of blood, a footprint preserved in ice, or a scrape across an icy surface.

Meanwhile, Coffee John warmed himself with rum from a disreputable flask. Again, we were unsuccessful.

"I must be going," Coffee John said. "Have t'ings to do. I'd like my money now."

I passed the note to him, and he stuffed it into his pocket. It was a sight to watch him descend the ancient ladder. He stepped in the boat and made his way to his nest quite nimbly for a man his size.

"Thank you, sir!" Barker called, raising a bowler to him.

"The Underground is due south," I muttered, stomping the snow from one of my boots.

"But it's such a fine day," he replied. "Why waste it in a sooty tunnel? Let us dockwallop."

"I'm a Welshman. Soot is my natural element. And what the devil is 'dockwalloping'?"

Barker knocked the ash from his pipe. It blew away long before it reached the ground. "Dockwalloping means exploring a dock you've never been to. You stop into shops and buy something small. You talk to people. You mill about and see what there is to see. Consider what it would be like if you were a sailor arriving in a new port. You want to explore the town."

"We were dockwalloping in the British Museum this morning, then," I said.

"We were."

"And I was dockwalloping in Charing Cross earlier."

"No, you weren't, lad. You were gone only briefly. A good walloping may take hours."

"Blast," I said. "I could have been gone for hours?"

"No need, because you know the booksellers' stock better than they," he replied. "Come along."

"Have you been here before?" I asked, turning my head, but he was gone. I caught sight of him out of the corner of my eye and trotted to catch him up, slipping on the ice. He turned back and helped me to my feet, brushing snow from my coat.

"I can see that dockwalloping is going to become one of my favorite activities," I remarked.

I will admit that though this was not the perfect time to see the Isle of Dogs, there were things to suit my imagination. We stepped into the opened door of a carpenter's yard and met a man who crafted figureheads of ships. We were both impressed with the attention he gave to the expression on the figure's face. I could not help but compare it to the old Viking longboats and their carved dragon heads.

Nearby was a shop with scrimshaw carvings and ship models made of bone. We put our heads into several public houses, but only to see what was inside. I bought lemon drops in a shop for Rebecca. She was currently in Wales. After a rupture from my family of many years' duration, I had agreed to take her to meet them for Christmas. They were impressed, as anyone would be, and she endeared herself to them to the point that when I had to return to London, they convinced her to stay another week. I've got dozens of aunts and cousins lying about in corners all over Gwent, and she was expected to visit each and every one of them. She had the patience of a saint, if I say so myself. Barker bought dried squid at an Asian stall as a snack for Harm. The Guv was perfectly content, but I wasn't.

"I don't see any connection here to the murder of Phillip Addison," I pointed out.

"Nor do I yet," Barker admitted. "And we might not, but this is where the trail has brought us, so look carefully. What was Phillip Addison doing here?"

I looked again, with more intent. I knew little of the schoolmaster, but I thought it likely he was never a sailor. This was not a place he would have come to voluntarily. Either he met someone here or he was brought here. He'd expected to return to his wife and go to work in the morning as he always did, but he met someone and his fate was sealed.

Everywhere we looked, we saw poverty. Boards were pulled off fences for firewood. A boy wore a shirt that I suspected was originally his sister's dress. One young man wore a garish tweed cap. When the weather was this cold, one would wear anything to stay warm.

However, I saw little sign of crime. The constables walking about did not sport battle-weary frowns, though I didn't believe there was a division constabulary closer than Wapping. This was a typical sailor town. There would be heavy drinking and not a few brawls when ships docked. It was a poor place to live, but people did it nevertheless. The question was would they die there, too?

Barker consulted his watch. Is spite of the cold he sat down with his boots over the side of the dock near the spot where Coffee John kept his boat. Reluctantly I sat beside him.

"It's near one," he said. "We'll have lunch and then report the sad news as gently as possible to our client. The Yard is efficient but informing women of their husband's demise is not high on their priorities. I'm sure you will agree with me that we should be the ones to tell her."

"Of course," I said. "It's our duty."

"Have you made any inferences now that you've toured the area?"

"Ask a question and I'll give you an answer, sir."

He lifted his collar against the wind. "Do you think Mr. Addison's body washed up here or was it thrown from the dock?"

"The latter, sir. Whoever brought him here wanted a quiet spot to question him. It's isolated, being a peninsula, and we're in the lull between holidays. He must have arrived in some kind of closed vehicle, since all public transport would have stopped by one."

"Good, Mr. Llewelyn. Pray continue."

"He disappeared last night and was found floating right below your boot there. I've been asking myself why he wasn't beaten. That would be the quickest method of getting information."

"Perhaps he was," the Guv said, kicking icicles off the dock below him. "There are ways to torture a fellow that leave few marks, Thomas."

"Please tell me there aren't many in London that know them, sir."

"Only the enforcers and bet collectors, lad," he replied. "Stay away from the horses. Pray continue."

"The fact that the ruby was still in Liam Grant's possession proves that they couldn't crack Phillip Addison's nut. I'm beginning to have some respect for the fellow. I doubt any of the paid employees would have given their lives for the British Museum. Of course, once they laid hands upon him, his life was forfeit. They were never going to let him go. Poor chap. If Hennings's assessment is true, think of what he could have accomplished."

"Think of what he did already," Barker said. "I'll talk to Mr. Thompson about the matter when this enquiry is done. Mrs. Addison deserves some kind of compensation for her husband's bravery."

"I wish you luck convincing the museum board of that, sir, but I applaud the sentiment."

The Guv grunted. "Tell me, lad, how do you suppose Addison was taken so quickly after discovering the ruby?"

"I can't work that out," I admitted. "Save that he told Grant there were some rough types in Russell Square."

"His nerves were a-jangle," the Guv replied. "More likely the ruffians were merely men leaving the Museum Tavern at midnight."

"No, sir," I insisted. "They got poor Addison in the end."

"The killers are always the quiet ones, Thomas," Barker said, kicking his heel against the dock, sending more icicles into Limehouse Reach.

"But it doesn't make sense," I argued. "Violent men don't hang about museums at night. You don't suppose the ruby had been hidden there by the killers and Addison stumbled across it? That's too unlikely."

"It is," he said. "But you've asked the best question of the day. It's time for lunch."

"As long as there is a fire nearby. I can't feel my ears."

"Ho's it is, then."

CHAPTER 5

We headed north on Bridge Street, skirting the river. Along the way we saw neither human nor animal, not a sprig of vegetation, not even a green stain left by algae along the edge of the docks. It was a blasted place. Even the rats had given up their scavenging. Creatures of the earth were never intended to walk solely on cobblestones their entire lives. It isn't natural.

We passed Lime Kiln Pier, below which I suspected Ho's tearoom lay hidden. Then we reached Narrow Street, which isn't, and soon stood in front of the anonymous entrance that led to the restaurant. It was an unmarked door in an unremarkable alley covered in rubble that was originally a Catholic church. Perhaps it was destroyed at the order of Henry VIII himself, that old reprobate. The door was scuffed, battered, and scarred. No respectable owner would allow such a door, but I assumed it kept those he wanted in and those he didn't out, which was its purpose.

Barker and I descended the stair and found ourselves in a tunnel that allowed two to walk abreast, lit by a single lamp in the middle. If one stood very still and held one's breath, the Thames could be heard gurgling above. I suspect the tunnel was originally a priest's bolt-hole during the dissolution of the churches. We climbed the stair at the far end and stepped into the tearoom.

As with Limehouse itself, there was nothing particularly oriental about the restaurant, save for the waiters and the food. True, there were some red lanterns overhead, but I knew they were left from the Chinese New Year celebration the previous year, and no one had gotten 'round to removing them. There were none of the charming little altars with their fierce or jolly gods that I've seen in some of the shops. There were no exotic landscapes painted on the walls, no photographs or maps, and nothing attempting to project any kind of emotion save perhaps despair. The furniture was worn and mismatched; that is, there were two sets that did not match, and the furniture was set out randomly. I suspect that all of this was due to there being no female eye to watch over everything. No doubt Ho wanted it that way. Once Rebecca said she'd like to see the tearoom and I told her, "No, no you don't."

There seemed no reason why anyone would come here, and yet the restaurant was bustling. There were tong men here sharing tables with solicitors, and young lords visiting the seedy end of town sitting comfortably beside dockworkers. There was an aroma in the room, a combination of all the dishes being cooked behind the kitchen doors, that entranced even seasoned customers like me. One can't normally find such Eastern fare outside of Asia.

When we arrived, a waiter led us to a table and left us, heading immediately to the kitchen. Ho's office was there. Barker and I discussed the case sotto voce while a second waiter shuffled by trying to listen to our conversation. Ho's is more than a tearoom. Information is collected here for the Blue Dragon Triad, whose tentacles reach all the way to Canton.

Ho himself arrived in a few minutes.

"So," he said.

"So indeed," Barker replied.

Barker's former shipmate cast a malevolent eye in my direction. I took no notice. A minute later tea was brought in a large cast-iron teapot along with several small, glazed cups without handles. I poured tea for them both, being their junior. One of the solicitors at a nearby table looked at me askance.

It wasn't that Ho didn't like me, although he probably didn't. He didn't approve of the Guv teaching Chinese boxing to a foreigner. That someone had obviously taught Barker was irrelevant. Also, I was still considered a student, though I taught classes now and then. Some martial masters—and here I am speaking of Ho, a master of Lion's Roar boxing—treat students with contempt until they become instructors. At that time, they welcome them with open arms, as if they'd just walked in the door that very moment, fully trained. The student had magically become a "person."

I've never heard Ho's first name, or if the Guv had mentioned it early in our acquaintance I didn't recall it. Of all the men in London to call a close friend he would be the last I would consider. Imagine a stocky Chinaman, his head shaved save for a thick queue which comes over his shoulder like a python and falls down his chest. Give him a number of gold rings in his ears, so that the lobes are stretched to his shoulders by the weight. Add black trousers gathered at the ankle, rope-soled shoes, and a singlet stained from cooking, though I've never actually seen him cook. Make your creation as ill-tempered as possible, and there you are, Ho in the flesh. How such a man had once been a Buddhist monk reels the mind.

"Drink tea! Drink tea!" he barked at me. I'd been watching them and thinking, and thus insulting the tea, which had been picked on a mountain in the north of China solely for my benefit. I will be the first to admit the tea was wasted on me. I cannot tell good tea from bad. I cannot even tell one type from another, no matter how hard I try. Barker assures me it is a curse.

"Who told you the body was nearby?" Ho asked my partner.

"The Thames inspector, Lamont," the Guv said. "I informed Terence Poole I was looking for a body. That is, I expected a man was dead."

"You found him. Is the enquiry closed?" Ho asked with an expectant look on his face.

"Not by a long chalk," Barker said, glowering.

"Who is the victim?"

"A schoolmaster who volunteers at the British Museum," Barker replied. "Last night, he made a discovery. He went to his superior in the middle of the night to tell him about it, but was rebuffed. Then he disappeared until an hour ago."

A tray of beef noodles arrived unbidden, followed shortly by buns and dumplings smothered in sauce.

"I'm told he was stabbed," Ho said. "How did he get here?"

Cyrus Barker shrugged his wide shoulders. He bit one of the buns in half and chewed it, his mind working. After a moment, he wiped his mustache.

"What do you know about a man named Coffee John?" he asked.

"He eats here twice a month," Ho replied. "He likes plum wine. Once he asked me to make an African dish for him."

"Did you?" I asked.

"I should make African food?" he snapped. "Do I look African to you?"

Ho's speech wanders between Mandarin, Pidgin, and English. He can speak like an Englishman when he wants. I've heard him do passable imitations of British dialects, and once I even heard him attempt an imitation of Barker's Perthshire accent.

"No, sir," I assured him. "In no way could you be mistaken for African."

"Do you know his origins?" Barker continued, ignoring Ho's rudeness.

"I do," the Chinaman said. "His name is John Cuffay. Since sailors cannot spell, it became John Coffee, and then Coffee John. I heard his father sold him to a Portuguese freighter as a lookout. He came into port here and stayed with the African colony in Canning Town. He never saw snow before, and he wanted to see it again. He must be pleased today. He can make a snow house."

"Igloo," I supplied.

Ho glared at me. "What you call me, boy?"

"Nothing," I said. "Nothing at all."

My partner had finished his bun and reached for another. I took one with the feeling that the owner wanted to slap my hand. However, I knew he was speaking English for my benefit, rather than the jumble of Mandarin and Cantonese he usually spoke with Barker. Ho was from Peking and the Guv had been left stranded as a youth in Foochow when his missionary parents died from cholera. He spoke Cantonese like the native he was.

"You think Coffee John is involved?" Ho asked.

"He could have killed Addison as well as anyone," Barker replied. "I know he must keep a knife on the boat. Probably a pistol as well. Did anyone witness John coming into Limehouse Reach with the body?"

Ho shook his head. "No, he found it in the river. We saw him discover it and haul it into his boat."

"You saw it by Millwall pier before Coffee John did?" I asked. "Why didn't one of you remove it from the river?"

"We saw he was dead. It's not our business. If we did anything, we would be blamed. We may still."

"Did someone inform Coffee John that a body was in the area?" Barker asked.

"No, he might be getting old, but his eyes are still sharp."

My partner nodded and poured a thimbleful of tea. He swallowed it and poured another. The cups looked as if they belonged to a child's tea-party set. In my opinion, men should have vessels fitted to their hands.

"Has anything unrelated happened in the last few days?" Barker continued.

A waiter came up to Ho then and murmured in his ear. The Chinaman frowned, then began barking orders at him. The waiter began kowtowing, receiving the abuse stoically. Finally, Ho waved him away.

"Not in Limehouse," he continued as if there had been no interruption. "However, there was an incident in Millwall last night. Everyone is still discussing it. There was a gang fight."

"Indeed?" the Guv asked. He put down his cup and moved his chair forward. "We haven't had a barney in some time. Between which two gangs?"

"One gang was the Millwall Boys," Ho said. "No one could identify the other."

"How many were involved in the fight?"

"Fifteen, perhaps twenty men," Ho said. He had that look of satisfaction one has when telling a story the audience wants to hear.

"Was it territorial?"

"The Millwall Boys thought so," came the reply. "One of theirs got cut and taken to London Hospital."

"Cut, you say?" my partner asked. "With a knife?"

"You can't cut with a spoon, though I'm certain this one has tried."

Naturally, that last volley was directed at me. I noticed Barker never takes my side in these criticisms. He ignores them. I must learn to fight my own battles.

"Here, now," I said. "There's no cause for that."

"I beg to differ, old boy," he replied in a credible Oxbridge accent.

"Was the young man stabbed in the same manner as Phillip Addison?" the Guv asked.

Ho nodded. "Close enough, I should think. The wound was on the left side of his chest."

"I see," Barker answered. He looked satisfied. He sat back in the old captain's chair.

"Do you have a description of the interlopers?"

Ho looked smug. Or perhaps insolent. They looked much the same on his face. "We do."

"And do you intend to share it with me or merely dangle it over my head?" my partner asked.

"I am considering. I could sell you the information, I suppose."

"You know I'd go down to Millwall and get an answer for free."

"As I am told they were nine men, some young and others over thirty," Ho answered. "They wore caps."

One of Barker's brows crested the top of his black-lensed spectacles. "Anything else?"

"Nothing."

"What kind of caps?"

"Country ones," Ho replied.

"Tweeds?" I asked.

"That's the word!" Ho said, snapping his fingers. "Tweeds. Only terrible ones. Hideous! That is what I was told. I didn't see them myself. Nor do I wish to."

"Did the Triad interfere?" my partner asked. "It's adjacent to your own territory."

"We considered it, but it was too cold. We decided to deal with the winner if necessary."

Barker leaned forward. "Have you? Dealt with them, I mean."

"We are looking for them. To my knowledge they haven't left, but there are many ways to get out of Millwall: the Underground at the bottom of Ferry Street, the ferry itself to South London, and private pilots like Coffee John. They didn't leave through Limehouse. However, it is merely a matter of curiosity. The Triad has had skirmishes with the Millwall Boys before. Why should we avenge them?"

"You believe they are here?" Barker asked again. "Where?"

"Must you badger me?" Ho cried.

"I shall until you answer my questions."

They argued then in a mash of language I didn't try to make sense of. I can speak a small amount of Cantonese but it makes my head ache. There are too many tones to learn.

"Very well," Barker said at last. "You don't know where they are. Where are they not?"

"They are not in Millwall or Limehouse."

"Could they be in Poplar?" he demanded.

"No," Ho said. "One of us would have seen them."

"Could they have left on the Underground?"

"We bribe the porters there."

"So that's it, then. You've lost them. There is a hole in your net."

The tearoom owner turned and bawled over his shoulder. In a minute or two a small water pipe was brought. Ho put a pinch of noxious tobacco in the brass bowl and lit it. I heard the pipe bubble.

"They come and go," Ho explained. "All day long, come and go, come and go. In pairs, or one at a time, never as a group. I think they have jobs or run errands. They are too industrious for a gang. Gangs are lazy. They sit and drink and complain. They flirt with local girls. They don't run about all the time."

"Perhaps they aren't a gang at all, then," I ventured. "Perhaps they are a crew."

"Perhaps," he admitted.

"Where haven't you looked?" Barker continued. "Or better, give us a spot to begin."

"I have a restaurant to run!"

"Give us a location and we will leave," the Guv growled.

Ho snorted. "Very well, impossible man! Cubitt Town. Try Cubitt Town."

"There," Barker said. "That wasn't difficult, was it?"

"Get out."

"Shall we go, lad?"

"Yes, sir," I said. We stood.

"You are in my debt!" Ho called after us.

'Try to collect," Cyrus Barker replied genially.

We walked through the tunnel, our voices echoing against the stone walls.

"I'd like to see those caps," I said.

"Not up close. Nine men armed with knives." Barker's stick tapped on the pavement. "Matching tweed caps could cost a good deal. Either they are young blades acting like a gang, or they are being provided for financially."

"They are cocky as well," I said. "They don't seem to care if they are seen by witnesses."

"Perhaps they are beginners. They didn't know, for example, that they were in someone's territory. Or they didn't care."

"All this is true," I admitted. "But it doesn't appear to have anything to do with Phillip Addison. There was no reason for him to be murdered."

"There was every reason," Barker said. "Or at least there was one, brick-shaped and glowing red."

"But they wouldn't know yet," I protested. "They wouldn't know at all. No one would."

Cyrus Barker suddenly raised a finger to his mustache. As we reached the steps leading to freedom we saw an old Chinaman sitting in a chair in the shadow of the stair, doing nothing, just staring blankly. We passed him silently and then stepped out into the light cast by a pale sun.

"Ho's got spies everywhere in Limehouse," I said.

Barker nodded. "Aye, and a few elsewhere. There must be three dozen opium dens in London."

He pointed south from where we stood, indicating the Inn of Double Happiness, a gambling parlor and den owned by a shadowy fellow called Mr. K'ing, who just happened to be married to Barker's former ward, Bok Fu Ying. Allowing her to wed K'ing was one of the few mistakes he had ever made, and he will admit it. The Guv mentioned him because not only did he own a casino, he was the Blue Dragon Triad's representative in London. I wondered if he already knew about the stone. He might be wise enough to hire English thugs to do his bidding instead of the Chinese. Tweed-wearing Englishmen, perhaps.

"Do you think that old man heard me?" I asked. "Have I compromised the enquiry?"

"I suspect it is already compromised, lad. If they didn't know by morning, they could guess. If they can't guess they can imagine. One cannot keep such a gem secret. It is impossible."

"Does Ho know?" I asked.

"Not yet, but he is certainly curious. I've seldom seen him come out of his office and sit by the fire. Of course, that doesn't mean I am obligated to tell him."

"That's a fine way to treat a former first mate with whom you plied the China Sea."

"Surely you don't suppose he told us everything, do you?" he asked with a twinkle in his eye. At least, there might have been one, buried behind those black quartz-lensed spectacles. One never knows.

CHAPTER 6

We were rattling toward Liverpool Street Station by Underground and the branch that would take us to Charing Cross. It's difficult to tell what Cyrus Barker is thinking. His expression is generally stoic, but I thought he looked dispirited. I won't say that after a decade I could read him like *The Times,* but I can assess his moods. I tried to imagine what could change his mood so markedly after leaving Ho's and it came to me. It was, quite literally, staring me in the face.

"We have to inform Mrs. Addison of her husband's death," I stated.

"Aye," he growled.

"Best get there and warn her before the Met arrives. They aren't known for their bedside manner."

"Certainly not," the Guv replied. "Addison's body should be at the morgue in 'A' Division within the hour."

"You should return to our chambers in case new information

has arrived," I said. "I'll go to Chelsea and break the news to our client that she is a widow."

The Guv was taciturn as always, but he looked a trifle relieved. "No. Thomas, I couldn't allow you to do so. It is my responsibility."

"Bosh," I said. "I'm part of the agency as well, and I'm sure you've got matters to attend to."

My partner nodded. "You'll question her thoroughly, I trust."

"Sir, I know how to do my duty."

He put up both hands. "Of course you do, lad. I wasn't suggesting otherwise. Be sure to mind the proprieties."

"I will."

"I shall inform the museum of young Addison's death by telephone," he said. "I'll see you back in Craig's Court."

We thundered into the station with a hiss of steam and a protesting squeal of brakes. On the platform, we parted company and I changed lines to the 2:10 headed west.

I planned the mission during my journey. The Guv was correct about the proprieties. First, I required a chaperone as I did not wish to be alone in a flat with a married woman. Perhaps I could find a constable on his beat. That might be worse, however, two men standing at the door and one of them a constable. I needed a female, a relative or friend. If Rebecca was in town, I could have brought her along, but she was off in the wilds of Gwent. It was me; just me. I arrived at Sloane Street Station and took a hansom to their address.

The Addisons' flat in Meek Street was a respectable if inexpensive address. My throat was parched, and I was apprehensive as I stepped out of the cab and paid the driver. I was in for it now. Whatever possessed me to volunteer? I stepped up to the door and raised my hand to knock, but it froze an inch away and would not budge. I stepped back and looked about with no small amount of concern.

We British are a reticent people. We do not knock on the

doors of perfect strangers. However, I would grasp any life preserver at that moment. There was a matching door beside Elizabeth Addison's and without thinking I stepped forward and knocked on it.

A voice called to me, telling me to wait. The door opened after a minute and a woman looked at me, trying to discern who I was. I might be a salesman traveling door-to-door, perhaps, or someone coming to the wrong address. She was plump and over sixty. She wore an apron as if it were a uniform, but I believed she was the woman of the house, or even its only occupant. By her features and the Star of David around her throat I could see she was one of the Chosen People.

"*Sholem Aleichem,*" I said, removing my bowler.

"*Aleichem Sholem,*" she replied cautiously.

"Tell me, madam, are you acquainted with your neighbor, Mrs. Addison?" I asked.

"A little," she replied. "We have spoken a few times. I met her when she and her husband first arrived last year."

"Are you aware that Mr. Addison has been missing since last night?" I asked.

The woman nodded. "Yes. Mrs. Clarence down the way informed me. Such a gossip she is!"

She was an Ashkenazi Jew, I deduced, probably born in a shtetl in Poland or Russia. Most of her Yiddish accent had worn away over the years. Some I've met at the Bevis Marks Synagogue, where my wife's parents attend, carry it as a badge of honor for the rest of their lives.

"Ma'am, I come with ill news for her," I continued. "Her husband was found this morning. I was hired by her to find him."

I handed her my card, which she took reluctantly.

"*Shammes,*" I said. *Detective.* It was one of the words I had learned in Yiddish.

"He is dead, yes?" she asked.

"Yes, ma'am," I replied. "Stabbed and tossed in the river."

"How terrible!" the woman exclaimed. "He was a fine young man and a good husband. The crime in this city grows worse every day. It is appalling!"

"It is indeed," I agreed. "I must tell her now, but there is no one to offer comfort. Also, I am a married man. You understand my dilemma. Could you possibly accompany me?"

She nodded. "I am an old woman and have seen everything. She is young and I have heard her crying through the wall. Of course, I will comfort her in her hour of need."

"Thank you, Mrs.—I'm sorry. I don't even know your name and I ask this of you!"

"It is Emma Lipinski."

"Thank you, Mrs. Lipinski," I answered. "Are you ready?"

"Mr. Llewelyn, no one is ever ready for these things."

She wiped her hands on her apron and we stepped up to the other door. This time there was no hesitation. I knocked and the door flew open as if Elizabeth Addison had been standing behind it waiting for someone to appear. Perhaps she had been. I dared not ask.

"Mr. Llewelyn!" she cried. "Have you found my husband?"

"We have, Mrs. Addison," I replied. "Unfortunately."

The woman screamed. Once I was unlucky enough to see a dog crushed under a cab wheel. It screeched, but the sound was cut off suddenly. I can never forget it. The woman gave such a screech and fell against the wall, sliding to the floor. Mrs. Lipinski helped her to a threadbare couch where our client began to cry, a full-throated sobbing that stemmed from intense pain. Her neighbor held her and rocked her in her arms.

"How did it happen?" Mrs. Addison eventually asked.

I told her the particulars, as we knew them. Her face went deathly white. She was clearly in shock. I must admit that I had avoided this duty until now. Generally, we leave it to Scotland Yard, though I suspect they are brusque in such matters. Elizabeth Addison put the palms of her hands against her eyes.

"My god, how I am I to live?" she cried. "Who will pay for Phillip's funeral? What's to become of me? I wish I were dead!"

I wondered what it would be like if Rebecca were gone forever but I couldn't imagine it. My brain refused to accept such a painful image, even for a second. I tried to imagine how this woman felt. In one fell swoop she'd lost her lover, her best friend, her confidant, her companion through thick and thin, and her financial support. She was left with nothing.

She continued to cry, leaving me to worry about what to do. I didn't want to leave Mrs. Lipinski with the duty of taking care of a perfect stranger. I waited for a few moments and then spoke to her.

"Mrs. Addison, you require help," I said. "Have you a relative in town or a close friend?"

She shook her head. "My sister, Millie. She lives in Southend-on-Sea."

"What is her surname?"

"It is Porter," she replied. "She and her husband, Franklin, own the Fox and Bear Public House."

"I shall send your sister a telegram now," I said. Then I turned to her neighbor. "Can you stay with her for a few minutes longer?"

"Of course, young man," she answered. "What sort of person would I be if I refused?"

I found a nearby telegraph office and sent a message to Mrs. Addison's sister. When I was done, I stopped at the public house at the corner and had a good stiff pint, and it required all my moral fiber not to have another. Now I knew why my partner hated this duty above any other.

A half hour later I stepped into the office, my head full of the events I had just witnessed. However, Cyrus Barker had concerns of his own. Our clerk, Jeremy Jenkins, nodded toward our office and as I headed through the open doorway a large constable appeared and filled it like a cork in a bottle of wine. I put my hands on my hips and stared up at him.

"Let him in, Cosgrove," a voice called from inside. I recognized that voice. It was Detective Chief Inspector Terence Poole of the Criminal Investigation Department. The PC opened like a door, and I entered our chambers. Poole was in our visitor's chair again, looking comfortable.

"Where is it, Cyrus?" Terry demanded. "You know it wasn't Addison's to begin with. It's British Museum property."

Barker glanced my way and I nodded slightly, just enough to show him I had completed my mission. "I am not in possession of it and do not know where it is currently stored."

Poole frowned, brushing a hand across his trim mustache, the kind that was de rigueur among the higher-ups at Scotland Yard.

"We'll return to that in a minute," Poole continued. "What is it? What was stuffed inside that old corpse's breast?"

The Guv stared at him a moment, deciding whether or not to tell him. I realized we could very well be warming a cell bench by end of day. Barker rarely lies to the Met, but he will withhold information if it suits his designs. He is not concerned about being placed in a cell for half a day, save that it slows our enquiry.

"It is a jewel," the Guv said. "A ruby. About that big."

He held up his hands, touching thumb to thumb and finger to finger. My hands could barely demonstrate the size, but his easily could.

Poole whistled. "Are you having me on? Tell me you are exaggerating."

"I am not," Barker answered. "It is uncut and roughly the shape of a human heart, resting on one side. I have no idea how large it will be when cut."

"Do you think it had been there since time immemorial, or did some smuggler stuff the old fellow?"

"It's a female," I told the inspector.

"Is it now?" Poole asked, turning to me. "My mistake. What do you call a female pharaoh?"

"I was thinking Zena," I replied.

"You're a card, Llewelyn, but no," he replied. "How about Cleo?"

I raised a brow, wondering if he already knew who the mummy was. Perhaps he didn't, but I swore to myself I wouldn't make an expression that gave her identity away. Barker was stone-faced as always, but Poole knew he might glean some information from my expression.

"I like it," I said. "Let's use that."

"The two of you were at the British Museum this morning," Poole remarked. "What was your opinion of Thompson?"

"He was cautious," my partner told him. "He seemed an honest and competent director in an unusual situation. I suspect he knew nothing, so he was vague about the events until he acquired more information."

"Probably wise," Poole admitted. "What of the other fellow? Hennings, I think his name is."

"He was more forthcoming," the Guv answered.

"Hennings has no record beyond a drinking-and-disturbing charge at Ascot when he was twenty-one. He is the second son of Lord Melvyrn. I'm sure His Lordship has given liberally to the Old Pile." Poole consulted his notebook. "Phillip Addison. Teacher at St. Olave's School. Volunteer at the British Museum. Original heir to the Addison fortune, Addison Industrial Tools and such. Got himself disinherited, and the line passed to his younger brother. Other than that, he appeared clean as a church on Sunday."

The Guv and I gave each other a glance at this, but our minds were racing. How had we missed this? There was nothing to suggest it save perhaps his surname, but then I did not keep the names of large manufacturers in my head.

"And his wife?"

"No information whatever," Poole said. "We're still looking. Perhaps his family knows. We can't find hers."

"We have a former heir living in reduced circumstances working as a schoolmaster and volunteering at the British Museum in hopes of earning a position there," the Guv stated. "He is cataloguing mummies, which must have been demeaning work, and in the process makes a discovery. He informs his supervisor at his home and leaves, and that is the last of him as well until he is found floating in the Thames the following day."

"Neatly put," Poole said.

"But who killed him?" Barker continued. "I doubt Hennings stabbed his volunteer with a clasp knife. He claims Addison wouldn't tell him what it was, and if he did, how would he carry the body all the way to Millwall?"

"And where is the ruby?" Poole asked. "It seems to have disappeared. Any man who has it now would be a rich man indeed, especially if he has a fortune already. Are you certain you wouldn't know where it is, Cyrus? You wouldn't fool an old friend, would you? I know you wouldn't be so stupid as to have the ruby in one of your drawers."

"Of course not, Terry," Barker answered, standing. "I presume you're going to search the room. We'll see you later. Have your lads be careful with the books. I despise a cracked spine."

Barker, Jenkins, and I left them to their work. Jenkins looked content. An unexpected pint in the middle of the day at his favorite public house would go down as a treat.

"Damn and blast!" Barker growled when we were in Whitehall Street.

"Tell me the ruby isn't in your bottom drawer and he just called your bluff," I said.

"There was no sign in the Addison home that Phillip came from a good family?" he demanded, ignoring my question.

"None at all," I replied. "The furniture was old, his wife's clothes threadbare. His own shoes and suit were worn and serviceable, but just barely. I assumed it was his best because he wore it to the museum. I suppose he'll be buried in it."

"There were no photographs in the house?"

"Not a one. Besides, why keep a photograph of a family who tossed you out on your ear? And why display a keepsake when you can pawn it for bread and sausages?"

"You are correct, Thomas," he said. "Forgive my sharp tone. I am merely frustrated. At least this opens another avenue of enquiry. After they are through with their examination of our chambers, let us lock up for the day. I want to speak to Addison Senior. We'll see if the Met has informed him of his son's demise."

CHAPTER 7

How did she take the news?" Barker asked after he whistled for a cab.

"It was painful to watch," I admitted. "His disappearance didn't prepare her at all for the news."

Barker shook his head. "You know what comes next, don't you?"

"I do. Telling his parents if they do not already know."

"Best get it over all at once," he replied.

While we were there, we hoped to learn what had happened between father and son that caused their relationship to rupture. From what I'd heard about Addison Junior, he was an excellent employee and a caring husband. He did not seem the kind of son who would anger a father enough to become disinherited.

The Addison residence was in Pont Street on the southern border of Knightsbridge. Industrial business must be lucrative these days. One would be hard-pressed to find a more prestigious neighborhood in London that did not belong to the royal family. Perhaps it is the coalman's son in me that wanted to find a flaw to prove that this nouveau riche family didn't know what it was doing, that they had no business being there. Those from low backgrounds can often be the most snobbish. However, the marble residence was beautiful, and my only consolation was that the house had been built in Regency days by someone else.

I overpaid the cabman and instructed him to return in half an hour. We walked up the drive to the elegant front door and as we did, I noted Barker's attire and could find no fault with it. He is always well-dressed. I had the same tailor, and I settled my coat a little and smoothed my muffler. Nouveau or not, one does want to look one's best.

"I'm sorry, gentlemen, but the Addisons are not taking visitors," the butler said upon opening the door. "There has been a death in the family."

He was a sturdily built old campaigner, with what I believed to be a saber wound on his forehead.

"Aye," the Guv said. "We are working with Scotland Yard and have been retained to investigate the younger Mr. Addison's death. We have a few questions for Mr. Addison Senior and have some information he might find important."

The butler inhaled and exhaled slowly, a ploy to gain time while he decided whether or not to admit us. I'm certain he wished we had used the tradesman's entrance.

"Stay here, gentlemen. I'll consult the master."

"Very well," my partner countered. "We shall wander about your pretty lawn."

The old campaigner stiffened. One cannot have private enquiry agents wandering loose among the hedgerows for all to see. It would be unseemly.

"Perhaps it would be best if you gentlemen waited in the hall," the old retainer said.

He retreated inside and invited us into the foyer. There were suits of armor lining the walls, a grand staircase that must be used as a showpiece once a year at most, a large bookcase full of neglected novels, and a coat of arms over the fireplace that, old as it appeared, had probably been forged in the past ten years.

We were left to our own devices for ten minutes. Finally, the butler returned and led us through a pair of French doors to a formal garden, which featured ornamental hedges in crisp geometric patterns, a mossy stone path, and newel post–shaped topiary. Though it lay dormant, one could not fault it. Barker gave a contented sigh. He does like his gardens.

"May I help you gentlemen?" a voice came from somewhere nearby. A man appeared from behind a tall yew bush. He was dressed in a formal day suit, though his knees were muddy. His cuffed trousers were stuffed into a pair of rubber Wellington boots, and his waistcoat had been used to wipe his hands. Addison Senior might be a serious and successful businessman, but at the moment his face was dirty and his hair unkempt. His eyes were glazed, I noticed.

Addison Pere was in his fifth decade and there was gray in his hair. He was sturdily built and had that look of prosperity that comes with too many rich meals and too few walks. He had a small mustache. His hands were red and chapped and made me wonder how long he'd been out wandering in the garden.

"Sir," Barker called. "We are working with Scotland Yard in the matter of your son's death. We have been retained by Mrs. Addison."

"That is a barefaced lie," he snarled. "My wife is upstairs, and she most definitely has not hired you."

"I was speaking of your son's wife, the second Mrs. Addison."

The man flushed. I suspected he must have been a tarter to work for.

"You are mistaken, sir," he said coldly. "My son was not married."

Barker and I turned and looked at each other and then back at him.

"I assure you, sir, we have met his wife," the Guv said. "Mr. Llewelyn has visited their flat, spoken to the neighbor, and seen her ring. Why would you claim they are not married?"

"Because I forbade it," Addison insisted. "I told Phillip in no uncertain terms that he was not to marry that little chippie. Was she blond-haired and pale, with blue eyes?"

"She was," my partner stated.

"That is no daughter-in-law of mine," he scoffed. "She was my wife's personal maid until I sacked her. She got her claws into my son but good. Smelled the money. She bided her time and then pounced. We had chosen a suitable bride for him, the younger daughter of an earl, but no. She had filled his head full of romantic notions. My son has always been easily led astray. They intended to run off together and live off Phillip's inheritance. She planned to buy dresses from the sweat of my brow and have a maid of her own, I'll be bound."

"You disinherited your son," Barker said. "Permanently?"

Addison had been holding some kind of bulb and a trowel in his hands. I don't know much about gardening, but I'm sure one cannot plant anything in midwinter. But then he wore no gloves and his patent leather shoes were covered in mud. There was a wild look in his eye. He was upset, and he must do something, and apparently gardening was that thing.

"You're damned right I did! She won't get a farthing of my money. I suspect the scheming wench had him murdered."

"Why, sir?" I asked.

"When she realized he was disinherited he became a millstone around her neck. I could have warned her he'd be no good as a provider. My wife pampered him too much. Spoiled him, made him of little use to the family business. I gave him an office and a position, but he had no drive. He kept a book in his desk. Always dipping into it. Archeology, if you can imagine a more useless subject to study. He had no head for figures whatever."

"And yet he was working day and night to support both of them," I interjected.

"Impossible!" Addison shouted. He was growing increasingly agitated.

I cleared my throat. "Sir, your son taught history at St. Olave's School by day and worked for the British Museum at night."

Granted, he hadn't been paid at the museum, but I felt a need to defend young Addison. I'd stood in their flat, saw the conditions under which he worked, and heard Hennings laud his work ethic. Just because the young man could not work under his father's supervision did not mean Phillip Addison couldn't make something of himself.

"The British Museum?" he replied "Are you joking? The boy was useless. Now, my second son, Eustace, he's got a head on his shoulders."

"Your son and his bride had a modest home in Chelsea," Barker said. "He supported the two of them. Times were difficult for them, and I suspect the wolf was often at the door, but they thrived unaided. So far in our investigation, your son's death appears to have been a random assault."

It was more than that, of course. He had discovered a priceless jewel, for one. However, the Guv felt the need to defend Phillip Addison from the slander put forth by his own father as much as I did.

"No," Addison Senior insisted. "She did it. She killed him! Hired someone to do it, one of her cronies, I expect."

"They didn't have two coins to rub together," I said. "And his wife is destroyed by the news."

"She's not his wife, I tell you!"

"They were common-law, at least," Barker replied. "Your son did not strike me as the sort that would live with a woman without marrying her. He was a schoolmaster."

"Enough!" Addison bellowed. "Leave my property immediately!"

Barker bowed. "Good day to you, sir. Come along, Thomas. We've finished our errand."

"Go, and don't come back!" the businessman cried. "Inform that seductress she won't get a brass farthing from me!"

We returned to the house. The butler was seeing us to the door as if we were a pair of young scamps caught stealing apples from the orchard. Then we heard a high, piercing scream. We all turned and ran through the French doors again. A wail was issuing from a high window above us, his wife. Addison Senior lay facedown in the dirt, the snow, and the muck.

"Murderers!" Mrs. Addison cried. "You have killed my husband!"

Barker rolled the industrialist onto his back and put an ear to the man's soiled chest.

"He is alive," the Guv called. "Best get him to a hospital or summon a doctor."

"Tabor!" the woman screeched at the butler from her window. "Stop that man! Don't let him touch my husband!"

The butler sprinted to Barker, but the latter had already stood and lifted both hands. There was nothing for the butler to do but step between them.

"I am calling the police immediately!" she continued. "I will see you in jail, murderers! Tabor, do you have their card?"

"The master has it, ma'am."

"Bring it here at once!"

The butler found our card in Addison Senior's waistcoat pocket. We quitted the premises and found our cab in the next street.

"If he dies we might find ourselves in a spot of trouble," I remarked.

"Nonsense," Barker scoffed. "One does not murder someone by talking to them. Did you take concise notes?"

"I always do."

"Excellent. That is our defense. Did you note how disheveled he was?"

"Yes, sir, I did."

"There you are, then," the Guv said. "The man was gardening in the middle of winter in a business suit. He was not in his right mind after learning of his son's death earlier today. This isn't our fault. All the same, we must go to Cusp's office at once and lay the record before him, else a barrister may contest that the notes were rewritten."

We found our solicitor out of his office. However, a young solicitor named Benton took our deposition. He was of the opinion that despite Mrs. Addison's assertions, we were not responsible for the industrialist's injuries or the loss of his life if it came to that. I gave him my actual notebook, which felt strange because it is like a part of my body. I carry it almost all the time. I had taken down Addison's words more from habit than from the notion that we might need it. Addison was blustering, and recording his reaction seemed a waste of my time, but I did it anyway. We each gave a relieved sigh as soon as we stood at the curb again.

"Which hospital is the closest to his residence?" I asked.

"Charing Cross, but it's possible the family sent for a doctor."

"It's also possible he might be en route to a mortuary this very minute," I said. "Poole could be looking for us even now."

"If so, he knows where to find us," the Guv replied. "We are not hiding. Let us return to the office."

It took Detective Chief Inspector Terence Poole about an hour before he strolled into our chambers again. He had a kind of world-weary savoir faire most C.I.D. men lack. He dropped into our visitor's chair, removed his bowler, and ran a hand over his thinning hair.

"Hello again, Cyrus, Thomas," the inspector said. "My, you two have been busy boys today. I can't leave the two of you for a minute. One second you're in Limehouse and the next you make some wealthy codger have apoplexy."

"I don't believe you can make another person have apoplexy," the Guv stated. "And if one does, he cannot legally be held responsible for it."

"Is he dead?" I asked.

Poole crossed a boot over his knee. "No, he'd just had a shock, his son dying like that."

"He was temporarily deranged, I think," I replied. "The man was gardening in the snow in his best suit."

"Thomas took notes," the Guv continued. "We immediately delivered them to Bram Cusp. They are at his office."

"I'll go later," Poole replied. "I'm sure they'll make interesting reading. By the way, we haven't been able to locate the widow so far."

"She was at home this afternoon," I told him. "Try the flat to the right. Mrs. Lipinski. She may be there."

"Thank you, I will. Who did you speak to at Wapping?"

"Inspector Lamont," I replied.

Poole wrinkled his nose. "Not the shiniest apple in the barrel. Lamont's just waiting for his pension, I think. Where did you go and what did you do?"

"Phillip Addison was found in the river near Limehouse Reach by a fellow named Coffee John," Barker said.

Poole laughed. "Coffee John! Is that old reprobate still plying the river for bodies? There are a lot of stories about him. As I heard it, he was hired on by a crew in Madagascar in his youth, and they were ever so glad to get rid of him when they reached London. He stole a chicken from the galley and sacrificed it to his gods on the poop deck, sprinkling blood everywhere. Then he drank the entire store of rum. They debated tossing him over the side. He's usually found by the West India Docks these days, where the rum is brought in. He does have a gift for finding bodies, though. I'm surprised you haven't met him before, Thomas, you being acquainted with so many colorful characters." He looked in my direction and smiled.

"Oi!" I said. "Why is everyone chaffing me today?"

"What's the widow like?" Poole continued. He rarely wrote things in his notebook, but he had a good memory.

"She was devastated by the news," I said. "And you should have heard the vitriol the senior Mr. Addison was spewing her way. If he could have, he'd have blamed her for the Black Plague and the Reformation!"

"Mr. Addison was very forthright," Barker noted. "His son's wife was a domestic in their home when she met her future husband."

"Forthright is an understatement," I answered. "You'd think she was the first maid to tempt away a son and heir. They cut him off without a farthing. Settled it on the younger brother. But you know, I think it only made the young couple stronger."

"I spoke to the headmaster of his school and Mr. Hennings from the British Museum," Poole said. "Neither had a bad word to say against him. Punctual, enthusiastic. A capital fellow."

"But his father said he'd never amount to anything," I said. "He didn't believe his son had an actual occupation."

"Mine was much the same," Poole remarked. "He wanted me to become a bootmaker."

"Coal miner," I stated, raising a finger.

"Evangelist," Barker grunted.

"Cyrus has us beat," Poole said. "Here's to not becoming what our fathers wanted us to be."

Barker nodded. "Each of us has our own destiny, Terry."

Poole gave me a look. "Spoken like an evangelist, eh?"

"Have you found any connection between Addison and Millwall?" Barker asked, sitting back in his chair, resting a heel on the end of his desk.

"Nary a one. Phillip Addison washed up by the docks. His body would have been swept east out of London if Coffee John hadn't swooped down like a seagull and snapped him up." He turned and cast an eye on the Guv. "Where's the ruby, Cyrus? You know we're going to find it sooner or later."

"If I had it, Terry, I'd give it to you," Barker said.

"I'll hold you to that, Cyrus, and if I learn otherwise, we shall have words."

CHAPTER 8

An hour later, I heard the scrape of a chair in the outer office. A drawer was pushed in and a throat cleared. For some, the workday was coming to a close. I was not among them.

"Cheerio, Mr. B., Mr. L.," Jeremy Jenkins called to us.

"Good evening, Jeremy," Barker rumbled from his chair.

"'Night, Jeremy!" I called to no one. Our clerk had evaporated. I fancied his foot was just that second entering through the door of the Rising Sun Public House and a pint of Watney's dripping with foam set on the counter for him.

Cyrus Barker came around the desk and stood in the bay window looking out at the late-afternoon traffic. It was at its busiest. He looked out for a good five minutes at the solid wall of vans and carriages. Meanwhile, I transcribed my notes with the aid of my Hammond typewriting machine.

Barker then crossed to the safe and pulled the hinged painting, *The Massacre of Glencoe*, to open it. He turned the handle and opened the safe. Inside were banknotes totaling a hundred and fifty pounds and a few odds and ends, which Poole had examined an hour before. The Guv closed it again and then reached his left hand up to a bolt on the safe. I stopped typing and watched as he tugged on the bolt until it began to descend. When it reached the bottom, he opened the safe again. It was empty except for the scarlet ruby lying lopsided on its base.

"That's quite a trick," I said. "Did you have that installed recently?"

"No," Cyrus Barker replied, removing the jewel. "I've never had a use for it before. It's a simple dumbwaiter built into the safe, with a false bottom."

He dropped the jewel into my lap. I held it up and turned it about. The gem was crystalline, like a geode, but its roughness and deep coloring reminded me of fresh beef and the makings of a roast.

"It's a bonny thing, no mistake," he said, staring at it.

"Thinking of keeping it, are we?" I asked, pulling the final sheet from the typewriter and placing it in a folder.

"I'm considering it," he admitted. "It's a matter of public good. Large stones like this tend to generate murder as a matter of course. It would be a service to hide it away again."

Jewels carry no allure for me. They are shiny baubles on which society sets an arbitrary price. I'll buy a ring or necklace for my wife but have no need for anything larger than a pea. I certainly wouldn't kill somebody over one.

"What do you suppose it's worth?" I asked.

"I'm asking myself the same question," he admitted. "There are too many factors to consider. I wish I had a lapidary at hand who could examine this without it becoming a matter of public record."

I rose and placed the jewel in his hand.

"Do you recall a young man in our first case named Ira Moskowitz?" I asked. "He was a rabbinical student and a friend of Israel Zangwill. Anyway, he decided that becoming a rabbi would be too demanding and joined his father's diamond firm, Moskowitz and Durham. We have stayed in touch all these years because Rebecca knew him as a classmate at the Jew's Free School. He might still be in his office."

"Call him."

I looked for his firm's telephone number in the Kelly's directory and was put through.

"Moskowitz and Durham," said a voice on the other end of the line.

"Ira, it's Thomas. Thomas Llewelyn."

"Thomas, my friend!" he brayed in my ear. "So good to hear your voice. How is Rebecca and that dybbuk of a partner you work with?"

"We are well," I answered. "Rebecca is in Wales visiting my family. How are Lydia and the children?"

"Healthy and happy!"

Ira had married a lovely dumpling of a woman and the two of them were a matched set of salt and pepper shakers. I've never met her when she wasn't with child and now there were five little Moskowitzes, with more to come. If we hadn't seen them recently it was due to their easy proliferation and our inability to produce a child. That and the fact that their house was in a constant uproar.

"Listen, Ira, might we be able to borrow your services for a couple of hours?" I asked. "We need someone in your line as soon as possible. We will see you're well compensated for your time."

"I don't know," his tinny voice replied in my ear. "I haven't had dinner. Lydia will be cooking."

"We have one of the best chefs in London at our beck and call. And remember, Mac, your old school friend, will be here to make certain everything is strictly kosher. I believe we're having turbot tonight. It's too much food for two of us. We'll just feed the rest to the dog or throw it out."

"I suppose I could send word to her, but she'll be put out."

"She won't be when you return with a cheque for fifty pounds," I said.

"Fifty pounds!" he shouted in my ear.

I looked at Barker. I hadn't asked before offering the inducement, but he nodded approval.

"Yes, Ira, but I'm not merely asking for your skills. We also require your discretion."

I heard a sigh on the other end of the line. "Thomas, why should a nice Jewish boy like you end up in such dangerous work?"

"I'm not Jewish, Ira," I reminded him.

"We'll make you an honorary Jew, then, for Rebecca's sake."

Cyrus Barker gave me a look of impatience. I'm sure he heard every word of the conversation, but sometimes watchers need to be coddled.

"So, are you coming, Ira, or will we be forced to feed this lovely turbot to the dog?"

"This case, this thing you need my services for, is it dangerous?" he asked.

"It is, but not for you," I admitted. "You come to dinner, you examine what we show you, you take your cheque and leave. It's that simple."

"I didn't ask if it was simple, Thomas," he said flatly. "I asked if it was dangerous."

"I'll have you back in your house safe and sound by bedtime, Ira. I promise."

There was a pause on the other end of the line.

"Ira?"

"What time?"

"Dinner is at seven. Three Lion Street, Newington."

"I'll be there."

Triumphant, I hung up the receiver on its hook.

"Dybbuk?" Barker asked.

"It's some kind of Jewish demon."

"I know what a dybbuk is," he snorted. "What made him call me a dybbuk?"

"I have no idea," I lied. "I'm mystified."

I lifted the receiver again and gave the operator our number in Newington. Mac answered on the second ring.

"Barker residence," he intoned.

"Mac, it's Thomas. Do you think dinner can stretch to four of us, yourself included? We're having an unexpected guest."

"Easily," he replied. "We've also got plenty in the larder."

"It's Ira Moskowitz," I told him. "He'll require a kosher meal."

"That shouldn't be a problem, but why in the world would anyone bring Ira Moskowitz to dinner?" he asked.

"I'll explain when we get home," I said. "Oh, and put out the best silver. I want to impress him."

"A banger on a bun would impress him," Mac stated. "Can you explain why you wish to do so?"

"He's doing us a favor, only he doesn't know what it is."

"Very well," he replied. "What time must this feast be served?"

"Seven."

"I'd better get started," he said as he hung up.

"Mac should like that," I said to my partner. "He enjoys a challenge. If I know Ira, he'll smell the food and lose any ability to concentrate."

"Was Mr. Moskowitz that stout fellow with the messy room and wild hair?" Barker enquired.

"That's him, but he's married now, so at least one of those problems has been rectified."

Jacob Maccabee met us at the front door at six in his best kit. He took our coats and hats. He always favored a green and silver vertically striped waistcoat, which I've never seen any other butler wear, but then Mac has always been a bit of a dandy.

"Sir, I have taken the liberty of overfeeding Harm. I assumed you didn't want him gnawing on our guest's ankle."

"That is sound judgment, Mac," my partner replied. He spoils that dog. Harm lay moribund on a large pillow in the front room, his tongue lolling. He cannot resist braised chicken livers.

The dining-room table was set as if we were expecting an earl. The cloth was a green brocade, the glassware and decanters crystal. There were three wines and a few bottles of Mac's home-brewed ale. Barker and I changed, but only into lounge suits. If we dressed in our evening kit Ira would be intimidated.

Our guest arrived at a quarter to seven, carrying a wooden box under his arm. Mac took his coat and hat, tipping him a wink. Ira has never been a handsome fellow. His wiry hair stands in all directions, and he wears a pair of round spectacles. His face is sallow and doughy. When he is fitted for a new suit it looks frowsy and ill-fitting, but then Ira didn't care much about his appearance.

"What's that wonderful aroma?" he asked.

"Consommé à la Brunoise," Mac answered.

The food had come from Le Toison d'Or, but Mac put his unique stamp upon it all. The three of us sat and Barker said a brief and ecumenical prayer. Then the courses came one by one at regular intervals. Ira declared that wine made him bilious, and since there was no female about to defer to, we chose beer.

Barker is not loquacious at dinner, and Ira is a trencherman, so I regaled our guest with a tale or two, though it is difficult to embellish when the man one is speaking of is seated before you. A light salad course came, then the dessert course, damson pudding with coffee. Ira was finally sated.

"Very well, gentleman," he said. There was a Yiddish cadence to his voice, though he'd been born and bred in London. "I am ready to sing for my supper."

Barker led him across the hall to the library. He pulled a chair beside a small table, then set a lamp on it, putting the plug into an electrical socket on the wall. From the box Ira removed a set of scales, calipers, various types of lenses, and several delicate metal rulers. He screwed a jeweler's loupe in his eye.

"Let us see the little beauty now," he said.

As if it were a conjurer's trick, the Guv produced the ruby and settled it on the table in front of him, the flat end on the bottom. Moskowitz immediately clapped both cheeks with his palms.

"What is this?" he demanded. "Have I gone mad? Where did this come from?"

"Best not to ask, Ira."

He moved both the jewel and the lamp closer to him. He examined the stone, turning it over in his hands to see every contour. His face was so screwed up his tongue protruded out one side, reminding me of Harm snoring in the hall.

"This cannot honestly be called a ruby," he said at last. "It is what is called an 'irregular cabochon red spinel.' The closest jewel I have seen to this is the Black Prince's Ruby now in the center of the Queen's imperial state crown, which is kept in the Jewel Room of the Tower of London. It is 170 carats. This is probably twice that size. In fact, I have never seen one this large. Of course, it is uncut, and it would take hours to determine what defects, if any, were inside."

He settled the jewel onto the scale and began to add brass weights to the other side. As he did so he kept shaking his shaggy head.

"It's 82.5 grams, gentlemen! If my father should see this he would drop dead! Even if it should have cracks or defects, it could be cut into smaller faceted gemstones. Dozens if not hundreds.

Necklaces, bracelets, rings. I must sit down. Wait, I am sitting down! How beautiful! Was it found recently?"

"Last night, in fact," Cyrus Barker said.

"And where was it found?" Ira asked. "I must know."

"It was found inside a mummy."

Ira turned to me. "Is he having me on?"

"No," I replied. "We saw it for ourselves."

"You have interesting problems, gentlemen," he remarked. "And just where is this mummy located?"

Barker coughed. "In the British Museum."

Ira rubbed a hand over his face roughly, then heaved a sigh over his stomach. "And how did you come to possess this jewel? No, don't answer that question. I don't want to know."

"It was stolen," Barker admitted. "But not by us. The man who took it is dead and we have no intention of keeping it. We were enquiring into his disappearance when we were given this for safekeeping. I intend to find the proper place for it to go."

"He is dead!" Moskowitz cried. "Of course, he is dead! This is the kind of jewel that people kill for. It drips with blood. That's why it is so red. Do you know its provenance? Where it came from? Who owned it?"

"Why should that matter?"

"It would be worth more if the owners were famous. For example, the Black Prince's Ruby was given to Abu Sa'id, then Don Pedro the Cruel, then Edward of Woodstock, the Black Prince himself, then Henry the Fifth. It goes on and on. Now it belongs to Her Majesty. Its history is part of its worth. Did this belong to someone famous? No, don't tell me. I don't want to know."

"Yes, you do," I told him. "You're dying to know."

"Very well. Tell me."

"The museum is determining whether the mummy the ruby was found inside was Cleopatra."

Ira's shoulders drooped. "This is exhausting. But you see,

it goes together. The gemstone proves the mummy is genuine, while the mummy provides the stone's provenance."

"How would you cut it?" Barker asked.

"Another excellent question. The Black Prince is irregularly shaped, being so old. They did not have precise tools. One could argue that this beauty should not be cut at all, but a gemstone this large can be cut into a number of shapes. It could be a tear shape, for example." He had lifted it and was holding it again. I took it from him, turned it over, and handed it back.

"It is a heart," I said.

"So it is," he said. "I see it now. So. Cleopatra. You mean the famous Cleopatra? Julius Caesar and so forth?"

"That is one of the questions the museum is trying to answer."

"They still have the mummy?" Ira asked. "Tell me you don't have that as well! You didn't carry it away in a hansom cab, did you?"

"Of course not," I replied. "That would be absurd."

"It is already absurd, Thomas! I could go and tell every man in England, and no one would believe me. Your secret is safe, I think." He screwed a loupe into his eye and examined the stone once more. His stubby but subtle hands were almost caressing it.

"It could be cut as a heart," he said after a moment. "A faceted one, I mean. Lodewyk and Bercken cut one for Mary Queen of Scots, but not this big, of course. Are you saying this gemstone came from Egypt?"

"We believe so."

"That's impossible. There are no rubies in Egypt. Maybe German East Africa to the southeast."

"You mean King Solomon's Mines?" I asked.

"Stop!" he insisted. "You're fraying my nerves! We really are in the realms of fantasy now, Thomas."

"Perhaps Solomon gave it to the Queen of Sheba, and later Antony presented it to Cleopatra."

Ira Moskowitz shook his head, refusing to consider it.

"Does this stone have a name?" he asked. "All stones this size must have a name, you know."

I nodded. "If it originally had one, it is lost to time. I suppose we could give it one. What do you think of 'Cleopatra's Heart'?"

"Heart of Egypt?" Ira suggested.

"Heart of the Nile," Barker rumbled. He'd been so quiet I nearly forgot he was there.

"That's it!" Ira exclaimed. "You have a way with words, sir. So, what shall you do with it? Make a doorstop of it?"

"I have not decided," Barker replied. "That's why I brought you here. I have no need of it."

"Allow me to take full measurements while I am here."

Barker nodded. "I will, sir, but you must leave them with me. As you said, people want it and have died for it. I do not wish for you to become one of them."

Ira swallowed loudly. "Nor do I, Mr. Barker. I thank you for your concern."

Moskowitz set to work. The smaller, more delicate tools were of little use. Also, it is difficult to measure a roughly spherical object.

"Pencil? Paper?" My friend demanded, now in his element. I tore a sheet from my notebook and gave him my pencil.

"No, Thomas," he said. "I need a proper piece of stationery if I am to produce an illustration to scale. This requires a diagram."

I looked through drawers in the library until I found one along with a box of sketching pencils in various shades. I'd used them once or twice on a case, but the set may have been in that drawer for a decade.

"Thank you," he murmured, distracted by his work. It was a side of Ira I had never seen before. He had found his niche, his competency. He was no longer the nebbish people once thought him.

"You've got somewhere else to be, gentlemen?" he asked. "I cannot work with people peering over my shoulder."

I carried our coffee cups into the kitchen and helped Mac with the dishes while Barker smoked in the front room. It took Ira half an hour, but when he was finished, it was professionally done. Every contour of the stone was shaded, and every detail measured.

"This is very fine work, Mr. Moskowitz," Barker said. "Thomas, I believe you will agree he has earned his fifty pounds. Would you prefer cash or a cheque, sir?"

"No, sir," Ira said, shaking his head. "I don't want your money."

The Guv crossed his burly arms. "This is absurd, sir. You have clearly earned your fee. Do not place me in the position of trying to force you to take my money."

"If you wish to be of service to me, request that whoever eventually receives the stone should have it cut by Moskowitz and Durham, Limited," Ira said.

"Indeed, I shall, but that costs me nothing. I still insist on paying you. Thomas, banknotes, I think. I don't want any obvious written connection between us."

I pulled Barker's wallet from my pocket and gave the notes to Ira, who looked dazed. Another of my partner's eccentricities is his dislike for carrying money. He does not even like to discuss it.

"Take Mr. Moskowitz through the garden and find a cab in the Old Kent Road. Wear mufflers about your faces so that you won't be recognized, as a precaution."

"Yes, sir."

"Thank you for coming, Mr. Moskowitz," the Guv said. "I am in your debt."

"You are not, sir," Ira said, putting the notes in his pocket. "We are square."

Barker turned to me, raising a brow. The term was unfamiliar to him.

"You are even, sir," I explained.

"Ah. Good evening, sir, and the most prosperous of New Years to you and your family."

"And you, sir."

"Bundle yourself, Ira," I said, leading him to the hall for his coat. We swathed our faces and stepped out the back door.

The oriental garden behind our house was dormant, but it was a beautiful sight in the snow. At least one photographer had come merely to photograph it midwinter. Ira walked right through it as if it wasn't even there. I supposed he saw beauty only through a jeweler's loupe.

I returned a quarter hour later, stamping the snow off my boots in the back passage under Mac's critical eye.

"Is all well, lad?" Barker called.

"Yes, sir. I put him in a cab. No one took any notice of us."

"I am certain you are correct, Thomas, but starting tomorrow, we must assume we are being watched."

CHAPTER 9

After Ira left, I went upstairs to my room. I was tired and tried to rest, but couldn't fall asleep. I missed Rebecca, her voice, her company, her soothing manner. It felt strange that she wasn't here. After a half hour tossing and turning, I climbed the stairs to the Guv's garret chamber. His lamp was lit and he balanced a book on his knee, a forgotten cup of tea on the table beside him. He wore a dressing gown and was warming his feet by the fire.

"Good evening, Thomas," he said. "Can't sleep?"

"No, sir," I replied. "I'm feeling agitated and was thinking of exploring Millwall at night. The tweed cap boys might be about."

He set the book aside. "Just the thing. I believe I'll join you."

I was not impressed by Millwall and the Isle of Dogs on my second visit. The pungent scent of tea in the air was stronger than the coffee and spices of the West India Docks. We took the Underground at the south end to West Ferry Road, which encircles much of the isle. Everything of consequence was there and anyway, one wouldn't want to visit the narrow alleyways even in daylight. Millwall does not have the reputation of White-chapel or the Jago, but one could die here as well as anyplace and better than some.

Barker knew his way about. The air was so cold there were plumes of vapor coming from our mouths, and my teeth began to chatter. We pulled our mufflers over our noses not only from the chill, but so as not to be recognized.

"Do you suppose the Millwall Boys use a pub as a base or have they a warren they work out of?" I asked the Guv.

"There are several public houses in the area, the Anchor and Hope, the Ferry House, the George, the Ship, and the Millwall Docks Tavern, to name a few. The Isle boasts some of the oldest in London because of the river."

"Are any of them particularly dodgy?" I asked.

"I should avoid the last."

"Then let us try it first."

The Guv nodded. "That's the spirit, lad."

We tried the Millwall Docks, the Ship, and the George before finally finding the Millwall gang in a seedy place simply called Dock House. We stepped inside and looked about and were in turn scrutinized by the crowd. The ceiling was low, and tankards hung from the ceiling above my partner's head. There was a roaring fire. Had I known we'd find ourselves in such a place, I'd have dressed less conspicuously. The level of conversation dipped as we entered and did not pick up again for half a minute.

Barker looked about. I don't know how he does it. The gas lamps were low, the room full of smoke from pipes and cigarettes, and he was wearing dark spectacles. They weren't even glass; they were shaved quartz. And yet he walked toward the bar unerringly, as if he'd been there many times before and the room lit like dawn. At the last second, he hiked a boot over the back of a chair and settled into the seat, facing a group of men at cards. It happened so quickly I almost ran into him. The denizens around the table scowled.

"Who invited you into this game?" one asked.

The Guv smiled or tried to. He's not particularly good at it. It's more like a dog baring its teeth.

"I invited myself," he said. "I'll buy a round of drinks if you will answer one question."

The leader, if that's what he was, had a neatly shaven head, but his scalp and chin had a blue sheen from the darkness of the hairs beneath his skin. His nose had been broken once and hadn't healed properly. There was a bandage around the hand that held his cards.

"I'm not answering questions for some toff off the street," he said. "Obviously you've walked into the wrong pub. Sod off."

There was a hiss and a small intake of breath from across the table. It caught my partner's attention. The hiss came from an old salt nearby, fifty at least, with a disreputable cap and gray in his scraggly beard.

"Ambrose Penn," Barker pronounced, his smile widening. "On the street again, are we?"

"As you see, Push," the man said, tugging on the peak of his cap.

"Still married to Katie?"

He shook his head. "No, sir, she moved along."

"Pity. She's a good woman. You're one of the Millwall Boys, now, are you?"

"Not as such," Penn answered. "I lend a little support. Offer advice. Mostly for drinks."

"What's your question?" the leader asked. I wondered if the two were father and son, but I couldn't tell for certain.

"What information can you provide about a group or gang of men wearing tweed caps?" the Guv asked.

In response the leader offered a string of oaths. He grew red-faced in the process.

"I'll tell you what I know!" he replied. "They come strolling into our territory without a by-your-leave two nights ago. We told them they can't just come and go without permission, and the man in charge pulls a knife and says, 'This here is my permission.' So, we get after it. One of my boys is in hospital, 'nother two injured. I got slashed in the hand here. Thought they was just toffs at first, out for a bit of fun, but they knew what they were about."

"Where are they now?" Barker asked.

"Now, ain't had that drink you offered yet."

Barker waved and the publican came out with a bottle of rye and a dozen glasses on a tray. Everyone was eager to participate. A glass was poured and given me but it was none too clean, so I passed it along. I suspected the rye inside did not match the label on the bottle.

"One question, one drink, two questions, two drinks?" my partner asked.

"Surely, if you're buying."

"Toffs, you say?" Barker said. "How many?"

"Eight or nine of them. Had knives, every one of them. Whoever they are, they were well trained. They thumped us proper, and we've won many a scrape protecting our quarter. We weren't prepared, but no one would be. Street gangs don't waltz in on another's territory, not without a shuffling about after."

Barker waved for another bottle. Two, actually. Now everyone in the tavern was drinking at our expense.

"When did you last see them?" my partner asked.

"They were here last night," he replied. "Might still be around. We ain't 'zactly looking for them if you take my meaning. Just want them to go so we can repair our reputation."

"Naturally," the Guv answered. "What did the leader look like?"

"Thirty years old, maybe," the man replied. "Yellow cap with red checks. Red hair and side-whiskers. Wore a ring, a horseshoe. Tried to punch me with it, to leave a mark, like. It might have had diamonds, maybe. They was tough, but still too posh for Millwall."

"What is your name, sir?" Barker asked.

"Hugh Chapman."

"Mr. Chapman, can you think of a reason why, having accomplished what they came for, they decided to stay and take the air?"

The leader of the Millwall Boys smiled. "Take the air, that's a good one, sir. They ain't dock boys, I know that for certain. They couldn't abide the stink, and they stepped over fish offal like they was afraid to get their precious boots soiled. Can't believe such fancy boys knew how to break an elbow."

"Break an elbow?" Barker asked. "You said nothing about breaking elbows."

"What did they call what happened to Jim's elbow, Ambrose?"

"Dislocated, Hugh."

"Right. He dislocated it. Or rather, one o' them done it for him."

"Did they seem professional?" my partner asked. "You gentlemen look more than capable of defending yourselves in a fair fight."

Flattery never hurts, especially when a man's fighting prowess is concerned. Respect breeds respect.

Chapman rubbed his bluish chin in thought and had another swallow of rye.

"Yeah. I suppose they could have been," he replied. "Tell you one thing, they done whatever that cocky posh boy told them to."

Barker turned to the older man. "Mr. Penn, were you involved in the fight?"

In answer, Penn removed his cap. There was a scrape across his forehead, and a sizeable lump. "I ain't past it, Guv."

"Obviously not. Did you recognize any of them?"

Penn thought for a moment. I felt sorry for him. He looked past his prime and had no pension. He was reduced to scraps and charity, though at least Chapman offered him some respect.

"I couldn't see everyone, Push, but one of them reminded me of a former jockey named Jack Hambly. I was occupied, but it looked like him."

Barker turned and addressed the gang leader again. "A final bottle for the room if you can add anything to what you've said. Any impression, any clue that might lead us to them. We suspect they might have killed the man found floating by Millwall Docks."

Chapman thought about it but could not come up with anything. That is, until we reached the door. Then something came to him.

"Oy!" he cried. "The leader, the one they answered to, he tried to be as rough as his boys, but he wasn't. He's a rich lad, proud of hisself, strutting around with his gang. Couldn't fight, though. I mean, he cut me, but only because he didn't know what he was doing. Cut himself as well as me."

"I see," Barker said.

"Oh, and the knives . . ."

"What about them?"

"Identical and new, they was, like new from a box. Black-handled clasp knives, probably bought in the West End. Sheffield steel. Whitechapel ain't got nothin' like it."

Barker and I returned to the bar and I paid the publican for another bottle. Someone had brought out an asthmatic concertina and began to play an old shanty. We were the most sober men in the room, save for the publican, who must have been feeling merry from the money I paid him. The Guv turned and we left. I laughed when we were in the street.

"Buying rounds of drinks in a low pub, and you a pious man," I chided in a low voice.

"I drank nothing," he said in his own defense.

The air felt bone-chilling compared with the moist heat of the Dock House. Icicles hung from the eaves of shops like the tusks of antediluvian monsters. I regretted suggesting we go out on such a night to such a place.

A lad ran up to us from the direction of the river, his feet bound in rags and a blanket covered in patches over his shoulders. The boy's towhead was covered in an oversized sailor's knit cap. He seemed to recognize us.

"Mr. Barker!" he called.

"Here, lad."

He thrust a note into the Guv's hand. I gave the boy a shilling and he was overjoyed. He stuffed the coin in his pocket then ran off again, a small spark of energy in the frigid darkness. At this hour, the boy should have been abed after a filling meal. However, this was the East End, and She is a flinty soul.

"It's from Ho," my partner rumbled. "He needs me at the restaurant immediately."

We hadn't gone a hundred yards when we saw a young man hurrying along in a green cap. He held the lapels of his coat up around his cheeks, but he did not notice us a few hundred feet away.

"A garish tweed cap," I noted. "One doesn't see such a thing every day. The world is the better for it."

"Decidedly, "he responded. "Perhaps Ho will wait a quarter hour."

"He wouldn't have sent a message if it wasn't important."

"I don't want to lose that fellow," Barker said. "He might lead us to the gang."

"You go on," I said. "I'll follow him and catch you up later."

"It could be dangerous, Thomas."

I had to decide immediately or lose sight of the dandy ahead.

"I'll stay at a discreet distance," I replied.

"Very well."

We parted, he going north toward Limehouse and me east toward the docks. I kept my White Rabbit in sight. Obligingly, he was smoking a Balkan Sobranie, so I could follow by scent as well as sight. I thought it likely that the gang, should they be here at all, would be on the less obvious east side, full of basins, wharfs, and docks. It was a maze and difficult to navigate, where even a group of men in outré hats might hide themselves away.

Fine crystals swirled around the gas lamps like airborne plankton in an icy sea. Meanwhile, the late December moon shone a pallid light on the icy streets, painting the snowy roofs blue.

My quarry abruptly turned right and disappeared. I approached the corner cautiously.

He'd entered a square, four buildings butted together with an arch in front, allowing people to come and go. I stepped back and considered leaving. There were too many factors that made me uncomfortable. I could leave and bring Barker back, now that I knew the general area where the gang might be staying, but I changed my mind. Perhaps I could discover something more.

I watched as he entered one of the buildings, never having noticed me. Cautiously, I stepped through the arch, looking left and right. There was no one here but me, endangering my life while Barker was having tea and thousand-year-old eggs, talking about old times with his former first mate.

I crept through the quad, headed to the dark stairwell where the lad had disappeared. The frigid snow crunched under my feet. It was the only sound I heard. I was nearly at the stairwell when a man with red side-whiskers stepped out, wearing a yellow checked cap. I knew immediately I was in grave danger.

"Pretty hat," I remarked.

"Thank you," he replied. "Handsome stick you've got there. It will go nicely with my cap. Boys!"

Men spilled from every entrance. Nine of them, as Hugh Chapman had said, all of them ready and confident, seasoned fighters save for the leader. He looked brash, erratic. He was enjoying this too much at my expense.

I was up against it now. The odds were nine-to-one with a brass-knobbed stick in my hand. They came forward cautiously, pulling knives from their pockets, new ones with black handles. My heart skipped a beat. I'd seen Julius Caesar murdered on stage this way. *Et tu, Brute?*

"Thomas Llewelyn," the leader said. "Some call you the Terrier, since you follow after your master. But you're off your lead now with no one to protect you. My, you are in a predicament."

"I'll give you five minutes to get out of Millwall," I said.

Everyone laughed, the leader especially.

"You do have brass, Tommy, no mistake. I heard you was cheeky. Boys, look at his suit. Now that's stitching. Savile Row. Class. Try not to get blood on the overcoat. I like it."

"Why the caps?" I asked.

"Never mind why the caps," he replied. "I know you're hoping Push'll come after you. I sent him that note. I hear he's mates with the Chinaman. I also hear you have a pretty little wife. Rich, too. I'll have to look her up when you're gone."

I shook my head and tsk-tsked.

"Now you've done it," I said. Pulling my Webley from my pocket, I shot him.

I never told them I wasn't armed. Let them learn that on their own, I say. It certainly got his companions' attention. They backed away and ran when I aimed at their heads.

Meanwhile, the cocky one was on the ground screaming. I'd shot him in the foot, dead center in his tan Italian vamp. The bullet had probably fractured a few metatarsals. I hadn't wanted to kill him, but I didn't intend to go back to Barker empty-handed.

"Oh, shut it," I said.

I seized the scruff of his collar and dragged him to a metal bollard erected to keep carriages out of the courtyard, as if any would dare venture into this quadrangle voluntarily. I reached into my pocket and retrieved a pair of darbies. They were not police regulation, just thumb cuffs, compact, like metal versions of a Chinese thumb trap. I thumped his head against the pole and circled his limbs around it. All the while he screamed and bled. Candles were lit in the rooms above us, and onlookers peered out of windows and from behind curtains.

I looked about. There were no gang members in sight. They had fled when their leader was shot. *Leaders are expendable*, I thought. Someone always wants to be the next one. I raised my bowler to the crowd looking down. Then I bent and spoke in the man's ear.

"Look up my widow, would you?" I asked. "You're lucky I didn't pip the ace in your eye."

I left him trussed there. It wasn't far to Narrow Street and Ho's establishment. I went through the tunnel and found the Guv sitting in one of three chairs by the fire, Ho sitting beside him. I fell into the third and put my palms to the blaze.

"I apologize, Thomas," Barker said. "I cannot believe I accepted the note at face value. It was written in English. Did you encounter anyone?"

"I did," I answered. "Shot the leader."

"Dead?" Barker asked, a brow appearing over the top of his spectacles.

"No. In the foot."

The Chinaman smiled. It looked even more unnatural on him than it did on the Guv.

"Intentionally, I mean," I continued. "I didn't want him going around causing trouble, so I wrapped him around a pole."

"Rope?"

"No, I used the thumb darbies you gave me. Had them in my pocket."

"I gave those to you as a curiosity," he said. "I don't know that they actually work. We should go speak to your new friend."

"He's no friend of mine," I said. "He made a rude remark about Mrs. Llewelyn."

"It's a wonder you didn't shoot him in both feet. Where was the shot precisely? Show me."

I pointed toward my right instep and he nodded.

"When it passed through, it probably ricocheted off the cobbles and shattered his heel as well. He'll limp for the rest of his life."

"He'll remember me, then," I answered. "I'm not greatly alarmed."

"You should be," Barker retorted. "I suspect he works for someone more powerful. You may have made yourself a new enemy."

We left and headed south again. I wondered how we would find our way back home in the dark, in the cold, in a dangerous part of London Town where cabs dared not go. I led Barker east to the square where I left the leader, but he was gone. There were gouts of blood on the cobblestones beside the bollard.

"Blast," I said, looking about.

"His friends were with him?" Barker asked.

"Nearby, I suspect. They wouldn't go far without him."

"They released him, then. If it is any consolation, I imagine they had to strip much of the skin from his thumbs to get those little darbies off."

"Thank you for the gift," I said as we walked about, looking for any sign of the gang. "It was certainly useful. However, we have a problem. The fellow knew me by name."

"Did he, by Jove?" Barker growled. "That makes this interesting."

"Interesting, is it?"

"Aye," said the Guv. "I'd watch my back if I were you."

CHAPTER 10

I'm not the sort of fellow who puts much stock in dreams. I know there are many that do, and I'll concede that the Bible speaks of Joseph interpreting the dreams of Nebuchadnezzar. I've met at least one society dame who claims she can interpret them, and there are some tarot card readers and spiritualists who I'm sure will claim to be able to do so for a small extra fee.

Personally, I believe dreams to be the ash can of the mind. Everything is tossed in willy-nilly: memories from long ago and yesterday; our greatest hopes and fears; something we read or experienced or ate. All of it is thrown together and our over-worked brain tries to mold it into a shape we can make sense of and accept. Oh sure, we all love to tell people our dreams if they are cohesive and interesting enough, but we never tell the ones that ramble, or make no sense at all, which is most of them. I've never had a dream that affected me emotionally or that I remembered long afterward. That is, until this enquiry. I put it down to overwork and to the strangeness of the case. Again, it signifies nothing, yet I felt it became a part of everything, if for no other reason than it shows how overwrought I was at the time. It was me entertaining myself with ghost stories.

I fell asleep in a chair after midnight while reading H. Rider Haggard's *Cleopatra*. It wasn't a patch on *King Solomon's Mines*, but it was the only book about the lady pharaoh on my shelves.

I was a quarter of the way into the book and it was rough going. Eventually, I fell asleep.

I dreamed I was walking along the Victoria Embankment with Rebecca on my arm. It was early spring, and the trees were filled with birdsong. There were already buds on the trees and tulips in beds, beginning to bloom by the river. My wife was in a jaunty new hat, white against her oyster-gray dress. She was telling me something completely inconsequential, and I was having trouble finding either a beginning or an end to the thread. I believe it had something to do with her sister.

"Let's stop here," I said, pointing to a bench facing the river. I offered her a seat and she continued the story. I saw something out of the corner of my eye and turned my head, realizing that we were sitting by Cleopatra's Needle, that strange obelisk donated to the king in 1819 by the Egyptian ruler, Muhammad Ali Pasha. It always draws my eye because it seems so out of place by the homely Thames, and I wondered what the architect would think to see his work standing in metropolitan Charing Cross, so far from home.

"Anyway," Rebecca continued. "Aunt Lydia said, 'What on earth?' and began to push my mother toward the broom closet."

I do like it when Rebecca chatters. I love her silvery laugh and how astute her opinions are. I half listened and let her voice wash over me, watching the sunlight play over the ancient stone monument. I wondered what the hieroglyphs meant. A yacht glided by, its sails billowing. It was warm and I wanted to remove my jacket.

"Of course, Mother wasn't going to let her have the last word on the subject . . ."

I glanced back at my wife. I thought it unfair that I could not remove my jacket while she had changed her entire costume. Still, it was more suited to the heat. Her white crepe dress set off the gold of her sandals and the elaborate necklace about her throat. It must have taken some time to outline her eyes in kohl and gold leaf like that. She looked fetching.

"What did your father say?" I asked, trying to keep up.

"You know poor Father can never get a word in."

I noticed her dress was cut rather low, but I sympathized. The heat was wretched this time of year. I finally removed my jacket while Rebecca kicked the bottom of the golden sandal against her heel as she played with the curls at the nape of my neck.

She continued her story. I watched as a royal barge rowed by, pulled by fifty slaves. I felt languorous and wondered what Barker was doing at that moment. It must be Saturday afternoon or Sunday if I wasn't working. I could tell my wife's story was reaching its denouement. A husband develops a sixth sense about these things. I turned in anticipation, but found it wasn't Rebecca next to me at all. It was Cleopatra herself.

Strange things, dreams. It did not in any way amaze me that I was sitting next to a beautiful Egyptian queen from two thousand years ago while she prattled and played with my hair as if she did it every day. She wasn't as beautiful as my wife, but she was alluring enough. One could see how she seduced Caesar and Mark Antony. She had a strong if regal profile and her eyes seemed flecked with gold.

I looked out on the lighthouse in the harbor of Alexandria, one of the wonders of the ancient world. Rebecca, or Cleopatra, or whoever it was, had stopped talking. It was almost unbearably hot. The dry air seized me by the throat as we watched a Roman galley sail into port. She put her head on my shoulder and stroked my neck. I had a premonition then of what was to come, and I stiffened as I realized her fingers had so little flesh on them, only dried leathery skin and wrappings.

I couldn't bear it anymore. I had to look. I turned my head and found a shriveled brown face with a rictus of a smile and eyes like old grapes rolling in their sockets. Her brick-colored hair was braided behind her ears. She seized the back of my neck in her terrible claws and began to pull me toward her face for an unholy kiss. I smelled her fetid breath, glared in panic as her desiccated and rotting flesh came closer. Her grin widened and then her lips came together to press against mine.

Cyrus Barker was shaking me awake.

"Thomas!" he yelled, slapping my face.

"What happened?" I demanded.

"You were screaming," he rumbled. "I thought you were being murdered!"

I sat up in bed and shook my head like a dog, bathed in sweat.

"I'm sorry to alarm you, sir," I said in a ragged voice. "I had a nightmare. A terrible one."

The Guv frowned. "Perhaps this enquiry is disturbing you, lad. I could continue on my own if you wish to withdraw."

"No, sir," I replied.

"There is no shame in it," he insisted.

"I'm fine," I told him, running a hand through my unruly hair. "It was a dream, nothing more. I'll be fine in a minute."

Barker crossed his arms and studied me. "You are overworking."

"I am not," I insisted. "We just started the case yesterday."

"Aye, but you shot a man."

"Yes, but in the foot!" I protested. "It's not as if I killed him. Besides, the blighter had it coming."

"When will Mrs. Llewelyn return?"

"New Year's Day," I answered. "Don't worry. I'll be right as rain in the morning."

"Very well," he said, studying me. "Get some sleep."

I tried to take his advice, but I was unaccustomed to sleeping alone and I've always been a troubled sleeper. Two hours later I was still staring at the ceiling, reliving the dream and trying not to think of amorous mummies. I couldn't recall if I had eaten anything that precipitated such absurdities. "'There's more of gravy than of grave,'" I thought. Dickens has a remark for everything.

I combed through the events of the day: Mrs. Addison's visit, the interviews with Thompson and Hennings, calling on Grant, and having a huge ruby thrust into our collective hands.

Then Addison's body was found, we were introduced to Coffee John, and after a walk we spoke with Ho. We informed the new widow and his family. Ira Moskowitz came to dinner.

Finally, I capped the day by shooting a man in the foot. I blamed myself. I shouldn't have suggested we go out after such a long day. A man makes poor decisions after nine o'clock at night.

I had no business being mesmerized by a long-dead Egyptian ruler. I was a respectable married man for one thing, and though Caesar and Antony had wives also, I was not the poor husband they were. I was beyond being flattered by a pair of fluttering eyelashes. She should try her Svengali tricks on someone else. She'd find no takers here.

I slept for a few hours then shaved and dressed and went down to breakfast with the hope of sucking down most of a pot of coffee. Barker came downstairs shortly after seven and had tea while glaring out the kitchen window at his dormant garden. If anything, he wanted spring to arrive more than I. On the way to our chambers in Whitehall, the Guv and I spoke little, and nothing was said about the dream the night before.

We arrived in our offices well before eight. Not long after, the front door opened and Clive Hennings entered unannounced.

"Mr. Hennings!" Barker boomed from his desk. He was bursting with rude health and vigor, while I was looking for an alleyway in which to die. "Come in and warm yourself by the fire."

Hennings came to the doorway of our office and peered in at the burning embers. "I don't mind it, sirs, if it's not too much trouble."

"Come, sit then."

The fireplace is to Barker's right. The Guv carried one of the visitor's chairs over and allowed Hennings to sit. Our visitor brought his boots as close to the fire as he dared without scorching the soles and held his hands in front of him.

"This makes me wish I were back in Luxor on a dig," Hennings said. "There's nothing like an Egyptian sun to warm an Englishman's blood."

"Alas, I've never been closer than the deck of a steamer headed for the Holy Land," Barker said.

"Go, sirs, if you can afford it," Hennings replied. "It will change your outlook on life. I first became entranced with Egypt as a child, but I never thought I'd visit the ancient cities or have the opportunity to plunge a hundred feet or more into an ancient tomb. It is exhilarating, but I must admit it makes London seem all the colder."

"Have you come to browbeat us again, sir, or compel us to give you what was inside the mummy?" Barker asked. He sat back in the recess of his chair, looking like nothing could compel him to do anything.

"Yes, sir, I have, but it isn't my primary purpose," he answered. "I've come to give you a warning."

"Very kind of you, sir," the Guv said in a gravelly voice. "Pray state it."

Hennings sat up in alarm. "My mistake, Mr. Barker. The warning is for your benefit. A fellow may come here soon who means all of us mischief. His name is Aamir Mahmoud. He claims to be a representative of the Cairo Museum."

"Why is he a problem?" Barker asked.

"To begin with, there is no Cairo Museum," Hennings stated. "It is still in the planning stages. He may be a member of the committee but he has no authority. He came in yesterday after-noon to ingratiate himself, but we soon realized his plan. He wants to thieve our museum of its treasures."

"Which treasures?" I asked.

"Anything and everything Egyptian, from the smallest scarab to the Rosetta Stone."

"Isn't it theirs, anyway?" I argued. "I mean, Cleopatra's Needle was a gift, but didn't we take the Stone?"

"We found it, sir," he argued. "It is ours."

"Regardless, gentlemen," the Guv interrupted. "What would you have me do with Mr. Mahmoud? Toss him out into White-hall Street and tell him to take himself elsewhere?"

"It is no less than he deserves," Hennings answered. "If a Cairo Museum is built, a law will be passed by the Egyptian gov-ernment making it illegal to carry antiquities out of the country. Then where will we be? There would be no digs, no expeditions, no discoveries. There would be no experts, no trained diggers, no engineers. There'd be no English Egyptologists. Nothing!"

"I see," Barker said.

Hennings shook his head. "Not to be rude, sir, but I fear you do not. Mahmoud has heard some of the rumors. The men working for me have been indiscreet, I'm sorry to say. In their defense, you cannot keep something this important from the public. Mahmoud wants what was in the mummy, and he knows that you have it."

"Mr. Hennings," the Guv remonstrated. "If you are attempt-ing to frighten me you aren't succeeding. An Egyptologist shall come here and berate me? Sir, I expect several will attempt to do the same over the next few days. Will he come armed? We are prepared for that. If he brings a solicitor, I assure you I have an excellent one at hand myself. What have I to fear?"

"The supernatural, sir."

Barker turned and looked at me. For once, I was speechless. We both turned and scrutinized Hennings more closely.

"Would you care to be more specific?" he asked.

"I am told that Mahmoud is a Blavatskyite. A Theosophist."

Again, the Guv turned to me. I am the Encyclopedia Llewe-lynia, as far as he is concerned. What he doesn't know I am sup-posed to supply, having attended Oxford. As it happened, I was on safe ground here.

"The late Mrs. Blavatsky was a believer in all religions and was attempting to combine them into one, which she called The-osophy," I explained. "She believed in mediums, spirits, card reading, table rapping, demons, and probably a hundred other things we've never heard of. She traveled around the world. Once or twice, she was caught faking a séance but managed to wriggle out of the notoriety. She was a fraud, sir, but a clever one. She fooled hundreds and gathered believers who would do or say anything she wanted. In fact, the believers in Theosophy are more ardent now that she has died, with her beliefs and reputation disgraced."

Barker looked amused. "What do you suppose Mr. Mah-moud will do?"

"She was a fraud, this is true, Mr. Barker," Hennings agreed. "She wrote her book *Isis Unveiled* with no more knowledge of Egypt than can be collected in an afternoon's reading and a middle-class steamer tour of the Nile. What frightens me is that if Mahmoud lays hand upon whatever it is you have, he will use it not only to justify the Cairo Museum, which is a travesty, or use it to revive Theosophy, which is even worse."

"What would Mahmoud do as far as the Cairo Museum is concerned?"

"He would use whatever you've got as a cornerstone for the museum, thus legitimizing it. It would ensure that others will donate monies for digs and artifacts. He might even attempt to purchase Cleopatra herself!"

As I watched him talk, it seemed to me that he acted as if he were under her spell, as if she belonged to him or he to her.

"Are you gentlemen acquainted with a man named Liam Grant?" he continued.

"We are, sir," Barker admitted.

"He believes that Mahmoud is attempting to reunite the factions that are the remnants of the Theosophy movement, such as the Society for Psychical Research and the British National Association of Spiritualists."

"Mr. Hennings, forgive me," my partner said, "but you appear to believe that some of their claims, curses, and demons are genuine, as if a group of middle- and upper-class citizens have the power to take back what I borrowed. Borrowed for safekeeping until this matter is resolved. I'm working to find Phillip Addison's murderer."

"Yes, we must not forget Phillip," Clive Hennings said. "I still can't believe he is gone. He was worth two of any of the fellows I have working for me now, and they with credentials from foreign universities and numerous digs behind them."

"You seem to know a good deal about Mr. Mahmoud," Barker said, steering the conversation back.

Hennings nodded. "I do. There are several articles written by him in various mystical publications that Mr. Grant claims is proof that Mahmoud is about to proclaim himself the High Priest of the old religion of Egypt, the High Priest of Amun-Ra. He also believes himself to be the thirtieth incarnation of the pharaoh, Ptolemy X."

"Cleopatra's husband," I said, pointing at him.

"Precisely," Hennings answered, nearly bouncing in his chair. "I suspect he's going to attempt to stop the presentation of the mummy to the public by claiming to be her husband and only relative."

I laughed. "That's absurd."

"It is, but his purpose is to halt the examination process until a better opportunity becomes available to him."

Barker pressed his fingertips together. Mahmoud's supposed

claims did not concern him. "Tell me, Mr. Hennings. You were the last known person to see Phillip Addison before he died. What did he say?"

"He was elated, of course. He said he'd made a discovery that I needed to see immediately. You see, gentlemen, the least important mummies are placed on the bottom shelves. Naturally I was curious, but someone had examined that specimen before and found it of little importance. He wanted me to see it for myself. Frankly, I thought it long odds that he had found anything important. I was upset at being startled awake as well, and the thought that I would have to go out into that dark night because of a volunteer's whim made me surly. Of course, I had no idea he was going to die, poor fellow. I must admit I feel responsible. If I had returned with him to the museum, he might not have been set upon. It's very hard. It seemed as if he were going to have a fine future, my protégé. He deserved one, poor devil. He and his wife were living hand-to-mouth."

He looked about the room as if attempting to screw up his courage. "Mr. Barker, you must give back what Phillip took. It is not your property. Whatever it is belongs to the British Museum, and we are a powerful force. Surely it is here now, or nearby. If you have it, give it to me. I'll see that it is returned discreetly, and no punishment will be forthcoming. Surely you see that this matter will reflect ill on Phillip's name. I'm sure your client would not want that to happen."

"Alas, sir," Barker said. "It is gone. I had it in my possession for a very short time."

"But surely you can get it back!" he pleaded.

"It is out of my hands, I'm afraid," the Guv said, holding up both palms.

"Director Thompson moves slowly but surely," Hennings insisted. "He will get the stone in the end. Surely you know this."

"Are you here on his behalf?"

"No, I'm here on my own," Hennings said. "Frankly, I've

been given a dressing-down for not believing Phillip that night, as if I were omniscient. Also for the lack of security by allowing a volunteer to work late. I supposed if I could convince you to give me whatever was in Cleopatra's belly, I could return it to Thompson and be restored to his good graces."

"What of Mr. Mahmoud?" my partner asked. "Was he a ploy to gain my cooperation?"

"No, sir. Watch for that fellow. He means mischief. He wants to lay hands on the stone."

Barker frowned. "Stone?"

"Yes, sir."

"What makes you believe it is a stone?"

"I'm not sure," Hennings said. "Something happened this morning in the director's office and now everyone at the museum is calling it a stone. There's a new fellow involved whom I've never seen before. I feared he was my replacement, but Thompson brought him in for something else."

"Yet you have not said 'stone' until now," the Guv replied. "Are you are trying to manipulate me, Mr. Hennings?"

"Sir," Clive Hennings said. "I'll be frank. I'm simply trying to retain my position."

"Very well, Mr. Hennings. Thank you for the word of warning. Good day."

Hennings stood awkwardly and bowed. Barker's was more perfunctory. I showed the Egyptologist to the door. He looked wan. I tried not to shut the door in his face.

"It sounds like his sins are finding him out," I remarked.

"They always do, lad," he rumbled. "They always do."

CHAPTER 11

After Hennings left, I made a stout fire in the grate. I'm a coal miner's son, so I know how to build a proper fire. Barker wouldn't notice the cold until the insides of the windows were laced with ice, and Jenkins lights a fire the moment he arrives, then doesn't think to stoke it again the rest of the day. It soothes me to set out the coal and tend it until it ignites.

I could see the Guv's mind turning. He alternated between scratching under his chin and drawing abstract designs on his blotter with the tip of his finger. I supposed it was a good sign, but I wondered what deviltry he was planning. One that would involve me getting shot at, no doubt.

It was just past eleven when a messenger arrived with a note. He was neither a child nor a pensioner, but a man in a proper suit and overcoat with an almost military bearing. He nodded at Jenkins, told him to give the note to Barker, and left, although the Guv was in view. Barker snatched the note from the salver and glanced at it. Then he crumpled it in a ball and tossed it. It bounced off the edge of his desk, I pounced on it and read:

13:00
.HoL
Come for lunch.
LG

It took about fifteen seconds to decipher the message. HoL meant House of Lords. LG was Lord Grayle, the well-known collector of antiquities whom my partner had banned from our offices for being a nuisance in a previous case. He and Barker had clashed over a biblical manuscript a year before. I heard his estate in Hampshire was like a museum, filled with glass cases and antiquities. There was even a rumor that he had a basement chamber full of Egyptian treasures, a replica of a tomb in Luxor with stone walls, gold-encrusted sarcophagi, and treasures to help while away the afterlife in comfort and style. In short, Grayle liked to play pharaoh when he wasn't at the museum or the House of Lords. I won't tell another man how to run his life, but it seemed to me that a part of him had never matured. He merely purchased larger and more expensive toys for his nursery. Cleopatra's mummy and a huge jewel were just the sort of things he'd desire and be willing to pay for. I haven't seen him reach a limit beyond which he would not go.

Barker exhaled a bushel full of air and frowned. He was sulking. He didn't want to go.

"Grayle's a lord," I counseled. "A peer of the realm. It would be bad form to refuse. Also, he might provide information, either intentionally or unwittingly. He's just the sort of fellow to hire a gang. I suspect if he wants something enough, he doesn't care what it will take to get it."

Barker crossed his arms. "Wealthy men acquire things. It is

in their nature. I own a fine home, but I could tear it down and build a grand estate if I wished to impress people. However, my home and garden contain all I desire. There are many charities in London that need our support, so many starving families that must be fed, which are more important than collecting things."

"Yes," I said. "And funding provided to places like the British Museum allow them to educate Britons and safeguard our history."

"Aye," he replied. "A public museum that all may attend. His Lordship doesn't understand. In my opinion, his type of collecting is just another form of grave robbing."

"I agree, sir," I said. "Yet we are going, aren't we?"

Cyrus Barker made an expression as if I had caused this predicament and then fished his watch from his pocket and consulted it.

"Half past twelve," he said. "The nerve of the fellow, believing we have nothing of consequence to do in the middle of a workday."

"I agree, sir. It shows a certain pomposity of manner. That being said, we don't have anything on."

"Yes, we do," he answered. "I was looking forward to some beef off the joint and a half pint of porter at the Clarence."

I shrugged my shoulders. "The choice is yours. My name is not on the invitation."

"Nonsense," the Guv replied. "If I'm going, you are as well."

"If you're punished, then I'm punished."

"Of course," he reasoned. "Someone must keep notes."

I rose and went to the coatrack. "At least we shall get a good meal out of it."

Barker stood, nodding. "One would think."

We shrugged on our coats. Jenkins was turning the pages of a new edition of *The Illustrated Police News*.

"We'll be back in an hour, Jeremy," I said.

"Yes, sir," he replied with a smile.

We gathered our sticks, hats, and mufflers and stepped outside. A frigid breeze brushed my face like the fingers of Death itself.

"I'll see if I can find a cab," I said.

"Don't bother," my partner replied. "We'll walk."

Barker is a proponent of the so-called strenuous life. I've heard that in Asia, monks stand under icy waterfalls, but I had no desire to become a monk. I thought of the wonderful fire I'd built for Jenkins to enjoy alone while I was being blamed for Lord Grayle's note. Perhaps it was because I had deciphered it so readily.

"You're responsible if I get frostbite and my fingers fall off," I said as we marched down Whitehall Street.

"Nonsense," he replied. "We will be like steam boilers, radiating our own heat."

"'The strenuous life is not worth living,'" I complained, misquoting Socrates. The Guv gave a rare chuckle, shaking his head.

The paving was treacherous, and at the cross streets I was nearly knocked off my feet by the wind. It was only a half-mile walk, however, and I survived with only burning ears and rosy cheeks to show for it. When we entered the building, Barker crossed to a tall porter's desk in the central lobby.

"We have been summoned by Lord Grayle," he stated.

The fellow consulted a ledger in front of him. Then he snapped his fingers and a second porter came trotting up and led us through the halls to a dining room. A gold and crystal chandelier glittered overhead and the white tablecloth had been starched and ironed. *If my grandfather could see me now*, I thought. You couldn't swing a stick without hitting an earl, a lord, or a duke. Everyone's ancestor had been the crony of a king. The Llewelyns had been kings in Wales once, but it wouldn't earn me tea and a bun now.

The room reminded me of my school days. The tables were

long and the wooden benches had no backs. Everyone sat elbow to elbow in the peer's dining room. We were led to where His Lordship sat and he nodded as we approached.

"Barker, glad you could come on short notice," he said. "Have a seat. Waiter, two more places."

Lord Grayle was not a remarkable-looking fellow. He was clean-shaven and well-dressed, between fifty and sixty, his hair receding at the temples. He did not appear raving mad. There was no obvious sign that he would sell his own mother for his latest acquisition, or the next, or the one after. But there was a sucking hole in the poor man's soul, and he spent his life rigorously trying to stop it with trinkets. I'd feel sorry for him if the fellow was not so avaricious.

"It should come as no surprise, Barker, that I am on the board of directors for the British Museum," he said. "Two nights ago, a volunteer left with an item that belonged to the museum's collection and subsequently disappeared with it. I was told the following morning that his body was found floating in Limehouse Basin. That afternoon you appeared and I was not especially surprised. You seem to turn up whenever matters get unpleasant. I think you have a nose for it. By the way, I must extend my congratulations to you for our last meeting. Posting a first-century gospel to the Vatican in a box of hosiery was truly imaginative."

"It was merely to hand," the Guv stated, as if it were a trivial matter. After a case is closed he does not think much about it afterward.

"Who hired you this time, if I may ask?" Grayle continued.

Barker looked about to tell him to jump in the Thames, which just happened to be outside the window, but the question had been civil, and my partner will answer a civil question truthfully.

"The widow, Mrs. Addison."

Grayle nodded. Actually, his name was Peter Ward Naughton,

Twelfth Lord of Grayle, I had discovered in *Burke's Peerage* during our last association. "A damsel in distress, then."

That last remark raised the Guv's hackles.

"What do you want, Your Lordship?" he rumbled. "I have matters to attend to."

"That should be obvious. I want to know what that chap, Addison, found inside the mummy. I want to estimate what it is worth. Almost anything belonging to Cleopatra would be worth a great deal, even the linen wrapping inside her, but I need to know how much to offer."

"Offer to whom, sir?"

"Whoever has it, of course," Grayle said. "I don't care who it is, although I suppose the amount would fluctuate depending on who has possession of it. I'm also gathering funds to buy the mummy itself. If it proves to be the real Cleopatra, I'll allow the museum to exhibit it with my name on a plaque. If the mummy is proved to be a fake, or a lesser member of the family, I'll still make an offer. I want her, Barker. I intend to have her. As for whatever little treasure she cradled in her bosom, I want that, too. I could hire you myself, I suppose. You could work for me."

"I am already engaged at present, Your Lordship," Barker answered.

"I didn't say you couldn't find that poor blighter's killer," he said. "Do both. I'm sure you have access to all sorts of information."

"I am already retained, Your Lordship, and my hands are full. There are still many questions I must answer."

Our first course arrived, a simple pea soup. I wanted to see how the food in the House of Lords compared to our nightly dinner from Le Toison d'Or, Etienne Dummolard's restaurant. It is difficult to ruin a pea soup, but the cook had triumphed spectacularly. It was full of lumps, partially cold, and the chef had managed to avoid his salt shaker entirely.

"Mr. Llewelyn," Grayle said, turning to me. "You didn't think

I knew your name, did you? I understand you have been working with Mr. Barker for ten years now. Isn't it time for you to spread your wings and soar? I could fund an office for you and get you started. In fact, you can work for me exclusively, hunting for curiosities around the world. You would have an interesting life, and Mrs. Llewelyn would drip with diamonds."

I invited His Lordship to jump up his own nose, but instead of getting angry the man guffawed.

"A man of the people as always, sir. Well, I can respect that. Not admire it, of course, but respect it."

Next came a course which proved to be ox cheek, braised in red wine and served with mashed potatoes. I don't understand how one part of an animal will be considered sweetmeats while others are deemed inedible. It looked appetizing on its bed of mash, but one bite informed me I would have been better served had it remained on the ox. I vowed that henceforth I could not eat any part of an animal above the neck. I barely managed to swallow it.

"Awful, isn't it?" Grayle asked, with some degree of sympathy.

"Very bad indeed," I agreed. "There must be an art to truly bad cooking."

"I'm sure," he chuckled. "This kitchen is famous for it."

The next course came. Beef marrow. It is one of Barker's favorites, although he prefers to break the bones himself with a nutcracker. These were halved and roasted. He was delighted.

"This is no way to win my favor, sir," I said, surveying the bones.

"Perhaps," Grayle replied. "But how often have you eaten with some of the most famous and powerful men in Britain?"

I looked about. I did indeed spy a half dozen men I'd seen in the newspapers that month tucking in.

"Why are they here?" I asked. "There are proper pubs nearby."

"Yes, but here you can eavesdrop on the opposition's conversation or try to convince a member to change his vote on a bill."

I looked about at the gold mirrors on the wall and the elegant moldings. Seldom has such an inedible meal been served in so distinctive and illustrious a setting, but apparently it occurred here every day.

The final course was a simple salad. I wouldn't think one could ruin that, but the amount of oil and vinegar in the dressing had been transposed. The lettuce visibly wilted in front of my eyes and lay like a fish gasping on the shore. I wondered how the aristocracy could still make decisions with such poor sustenance to fuel them.

Barker had eaten everything placed before him. He took a satisfied sip of his coffee and I dared try mine. It was the worst coffee I had ever had in London and that is saying a great deal.

"Your Lordship," Barker said. "I thank you for the meal. There isn't enough good, plain fare anywhere in this country. It was a privilege to be your guest."

"However . . ." Lord Grayle supplied.

"However, this does not mean I will help you to acquire the missing artifact."

Grayle sighed. "Can you at least tell me what it is?"

"Alas," the Guv said.

His Lordship put up a hand. "Just answer this one question for me, please. Should I wish to gather monies to acquire the object in question, would it be necessary to gather or borrow a large sum?"

"I suspect it would be a price even you couldn't afford," Barker replied.

"Ha!" Grayle bellowed, slapping the table with the palm of his hand.

Three dozen pairs of cool, disapproving eyes turned in our direction. His Lordship cared not a whit. He'd received a challenge and relished it.

"Very well, Mr. Barker," he said. "We shall see."

We stood and prepared to leave. The strange thing was that

the food in front of us smelled unaccountably marvelous. My stomach rumbled under the mistaken impression there was food nearby.

Lord Grayle put out a hand. Barker bowed instead. He and I donned our hats and left the relative warmth and comfort of the Palace of Westminster for the polar winds.

CHAPTER 12

The snow fell in large, tenuous flakes, the kind that makes one feel nostalgic for a home and a world that never actually exists outside of Christmas cards. It was beautiful when seen from a bow window with a warm fire at one's back, less so when one is, for example, a messenger boy with rags for shoes. Forgive me for sounding like Mr. Dickens. As snows fare, this one was pretty without being harsh. All the same, I'd have preferred to remain in our snug chambers for the remainder of the afternoon.

I heard the door open. I've tried in vain to convince my partner we need to hang a bell over it, like many establishments in London, which alerts the merchant that someone is in their shop. Our clientele sometimes carry pistols and infernal machines containing dynamite and timers. Barker refused, however, claiming it would make us seem like merchants. I countered that, in point of fact, we were merchants, offering our services for vulgar money. He argued that one should inject a little taste and professionalism to our occupation, and I insisted that there is nothing tasteful or professional about shooting a fellow or breaking his elbow. His only response was that we had not broken a man's elbow in months. I did not belabor the point.

Jenkins keeps the hinges well-oiled, but the sound of traffic in Whitehall is appreciably louder when the door is open. A man entered the premises and I could just see his profile at Jeremy's desk from my own. As Hennings predicted, it was Mahmoud, or some other Near Eastern gentleman. He gave our clerk his card and I heard him shrug out of his greatcoat and hang it on the coatrack while the card was carried to the Guv. When he sat, I could just see the tip of our visitor's boot, highly polished, the vamp covered with a pair of stylish spatterdashes. The boot swayed to a song in his head. I heard the flair of a match and the sizzle of the flame being sucked through a cigarette. It was Turkish tobacco.

Without looking at our visitor, I stood and snatched his card from the tray where it had been left. The card was printed using English letters with Arabic script underneath. It read:

MUSEUM OF EGYPTIAN ANTIQUITIES
CAIRO, EGYPT
AAMIR MAHMOUD,
COLLECTIONS CURATOR

Barker stood. I didn't especially like Hennings, but he had put me on my guard about this fellow. Mahmoud stood and bowed and we bowed in return.

"You are Mr. Barker?" he asked. "Thank you for seeing me without an appointment. I won't take up much of your time."

"Not at all, sir," Barker said. Sometimes his deep voice makes the floorboards vibrate. "Won't you have a seat? What can I do for you?"

Mahmoud sat and crossed a boot over his knee. He puffed his cigarette and took in our chambers but showed no indication if he approved. He was a little under six feet in height and rail thin. His shoulders were narrow, his hips even more so. He was very elegant. He wore a cutaway coat with a double-breasted waistcoat, gray-striped trousers, and a pair of tan kid gloves.

Mahmoud had a mop of black curls not unlike my own save that his were surmounted by a fez. His eyes were large and dark, his lashes long. His nose was aquiline and his lips full, which combined with his lashes and his obvious fastidiousness, gave him an almost effeminate air. However, he wore a short beard, black as pitch. He was an exotic creature.

"How is the Cairo Museum coming along, sir?" the Guv asked. I suspected he had not known about it until Hennings complained of it a few hours before.

"Splendidly," the man replied. "The collection is currently housed in the Kasr al-Incha Palace until the museum is finished. We've hired a French architect and an Italian builder and we hope to open our doors on the first of January 1900."

His voice was as unusual as his appearance. It was rich and cultured with little touch of an accent. It reminded me of something, but it took a moment to place it. He was aping Oscar Wilde's honeyed baritone. I noticed because I have used it myself on more than one occasion. It was de rigueur when I was at Oxford and the poet was an upperclassman, either out of respect or mockery. Perhaps both. There is only one thing in the world worse than being talked about, and that is not being talked about, as he has famously said.

"How may we help you, sir?" Barker continued.

Our visitor allowed a little smoke to escape his lips and then sucked it into his nostrils. Then he blew a gust of it out his mouth. Barker raised a brow.

"I am here in London on a diplomatic mission, I suppose you could say," Mahmoud said. "I've been passed from one government agency to another, until I feel like a pail of water in a fireman's bucket brigade. Unfortunately, Egypt has no embassy or minister in London, so I'm forced to forage for myself."

"Forage for what, precisely?" I asked.

"For what has been thieved from my country by your government: our heritage, our birthright, our treasures," he claimed. "They've been funneled from my country to yours piecemeal for centuries. Of course, they are purchased and sold privately, and my country has not had the power to stop it. However, it will be stopped when the museum is finished, and all discoveries must end at our borders. It is time to regulate the sale of antiquities. These fleas, these maggots on the hide of my country won't be able to feast much longer."

"Do you consider the British Museum to be one of those fleas?" the Guv asked.

"The biggest of them all, though I haven't singled it out from the others. There is also the Louvre, the Neues Museum in Berlin, and the Metropolitan Museum of Art in New York City. I lead a peripatetic life, Mr. Barker, but today I am concentrating my energies on London."

"Why?" Barker asked. "Or perhaps I should ask, why now?"

"Oh, come, I know you're not a simpleton," Mahmoud replied. "I'm speaking of the mummy. An unfortunate duty of my position is to act as a showman. When the Cairo Museum finally opens its doors we will require some major item of antiquity or we will become the laughingstock of the archeological world. You understand my predicament. The mummy of Cleopatra XII is just the sort of item we need."

"And how do you intend to acquire this item?"

"Does it really matter?" he asked. "Any way I can, I suppose. I will bully and cajole. I'll threaten through diplomatic channels. I'll bribe and steal. Whatever is required to secure it for my country."

"Forgive me if I say that sounds unscrupulous, sir," Barker said.

"Does stealing from a museum that plunders my country's heritage make me a scoundrel?"

"Semantics is Mr. Llewelyn's field of expertise, not mine," my partner said, sitting back in his chair and resting his fingertips on the glass sheet covering his desk.

Mahmoud exhaled a final gust of his Turkish tobacco in his direction and put out the fag end of his cigarette in a crystal ashtray. "Is your reticence about the mummy or your own involvement?"

"My involvement?" Barker asked, more intrigued than frightened.

"I've heard that Thompson has called the Palace about your royal warrant, hoping to get it rescinded, but was rebuffed. You must have friends there. Thompson's all right. He knows how to play the game. I'd even call him canny. Hennings is an ass."

"Mercy, sir," my partner said. "You sound as if you have spies there."

"I needn't bother," Mahmoud replied. "Archeologists are the worst gossips. They are like society beauties, looking for rich husbands and jockeying for position. There is a good deal of backbiting. I'm sure someone has been telling tales about me."

"They have," Barker admitted.

"How am I characterized today?" he continued. "Am I a spy for the Ottoman Empire? A threat to Christianity? High priest for the return of Ra worship?"

"The latter, I think," I told him.

"No doubt," he said, shaking his head. "It is the most colorful and requires the least amount of thought."

"You aren't a Theosophist, then?" the Guv asked bluntly.

"No, sir," he replied, shaking his head. "I am a Muslim. A Mussulman, you English call us. To resurrect the Old Religion of my country would be blasphemy to me. Allah is my god and Mohammed is His Prophet."

"Your English is excellent," I remarked.

"I would hope so. I'm an Oxonian."

I sat forward. "What college?"

"Balliol."

"Magdalen," I said, pointing to myself.

"Dominus Illuminatio Mea," he replied.

"As illuminating as this might be, gentlemen," Barker said, clearing his throat. "Let us get back to the matter at hand."

"Very well, sir," Mahmoud continued. "I am here to make an offer on whatever was inside Cleopatra's mummy. It was part of her. As famous as she was, we could not exhibit the mummy without this mysterious object, whatever it is."

"I am no longer in possession of it," Barker said.

"People are shouting from the rooftops that you have it," Mahmoud accused.

"Which people?" the Guv enquired. "No, you need not answer that."

Mahmoud smiled. "It is not particularly a secret. Mr. Hennings's assistants have been singing like nightingales. They would sell out their superior for two shillings. But as I said, they have little cause to respect him."

"How so?" Barker asked.

"It's well-known in Egyptological circles that the fellow can't even step down into a cellar, let alone a pharaoh's tomb a hundred feet below the ground. During digs he sits in a tent on the surface and sends his workers down to do the dangerous work. What sort of fellow becomes an archeologist with such a handicap, I ask you? Have you been in his office and seen the painting? It's worse than grotesque, but unknowing strangers are impressed by it."

Barker grunted in reply.

"Answer this, if I may ask it," the man continued. "Could you get the object back? I'm certain we could offer a fair and honest price. Of course, we cannot match the price of France or America, but the mummy was ours to begin with. I appeal to your sense of fair play."

"Alas, sir, I no longer have it or I would take your argument with the seriousness it deserves."

Mahmoud took a deep breath and slowly exhaled. He looked frustrated. He didn't expect to face someone as adamantine as my partner.

"Look, Mr. Barker," our visitor said. "As I understand it, the British Museum will bluster and threaten you. They'll consult their solicitors and take counsel. Then they'll vote upon the matter. They want it back even though none of us knows what it is. I have had to send a telegram south to say that so far I am empty-handed. My reputation is at stake. That won't matter to you, but it is all I have."

Barker said nothing, but Mahmoud was undaunted.

"Where was I?" he asked. "Yes, they want it back, though they have no idea what it is. You should hear the speculations Hennings and his crowd have made. One claims it contains Cleopatra's unborn child. Another claims it is a codex of some sort. A third, imagine this, believes it is the mummified asp that bit her, which is absurd, of course. She was never bitten by an asp. It is incredibly painful and would have taken hours to kill her. More likely, she poisoned herself with one of her own concoctions."

Mahmoud uncrossed his leg and sat forward. "Name your price, Mr. Barker."

"You could not afford it, Mr. Mahmoud."

The man sat back in his chair, his eyes like two boiled eggs. "That deep, eh?"

Barker nodded. "Far deeper than the British Museum will ever go."

"I am empowered to bid to a certain price, but not over," Mahmoud continued. "After that I would need to wire Cairo and see what funds can be gathered. The museum is closely allied with the government, you know."

"I no longer have the object in question, as I said," the Guv stated. "I cannot sell what I do not possess."

"I feared you would say that. How tiresome." The Egyptian removed a watch from his pocket and consulted it. "Perhaps you are telling the truth. I will believe you are because despite your deplorable profession, you have been represented to me as an honest man. However, I've also been informed that you belong to a secret society with power and perhaps access to great resources. If you passed it on to them, you would no longer possess it but might be able to broker its sale. I would speak to someone of authority."

"You are, Mr. Mahmoud."

For a moment I felt as if we were playing a card game without cards. Our visitor had just been trumped.

Barker burrowed back into the tufts of his green leather chair and rested his elbows on the arms. The chair was on a swivel, and he listed from side to side. His manner changed. He did not come forward, but Mahmoud quickly moved back.

"Where did you get your information about a secret society?" the Guv asked.

"Here and there. I have resources of my own."

"Tell me, Mr. Mahmoud, are you a representative of the museum, working with the government, or are you a spy for your government who acts as a representative of your museum?"

"Mr. Barker, why should I answer your questions if you won't answer mine?" He slipped his finger under the kid leather of his glove and lifted it a little. "Sometimes it is difficult to tell the hand from the glove."

"You must play chess, Mr. Mahmoud," I ventured.

"Mr. Llewelyn, it was invented in my country. I won a tournament at university but ultimately found it unsatisfying. There are no stakes."

He pulled a notebook from his pocket and wrote on it with a pencil. The he ripped out the sheet and placed it on the Guv's desk. The latter did not seem inclined to look at it.

"If you will not bargain, then allow me to place a bid, if not to you, then to the group you represent. Consider our plight. We have the right to this object, but our pockets are not deep because your country has their boot on our necks."

The group to which Aamir Mahmoud referred was the Knights Templar, an organization composed of government officials, civil servants, aristocrats, and former military officers. The duties as leader were split between Barker and James Munro, the commissioner of Scotland Yard.

"They might have considered such an offer," the Guv admitted. "But unfortunately, they are not in possession of the item, either."

Mahmoud turned to me as if I were a coconspirator. "Isn't this exciting? The stakes are high. Where could this object be? In the locker of your boxing school? In the offering box of your chapel? Perhaps Mr. Barker posted it to his brother in America."

"You are beginning to weary me, sir," Barker said. "I don't have it, I can't get it, and the person who possesses it will not give it up to you."

"So, there is a person then. Such subterfuge! The answer might be under my very nose. Did he give it to you, Mr. Llewelyn? Does your clerk even now have it in his drawer?"

I was growing tired of him as well. If he mentioned my wife's name, or that of Barker's lady friend, Philippa Ashleigh, we would toss him out the window into a snowbank. He did not mention their names, but they were implied.

"Be careful, Mr. Mahmoud," I said. "Touch not the cat without a glove."

Our visitor raised his hands.

"I've brought two," he said. "I came prepared."

"You are not nearly prepared enough," I replied. "In fact, I believe you're in check."

He laughed. He didn't know what he was doing. I've said before that Cyrus Barker was the most dangerous man in London, and I stand by it.

"Very well, gentlemen. I concede," he said at last. "But I may wish to play again if conditions change. Should an auction occur, by all means, call upon me. I am staying at the Carlton."

"Of course you are," I replied. It was the finest hotel in London.

"Not of course, Mr. Llewelyn," Mahmoud answered. "I know what they call me behind my back. But I try to lead an elegant life. What's that old Wilde says? 'Nothing succeeds like excess'?"

Barker rose from his seat. Somehow the room seemed smaller. "You gentlemen may banter, but I've got a murderer to track. It was interesting to meet you, Mr. Mahmoud. I am not without sympathy. In the unlikely event that an auction occurs, we shall leave word at the Carlton. Good day."

I led our visitor to the front room and helped him on with his coat. I wanted to make certain he left. I even thought of locking the door behind him.

"Mr. Llewelyn," Mahmoud said. "May I buy you a drink?"

"You are tenacious, sir, but unlike my partner, I am without sympathy."

"Ah," he replied. "We must agree to disagree, then. Good day!"

Returning to my desk, I fell into my seat.

"That was exhausting," I said.

"I don't like his knowing so much about us while we know so little of him," Barker agreed.

"Perhaps we've been tracking the wrong people," I answered.

"He could have stabbed Addison and dropped him in the river, and our colorful street gang had nothing to do his death."

"We never heard of him until this morning," the Guv replied. "I don't care for suspects who arrive late in the case."

"Pushy cove, wasn't he?"

"It was wise you didn't take up his offer," Barker rumbled.

"I don't necessarily trust a man who quotes Wilde, no matter how popular he becomes."

The Guv smiled. "I'm certain you've dropped one or two of his bon mots yourself."

"Case in point," I said.

CHAPTER 13

An hour later, Elizabeth Addison arrived in our chambers with her sister, Mrs. Millicent Porter, of Southend-on-Sea. In contrast to our client, Mrs. Porter was a sturdily built woman with a capable air. Our client looked haggard and withdrawn, as expected. We were surprised to see her on our doorstep a day after learning her husband was murdered.

"Mr. Barker," she said, nodding solemnly. "Mr. Llewelyn."

"Good day, ma'am," Cyrus Barker replied. "Won't you have a seat?"

The two women sat in our pair of visitors' chairs. Mrs. Addison spoke first.

"I am leaving London, sir," she managed. "My sister has arranged everything. We've sold the furniture and closed my accounts. I'm ready to settle my bill with you."

"But, ma'am," the Guv protested. "Thus far we have been unable to find your husband's killer."

"It doesn't matter anymore, Mr. Barker," she replied. "It won't bring him back. Millie has arranged for me to stay at a convalescent home near her, to rest and decide what my future shall be."

"A month's rest and she'll be as right as rain," Mrs. Porter insisted.

Perhaps she would and perhaps she wouldn't. Personally, I thought it would take a couple of years, at least. Elizabeth Addison and her husband had grown together like a pair of trees one sees in the forest. Now that tree was half dead. Perhaps more than half. However, a month of rest was a good start.

"Southend's gain is London's loss," Barker stated. "When is the funeral?"

"I have no idea, sir," the young widow replied. "Phillip's family has taken possession of his body."

"What?" Barker rasped, his nostrils flaring.

I heard a squeal from our waiting room. It was Jenkins's chair leaning forward. He'd heard the tone in the Guv's voice as well as I.

"Was this with your consent?" he demanded.

It was somehow appropriate that when I looked at him the fire in the grate was reflected in each of his spectacles. I was staring into the flames of Hell.

"Mrs. Addison, I can stop this miscarriage," the Guv continued. "You'll have possession of your husband's remains by end of day, I swear it."

The widow shrugged her thin shoulders. "It isn't necessary, sir, but thank you for your offer. You've been most kind, but it's best this way. He'll have a proper gravestone. What can I give him, I who own nothing?"

Cyrus Barker seemed to swell in his seat. I knew the man. He wanted to pay for the funeral himself. Blast it, I wanted to pay for the funeral, too, but the decision had to be Mrs. Addison's and she was a spent match. I suspected her sister would not

allow her to accept charity, which meant that if we were successful in halting the family's cruel plans, the cost of the con-
valescence and funeral would fall on the shoulders of Millicent
Porter and her husband. To add further insult, there was the
matter of our bill.

Barker leaned forward. "Mrs. Addison, surely you will want
to be buried next to your husband."

"Oh, Mr. Barker," she said with a faint smile. "We'll be together always. The grave is mere dirt, the coffin a box, and
Phillip's body clay. His soul is in heaven, but his love will be
with me forever. I have a few things of his: books, some photographs of us together, his favorite pipe. I have letters and many
sentimental things to remember him by."

"There's one thing you haven't got yet, Mrs. Addison," the
Guv said, reaching into his waistcoat pocket. He retrieved the
watch he'd taken from Coffee John. Seeing that it had tarnished,
he pulled a handkerchief from his pocket and began to burnish it.

She started, giving me a momentary feeling of dread.

"Oh, you wonderful man!" she cried. "Thank you! This is
now the most cherished thing I own."

Barker is naturally sallow-faced and rough-hewn, but at the
sentiment he colored a little. As for her, I noticed a spark in her
eye that hadn't been there before.

"Mr. Barker," Mrs. Porter interrupted. "We are leaving in a
couple of hours. There is nothing to detain us in London any
longer. We have received Phillip's pay from St. Olave's and I
am here to notify you that your services are no longer required.
Please tell me the amount we owe you."

Barker opened his mouth to speak but the woman gave him a
look of warning. I knew he intended to say she owed us nothing.
He dared not say so now.

"Mr. Llewelyn," he said. "Tally our services."

"Yes, sir."

I pulled my notebook from my pocket.

"Let's see," I said. "There were the hansom fares, the rides on the Underground, telegrams and messages. Then there are the lunches—"

"No lunches," Barker interrupted. "We would have eaten, anyway."

"True," I answered.

"Ma'am, we accomplished little," Barker said. "We did not find the body. We have not found Mr. Addison's killer. There is a gang of men who may be the culprits, but we have not successfully questioned them. We assumed we would have more time to question all the witnesses."

"Name your price, sir," Millicent Porter said. I'll say one thing in her favor: the woman had backbone. Many a man has paled in front of my partner's glare.

"Very well, ma'am. Ten pounds."

"I'll ask for no charity from you, Mr. Barker. Thirty."

"That is not how one haggles, Mrs. Porter. Quite the reverse. Fifteen."

"I know the price of things," she said with a belligerent air. "Just because I own a public house and know how to squeeze a penny, don't think I can't pay a big-city detective a proper wage. Twenty."

"Really, madam. This is absurd," the Guv said. "I am ashamed. I should be paying you."

"Twenty and done, sir. I will pay in cash. Mr. Llewelyn, may I have a receipt?"

"Of course."

She opened her reticule and counted out the notes. If she thought she knew what we charged, she had little idea. Some of our fees in those days hovered around a hundred pounds, at least, and with the new warrant it was certain to rise. Barker was known to do away with a fee entirely when the mood suited him or if a case interested him, which I suspected this one did. Mrs. Porter had been adamant, however, and that was that. It was a good thing, too, because I had recently lectured him about declining fees. Personally, I liked them. Our agency is not a charity, and I'd wanted to know I was risking my neck for something besides a pat on the back and a thank-you.

Another thing they did not suspect is that an enquiry is not over until Barker says it is. He does not relinquish a case until the matter is settled to his satisfaction, either in a court of law or a morgue. He is relentless. I've tried to convince him to stop when we have worked several days in a row without a proper culmination, but I might as well have been talking to a block of granite.

"Mr. Llewelyn has already drawn up a contract," Barker said. "If your sister could look it over and sign it?"

It was telling that Mrs. Addison didn't even think to look at it until her sister examined every jot and tittle. Mrs. Porter pointed to a vacant space, and Elizabeth signed her name. She didn't have the slightest inkling of how commerce worked, and I suspected her husband was not much wiser. They were a pair of innocents loose in a harsh world. It appeared the world had won.

"Mrs. Addison," Barker said after the document was signed and returned. "You should know something about your husband and his connection with the British Museum. So far the museum staff has gone out of its way to keep your husband's movements during the last hour of his life hidden from you. I believe you should know what they were. On the night your husband died, he was cataloguing mummies. He found one on a bottom shelf, dusty and forgotten. While he was weighing it, he discovered that it was heavier than the others. There was a weight in the chest, something which may prove valuable to the institution."

This left both women blinking. It was clear they were trying to work out how Elizabeth's steady husband was involved with this intrigue.

"According to a witness, your husband decided to take it to his superior," Barker continued.

"Mr. Hennings," she replied.

"Aye, but after Mr. Addison left the museum with the object he realized that it might be construed as theft, even though they did not know anything of it. Luckily, he had a friend nearby."

"A friend?" Elizabeth Addison interjected. "I didn't know he had friends there. He never spoke of any."

"Let us call him an acquaintance, then," my partner continued. "Phillip gave him the object, promising to return for it soon. Then he went to his superior's home at approximately one o'clock in the morning."

"While I was waiting for him to return!" our client said. That glimmer of interest was still in her eye.

The Guv nodded. "Exactly. Your husband traveled to Mr. Hennings's home to speak with him but did not tell him what he had found. He only said there was an unusual mummy at the museum that Hennings needed to see immediately."

"And did he?" Mrs. Porter asked, as caught up in the story as her sister.

"No, Mr. Hennings refused to return to the museum in the middle of the night."

"But what of the mummy and the valuable object?" Mrs. Addison asked.

"As I said, your husband feared being accused of theft. When he couldn't convince Hennings to see it that evening, he was sent home."

"But he didn't come home," the widow protested.

"No, ma'am," Barker said, nodding. "He died somewhere between Hennings's home and your doorstep."

Mrs. Porter was the first to say anything. "Is that all?"

"Not by half, madam," the Guv said. "You see, the mummy itself may have been a famous Egyptian queen. Have you heard of Cleopatra?"

Both women shook their heads. Orphans, maids, and publicans are not taught ancient history or English literature as a matter of course. Such knowledge won't, for example, help one to find a position in service or to pull a pint.

"She was very famous," he continued. "And people have been searching for her mummy for two thousand years."

"And Phillip found it!" Mrs. Addison exclaimed with pride in her voice.

"Aye, he did, ma'am," Barker answered. "If this was proved to be Cleopatra it would be the find of the century. The reputation of the British Museum as the premier museum in the world would be enhanced. There would be an exhibition in London and all other countries would be envious. You understand we are talking about a lot of money."

"You're saying Phillip found something rich men would kill for," Millicent Porter stated.

"That is correct," Barker replied.

"But what happened to the valuable object?" Mrs. Addison asked.

"It is being kept out of harm's way for the time being. I must tell you that your husband will be given credit for the discovery, not only of the mummy itself but for the object as well."

"Thank you, Mr. Barker," she replied. "It matters little to me now, but Phillip would have been proud."

"Give it time, madam," the Guv said. "It will matter over time. Now, Mrs. Addison, I have some questions for you. Understand, I am in no way accusing your husband of anything. I'm merely trying to put pieces of a puzzle together. Do you understand?"

From where I sat, I could see that both women had moved to the edge of their seats.

"First question: Did your husband know anyone who is Egyptian?"

Elizabeth Addison looked bewildered. "No, sir. He never spoke of any. He would have told me about that, I'm sure."

"Did he visit the East End occasionally?" he asked.

"He's never been there," she stated. "I wouldn't let him. My dreadful childhood was spent in that awful place."

"It's a pestilent place, Mr. Barker," Mrs. Porter said. "I can't work out how Phillip was found there."

Barker sidestepped the question and continued. "Did your husband ever gamble?"

"With what?" Mrs. Porter asked, astonished. "The poor soul didn't have two farthings to rub together. I'll wager whatever the two of you have in your pockets right now would be a fortune to him. He couldn't afford a cab and had to walk all over London."

"Did he?" Barker purred.

"Mr. Barker, why are you asking me these questions?" Mrs. Addison asked. "This is museum business and the information can do nothing for us now."

"True, ma'am," he replied. "But you deserve to know that he was an honest man to the end. Also, there is little chance the museum will be able to keep the story out of the newspapers. As early as tomorrow, reporters may come to your door, even Scotland Yard."

"But they came and questioned me already!"

"Did they? They will no doubt return to question you again. Go to that convalescent home and stay there. Answer no questions, if you can. I encourage you to get some rest. Grieve for your husband. Consider what you wish to do with your future. Mr. Addison sounded like a fine fellow. It's comforting to know such men still exist in this town."

"He gave up a family fortune for you without a second thought," I said. "He must have loved you very much, Mrs. Addison."

"He did, Mr. Llewelyn," she replied. "No one could keep us apart."

The Guv swiveled his chair toward our other visitor lest the conversation descend into sentiment. "Mrs. Porter, be prepared for reporters coming to your public house. They might offer you money for your story."

The woman nodded. "Mr. Barker, I have many friends there, including some strapping lads who will protect us. I'll not take sixpence. We shall put a flea in their ear and I'll take a broom to them myself."

"We'll see you ladies out," he said, rising from his chair. "Mr. Llewelyn will summon a cab. It was a pleasure meeting the two of you. I wish there was more I could have done."

I stepped outside, crossed to the curb, and raised my hand. Despite the weather a cab pulled to the curb. For once, I felt lucky. Then I saw the glint of a pistol in the darkness of the cab. Without thinking—something I do more often than I like—I ran forward waving my arms. I don't know why I did it. I had a perfectly wonderful life and no reason to endanger it. I assumed the bullet was meant for me, retribution for the one I'd put in the gang leader's foot. I may have realized there were women present who must be protected. Or perhaps I am a total idiot. In any case, I ran toward the gun, and it went off.

People often exaggerate how quiet it can be sometimes, but that was not my experience. First, I lost my hearing. My ears rang for several minutes. I could no longer hear the traffic in Whitehall Street, one of the busiest in London.

I felt my shoulder. No, nothing. I looked down at my stomach, expecting blood, but there was none. I ran my hand through my hair, looked at my knees and elbows. *My word*, I thought. *They missed at not more than five feet!*

I looked over my shoulder at Barker, but he was turned away and kneeling. Had he been hurt? Then I saw the boots on the ground, the soles facing me, the toes at a ninety-degree angle. Elizabeth Addison's boots.

I saw but could not hear Mrs. Porter scream. Barker glanced back at me, and I looked back at the cab. The bat-wing doors closed, and the cab bowled off quickly. The cabman cracked his whip. I considered giving chase, but I lost sight of it immediately among a half dozen identical vehicles. The shooter could be anywhere.

I nearly slipped on the ice as I turned back toward our offices. Mrs. Addison was not dead but losing blood quickly from a wound in her temple. It stained the snow about our freshly painted front door. Barker and Mrs. Porter were attempting to stanch the blood with handkerchiefs, but they were ineffectual. I handed my own to the Guv. I realized if they could not stop the hemorrhaging, she could bleed to death there and then. People had stopped to stare in disbelief. I could not believe it myself. I had never heard of a woman shot before. It didn't happen.

"Come, Thomas!" Barker bellowed. Now, that I heard. "Help me carry the poor girl into our chambers. She cannot be seen like this!"

Elizabeth Addison's face was bathed in blood to the point that she was unrecognizable. I told myself she could not possibly survive. Barker lifted her and carried her inside.

That poor, ill-fated woman. She had been orphaned, then separated from her sister. She was forced to go into service to keep from starving. She met a boy, then was responsible for a rupture with his family and financial ruin. The pair lived in poverty. One day he was shot, and she became a widow. Then she was shot as well. She was not Mrs. Addison in my mind any longer. From that day forward, she would always be "Poor Mrs. Addison."

CHAPTER 14

The Guv carried Elizabeth Addison into our office. A trail of blood beaded on the polished wood floor. Carefully, we laid her on the rug in front of the visitor's chair. "Thomas, send for an ambulance," Barker ordered.

I seized the telephone set from the desk and called Charing Cross Hospital.

"Hello," I said. "We have a woman here in Whitehall who has just been shot. No, not a man. I said a woman, yes. We are in Craig's Court. Number seven. My name is Thomas Llewelyn. . . . How do I know how bad the wound is? There's blood everywhere and she's moaning. Better hurry or you'll be too late."

I hung the receiver back on the stalk. "Five minutes, he says. Will she last five minutes?"

"Aye," Barker pronounced. "She was grazed on the forehead, near the hairline. Head wounds always bleed heavily. I suspect her life is not in danger, but she'll have a splitting headache when she wakes."

Barker had a rudimentary knowledge of medicine, but now I doubted that knowledge. The blood was not merely dripping, it was spraying in tiny droplets from her head, spattering her face and dress like paint flicked from a brush. Barker held a handkerchief to the wound as Mrs. Porter cradled her sister on the floor.

I was incensed. Indignant, in fact. In all my years as an enquiry agent I could not recall a woman being shot. Poisoned, yes. Stabbed, strangled, certainly. But shot? It didn't happen. There are rules, of a sort, and even criminals know them. Whoever did this was going to swing for it. That is, unless we caught hold of him first.

"Thomas, a towel and blanket, if you please!" the Guv ordered.

"Yes, sir!"

I ran to the lumber room behind our office and brought them to my partner. We wrapped the blanket around her and cradled her head with the towel. Our client continued to moan.

"It's all right, Lizzie," her sister whispered in her ear. "The doctor will be here soon."

I noticed that she was covered in her sister's blood. Barker and I were as well. Looking up, I saw Jenkins standing in the doorway, his eyes round as saucers, unable to help, unwilling to step into the room. I waved him back. There was nothing he could do.

"Ma'am," I said to Mrs. Porter, "the ambulance will arrive soon. There is a water closet through that door, with a bowl and ewer. You may want to make yourself presentable."

Reluctantly, she relinquished possession of her sister. There was a small cushion on one of the chairs and my partner put it under Elizabeth's head. It was soon covered in blood. The room looked like a charnel house, and we like corpses.

An ambulance arrived from St. John's Priory. The driver directed two orderlies to load Mrs. Addison onto a stretcher.

Meanwhile, Mrs. Porter had returned and Barker wrapped his coat around her. As Elizabeth Addison was loaded into the ambulance, I put her sister into a cab after scanning the street once again. A gawking crowd had gathered, attracted by the ambulance. I was relieved when a constable arrived.

We explained who we were, who the victim was, and how she had been present at our offices. The constable went over our story several times while blood was drying in the crevices of my hands. Finally, he closed his notebook and put it in his tunic pocket. I tapped my jacket to be sure I still had mine.

"Thomas, you change first," my partner ordered, his voice gruff, when the constable and ambulance had gone.

"Yes, sir."

I went to the water closet and carried the ewer Mrs. Porter had used to wash her face into the yard behind our offices. I tossed the water on the tinged cobblestones and pumped some more into it.

"Thomas!" he called. "Don't dawdle!"

"Yes, sir!" I replied.

In the water closet, I stripped down to my singlet. Opening a box of Pear's soap, I washed my face and hands. Then I pulled up my braces and went into the lumber room, which contains dozens of hats and clothing of various professions to be used when we were trying to remain anonymous. There, I donned a new shirt and tie, a brown suit, and a thick tweed overcoat. A wide-brimmed hat and I was ready.

Barker and I changed places and I went back into our chambers.

"What a mess," I said.

Jenkins gave me a dolorous look. "I'll have to get the mop and bucket, roll up the carpet, and have it cleaned. And look here! There's blood on the chairs and even on Mr. B.'s desk!"

"It wasn't my fault," I said to him, but the truth is I wondered if it was.

Barker was gone for nearly a quarter hour and when he returned, he had undergone a transformation. He wore an astrakhan coat and a glossy top hat. He was resplendent, but we were entirely mismatched. However, we were going to a hospital, not a charity ball. We swathed our chins in mufflers, gathered our sticks, and launched out into Craig's Court again, ready to avenge our client, for such she still was in Barker's eyes.

It was nearing four and traffic in Whitehall was slow. We found a cab, each of us with a hand on the pistol in our pocket as we climbed aboard, just in case. I pulled my muffler up over my nose, thinking the Underground might have been faster and warmer as my heart was beating a brisk tempo.

"This is my fault, isn't it?" I asked.

A very dapper Cyrus Barker turned my way.

"How so?" he asked.

"Obviously, the bullet was intended for me, in retaliation for shooting that fellow in the foot."

"Was it he who shot at you?" he asked.

"I don't know," I said. "I didn't see his face, just his arm."

"Do you remember any details?"

I closed an eye for a moment and tried to concentrate.

"I can't say," I answered. "I was focused on the pistol."

"It was brave of you, lad, charging the cab, waving your arms like a windmill. For a moment, I thought I would be without a partner again. Then I'd have to change the new sign over the door."

"Not to mention purchasing new visiting cards," I said. "And the advert in *The Times*."

It was banter, but it was serious as well. In an unspoken manner he was saying he was glad I had survived the incident. I, in turn, was thanking him for the distraction.

"Let me put it another way," he continued. "Whom do you suppose was the shooter's target?"

I closed both eyes this time and tried to think even harder. One "I can't say" can be forgiven, but two is letting down the side.

"If I was charging him and waving my arms, he was a poor shot if he missed me," I stated. "On the other hand, if Mrs. Addison was the target, he was rather good. The bullet needed to pass between both of us and Mrs. Porter to reach her. Also, she was moving, and the head is a small target, best avoided for a pistol."

"I suppose I could have been the target, as well, although I don't see why," the Guv said. "I've done piteously little so far to warrant an assassination attempt. I've merely gone places and asked questions. And he must know that had he been successful you would not rest until you found him."

"Of course," I replied. "And neither would Harm."

No one was as close to Barker as his prized Pekingese, given to him by the Dowager Empress of China. I had no trouble picturing the little brute stalking London for the killer. The first bite might be on the ankle, but the second would tear out the jugular.

"Was I wrong to shoot that fellow?" I asked.

Barker exhaled and frowned. He doesn't give opinions cavalierly.

"Several men came toward you, knives drawn," he replied. "Granted, you could have shot your pistol into the air, but in my opinion, it would have been a waste of a bullet. I would not have hesitated to blow his head from his shoulders."

"I'm regret he got away, sir," I said. "I didn't think he'd get out of those restraints so quickly."

"Not to worry, Thomas. He'll return, mark my word."

"He already has," I said.

We arrived at the hospital twenty minutes later than the ambulance due to the traffic. My partner jumped down with a rocking of the springs and hurried into the building while I paid the fare. Inside, I found him in conversation with Mrs. Porter, who still wore his coat over her bloodstained dress.

"What's the news?" I asked.

"Lizzie has been given a tot of laudanum," she said. "Doctor says the bullet glanced off her skull, but she'll need a dozen stitches. I'll reckon she'll be more concerned that he'll have to shave the area."

We found some chairs in a corner and sat.

"You're seeing her at her lowest, gentlemen," she continued. "Normally she's a vivacious girl, is Lizzie. Bright. Humorous. She could get you laughing in half a minute. But not without Phillip. He was her world and she his. They went through such trials and tribulations for each other, and the problems never stopped following them. If his parents had given her a chance, they'd thank their stars to have a daughter-in-law like her."

"Did you attend their wedding?" Barker asked.

"Oh, they came to Southend. I was maid of honor and witness rolled in one. No one else was there, but then it was an elopement of sorts. We watched the main road for any Addisons who might try to stop us, but none came."

Barker's mustache bowed a little. He approved of this publican from Suffolk. She was forthright and afraid of no one, not even him.

"Did you ever meet the Addisons?" he asked.

"Did more than that," she said. "Saw Phillip's mum once in Hyde Park when I come up to visit. I cornered her and give her my opinions, first to last. She's no lady. She was born in Cheapside. But she wants respectability like a fiend craves opium. You know, between us here, I wouldn't put it past the Addisons to do Lizzie in now that their son is gone."

"Why would they do so?" I asked. "They passed the inheritance on to the younger brother."

"Have they?" asked Mrs. Porter. "How do you know? Have you seen a legal document? Eustace Addison is a wastrel and capable of doing far worse than his brother ever could. I reckon that once you cut off a son from his inheritance it's dreadful hard to give it back to him. I think they was hoping to drive Lizzie off and get Phillip to return, so they didn't have to change the will at all."

"Why didn't Phillip publish the banns?" I asked.

"Phillip loved his parents despite everything," she said. "He didn't want them to learn about the wedding from the newspapers."

Barker raised a calloused hand. "Wait. If the Addisons have not legally passed the inheritance on to the younger son, and your sister is a widow . . ."

"She'd inherit everything!" Mrs. Porter said, nodding. "Or at least some of it. Enough to live on for the rest of her life. Enough to tweak the Addison noses no end. Can you imagine? Lizzie starting as a tweeny and ending up with the lot?"

I blinked. Could the Addisons be desperate enough to kill their own daughter-in-law after their son died? It didn't seem possible, but that only made it worse. Someone killed Phillip Addison and now someone else might be trying to kill his wife. Call me old-fashioned, but I prefer one assassination at a time, and for one reason. I reached for my notebook but found I'd left it in my other jacket pocket. I hated being without my notebook. Someone might say something important such as the possibility that the Addisons were after our client. That's something I might want to jot down.

Listening to Barker and Mrs. Porter talk, it finally struck home that I had just tried to jump in front of a bullet. Barker called me brave, but I was certain my wife, Rebecca, would have another word for it, and a few extra ones in the bargain. She and the Guv have differing ideas of my purpose in life.

Me, I'd rather be sitting in a comfortable chair with a cup of coffee and a good book. A *pain au chocolat* wouldn't go amiss, either.

The surgeon spoke to us in about a half hour, a broad, burly fellow who looked like he should be a steamfitter instead of a surgeon.

"Mrs. Addison required twenty sutures," he stated. "The bullet had gouged a small trough in the bone, which will probably cause her headaches for several weeks, but she should recover without any ill effects. Mrs. Porter has told me a little of how she came to be wounded. I've never worked on a bullet wound in London before, only in the Sudan. A young lady shot in the head is the last sight I expected to see today."

"Have you rooms available?" Cyrus Barker asked. "Private rooms, I mean. I'll pay."

The man put a hand on each brawny hip. "We do. They are rarely used. Flowers are included."

"Excellent. Have her moved when she is ready, Dr. . . ."

"Crankshaw. Edward."

"Cyrus Barker."

The doctor pointed at him. "Glasshouse Street. You have an antagonistics class."

The Guv nodded. "I do. Come and I'll give you a free lesson."

"I may take advantage of your kind offer."

"And I yours," my partner replied.

We left him to his work and gave our adieus to Mrs. Porter.

"Please keep us informed of her progress," Barker said.

"I shall," Mrs. Porter answered. "About the private room. You needn't bother. A regular room or the ward is fine."

"Ma'am, your sister was shot on my very doorstep," my partner insisted. "She is my responsibility. They might try again. And as you heard, free flowers!"

Out in the street we summoned a cab, which stopped automatically at our feet when its driver saw Barker's expensive coat and hat.

"I must say, you look natty today," I remarked.

"We really should stop in Petticoat Lane soon and buy more apparel. It was either this or the uniform of a railway platelayer."

"Wise choice," I decided. "Had you worn the other, they wouldn't have offered the flowers."

We made our way back to Whitehall and our narrow court. The spray of blood on the pavement had seeped into the snow and needed shoveling. I knew Jenkins wouldn't do it. He raises laziness to an art form. I stepped inside, expecting to have words with our clerk. Instead, I found him on the floor. He sat with his ankles spread like a child's doll and a dazed look on his thin face.

"The policeman," he said. "He weren't no policeman at all."

We looked around our chambers, which was a shambles. The room had been torn apart, and when the ruby was not found they destroyed things merely for the enjoyment of it. Every drawer was opened, its contents thrown on the floor. Barker's ancient coat of arms lay on the carpet, the claymores that flanked it taken away as spoils. Books had been pulled from the shelves in the vain hope of finding a secret compartment. The cigar box was open and empty, and the silver tampers and other expensive equipment in the smoking cabinet stolen, presumably to sell.

"My word," I murmured at the damage. "It will take days to repair this."

By then, poor Mrs. Addison's blood had soaked into the carpet or dried on the wood floor. We would need to purchase a new rug. The current one was expensive and had a pleasing oriental pattern. Furnishings are not as important as human life, I knew, but damn and blast, I was going to miss that rug.

There's a feeling one has when someone goes through one's personal things. There was nothing of importance in my drawers, and I'd taken my pistol with me. But there was a small vase Rebecca had given me to keep for boutonnieres that had been dashed to the floor and shattered. It wasn't expensive but it mattered to me, because she mattered to me. If that fellow were to walk in now I'd have shot him also, and not in the foot. It was out of all reason, but I didn't care.

"Was it the gang from Millwall, do you think?" I asked Barker.

"Probably."

"Was the man who shot our client among them?"

"It is possible."

I put my hands on my hips. "Why aren't you angry?"

"They are just possessions, Thomas, and I can replace them," he rumbled. "As for Mrs. Addison, we'll get our just due and heaven help them all when we do. Jeremy, are ye hurt?"

"One of them hit me with the butt of his revolver," Jenkins answered, pointing to the top of his head. "They are armed now, sirs. Pistols. I didn't recognize the brand. They was all new-looking."

"Like the knives," I replied. "These boys are being privately funded."

We set to work. I organized and returned the pens and other detritus in my drawer. Then I filled the cubbies in my rolltop desk. *Perhaps this was a good thing*, I told myself. It was a chance to get organized. When I was done, I turned to the books. Jenkins was at the other end of the room, but it would be a new century before he finished.

"I'll start here, then," I stated.

The spines on several were broken, and a few had lost their binding. Luckily, most of the reference materials were undamaged: atlases, street maps, Kelly's telephone directories, along with a *Baedeker's* and timetables for individual railway lines. A shopping guide to London, divided by subject. *Burke's Peerage*.

Crockford's list of clergymen. On and on. You never know what information an enquiry agent may require to fulfill the needs of an enquiry.

Then I picked up a copy of the *Works of William Shakespeare*. I'd purchased it myself after a client quoted him, because I felt we needed one. It was published in 1813. The collection did not withstand being dropped four feet. The boards split and the pages came apart. It could not be repaired. Were it an animal, I'd have had to put it down. This book was printed when Jane Austen was alive, and Scott, and Shelley.

Barker suddenly raised his head.

"It didn't matter who was shot," he stated. "The purpose was to remove us from the office to search for the ruby."

That did it. I turned and walked out the door. I didn't say a word, didn't say where I was going. I merely went. I waved at a cab and climbed into the seat, glad for once that I didn't have to share it.

"Where to, Guv?" the cabman asked. For a moment I thought he was talking to Barker.

"The choice is yours," I answered. "Just get me away from here."

He pushed off and our little urban gondola floated out into traffic and slipped upstream toward Nelson's Column. I didn't mind the cold now. It felt fresh on my cheeks. I took in a lungful of air and tried not to cough.

"Now where?" I asked myself.

Did I think the gang would suddenly appear for my benefit? I began to feel foolish. Now I'd have to return and give an explanation to my partner. I'd been upset when our chambers were tossed, even if Barker wasn't. I didn't have a master in China to teach one patience. I am a passionate Welshman. We feel things more than others.

The cabman drove while I watched traffic: omnibuses,

delivery vans, the odd hackney or brougham, and enough cabs to choke the Thames. So many people; eight million souls, or so I've read. My mind couldn't fathom that many, yet here they were, swirling past me. We are ants in an anthill, every bit as self-important, rushing toward nowhere.

CHAPTER 15

When my temper had cooled, I tapped the trap overhead and ordered the cabman back to Whitehall.

"It's your shilling, sir," he answered, shrugging.

Barker said nothing when I returned to our chambers. He stood by his newly arranged smoking cabinet and stuffed his pipe. Sometimes after a day in Craig's Court Rebecca tells me I reek of tobacco, though I haven't smoked. Working with the Guv has its advantages and disadvantages.

"Did you enjoy your ride, Thomas?" he eventually asked.

"It was fruitless. I was out looking for Mrs. Addison's shooter."

"He is about his business and we are about ours," the Guv said. "However, I believe it is inevitable we shall meet again."

"I hope so," I replied. "If it's that miscreant I shot in the foot, I'd like to renew our acquaintance. I wish there was a way to know where he went."

Barker looked at me levelly.

"Of course!" I exclaimed. "The hansom cab headquarters in front of Scotland Yard. Sorry. I'm a bit rattled today. Shall I go there now?"

"You can, lad," he said. "But only to deliver a message. The driver of Mrs. Addison's shooter won't return until after his shift."

"Perhaps he started this morning," I said. "It's worth the effort."

"It is," he agreed. "We must leave no stone unturned."

"I'm off again, then," I told him, donning my tweed coat. "I won't be long."

I stepped out the door only to be pushed back in by a firm hand.

"What's your hurry?" Detective Chief Inspector Terence Poole asked as he entered our chambers. It wasn't really a question. With a sigh, I turned about.

"Afternoon, Cyrus," he said. "You've got a bloody mess by your front door. Thought you should know. How is your client?"

"Well enough, Terry," Barker rumbled. "She is sedated in Charing Cross Hospital. The bullet grazed her temple."

Poole shrugged. "Perhaps, but she's bled all over a public thoroughfare. It's your shop and you're responsible."

"It's hardly a shop," I said.

"Then you won't mind cleaning it up."

Somewhere in London, someone was having a fine day. Unfortunately, it wasn't me. I went to the lumber room and retrieved a shovel.

"You've redecorated," I heard Poole say to the Guv.

"Someone did it for us!" I called.

"The rooms were tossed while we were at Charing Cross," Barker explained. "Jeremy was knocked on the head."

"You chaps are having a lively time of it," our friend observed.

"One of them was dressed as a constable."

All the humor in Poole's face evaporated immediately. "What?"

"You heard me," Barker answered.

Poole sat in the visitor's chair, perched on the edge. "Tell me, Cyrus. Tell me everything, and spare nothing!"

Barker did as he was asked. The Yard takes impersonating an officer of the law very seriously. A lord's son at Cambridge dressed for a pantomime once found himself in a cell for as long as he could legally be held for thumbing his nose at 'A' Division. Worse still, Mrs. Addison's attack was nearly in sight of New Scotland Yard itself.

Terence Poole frowned. "One man, you say?"

"More than one, I should imagine," Barker answered. "He was professional. His uniform looked genuine, and he even wore a regulation mustache."

"False, I suppose."

I snorted. "A fine thing if an experienced enquiry agent can't tell a false mustache from a real one."

"Don't get shirty, Thomas. I'm only theorizing. I promise you one thing: if it was a real constable I'll have his badge and toss him in stir 'til he grows moss."

He looked at me as if I'd just walked in the room. "You still here? What are you, deaf?"

"Everybody's in a foul mood today," I said, leaving with the shovel.

It was cold but not freezing. Melting snow gurgled in the gutter, but the bloody patch was hard enough that it wouldn't budge. I hit at it with the shovel, trying to break it and push it into the grating. It was slow work.

After twenty minutes, I returned, all vestiges of the tragic offense upon Mrs. Addison now in the sewer. Terence Poole had gone.

"I'm going after that cabman," I told the Guv.

"Be vigilant," Barker said, nodding. "You've survived one attempt already today."

I was wary as I walked toward Great Scotland Yard Street, watching the afternoon traffic coming toward me, not that it did any good. Suppose he did appear again, waving a pistol? How would I react? Would I run forward again, arms waving, or duck into an alley like a coward? I scanned the opposite pavement looking for faces I recognized. It was what my assailant wanted me to do, I thought, to wonder where he was. He was probably miles away by now, sitting and drinking in a public house while I was looking over my shoulder.

I found the hansom cab office and went inside, crossing directly over to the cashier's cage.

"How can I help you, sir?" a man asked behind the counter, ensconced behind glass.

"A cab was taken a little over three hours ago," I replied. "I need to track down the driver."

"Do you recall the cabman's number, sir?"

"I'm afraid not," I answered. "I was otherwise engaged."

The gentleman frowned. "I see. Did he not give satisfaction?"

"Perhaps to his fare, but not to me."

"You were not in the vehicle?" the man asked, eyeing me closely.

"I would have been if I'd had a few more seconds."

"Was he rude to you?"

"Not the driver. His fare."

The clerk gave me a condescending look. "Sir, we have little control over our customers."

"Very well," I said. "I'm looking for a cab that left here about two hours ago. He slowed to the curb in front of Craig's Court. Do you know where that is?"

"Of course, sir. It is the next street north. Did the driver splash you with snow?"

"No, sir. The passenger shot a woman in the head."

The clerk stepped back. There was a lunatic in the building, or it was someone's poor idea of a joke. I pulled my card and slid it under the glass. I'm not saying he recognized my name, but he must have passed our sign on the front of our building once or twice a day. I had the veneer of trustworthiness.

"We had an ambulance take the victim to Charing Cross Hospital," I continued. "She bled all over Whitehall Street but is expected to live. I've just been speaking to Detective Chief Inspector Poole from the C.I.D. He should come 'round soon if he knows his onions."

The clerk disappeared like a marionette in a puppet show. Nothing happened for several minutes. Then an older gentleman walked through a door and came over to me.

"I'm Horace Holcomb," he said. "I am the manager here."

"Thomas Llewelyn of the Barker and Llewelyn Agency," I stated. "Private enquiry agents. May we retire to your office, sir? What I have to say should not be heard by cabmen or fares."

"Of course," he said, leading me through the door and down a hall to an office the size of a broom closet. There was a half-eaten pork pie on his desk on an oily bit of newspaper. It was obvious I'd interrupted an early dinner. He moved it to a filing cabinet and motioned me to a chair before sitting behind the desk.

"Please start at the beginning," he said.

I gave him an expurgated version of the events, not including the British Museum or the attack in Cubitt Town. It was enough of a concern, a husband stabbed and a wife shot between Christmas and New Year's, the year's most joyous season. I implied that I was working with Scotland Yard, which was marginally true, and that they would call.

"Can you help?" I asked.

"Sir, normally I would refuse, but these appear to be extraordinary circumstances. When someone hires a cab here on the premises, we write their names and address in our ledger book, along with the destination and which cab was taken. We keep meticulous records. Obviously, the cab was heading north and had just left the ranks here. If you can furnish a time, I can consult our records for this afternoon."

"Excellent," I said. "It was a quarter past two. I am in the habit of keeping records for my reports in case my partner or the Criminal Investigation Department requires them."

"Let me look at the ledger and speak to my staff," the manager said. "I'll be just a few minutes."

It isn't wise to leave an enquiry agent in an empty office. We'll toss it for information. I noted that Mr. Holcomb sketched in the margins of his desk blotter, was married with no children, and had a fondness for horehound sweets. That's how much I had discovered when I heard his step in the hall, and I just had time to return to my seat.

"I have some information for you, sir," he said, closing the door behind him. "Two cabs left our queue at two ten with destinations to the north. One is a Mr. Samuel Jowett of Battersea. I believe I know him on sight. He uses our services often and has an office here in Whitehall. He's in insurance, Lloyd's of London, that sort of thing. His destination was Leadenhall Market."

"I see," I replied. "And the other?"

He frowned over the entry, then sat back in the chair. "I'm afraid you're not going to like this, sir. He said his name was Thomas Llewelyn and his destination was Charing Cross Station."

I stared at him. "What did he give as his personal address?"

"Camomile Street, the City."

A chill ran down my spine. This fellow, this murderer, knew my personal residence. My wife and I split our time between one, which originally belonged to my wife, widowed by her first husband, and 3 Lion Street, Barker's residence. I was relieved that she was out of town. This man knew too much about our movements and private life.

"Thank you," I said, nodding. "A final request and then I'll bother you no further. Can any of the clerks recall the man who hired the cab?"

"I've questioned them already," Mr. Holcomb said. "The man who requested a cab in your name came in person. He was young with red side-whiskers. The clerk remembers him because he wore a tweed cap. He also said the man walked with a limp."

"That's the fellow," I muttered. "It's amazing we share the same name and address. One would think we'd meet occasionally. Actually, we did meet once when he threatened me with a knife."

"Not the best of friends, then, sir?"

"Decidedly not," I answered. "I imagine the Yard will want to see this ledger. Do you have the cabby's name?"

"Danny Pepper, sir. He's a good one."

"If his shift is over before six we'll be in our offices in Craig's Court," I told him. "You have my card?"

He held it up. He must have taken it from the clerk, clever man. "I do."

I nodded. "Thank you for seeing me, Mr. Holcomb."

"I hope the lady recovers quickly," he said solemnly. "I regret our cab was used for so heinous a crime."

It had stopped snowing, but the sky was leaden. I trotted to Scotland Yard but stopped before reaching the gate, in case they might think I was making an affray. I stepped inside, waved to the desk sergeant, a friend named Kirkwood, then nipped up to Poole's office. He wasn't there, but I eventually tracked him down. I told him what I'd just learned.

"The fellow you shot in the foot?" he asked.

"Yes," I said.

"You need shooting lessons."

"I intended to shoot him in the foot," I argued. "His gang was coming at me with knives."

"I don't blame them," Poole replied. "Thank you for the tip."

"The manager there is named Holcomb."

"Holcomb," he wrote on his cuff with a pencil. "Got it."

I turned and made my way back into the street. There was a crime to solve. No, it was more than that. I was going to get this blighter.

CHAPTER 16

I related the information I discovered at the cab's office to my partner.

"Oh, by the way," I said. "There is a gentleman by the door of the Shades public house, hiding behind a copy of *The Times*. He's not the shooter or the constable who tossed our rooms."

"What did you notice about him?" Barker asked.

"He's reading while standing," I replied. "Reading is a seated activity. And it's cold. Also, the Shades doesn't carry *The Times*. It's too conservative. However, there is an advertisement for our services therein. I suspect he has been getting up the courage to enter."

"Sound reasoning," Barker stated. "Do you recommend pistols?"

"Better safe than dead, I say."

I retrieved my bulldog pistol from the cubby in my desk.

Barker's Colt hung by its ring from a hook under his, where he could get to it quickly.

We waited for nearly five minutes before he entered and stood before Jenkins's desk. He gave our clerk his card, and the latter brought it to the Guv while our visitor waited in the front office. My partner glanced at it and shrugged, passing it to me. I glanced at it but did not shrug. Instead, I gave a low whistle.

Our visitor was Andrew Cullen Davis, a popular writer of sensational fiction. His omniscient detective and befuddled narrator were very much in vogue. Barker stood and bowed.

"Have a chair, Mr. Davis," he said as our visitor approached. "How can our agency be of service to you?"

Davis crossed one knee over the other. He was near Barker's equal in size and weight. He looked more rugger than writer, I thought. He studied us both. Taking impressions, I thought.

"You are an interesting pair, gentlemen," he said. "I've asked some of my acquaintances about you and heard the most out- landish tales."

"Do you intend to put us in one of your novels, sir?" the Guv asked.

Our visitor laughed. "Certainly not. Not without permission. I suspect no one will believe it, anyway. The reading public will never know how many tales have been altered to make the truth more palatable for them. I've had trouble believing some of your adventures myself."

"Have you a point, sir?" the Guv asked, already looking a trifle bored. If Davis had no work for him and was not a witness, he ceased to be of potential interest.

"You must understand, Mr. Barker," Davis continued. "Many people are content to be acquaintances of a famous author, whether it is the bootblack that polishes his shoes or the MP whom he meets at table during a dress ball. An au- thor benefits from these acquaintances by collecting tales, true tales that he can embroider for drama or strip for starkness. I need a constant supply of them, you see, as fodder for my stories. Sometimes I can assemble them, borrowing a snippet from here, a fact from there, and using my own imagination to craft a story that a popular magazine will want to publish. It's how I do things, you see. I start with the truth, then twist it like dough into a story."

"Fascinating," Barker said, sounding anything but fascinated. "What is it precisely that you want of us?"

Davis cleared his throat. "A tale came to my ear yesterday thirdhand, as they often do. It was a corker, having to do with an ancient Egyptian curse and a mummy with something hidden in its breast. Some say it was a ceremonial dagger, or a chest of jewels from Solomon. This morning I learned that the man who found the mummy has been murdered. One even suggested the mummy rose from the tomb and strangled him. And do you know where all these tales from various sources led?" Davis leaned forward and tapped the surface of my partner's glass-topped desk. "Here, sir."

Barker made no reply.

"You run a warranted enquiry agency but no one seems to know what you did to deserve the warrant," Davis continued. "You own an antagonistics school teaching Chinese boxing and Japanese wresting, the only one in Europe. I've heard the most interesting tales about you, sir."

"Bosh," Barker said. "You've heard very little about me. My friends know how to keep secrets."

Davis laughed. "You've caught me in a fib, sir."

"You trade in them, Mr. Davis."

"When I began asking about it in the clubs of Pall Mall, your name came up but no one would speak of you. It's as if they were sworn to silence. One fellow even tapped the side of his nose as if to say, 'I could tell you tales.' But I have many friends as well, sir. I'll draw it out of them eventually."

"What sort of friends, sir?" the Guv asked. "Friends at the British Museum, perhaps?"

"Friends everywhere," Davis replied, nodding. "Everyone wants to meet a famous author, even other famous authors. Everyone but you, apparently, Mr. Barker. You seem to be impervious to my charms."

Barker smiled. "Let us say I am suspicious. Why ask us for stories? 'A' Division is just down the street."

Davis gave a rueful look. "Scotland Yard as an organization is being surprisingly precious."

"I've read some of your stories," I said. "You call their inspectors dolts and dullards."

Davis missed the last remark because he was fixated on the first. "You've read my stories, Mr. Llewelyn? I am flattered."

"Don't be," I answered. "I also read *The Illustrated Police News.*"

"What would you do if we told you all the events as they happened, Mr. Davis?" Barker asked.

Davis recrossed his limbs and looked at the ceiling. "I'd probably write something close to the truth, at least until the end. I reserve the right to end with a flourish."

"Would you use our names?" the Guv asked.

The two looked at each other for a moment.

"I assume you do not want me to," Davis said. "No, I would have my own fellows solve it. Not out of vanity, however. It is in my contract that I cannot begin a second series until my first one has run its course. As my agent says, I already have a goose laying golden eggs. There is no need for a second."

Barker grunted. "What do you hope will happen if you write such a story?"

"It would be published and become a minor sensation for a few days, which my agent would make use of when it's time to renew my contract," he admitted.

"And if we refuse to aid you?"

"I have enough information to write something now, but I don't wish to slander someone's reputation. I would not sink so low. However, I prefer not to write a story without a kernel of truth. It's no fun to write, and my readers, the ones who matter to me, like to work out what actual events I'm writing about. I'm speaking of my contemporaries. Nothing pleases me more than to hear another writer say 'I wish I'd written that.' Good heavens, I don't know why I'm telling you all this. I suppose it is the detective in you."

"Private enquiry agents," I corrected.

"I must confess, sir, that I do not read sensational fiction," the Guv rumbled.

"Nor do I, Mr. Barker," Davis acknowledged. "I'd prefer writing about King Arthur and Robin Hood, or the Battle of Hastings. Unfortunately, that sort of thing doesn't sell in this modern age. I wish I were writing fifty years ago. I'd give Sir Walter Scott a run for his money!"

"Brave words," I said.

"Yes, aren't they? I've a second reason. I have a large and expensive house in London, and a wife and children to support. All authors live beyond their means. It is practically expected of us. Mr. Barker, have a heart! Give me something I can use."

My partner stared at our visitor for a few seconds and then looked at me. Cautiously, I nodded. This fellow was all right, I supposed. He would tell a thrilling tale, but few would link it to historical events. The Guv cleared his throat.

"Very well," Barker said at last. "These are the facts I am willing to give you. Three nights ago, around midnight, a volunteer at the British Museum came upon a discovery, a mummy containing something in its chest. He went to his superior and tried to convince him that what he found was significant, but the man suspected he was overexcited and refused to go. The next morning a mummy was found with a cavity in its chest, but the volunteer was missing, at least for most of a day. His body was found floating in Limehouse Reach."

"The poor beggar!" Davis exclaimed. "Was he married? Are you working for his widow?"

"He was and I am. I can say no more."

Davis leaned forward. "What sort of discovery was in the chest?"

"You are a writer, Mr. Davis," the Guv said. "Choose something. Now, we have work to do."

"One more fact, Mr. Barker," he begged. "Any fact."

"Very well, the mummy was female."

The man smiled. "Perfect. Thank you, sir. I'll take up no more of your time."

"Regarding my client, Mr. Davis. I will be very unhappy if she is discomfited by what she reads. Promise me you will not question her. In fact, I insist upon it."

"I promise, Mr. Barker, and my word is my bond. Good day."

He left, eager to begin his work. I followed him to the door and watched him launch himself into the crowd of people walking down Whitehall Street.

"You left out as much as you told him," I said.

"He's fortunate I gave him that much," he replied.

I put my hands on my hips. "Wait. Are you saying you consider him a suspect?"

"Perhaps the gang works for him and he wanted to see what sort of opposition we are."

I shook my head. "He's a writer, nothing more."

"You heard him say he is living beyond his means. He's also a boxer. I can tell by the knots on his knuckles and how he is built."

"He did have information about the case very early," I agreed. "If you suspected him, why did you tell him about the case?"

"I only told him what he already knew or suspected."

"You were whetting his appetite," I said. "Baiting him, in fact."

"We'll see what he'll do next."

A half hour went by when a note arrived from British Museum director Thompson, requesting that we meet him at the Oriental Club in Hanover Square. It arrived in the hands of a commissionaire, and Barker signed for it and sent him back with an assurance we'd be there. He gave the gentleman a generous gratuity. My partner has great respect for former servicemen.

"I wondered how long it would take before the director gathered all the facts and started casting about for new ones," he said.

"Shouldn't you just give him the ruby?" I asked. "It is museum property, and Addison's no longer in danger, poor fellow."

"I might consider it if it were still in my possession, but it isn't, and I can't get it back."

"Gave it away already, did you?" I asked.

"I don't want it," he replied. "And I could no longer keep it here. There are too many others that want it and are willing to do anything to acquire it. And what is it, after all? A shiny red bauble."

"Not even that," I said. "It could do with a good polishing."

"Exactly."

"Why not break precedent and actually tell me what you've done with the thing?" I asked.

His mustache gave a slight bow. "I'm certain you could work out its location if you put your mind to it."

"Thank you for the vote of confidence," I said.

"You're welcome," he replied. Barker's mind doesn't register sarcasm.

At six-fifteen we were in Hanover Square in front of the Oriental Club. We murmured our purpose to the porter and were led to the strangers' coffee room. I was expecting a loud café atmosphere, but the room had Adams chimneypieces, comfortable leather sofas, and shaded lamps. The walls were covered in relics from the East India Company. The room was only partially full. We were led to a near-empty, shadowy corner.

Thompson stood. "Thank you for coming on short notice, gentlemen. The situation at the museum is in something of a mess. Coffee?"

I accepted. Barker requested tea.

"Mr. Thompson," he said. "What has happened since last we met?"

"To begin with, I've given Hennings a stern talking-to. He's given volunteers the run of the place and made major discoveries without bothering to inform me. I shall be keeping a close collar on him from now on."

"Have you discovered the identity of the mummy?" the Guv asked.

"I thought it best to hire an up-and-coming Egyptologist named Flinders Petrie to decide if the mummy is the real article. The Egyptology field is full of fakes, I'm afraid. He'll give us an expert opinion."

Barker nodded and ran a finger across his cheek. We don't generally use signals in our profession, but I knew that one. Be vigilant. Casually, I glanced about. There was a man seated not far behind us, reading a book. The front of the coffee room faced windows, but in the corner, it was dark, with covered shades. I glanced in the opposite direction. I saw no sign of a constable, but I suspected a trap of some sort.

"Why not invite him over?" my partner asked.

Mr. Thompson was nonplussed, but I wasn't. I stood and waved the man over, as if we were old club mates that happened to be in town and met accidentally. Petrie seemed unsure and glanced at the director, but the fellow was still flummoxed. I turned to the waiter at the far end of the room.

"Four sherries!" I called.

Thompson's plan was temporarily thwarted, but he still rallied. He introduced us to Petrie, who then sat opposite us on a matching sofa. He was holding a box approximately eight inches square.

Petrie was a good-looking fellow with the requisite archeologist's short beard. He was thin, tanned, and confident, but there was also the look of a scholar about him. I put him at no more than three years older than myself, which made his mission of identifying Cleopatra's mummy remarkable. The old fellows generally kept the juiciest morsels for themselves.

"Mr. Barker, I believe you have the object that was contained within the mummy Addison found," Thompson said. "We want it back. If you return it to us by noon tomorrow all will be well. If not, we will have no choice but to have you arrested. We certainly don't want that outcome, but you've given me no alternative. I have board members to whom I am responsible."

The Guv shook his head slowly like a schoolmaster with a slow student. "Mr. Thompson, if I had possession of the object you mentioned it would be out of Europe by now, in the Indian Ocean, where it would never be found. I would have vanished as well, never to be heard from again. I own my own boat and speak several Asian languages. The fact that I stand here before you is proof that I don't have it."

Thompson pounced. "But you know what it is!"

"Sir, I don't care what it is," Barker rumbled. "It isn't mine and it doesn't concern me. I want to find whoever killed Phillip Addison. I've been hired to do so, and I intend to because his young widow is in a poor condition. As we entered just now, I saw the shadow of a policeman's helmet in the lobby below. If you arrest us, you will hamper our enquiry and any chance to get the object back again. Then there would be no reason why I would continue funding your institution, or for that matter this club, of which I've been a member for fifteen years."

Barker's voice is low and loud and it carries far, as anyone who has attended a church service with him will attest. Everyone drinking coffee nearby could hear us. I knew because several visitors stopped their cups in midair.

"We are not accusing you, Mr. Barker, I assure you," Thompson said. "We simply want whatever it is back."

"But you don't know if there was an object," he argued. "The cavity may have been empty."

"Addison . . . Mr. Addison broke the wrappings to get inside."

"Aye, but that did not mean he found anything there."

Thompson's shoulders slumped a little. This was not going as he'd hoped. Perhaps he thought we'd confess immediately and pass over the fabulous object, whatever it was.

"What do you believe was inside it?" I asked innocently. I have an innocent face.

In answer, Thompson nodded to Petrie, who raised the top of the box in front of him and set it on the table. It looked like a model of an iceberg, snowy white.

"Dr. Petrie carefully pulled the hardened wrappings from inside the mummy," Thompson said. "He assembled them again and covered them in plaster of Paris. He then filled the mold with papier-mâché. This is what was inside, gentlemen, but we have no idea what it is."

I looked at the object he held out for our inspection. It was a near perfect likeness of the stone, save that it was white. That luster, that reddish glow from within was gone, leaving the mere shape. I wondered how much Barker would reveal.

My partner lifted the plaster cast and moved it around carelessly. It made Petrie nervous. I suspected he could not duplicate the process. At last, he flipped the irregular shape upside down, so that the wider portion was at the top.

"It is a heart," the Guv said. "I suspect you didn't consider the position of it in the cavity."

Petrie took it from him carefully and held it up.

"It is not heart-shaped," he said.

"It is not the symmetrical shape given in valentines," the Guv agreed. "That is a European concept. No, it represents a human heart."

Now Thompson took it and examined it.

"So it does," he said. "This is such an unusual shape. It looks natural rather than man-made."

"I wish I knew what it was for," Petrie said.

"I know little of Egyptian death rituals, doctor," Barker replied. "Aren't the mummies of pharaohs buried with gold and precious stones and other fine things?"

"Yes," Flinders Petrie said with awe in his voice. "Gold. To carry into the afterlife."

"What?" Thompson exclaimed, and they stared at the casting as if it would suddenly turn to gold, like Midas's daughter.

"Thomas was telling me something just the other day about King Solomon and his gold mines," Barker said. "Where did you say they were?"

"East Africa, sir, or so I've heard, but that's just speculation," I replied.

"It would be awfully heavy," Petrie said, staring at the creation.

"According to Hennings, Addison said he first noticed the mummy because of its weight," Director Thompson said.

"Traditionally, the hearts of mummies are not removed," Petrie continued. "They are weighed in the afterlife against something called the Feather of Ma'at, to see if the noble is worthy to step into the afterlife."

The archaeologist was getting excited now. "There are so many things about this mummy that are different. The brain was not removed, but the heart was. I've never heard of a mummy retaining its brain before, but Cleopatra was the most intelligent woman of the ancient world, gifted in history, diplomacy, war strategy, all the sciences, and even seduction. The ancient embalmers removed all the organs through the perineum, as Addison did three days ago, and a plaster plaque was affixed. All these things are unusual. However, they were living under Roman rule then, and everything had gone slapdash since the glorious days of the pharaohs. She was the last."

"Roman rule," I said. "That was Cleopatra's time."

Petrie waved a hand in the air as if he were erasing a blackboard. "No, no, I am not yet prepared to claim that the mummy is she."

"The doctor is fastidious and exact, gentlemen," Thompson stated. "That is why I hired him. Hennings was prepared to announce her identity to the press immediately, but I ordered him to wait until we are certain."

"Mr. Hennings is a relic of the past," Petrie said, sounding peeved. "There is no telling how many potsherds he crushed underfoot, how many seals he broke with a hammer. Egyptology is changing, gentlemen. Such rack and ruin shall soon be a thing of the past. There is more to discover about the Old World in a clay inventory tablet than a . . . well, than a lump of gold, whatever the size."

We sat for a moment, each lost in our own thoughts.

"Mr. Barker," the director said. "Are you still working for Mrs. Addison?"

"I am, sir. On her behalf, at least."

"Forgive me for saying it, but she cannot possess much money."

"Barely a sou, sir, but she vowed to sell everything she owns to pay my fee."

Thompson shook his balding head and his fingers played with his beard in thought.

"Phillip Addison was not officially working for the museum, but as far as the British Museum is concerned, he was performing our work when he died. We'd like to pay for your services, to find the criminals who killed him. If in doing so you uncover the trail of the stolen heart, so much the better. In addition, we shall also take up a subscription for his widow, privately of course. The poor woman has been through enough."

"Quite right," Barker rumbled. "But we already have a client."

Petrie lifted the white casting and peered at it closely. "No, it wasn't gold. It's too jagged. It's some sort of crystal, quartz, perhaps, or agate. Some sort of semiprecious stone, perhaps."

"This isn't fair, Barker," Thompson said. "We have been more than patient. What is it, and where is it? We demand to know."

"It is not my intention to be coy, gentlemen," the Guv replied. "It will return to you in the fullness of time. As to what it is, Mr. Petrie, what color is a heart?"

"Red, obviously." The man's eyes widened. "What . . . a ruby? Is it a ruby?"

"I've heard the term is 'spinel,' but aye, it's a ruby."

"My God!" Edward Maund Thompson cried. "A giant ruby inside the mummy of Cleopatra? This could be the greatest find of all time! Sir, give us our property at once!"

"No, sir," Barker replied. "It is in a safe place and will be returned to you soon. Whoever possesses it is in danger. Mrs. Addison is in hospital. She was shot in front of our offices this very day. I thought it best to take it out of play, so to speak. I alone know where it is in order to make certain it is safe."

"We can safeguard it ourselves," Thompson argued.

"You did. It languished in your cellar for years."

The director made a sour face.

"Be patient, sir," Barker said. "You'll get your reward."

"Have you made any headway in your investigation?" Thompson cried. "Tell me you have!"

"Yes indeed," the Guv replied. "Addison was killed by a gang, but we have not yet uncovered who hired them. As it happens, Mr. Llewelyn shot one of the members last night."

The two men looked at me with sudden respect. I attempted some sangfroid. Grinning like an idiot would have spoiled the effect.

CHAPTER 17

We'd had our fill for the day, or at least I had. Barker released Jenkins, who fled to the Rising Sun. My partner locked the doors, and I summoned a cab, keeping a watchful eye. It would be a while before I would be able to jump into a hansom without thinking.

A half hour later, having fought our way through traffic, we alighted in Lion Street and entered the house. Mac met us in the hall with a bow for Barker. Harm skirted my legs and hopped up to rest his paws on Barker's knee. I missed Rebecca. It would have been nice to have someone who actually cared about my welfare. *How are you, Thomas?* I said to myself. *Fine. I wasn't shot today. Well, shot at, but they missed.*

Dinner was excellent. Pot-au-feu, shoulder of mutton, sturgeon cutlet, potatoes, and stuffed mushrooms. Mac had made strawberry ice cream, so I forgave him for cutting me dead in the hallway. Afterward, I returned to my room and tried to choose a book from my overstuffed shelf. It was either *New Grub Street* or *The Odd Women*. I like George Gissing. He is delightfully melancholy. However, I couldn't decide which to choose, so I read them both back and forth, which I do not recommend. It only gets them muddled. Around nine o'clock, the telephone set rang. I heard Mac speak. I needed a moment to clear my head anyway, so I went down the stair.

"It's for you, sir," Mac said, handing me the apparatus.

"For me?" I asked.

"I believe so. It was difficult to make out. The fellow mumbles."

"Hello. This is Thomas Llewelyn speaking."

There was silence on the line. I thought I heard breathing, but I wasn't certain.

"Hallo!" I said. "Is someone there?"

"Thomas," a voice whispered. It sounded slurred, but at the same time I seemed to recognize it. I ran through dozen possibilities before it came to me.

"Liam?" I asked. "Is that you?"

"Yes," he murmured again.

"What's wrong?" I asked with a feeling of alarm.

"They got in," he said. "They destroyed everything. My collection. My books."

"Are you hurt?"

There was a pause. I believe it was shame. Every man is supposed to be able to defend his own castle. "They beat me."

"Who did?"

"Several men in tweed caps."

"We'll be right over!" I cried.

"Do hurry. I believe I've been stabbed."

I hung up the receiver.

"Sir!" I called up the stair. "Liam Grant had just had the Tweed gang break into his flat. He's been stabbed."

"I'll be right down," he called.

It took us only a few minutes to leave. We trotted to the

Elephant and Castle and hailed a cab. Barker carried a small leather bag containing bandages and medicine bottles. I repeated what was said between us for my partner's benefit.

Eventually, the cab burst into Russell Square and skidded to a halt in front of Grant's door. We rushed inside the well-appointed building where we found Liam's door partially open. Cautiously, we stepped inside. The first thing I saw was that the contents of the filing cabinets had been emptied onto the floor. It was obvious the gang was looking for the ruby.

"Liam!" I called.

"In here!" he cried.

I hurried to the fireplace where he was slumped in one of the old and cracked leather chairs. He held a towel to his stomach, which was spattered with blood. A welt under one eye was swelling and his lip was cut. Normally he was groomed immaculately, but he was in as poor a state as his flat. His grizzled hair was sticking up in every direction, his shirt and waistcoat stained. We bent and examined the wound. He had been slashed, six inches across. One end was half an inch deep.

"You'll live, Mr. Grant," the Guv said. "I'll treat this with a clean bandage and some carbolic. Tell us what happened, sir."

"I came out of the museum around six and saw that the light in my room was lit, so I ran inside," Liam said as Barker probed the wound. "When I arrived, I found my door open, and men were ransacking my files. When they saw me, they seized me and demanded to know where the ruby was. I told them I didn't know what they were talking about. They beat me. I think one of my ribs is broken. The leader . . ."

"Ugly fellow, red hair?" I asked.

"Yes! He threatened to cut my gizzard when I couldn't give them the ruby."

"Look what they did to this room," I muttered.

Old and rare tomes were strewn about the floor. Curios and knickknacks from various centuries had been broken and ground into the carpet. The owl was flying about the room in a panic and the crocodile hung by one chain. Some of the items could be set right, but not Liam Grant's psyche, I feared.

"We'll set everything to rights," I promised, touching his shoulder.

He seized me by the wrist. "First the museum and now this!"

"The museum?" I asked. "What happened there?"

"Director Thompson banned me for life. For life, Thomas! There's no longer a reason to be in London anymore. I'm leaving for Aberdeen as soon as I rid myself of all this! It's been tainted, anyway."

"No," I said. "It will be fine. We'll clean the place and fix things. You'll burn some incense, say a druidical prayer or something, and everything will be fine. You'll see."

"My nerves can't take it," he insisted. "Me, stabbed and beaten! My sanctuary has been defiled. I can never come back here again."

"London wouldn't be the same without you," I told him. "You can't go. Rebecca and I couldn't visit the Museum Tavern without you there. We wouldn't."

"How do you stand it, Thomas?" he asked, nearly a whisper. "I know you've been shot before. And stabbed. How can you do such dangerous work? Why in the world does your wife allow you to risk life and limb for clients you don't even know?"

"Barker's a bit of a Galahad, always looking for a quest," I said. "He likes the freedom and the danger. It's also something he's very good at, a vocation of sorts to him."

"I'm sure it is for him, but what about you?"

"Let us say my career as a poet was short-lived," I told him. "I'm established in this field now. People know my name."

"I couldn't do what you do," he said. "It's a mad business."

"No one expects you to, Liam. You are a natural scholar. You have other strengths. Now come, let's see if we can get a clean shirt for you."

It took Barker a quarter hour to patch him up. He put a sticking plaster on Grant's ribs. I helped him change his clothing but could not button his waistcoat over the bruises on his torso. He had a small bottle of laudanum he'd purchased for a toothache, and I convinced him to have a spoonful for the pain.

Barker finished and closed his case. He turned and regarded the state of Grant's shelves. When Liam returned to the sitting room, I helped him to the other chair, the one not stained with blood. Barker began to put the books back on the shelves, though a book lover always prefers to have the final say in placement. He gathered a stack of books that would require the services of a bookbinder. Many of those were the oldest, and I know Liam would want them repaired. The floor was still littered by debris, but the Guv had not found a broom or brush.

"You can't leave London," I told him again. "I won't stand for it. Even if I did, Rebecca wouldn't. This is your home. We'll get those blighters and when we find them, they'll never bother you again."

"But we're right across from the museum, Thomas. I've been banished. Every time I looked out the window, I'd see the site of my disgrace. Every time I went to dinner, there it would be. My friends are either patrons or employed there. I read there. There are still hundreds of volumes I haven't read. My life is there."

"Move across from the London Library, then," I counseled. "I'm sure you would be appreciated there. Russell Square's loss would be St. James's Square's gain."

"You'll barely notice I'm gone," he stated. "Come back in five years and no one here will have ever heard of me. I do nothing. I serve no purpose. I offer answers if someone asks me questions on a particular subject. Mostly, I just read all day."

"I think we need you for that most of all," I said. "For those of us who wish we could afford to read all day, you are an inspiration. Surely you don't really believe you are doing nothing, do you? You know more about the book collections in the British

Museum than anyone. You've read most of them. You know the answers people are looking for. You rescue books that the museum foolishly withdraws. You tell anyone who has questions where to find the answers. You are an ambassador for the place. That isn't nothing. Far from it, in fact."

Inwardly, I wondered if Grant had the nerve to stay. He hadn't left this neighborhood or this street in years. He lived in his small but pleasant world, with his flat, his museum, his books, and his independent means. He was a bachelor because he was shy around women, though Rebecca thought him quite the charmer. In fact, she told me she must do something about that.

Most of all, Liam Grant was kind, though kindness doesn't get one far. People can't make a living at it. Some would not recognize it, while others consider civility a relic of the past. People rarely talk of it, but if it is taken away, the world is colder and meaner. Not having kindness can damage the soul.

"I feel terrible about it," I said. "Whoever did this could only have learned of your location because we went to your door. Somehow, we were seen."

"It wasn't you, Thomas," he replied. "I suspect it was Phillip. And I do not blame him. He was in a serious predicament. We must have been seen, that's all. He said there were suspicious men in the street."

"Yes, but criminals don't loiter by the British Museum waiting for someone to find a ruby," I reasoned.

"True."

Barker lifted an overturned table and righted it. "Do you think you need to go to hospital, sir?"

"No hospital," Grant said.

"Would you like us to call Scotland Yard? I recommend it."

"I suppose I should," Liam said. The idea had not occurred to him.

Barker found his telephone set under a table and called Scotland Yard to explain what happened. Then he tapped the receiver to end the call and made another call.

"Mac, I need you to gather some cleaning supplies and come to Russell Square." He gave the address then hung the receiver on the stalk.

"Mr. Grant," the Guv said over his shoulder. "I have taken the liberty of calling my butler. He is a marvel, particularly in matters such as this. Our offices have been assaulted many times, including this week. He'll have these rooms looking better than new."

"Thank you, sir," Liam said.

"Lad," Barker growled suddenly, looking at me in warning. He gestured toward the window.

A group of men were coming up the walk. The gang had returned. Barker and I reached for our pistols. We looked at each other and then at Grant, who had gone deathly pale.

There was a loud thump on the door. Barker crossed to it, lifted his Colt, and flung it open. A group of men stood frowning, first at the state of the room, then at Barker, and then at my friend standing behind him. They were not wearing tweed caps but more respectable top hats and bowlers. A few even looked familiar.

"Gentlemen!" Grant cried. "Come in!"

I recognized them then. They were from the museum, librarians and guides. They entered and demanded to know what had happened to their friend. It was obvious they thought we had destroyed the place. Of course, they could not have done much if we had. Grant explained the situation. Everyone sat, claiming every chair in the room. Others sat on the stone hearth or on the rugs.

Scotland Yard arrived about five minutes later. They interviewed Grant and took down a description of the perpetrators. Barker hung back, and the Yard inspector did not recognize him.

Shortly after, Jacob Maccabee arrived. He said nothing, but glanced at the crowd and then began cleaning, beginning with the files strewn by the front door. By the time he was done I knew they would be far cleaner and more organized than they had ever been.

At that point one of the men spoke. He was a solemn-looking librarian with white hair and a walrus mustache. He had obviously been chosen from among them to speak to their friend.

"Mr. Grant, we feel the treatment of you by the director is cruel," he said. "You are more than a member of the public; you are a friend. You have touched our lives. We heard what happened with poor young Addison, and you can't be held responsible for helping him. Thompson has made a blunder. We won't allow you to be banned."

"Hear, hear," I said.

"They can't treat one of our own like that!" the man continued. "Russell Square is ours and we'll protect it to the bitter end. We won't put up with ruffians near the museum."

A thought occurred to me and I went to the telephone and asked the operator to connect us to the Museum Tavern. When the call went through, I asked to speak to the publican.

"Sir," I said in a low voice. "My name is Thomas Llewelyn. Do you know a patron named Liam Grant?"

"Of course, sir," came the reply. "He is one of our best customers."

"I suspected as much," I told him. "Sir, Grant's home was ransacked tonight and he was injured. He has also been banned from the museum by the director."

"What!" the publican cried. "Director Thompson? Surely there has been some kind of mistake."

"Perhaps, but right now his flat is full of outraged museum staff. There are more than ten of us, and we are trying to sort this matter. Some kind of decision must be made tonight about the museum's ill treatment of Mr. Grant."

"How can we help, sir?"

"We require ale and sandwiches, or whatever you have left at this time of night," I told him. "I will pay for everything."

"Anything for Mr. Grant. Give us ten minutes. Do you require anything stronger?"

I looked about at the group of men, trying to decide how to deal with this situation. "No, just the ale, I think. I don't want to have to deal with a roomful of drunken and angry librarians."

"Good thought, lad," Barker murmured in my ear. We turned to the group.

"I say we should strike," one of the men said.

"That's easy for you to say, Neville," another argued. "You don't have a family to feed."

"We should tell the newspapers!"

"Gentlemen," Grant stated, holding up his hands. "I don't want you to get into any trouble on my behalf."

"It isn't right how they treated you, acting as if you were a common criminal causing a nuisance!"

"What we need is a librarians' union. They can't push us about."

"Gentlemen, I'm not a librarian," Grant insisted.

"Well, you should be. You're there twelve hours a day like me, helping people all the time. If you're doing it, rich man or no, you deserve to be paid!"

There was a pounding on the door ten minutes later. I answered it. The publican stood on the other side.

"In here!" he called to a troop of people carrying trays full of pint glasses of ale. They were followed by plates stacked with sandwiches.

"I shut down the tavern early," the publican said. "Would you mind if I sit in on the meeting? Good to see you, Mr. Grant."

"You needn't go to all this trouble, Mr. Halliday," my friend said.

"I reckon you are my steadiest customer," he replied. "I've

a mind to demand payment of the directors' tabs immediately. We'll see how much they enjoy that."

"We should go on strike, I say," one of the men repeated.

"We need a union, I tell you. We'll get the Socialist League involved."

"Henry, if a group of librarians can't organize a union, what good are we?"

The man who first spoke up raised his hand.

"Striking sounds drastic," he said. "Suppose they call? Suppose they sack us all?"

"What do you suggest, Bob?"

"I suggest we all call in tomorrow, due to illness," he replied. "The director will understand our meaning."

"We have mouths to feed," another cautioned.

"If you are worried about a day's wages, I will pay for them myself," Barker said. "And if they threaten you, I shall take my name off the subscribers' list. That will hurt far worse."

I stepped over to where the publican sat.

"I've got your money," I said.

"Keep it," he said. "I'm in this now. Thompson can't do this to my best customer."

Everyone took a pint in one hand and a sandwich in the other. I got Mac's attention with a wave, but he shook his head. No, he would see this mess through even if it took until morning. My partner and I slipped out into the night, while the librarians plotted vengeance for one of their own.

CHAPTER 18

We were back in Millwall the next morning, although I didn't know why. Cyrus Barker was dissatisfied. The Tweed Cap Gang had disappeared in a puff of smoke. They hadn't returned to their squatter's flat in Cubitt Town and had not been seen in the area. Perhaps they had moved to the West End now.

Barker frowned. In his black coat and bowler hat, his sober suit, and black-lensed spectacles, he looked menacing. However, he was just in an ill mood.

"Today we are going to hunt the gang instead of them hunting us," he said.

"Very well," I said. "But how?"

"Let's begin with the Millwall Boys," he replied.

"I don't like buying information, even if it's just drinks," I complained. "The other offices in Craig's Court can't afford

192 • WILL THOMAS

such luxuries. I'd like to feel we are at least giving them a sporting chance."

"Very well. We can work under those restraints."

We found Dock House again and stepped inside. It was dark and nearly empty. The gang was nowhere to be seen. Outside again, there was a fine snow falling.

"That didn't work," I said as we left the establishment. "What's the next move?"

"One I was hoping to avoid."

We were on the dock, directly above the spot where Phillip Addison had been found and Coffee John had secured his boat. Barker turned and faced north. I followed his line of sight.

"The Inn of Double Happiness," I guessed. "Mr. K'ing's domain."

My partner scowled and I couldn't blame him. It's best to avoid Mr. K'ing, to disavow him, to not even claim that he exists. He is a specter, a spook. He is the toehold that China has in Jolly Old England. Everything coming from Canton flows through his fingers, from rice to opium, especially opium. There is a den under the inn and now K'ing had expanded into gambling. Rumor had it that he was creating a house of assignation next. Whatever weakness a man has, he will exploit it.

"Blast, I was hoping I wouldn't have to do this," the Guv said, trudging north. "Let's get it over and done. He's a stone I cannot leave unturned."

"Do you think he'd know something Ho doesn't?" I asked, as reluctant to cross the threshold of his establishment as Barker.

"They exchange a great deal of information, but K'ing would be a fool to give away all he knows, even to a lieutenant."

"Is Ho a lieutenant, then?"

"Best not to ask," he answered. "I no longer attend meetings of the Chee Kong Tong."

Barker began to explain the difference between Chinese Masonry, the so-called Heaven and Earth Society, the Blue Dragon Triad, and the benevolence societies. He only succeeded in giving me a headache. K'ing belonged to all of them. It is easy to paint the man as a villain, but it wasn't entirely so. He looked after Asian interests in the West. I believe that is all I needed to know or, in fact, wanted to.

The inn was on the shore of Limehouse Basin, a nondescript building with no sign of its purpose. The façade boasted pillars, roof-tiled eaves, and a round door. Inside, I found a reception desk and a large plaster dragon coiled against one wall. The desk was staffed with hostesses, three of them. They wore robes with long sleeves and decorative pins in their hair. Aside from Barker's ward, Bok Fu Ying, I had never seen a Chinese woman before. Most of the Asian residents are sailors and thus transitory. Their wives lived in the Pearl Delta with their families.

"Welcome!" one of the women chirped. "How can we be of service?"

"We would speak with Mr. K'ing," Barker said.

All three women smiled at once. "Mr. K'ing, he is not here."

"He is here," Barker insisted. "He is always here."

"He is here, it is true," she acknowledged. "But he is very busy. So busy. Perhaps another time."

"Perhaps now," Barker said. "Tell him Shi Shi Ji is waiting. Impatiently."

Suddenly the girl in the middle disappeared, and the other two came together like sliding doors. I saw the other slink up some stairs in a corridor behind. I suspected this was the procedure if, for example, a pair of drunken sailors became rowdy or a Scotland Yard inspector appeared. If some of K'ing's bodyguards appeared, a fight might ensue.

Barker turned toward the door and leaned against the counter, crossing his arms. He was in the lane of commerce. People were entering the lobby, expecting to be helped. The two young women fluttered around him like butterflies greeting the customers, although it was awkward. The Guv is not the most welcoming of men.

I looked up after a moment, and there was only one girl left in the lobby. I supposed the other had been sent upstairs. Barker pulled out his watch and noted the time as a pair of Chinese sailors entered. He spoke to them in Chinese and they turned and left. The lone girl became flustered, smiling politely, not certain what to do. Finally, the other two young women returned. One bowed in front of my partner.

"Mr. K'ing is most anxious to see you," she said. "Please to step this way."

She turned to lead him and I followed. The second young woman reached out a hand to stop me. Apparently, I had not been invited. I frowned at her and followed my partner up the stair.

K'ing's office was on the top floor. Like Limehouse itself, the room was a combination of oriental and occidental: a Chinese rug, an English desk. European bookcases filled with Chinese classics. Beautiful rosewood chairs drawn up to a fireplace that once graced an English manor house.

K'ing was sitting behind the desk. When I first met him, he wore a Savile Row suit and had an English haircut. Now he wore a gown and skullcap, both of blue silk. He had a black mustache, and there was a large burn mark on the side of his face, like white webbing. He was not yet forty, but he looked older than he was. He set down a pen when we arrived and removed a pair of pince-nez spectacles.

"Father-in-law," he said in greeting.

Barker lowered himself into a chair in front of the desk.

"I am most certainly not your father-in-law," he said.

The Chinese leader turned to me. "Thomas, you are looking well. I understand our wives have become friends."

"Indeed," I said. "How is Foo Ying?"

"Well enough, but her guardian neglects her terribly," he

replied. "Soo is taller every time I see her. I doubt she would even recognize him."

He was referring to their daughter, now three years old. It was true that Barker had not visited her home in 3 Colt Lane in a while, but K'ing had not, either. It was a marriage of alliance, and rather than living with his wife, he lived here on the premises, the base of his operations.

"You have not come to discuss family," he continued. "How can I be of service to you?"

"A body was discovered in Millwall two days ago," the Guv said. "I believe I can see the very spot it was found from here."

"Englishman?"

Barker nodded. "Yes. He was a schoolmaster, who also worked for the British Museum. His name was Phillip Addison. I am working for his widow."

"The name is not familiar," K'ing said. "Did he gamble?"

"No, but he did discover a mummy recently that may be Cleopatra."

K'ing shrugged his thin shoulders. He had no interest in Egypt.

"Near Christmas, a gang moved into Cubitt Town and there was a fight with the Millwall Boys. You are familiar with them?"

"I know the Millwall Boys," the Chinese leader said. "If they were beaten, I am not surprised."

A houseboy entered with a tray of tea. K'ing waved him away and poured three bowls, setting them at the edge of the desk. We raised ours and drank.

"The other gang we know little about," Barker said, setting down his cup. "They wear tweed caps and appear to come from nowhere. I was wondering if you have encountered them. I know that what happens in the area matters to you."

K'ing gave a thin smile. "It does."

"I assume you spoke to them, then," the Guv said.

"I did not. However, they encountered a few of my sailors. More than a few, in fact."

"I wish I'd been there," Barker said, giving him a sanguine look. "Did you chase them out or do something worse to them?"

"I understand they were armed with knives," K'ing replied. "The leader was inclined to be bellicose. Someone had shot him in the foot."

Here K'ing turned and regarded me approvingly from his chair. Then he turned back to Barker.

"Fascinating," my partner rumbled. "What was the outcome?"

K'ing shrugged. "I sent some of my sailors after them and they have not returned since."

The Guv glanced at me. That was one mystery solved.

"Do you know who they were?" Barker asked.

K'ing shook his head. "Good fighters for Westerners."

"Where did they go afterward?" Barker pursued.

"North London," K'ing said. "We made certain they were gone."

"Why do you suppose they came here in the first place?" I asked.

"I don't know and I don't care," he replied.

There was silence for a moment. I suspected some of K'ing's hatchet men were nearby. We had barged in uninvited. There must always be a show of strength after such an occurrence.

"You are doing well here," Barker noted. "When were you in Canton last?"

The Chinaman sat back in his chair. "More business is done in Hong Kong and Macao these days, but I was there three months ago. It hasn't changed, though there is talk of a railway to Kowloon. I have purchased shares."

Barker stood. "Thomas, we have trespassed long enough on this gentleman's time."

We bowed and opened the door. I noted a guard in the hall who hadn't been there when we entered. As we descended the stair, I felt a prickling between my shoulder blades. We were several streets away before I stopped holding my breath.

My partner began meandering through Limehouse without any obvious purpose, as he had done in Millwall. He was dock-walloping again. I assumed he was headed toward Commercial Road, where we could find a cab to take us back to Whitehall. If he had a destination in mind, however, it wasn't obvious to me.

"Wait here, Thomas," he ordered before ducking into a shop. The hoarding overhead was written in Chinese, and I couldn't tell what kind of establishment it was because the windows were so filthy I couldn't see inside. He did not return for ten minutes, leaving me shivering in the cold.

"Let's go," he said when he stepped out into the street again, as if it were I who had kept him waiting. A few turns told me where we were headed. We were going to 3 Colt Lane to see Bok Fu Ying. The few words K'ing had said to Barker about his ward must have stung. Once at her door, we adjusted our ties and mufflers and knocked.

An elderly Chinese woman answered the door, frowning as if trying to work out why two British men were at the door. She called back over her shoulder, and a few seconds later I heard the sound of slippers on the stairs and Fu Ying appeared, out of breath.

"Sir!" she cried, overjoyed. She pulled us in by the sleeves and took our hats and gloves. She wore a silk blouse with frogged but-tons and a long skirt, both in an aqua color. She looked well. In fact, she had hardly aged in the ten years I had known her. There was a time in my single days that I considered getting to know her better, but matters had worked out perfectly for me. Not as well for her, obviously, with a neglectful guardian and a delinquent husband. I'd have rather seen her married to any Chinese sailor in Limehouse than the opium king of the East End.

As we climbed the steps, she patted us on the backs as if urging us to move faster. I'd never seen her look happier. She had always been a serious person, like her guardian. When we reached the first floor, she called to the old woman for tea. I glanced about the parlor, which had changed little since I saw it last. There was one addition, however, about two and a half feet tall, with pigtails and an elfish face. Fu Ying's daughter was sitting on the floor with paper and some colored pencils.

"Sir!" Bok Fu Ying whispered. The girl jumped to her feet and ran to Barker. She stopped in front of him and bowed in the Chinese manner, one hand cupping the other.

"Sir," the child crooned. This was he, the famous Sir her mother had always told her about but had rarely, if ever, seen. I believe she was frightened, and with good reason. Being distant and imposing are two of Barker's key traits.

Meanwhile, the Guv regarded the little morsel with some suspicion, as if she were an Irish bomb set to go off at any moment. Both stopped and looked at each other, not sure of what to do next.

Barker cleared his throat then, and in the blink of an eye Soo was standing before him and bowing again. He reached into one of his coat pockets and handed her a cube of wood painted red. She bowed in thanks and took it to a corner, not sure what to do with it. He cleared his throat a second time. She was back again. He pulled another piece from his pocket, a blue triangle. She understood then and made a dash for his pocket. The rug was soon littered with blocks: green rectangles, purple ovals, and every other shape and color. Soo was delighted and began putting them together and stacking them on the floor.

"It was very nice of Sir to bring presents," Fu Ying observed.

"I didn't want the girl to feel neglected."

Fu Ying nodded. "Of course not."

"Nor her mother." He reached into his coat pocket and handed her a small box. Our hostess was nearly overcome and hid her mouth behind her hand, but of course the temptation was too great, and she opened it. Inside was a cloisonné pin of a dragon, beautiful and delicate. She gave him an awkward curtsy and then ran to a mirror to pin it on.

"Who is this?" Barker demanded of Soo, pulling an Asian doll from his other coat pocket. The girl looked up from her blocks and stared, as if she'd been caught doing something wrong.

"Sir!" she cried, running to him. She caught up the doll, which wore a silken dress and clips in her hair, hugging it close. If she held it any tighter it would break.

Tea was brought, and shortbread, which Fu Ying knew was the Guv's favorite. She served, of course, her cheeks flushed. She may have felt she was not worthy of such joy. If so, she had reason. Bok Fu Ying had been given him by the Empress Dowager of China for his services to her, along with Harm. She was a slave, although not of Cyrus Barker. She belonged to Harm. If the prized Pekingese died, she could be put to death for negligence in China. He had been unprepared to be placed in charge of a fourteen-year-old girl. When he came to London, he had papers drawn to make him her legal guardian and bought her the house at 3 Colt Lane. Then he went about his business. I suppose he thought she was like a flower that didn't need tending. I'd remonstrated with him about her more than once. Like most of us, he is as ignorant in some ways as he is wise in others.

It was Rebecca who first noticed Fu Ying's plight. Now the two women were friends and she was an occasional visitor in Camomile Street.

While we talked, Soo built the blocks into every shape imaginable and had undressed and redressed the doll. The only new thing in the room left to explore was Barker himself. Currently, he was discussing Chinese boxing with her mother, who trained under him. As they were talking Soo crawled into his lap with her doll. Barker froze. Men he could wrestle to the ground, but what was one to do with a little girl? She took his immobility as a sign she could make herself comfortable.

Fu Ying caught my eye, raising a brow. She knew what was happening. This was a part of his life he must improve. He knew, as Rebecca and I did, that the domestic life here was not on solid ground. By tossing her at him like an afterthought, the Empress Dowager Cixi had made him responsible for Fu Ying for life. By allowing her to marry the wrong man, he had insured she would need his help for years to come. On the other hand, the changes she brought to his bachelor life were for the good as well, changes like the little girl in his lap, who had just fallen asleep.

Everyone lowered their voices. We talked about Harm's health, of Rebecca in Gwent with my Methodist family, of New Year's plans and hopes for the coming year. We would talk of anything but the matter that brought us to Limehouse.

Eventually, the old woman came and collected the sleeping child. Bok Fu Ying held Barker's hand for a few minutes afterward, talking of nothing important. It was the communing rather than the words. She realized before he did that he must be about his business. She brought his gloves and bowler hat to him. I thought something should be said, but I wasn't the one to say it.

"Fu Ying," Barker said. "When Mrs. Llewelyn returns from Wales, you must come for dinner. The two of you may work out the details with Mac. Of course, you must bring little Soo."

Impulsively, she kissed him on the cheek. The Guv was astounded. Even I was surprised. Then she was so mortified at her own action that she nearly slammed the door in our faces. We stepped back and looked at each other.

Cyrus Barker harrumphed and reset his bowler and the lapels of his coat. If I'd have made any remark or even smiled, he'd have boxed my ears.

"Cab or Underground?" he asked.

"Cab, I think," I said.

"Commercial Road it is, then."

CHAPTER 19

Two hours later, a man in his late fifties shuffled into our offices wearing a flat cap and a sailor's pea jacket. His name was Ambrose Wheeler. The Guv greeted him as he entered and they spent a few minutes reminiscing before I realized he was the detective whom Davis had hired to track down information about us and the mummy.

"I hope there's no hard feelings about me taking the work, Push," he said, kneading his cap in his hands. "Times are hard this time of year with the weather and the holidays. People don't hire detectives in late December."

"Not at all, Ambrose," Barker replied. He wore an expensive suit while Wheeler's boots were scraped and dirty, but there was a camaraderie between them. They talked of old cases and Scotland Yard, where Wheeler had formerly worked as a sergeant. The stories they shared were good enough that I wanted to take notes, but this was one time I couldn't. Finally, Barker arrived at the reason why he was there.

"Tell me, do you recall a jockey named Hambly?" the Guv asked.

"Sure, I know him," Wheeler said. "He won a few races up Yorkshire way. Talented jockey. Then he fell off his mare, Lady's Choice, in the third race at Epsom Downs and got stepped on proper. Both his knees were fractured, I think. That was 1889, as I recall. Maybe 1890."

"What has become of him?"

"Last I heard of him he was working for Cargill at Ally Pally. That was, what, two years ago?"

"Doing what?"

Wheeler shrugged. "Oh, this and that. Nobbling. Messages. Muckin' out. That sort of thing."

"Do you think he's still there?"

The detective shrugged his shoulders. "Probably. He's got a problem with the bottle, I hear. It's getting the best of him. You fall off one horse and that's it. There was your chance."

"I appreciate the information," Barker replied. "And no, there are no hard feelings at all. It's good to talk with you again."

"I must say, I never thought to see a royal warrant in this court," the man answered. "Congratulations."

"Give the gentleman a finny, Mr. Llewelyn."

I handed Wheeler a five-pound note from our collective wallet. I wondered if this fellow, too, was a victim of drink. For many, detective work can be an unstable profession, peopled by bachelors, widowers, men dismissed from the Yard, and sots. Barker was nothing like them. He was trying to elevate the profession, though he treated them as colleagues.

"Ta, Push," Wheeler said. "I'm off, then."

When he was gone Barker turned to me. "Do you fancy a trip north?"

"Scotland?" I asked.

"Haringey. North London."

"As long as we take the Underground," I replied as we donned our coats. "What's 'Ally Pally'?"

"You're getting too posh, lad," my partner rumbled. "You need to spend a week in the East End and learn some new cant. It's the Alexandra Park Racecourse. Have you heard of Alfred Cargill?"

"The name sounds familiar," I answered. "I believe there was some sort of scandal. Fraud?"

Barker nodded. "He fixed the London Cup. He was indicted but they couldn't prove the charges."

"That's right!" I said. "He's a showy fellow. Diamonds on each finger. The newspapers claimed he'd bet on anything. I seem to recall he once bet a thousand pounds on whether a leaf would blow through or over the fence outside of Kensington Palace. He probably did. He's very lucky."

"Luck is a mere notion, and a poor substitute for prayer," the Guv said.

I should have known better. "Luck" was one of those words that set him off.

"Interesting," he continued. "We began with a young man examining mummies in the British Museum, and now we are visiting an infamous bookmaker. I wonder where this trail shall lead."

Barker consulted a Kelly's directory and found the address. When we took the Underground to Haringey I found the district looking more prosperous than I had assumed. I had rarely been in north London. We considered it the sleepy end of town, where our work seldom took us. If Cargill was there perhaps there was more to the borough than meets the eye.

The track was well kept, and ringed with trees, now bare. Sliding gates were partially open as we stepped into the stable area. The oval ring that circled the track was laid with shavings and fog nestled in the rafters. There were no horses nearby, but then it wasn't racing season. We walked along the outer track and just when we were about to give up, we discovered an office in a place where one expected stalls. It wasn't a dodgy-looking business, either. The hand-lettering was fine, the woodwork in mahogany stain. If one did not object to the smell of horses and all that goes with it, it was a snug little office.

The sign read ALFRED CARGILL & ASSOCIATES, LICENSED BETTING OFFICE.

As we neared the door, we could hear a typing machine tapping steadily inside. Cautiously we opened and stepped through the door. A man sat at a desk typing as rhythmically as a metronome. He did not look up as we entered. Several chairs lined the walls, all the seats empty. The chalkboard across from them had a series of numbers written on it I could barely understand. I only bet at large public events and almost never win. Math was never my strong suit and I had no expertise in horse racing to rely upon.

A large desk sat in the middle of the room, on top of which was a chaotic mess of ledger books, betting forms, and a spindle full of notes spilling over. In the midst of all of it sat a man with hair and side-whiskers still black as night, though he was approaching sixty. His jacket was hung on a hook, and he sat in his waistcoat and shirtsleeves, his tie loosened. He was talking into a telephone receiver, in no hurry to end the conversation, but he waved us to a pair of chairs in front of his desk. I noticed his hands were covered with rings glittering even in the dark coolness of the room. The Persian carpet under our feet was littered with more shavings. An ancient basset hound reclined on a cushion in a corner, but the creature had no more interest in us than the secretary. I placed our card near Cargill and he took it up and read it while finishing his call. Finally, he set the receiver in its cradle.

Cargill examined the two of us, Barker especially, while tapping the card against his lip. I thought he was trying to work out what we were doing there, but he surprised me.

"Cyrus Barker," he exclaimed. "Weren't you Andrew Mc-Lean's mate? You boxed bare-knuckle for a year or two, didn't you? It must have been ten or fifteen years ago. I remember you. You wore goggles with green glass. The officials . . . well, we couldn't call them officials, the fight being illegal; they argued about whether you could wear them or not. You had to take them off and you were angry. You charged in the minute the bell rang and took Leonard McGillis down in fewer than a dozen punches. It didn't matter that you didn't wear the goggles. You could have worn a tiara and it wouldn't have made a bit of difference."

"You have an excellent memory, Mr. Cargill," Barker said.

"I do, sir," he admitted. "I trade on it. In your case, I lost twenty-five pounds. I'll take a cheque."

We stared at him. He threw his head back and laughed.

"A bit of humor there, gentlemen," he said. "Private enquiry agents. Is that 'to the Queen'? I see the warrant on your card. You must be doing well for yourself these days. Anything to pad the bill, I say. What brings you to my humble office, gentlemen?"

Barker cleared his throat. "I'm investigating the murder of a teacher and volunteer at the British Museum. He was stabbed and dropped into Limehouse Reach."

"And?" he said.

"A number of young men were spotted in the area. A witness claims that one of them was a former jockey named Hambly. Mr. Llewelyn here was attacked by the gang with knives."

"Continue," he said.

"The night before there was a fight between this gang and the Millwall Boys," the Guv replied. "One of their men was also stabbed. We suspect the victim might have been killed by a member of this gang."

Cargill raised a brow. "How do you think I am involved?"

"A witness claims one of the men was Hambly, who works for

you. They were followed to this area after being chased out of the Isle of Dogs."

"Chased by whom?" asked Cargill.

"The Blue Dragon Triad," Barker rumbled. "Your boys left quickly."

"Why would you think I have boys?" he asked.

"You're a booking agent," the Guv said. "Sometimes people can't or won't pay their debts. Gentlemen like you who accept such bets require strong, fit men to collect these debts. I am going to infer that your offices require them as a usual part of doing business. I have not come to accuse anyone or to interfere in your operations. I'm looking for those fellows to question them about the stabbing. I work for the victim's family."

The two men stared at each other. Barker was waiting for Cargill to start answering questions instead of asking them. Goodness knows what Cargill was thinking.

Cargill cursed, then raised his head as if his neck hurt and sighed.

"Yes, they're mine," he said. "But they're not a gang. They collect debts for me, not as a group, but in pairs. I've never sent them to Millwall. Who has money in Millwall? It's an ash heap. That's a cheap way to die, floating in Limehouse Reach. How many of these lads were there? Did anyone say?"

"There were nine," I said.

"That's the lot of them," Cargill pronounced. "And they tried to take on the Triads? Those are K'ing's people. It's a wonder they aren't in a soup somewhere, the idiots! No one told me about Millwall or K'ing. Nobody said anything to me about a man getting stabbed and tossed in the river. Gentlemen, I've told my boys one thing all their lives. I've told my staff and secretary, I've told the jockeys I work with. I told everybody: don't tell lies. Lies will find you out, trip you up, and send you to prison. It's better to admit your transgressions and take your punishment than to get yourself in more trouble. It don't end well."

"We regret being the bearer of ill news," the Guv stated.

"I should have known something was amiss," Cargill said, shaking his head. "Reggie came in a few nights ago with an injured foot."

"Reggie?" Barker asked.

"My eldest. I've warned him to stay out of the Docks."

"What about the caps?" I asked.

"A vendor has been selling them in Petticoat Lane. Reggie liked them. He wanted his boys to look different, to be recognizable. I told him it was the stupidest idea I've ever heard. Constables have eyes, you know. People will be watching you. He didn't listen."

"It sounds to me that your son is trying to take your associates and turn them into his own private army," Barker said.

"Perhaps. Reggie is getting cocky. He's worked for me since he was a nipper. I think he's tired of taking orders from the old man. It makes me wonder why K'ing used a pistol instead of his usual hatchet men. If he is modernizing his methods, he could take over the whole of the East End. Now, that doesn't affect me in particular. I'm just a businessman. However, my boys have to go into those neighborhoods."

"How many sons do you have?" the Guv asked.

"Three," Cargill said. "Reggie is the eldest. He's twenty-nine."

"Mr. Cargill, it is not my place to offer you advice, but you might consider finding better work for your sons and hiring more reliable help for yourself."

"Reggie won't leave the work," he argued. "He likes the prestige, the power."

"Is he attempting to strike out on his own?" Barker asked.

Cargill went to the window and drew open the blinds, looking out on his fiefdom. I supposed we had come hoping to end this with an arrest, but everything had changed.

"Sir," I asked. "Do your sons live nearby?"

"They do. Reggie shares a flat with Michael, and Benjamin still lives with us."

I steeled my courage and spoke. "Mr. Cargill, I was cornered and attacked by your boys in some flats in Cubitt Town."

The gambler gave me a questioning look.

"Cubitt Town? Where is that?" Cargill asked, frowning.

"It's on the Isle of Dogs by the West India Basin," I answered. "On the east side."

"To my knowledge there is no gang that claims it," he replied. "Perhaps he knows that and intends to take it, and then push the Millwall Boys out of the area. Why did they attack you?"

"I'm not sure, but they knew me by name," I replied. "I was enquiring after a young man found floating nearby in the Basin. Mr. Barker and I separated, and I followed one of your men to the Cubitt Flats."

"I've never heard of Cubitt Flats."

"Believe me, sir," I assured him. "They are not worth knowing."

"What happened then?"

"I followed one into a courtyard. Then all of them came out of the flats and surrounded me. They had knives. New ones."

Cargill frowned. He scratched his forehead and cleared his throat. "I bought a boxful last week. Reggie had complained about the quality of their equipment. Two days ago, I purchased some pistols for them. Cheap ones, European made. More for waving about than using. He claimed his work was becoming more dangerous and he had the bullet wound to prove it."

"That makes our work more difficult," Barker said. "Thank you for warning us. It saves us from walking into another ambush. Now, sir, we have a second matter to discuss. Yesterday a hired cab arrived in front of my offices as we were leaving with my client. Your son, who was inside the cab, fired at us. He fired specifically at Mr. Llewelyn, but he missed him, much in the way someone not familiar with firearms would miss a target. However, he shot the victim's young widow in Whitehall Street in front of everyone. Have you any idea of what you plan to do about your son? He has come dangerously close to slaughtering an entire family."

"How do you know it was Reg?" he asked. I could see he was trying to build a defense for his son.

"He hired a cab," Barker answered. "The cab driver gave us a description. The man had a tweed cap with ginger side-whiskers. That's your eldest, isn't it?"

"Yes, but he was injured," Cargill said. "He had a horse step on his foot."

"No, he didn't," I said. "When he and his boys came after me in Millwall with knives, I was obliged to shoot him in the foot."

Cargill's face went slack. "You shot my son?"

"I did, but only in the foot. He and his boys were menacing me with knives, all nine of them. They surrounded me, so I shot him to make the others scatter. I wasn't trying to kill him, just protect myself."

Cargill ran a palm over his forehead and sat back in his chair. "If there is a mistake to be made, that boy will make it. You say he stabbed a man three days ago and shot the man's wife today? Was he sparking her?"

"No, the two were happily married," the Guv said. "However, her husband was last seen with a very expensive jewel."

Cargill smote the top of his desk with the flat of his hand.

"He's trying to go out on his own," he growled. In his anger, the Cockney came out in his voice. "I knew this would happen, that whelp of mine, allus thinkin' himself smarter than me. You've come to arrest him, haven't you?"

"We haven't the right to arrest him," Barker said. "We are private enquiry agents. We are merely trying to find him and warn Scotland Yard."

"Now I know why I haven't seen him lately." Cargill stood and began pacing the room in agitation. "If these few damning facts are evident, what else has he done I haven't heard about?"

"You must convince him to turn himself in, sir, and your

other sons as well, whom I assume were witnesses. The man who murdered that young teacher and injured his wife is whom I am looking for. I hope for your son's sake that I am wrong, that another man is responsible and Reggie being nearby was just an accident. I've come to warn you because the young man who was murdered is from a very powerful family."

My partner rose and turned to me.

"Come, Thomas," he said. "We must be about our business. Good day, Mr. Cargill."

We left the gambler speechless. Barker walked along the shavings-covered track and then stepped out into the cold again. We lifted our collars against the chill. By the way he walked, I could tell he was tense.

"Why does this pattern continue to happen?" he asked. "A man works for years. He scrimps and saves, gives all for his family, and plans to give it over to his son. At the same time, he spends years ignoring that very son and giving him no reason to interest himself in the business. He spoils the boy and leaves him at home with his mother, who has no more knowledge of her husband's occupation than he. She dotes on her son and gives him anything he desires, and the boy can never grasp what his father's interests are. Then the young man becomes frivolous, he and the father fight, and in the end the one dies and the other lets his father's hard-earned money slip through his fingers. It is happening all over London. I have seen that for years, but until today I had not realized that it has happened even to fathers such as that man, who thrives upon the weakness of others."

"What is your opinion of Cargill?" I asked.

"I take nothing he said at face value. For all we know, he deliberately sent his son to murder our client and her husband."

"But why?" I asked.

"I don't know at this point," he replied. "But I intend to find out. The killer will tip his hand and reveal himself one way or another."

We reached the Underground, descended the stairs, and waited for a train. An engine came 'round a bend and began to slow.

"What if he doesn't?" I asked. "Suppose he's more intelligent and crafty than we realize?"

Barker frowned as the train stopped in front of us with a hiss of steam.

"Then I will track him down like a dog," he answered, climbing aboard.

I stepped up and seized the handrail as the door closed behind us. "Better not let Harm hear you say that."

I was almost certain the Guv gave me the ghost of a smile.

"Back to the offices, then?" I asked.

"No. Young Reg's gang may have left the area, but there still may be signs of them. Let's look into Cubitt Flats."

CHAPTER 20

Cubitt Town was the invention of William Cubitt, once Lord Mayor of London. It was a development of inexpensive flats meant to house shipbuilders and dockworkers employed in the area forty years earlier. The area was shabby now; wood tends to warp and wear by the river, but it was still respectable enough to attract a thriving population because rent was cheap. When built, it was the pride of London, but now it was up to the hardworking and economizing residents to maintain its upkeep.

We stood in the doorway of the development where the gang leader had surprised me. It wasn't as rough-looking by light of day, though it could use a new coat of whitewash or two. It was merely an entrance to a down-at-heel but respectable building of flats. One could hardly believe that thirty hours earlier a gang of violent men had caused an affray on this very spot.

"The man was in this doorway, you say, and the others came from the surrounding entrances?" Barker asked.

"They did."

"It doesn't make sense, Thomas. How would they already know your name? Why would they lead you here?"

"To kill me, obviously."

"Were you the target in particular, or could it have been both of us?"

I thought about it a moment. "Aside from what came after, I haven't done anything lately worth killing for. Perhaps it was their plan to separate and dispatch us singly, rather than fight both of us at once."

"I was a fool to fall for that false note," the Guv muttered. "Ho doesn't write in English."

Barker hates to make a mistake in reasoning. He holds himself to a higher standard. He turned and entered the building, knocking at the first door in the hall. There was no answer. He tried another and fared no better. However, a thump at the third brought an occupant almost immediately, a young woman of perhaps thirty years in a delicate condition wielding a broom.

"Here, now, who are you?" she demanded, brandishing her weapon. "The rent is paid!"

"We are not collectors, ma'am," Cyrus Barker assured her. "We are looking for a group of men who have been causing a disruption in the area. They were wearing tweed caps. Have you seen them?"

"I should say I have!" she replied. "They were here a few days. Rough types, they were."

"Did they take rooms in the building?"

"Not as such," she responded, pressing a hand to her aching back. I could hear children arguing in the back room. "They were squatters. Waltzed in and took what they pleased. Haven't heard them recently. If they're gone, I won't cry over it."

"Which room did they commandeer?"

She puffed a length of lank hair out of her eye. "Eight B."

"Thank you, ma'am," he said. "I won't trouble you further."

"Who are you?" she asked.

"Exterminators," the Guv replied, raising his bowler to her. "Nothing for you to worry about."

When we found 8-B, we each stepped to one side and flung open the door. The room was vacant but there was trash on the floor, empty tins on a table, and newspapers fanned loosely across a table. Barker inspected the last.

"There are newspapers from the last week, but not yesterday's," he said. "They have vacated the building."

"There is nothing of any value left behind," I replied. "It looks as if they were biding time for some reason."

"There are a number of possibilities," Barker said, rummaging through the newspapers. "They could have returned to wherever they came from or rented a more permanent flat nearby. It is also possible they found the area disagreeable and decided to move elsewhere."

"I certainly would," I replied. "Let's say they decided to settle nearby. If so, why here? There isn't much commerce in the area, save for cargo, and that goes to merchants on the other side of town."

"That's not poor reasoning, Thomas, but Cubitt Town is the only place in London that doesn't have a gang. Tell me, if you and your associates moved to a new area, what is the first thing you would do? How would you announce yourselves?"

"By attacking another gang, I suppose," I said. "A show of force."

"Exactly," Barker replied. "And what else, lad?"

"A gesture to show they are serious about their intentions," I answered. "Like leaving a body in your neighbor's territory as a warning. But why Addison from Chelsea? What's his place in this?"

"He was a victim, obviously, just walking through neighborhoods after midnight on his way home. Perhaps he was to hand."

"He wasn't a big, strapping fellow," I agreed. "A group of men with knives could capture him easily."

"True," Barker admitted as we left the flat. "What are the chances someone who found a ruby worth a fortune half an hour before would be set upon by a gang and murdered?"

"Perhaps Hennings hired them," I answered. "It is possible they work for him."

"Lad, how many museum directors have their own gangs, or how many museums, for that matter? Is there a Louvre gang in Paris, for example?"

"Hardly," I admitted. "Or if there were, they wouldn't frighten me, which takes me back to the tweed caps. What is their purpose?"

"Most gang members are followers. They do whatever their leader tells them to." We heard a noise and the Guv turned. "What's that?"

We'd been walking along the dock on Ferry Street. Something was happening on the south bank of the Isle of Dogs. A group of men were struggling with something by the water. We hurried in their direction to lend a hand, although I couldn't see for a minute or two. Someone's head or shoulder was always in the way. Suddenly, the small crowd parted.

"Coffee John!" I cried.

In death his complexion was an ashen gray, his expression dolorous. I looked along the Thames.

"There!" I said, pointing. I spotted the boat floating abandoned in the river.

Someone brought a cart and the group of men, at least seven of them, struggled to lift him onto a litter. The body was frozen and difficult to move. Grimy water seeped from the plaited hair and sodden clothes. It was a sad end for the man, but then he died as he had lived and he had no doubt expected to die on the river one day.

"Blast," I said. "I liked him."

Another death. This time it had happened to a man so full of life. It doesn't seem fair, but then Barker is always telling me that fairness is something we invent. It's not my business to decide who lives or dies. Not if I can help it, anyway.

Inspector Lamont arrived with a couple of constables in tow. It would take half an hour to get the steam launch ready to prowl the river, but it would be necessary to inspect the area for evidence. Meanwhile, a lighterman in the crowd took his own boat to Coffee John's and hauled it back to the dock.

Coffee John's body was taken to the same table that had held Phillip Addison just days before. We looked him over. In addition to the body being frozen, rigor mortis had set in. With the help of a burly desk sergeant, we rolled him onto his side. We couldn't find the wound for several minutes. I began to wonder if his heart had given out under all that weight.

"Have you a tool chest?" Barker asked.

The sergeant went to get it while the inspector gave him a pondering look. Barker lifted the stomach and showed us a purplish wound under it. When the sergeant returned, the Guv looked through the tool chest until he found a set of pliers. He dug into the wound with them, a grisly sight, but then pulled a long, thin shard of metal from it. I had to look at it a moment to realize what it was: a fileting knife. It was but an inch wide, but at least six inches long with a serrated edge. The handle had snapped off in the struggle. At least that was the only explanation I could fathom.

"A knife made for separating a fish from its ribs was not meant for frenzied stabbing," Barker stated. "It was not up to the task."

"A poor weapon," the inspector agreed.

"It may have belonged to Coffee John himself and was used against him."

Inspector Lamont played with his mustache for a moment. "I believe I'll suggest to the Yard that they interview all of this fellow's contemporaries," he said. "There may have been a drunken fight aboard his boat. Let's see what we find there."

We spent the next quarter hour examining Coffee John's rowboat. Most everything was stored under a shelf in the stern behind him. We found a coat and knit cap, a pillow and blanket, various ropes, a net, fishing tackle, and a small chessboard.

"We'll find whatever warren he was staying in," Lamont said.

"He said Canning Town," I told him.

"Much obliged."

"There was no knife on the boat," Barker noted. "Surely he must have owned one. It was necessary for his work."

"What about this?" the inspector said. "Coffee John is at one of the huts by the river last night with a friend or two, having some grub and a few bottles. They get in a drunken fight and John is killed. They roll him into the water, which was easier than trying to lift him into the boat, then they set that adrift as well."

"That's not a bad theory," the Guv admitted.

"He didn't have any money," the inspector continued. "I heard an old salt say he had seen a wooden box full of coins in the boat once. There was a rumor John was secretly well off and intended to return to Afriky a rich man."

"That's mere rumor," Barker dismissed. "I've heard that same tale about most old salts on the river. He lived here, he died here, and he'll be buried here. However, your theory will be easy to determine. His stomach would be filled with undigested food and alcohol."

"Exactly!" Lamont cried.

"Inspector!" the desk sergeant called from inside the station.

"Now what's happening?" the inspector muttered, walking inside.

"Do you really think he died in a drunken brawl?" I asked the Guv.

"It's how many a sailor meets his end," he answered. "At one point in my life, I felt destined for such an end myself."

The inspector returned with a sour expression on his face. He stepped to the edge of the dock and spoke to the officer who had been preparing the launch for service. Then he walked over to us.

"Your client, Mrs. Addison—" he began.

"She is our client no more, as of this morning," I said.

"Were you paid?"

"We were."

"Good, then," he replied. "She jumped off Waterloo Bridge about a half hour ago. We must take the launch to look for her. Can I offer you a ride?"

"Please," Barker said.

"Come aboard, then."

We climbed into the police launch and a moment or two later the boat surged forward. Barker was as steady on his feet as if he was part of the deck itself, but I fell back a few steps and nearly stumbled over the portside.

Waterloo Bridge is but two miles from Wapping, but by the time we arrived there were already a half dozen boats circling the area, and people lining the bridge, peering down expectantly. Waterloo has a reputation as a suicide bridge. People come here to end their troubles.

I'd stood on that bridge myself once, trying to pluck up the courage to jump. At the time I hadn't a penny to my name, not a blessed one. Luckily for me, a constable came along at the proper moment and moved me along. Within half an hour of being ordered away, I applied for a position as a private enquiry agent's assistant and met a very odd fellow named Cyrus Barker. I met the constable again years later and bought him a pint. It was the least I could do.

The steam launch circled the area a half dozen times, but so far the corpse had not surfaced. The water moved swiftly and was flowing with ice. I leaned over the side looking for the blond hair and pale features of Elizabeth Addison.

I turned to the Guv. "Do jumpers survive sometimes?"

"They do, now and again, but not in winter," he said, his hands on the gunwale of the launch, his eyes searching. "Striking such cold water can cause a rupture of the heart. Or she may have struck her head on the ice."

"Do the bodies disappear?"

He nodded. "Aye, quite often. They might come to the surface a mile downstream, especially in weather like this. It is possible she is following the same path her husband took and will find herself at the same destination, Millwall."

"I suppose she would have preferred it that way," I said. "She knew she wouldn't be buried with her husband. This has a certain poetic justice."

The Guv looked at me sharply. "I disagree, Mr. Llewelyn. Suicide is neither poetic nor romantic. God may have had plans for her. Possibly great ones if she had risen above such tragedy. Besides, she would never have had the opportunity to lie beside her husband, anyway; suicides are not accepted in Anglican churchyards."

"Poor woman," I said. "It was a hard life and a short one."

Barker seized my shoulder and pointed overhead. I saw a figure in the crowd waving a handkerchief. It was Mrs. Porter. My partner spoke to the inspector and had the launch bring us to a small dock on the side. There was not a steady path to the bridge but we made our way to it eventually.

Millicent Porter was waiting for us, a blanket thrown over her shoulders. Strands of hair loosed from her bonnet were being batted about by the wind. Her eyes were not red with crying, but her face was blanched and waxen.

"I didn't know!" she cried. "I'm not from London. I had no idea there was a suicide bridge! I've never heard of such a thing."

Barker took both of the woman's hands, which must have been freezing. "Now, ma'am, you're not to blame yourself. The decision was hers. If it weren't the bridge, it would have been some other method. You said it yourself, she wasn't strong."

He caught my eye and pointed to an A.B.C. nearby.

"Let's get you some tea," he said, leading her to it.

Inside, it was warm, the windows fogged, masking the spectacle on the bridge. The room smelled of fresh bread. God bless the Aerated Bread Company, whose strong tea has gotten all of us through crises at one time or another.

"We were passing by the bridge on the way to the station," she said, taking her cup in her hands. "I'd bought her a new hat to lift her spirits after part of her head was shaved. Lizzie was subdued, but I had no idea she'd do something so drastic. She suddenly opened the wing of the cab and jumped down. While it was slowing, she circled around behind it and ran for the bridge. Ran straight for it, she did, right through traffic, as if it wasn't there, and when she reached it, she didn't hesitate for a breath. She stepped up at the ledge and jumped. I watched her sail over, arms spread, her new hat in one hand and an umbrella in the other."

"It was the bullet, ma'am," I said. "It must have affected her reason."

"No doubt," Barker agreed. "There were too many calamities for her to withstand."

"I was looking forward to having her in Southend," she said. "I made plans. She could have worked with me. There are many positions for a well-spoken young woman in town. She likes my boys and always got along with my husband. I can't believe it! What was she thinking?"

"She wasn't," I said. "Possibly she couldn't."

"But, a suicide?" she moaned. "Where will she be buried? Not beside us, surely."

"You heard her say it didn't matter to her where she was buried," Barker rumbled.

"She will be found, won't she?" she asked. "My sister won't just float out to sea?"

"I'll find her, Mrs. Porter," Barker said. "What color was her dress?"

"It was gray. The new hat was violet with grouse feathers."

It began to rain outside. I suspected the umbrella our former client clutched had been Mrs. Porter's. Soon it became a downpour. Thunder peeled. It was as if London were mourning the loss of Elizabeth Addison.

"It would be best, Mrs. Porter, if you spent another night in London. Perhaps she'll be found by morning. The police will search all night."

I thought of the trawlers who might find Mrs. Addison in the frigid river.

"I can't think about that now," she replied. 'Can you get me on the river?"

Barker shook his head. "I fear not, not in this weather. Scotland Yard will have just the one launch from the Thames Police, and they don't take civilians."

The door to the A.B.C. opened and Inspector Poole entered, water dripping from his bowler. He searched the room until he found us. He ordered a cup of tea and sat down with us at our table.

"Have you found her?" Mrs. Porter asked.

"No, ma'am," he said. "Not so far. Most of the boats have left because of the steady rain. We have the launch for the rest of the day. I suggest you come to Scotland Yard. If she can be found, we'll find her."

For once Mrs. Porter was at a loss for words. She merely

nodded. I paid for the tea while Barker gathered her blanket around her. Poole stepped outside, right into traffic, and held up an arm. A cabman reined his horses to a stop with a volley of cursing. In turn, Poole flashed his badge and he and Barker helped Mrs. Porter into the cab. She and the inspector bowled off.

We were not so fortunate. One would think cabs were made of newspaper the way they dissolve in the rain. Luckily, our offices were not far. Barker and I settled our bowlers on our heads, lifted our collars, and began to walk along the Embankment. We passed Cleopatra's Needle, but I ignored it completely. I'd had more than my share of that famous woman at the moment. We walked along the Strand, ducking from one shelter to another and eventually reached our offices.

Inside, Jenkins went to work. He brought us dry towels from the lumber room. Then he carried our coat stand to the grate and hung our coats to dry. As if performing a conjuring trick, he produced some bottles of ale and glasses. The label was from Watney's, which meant they came from the Rising Sun. We took the drinks eagerly.

Meanwhile, the storm grew in volume. Lightning flashed across London Town, and you could hear the thunder rumbling from one district to the next. The room was dark, then suddenly illuminated by the storm. We sat in our seats before the fire and watched the storm pass as we drank our ale.

"Two deaths in one hour," I commented, shaking my head.

"No client," he replied. "No answers, only questions."

It wasn't true, but it felt true, which is much the same.

CHAPTER 21

The next morning, I awoke with the tip of a cane in my stomach. It pushed, not painfully, but insistently into my navel. I squirmed and rolled onto my side. Sleep is important to me because I get too little of it. Between having insomnia and working for a man who enjoys moving twenty-four hours a day, I count myself fortunate to get five or six hours per night. After a moment, the tip was pressed into my kidney.

"What o'clock is it?" I asked into my pillow.

"Just six," came the answer.

"I don't keep Barker hours."

"You should," the Guv insisted. "It is a fine, brisk morning, the storm is gone, and it is time we were about."

"Brisk is an elastic term. I am hibernating."

He poked me twice in the small of the back. "Get up."

"Give me a reason."

"Petrie is to give a pronouncement today," he said. "He is offering us a private audience in half an hour, sub rosa."

I lay a moment, considering, and then lifted the pillow. "Out of the goodness of his heart? He doesn't even know us."

"He requires funding for his next expedition to Alexandria. I suggested I might be of service."

I pointed at him. "I told you we shouldn't take advantage of your private funds while detectives in Craig's Court are struggling along."

He stood at the foot of my bed, menacing me with his stick. "I did not bribe him. Come, you've got a quarter hour to shave and dress."

Reluctantly, I rose and was dressed and ready in twenty minutes. Breakfast was out of the question. The Guv waited for me impatiently at the front door. We stepped outside in time to meet our chef, Etienne Dummolard, as he arrived. In addition to cooking our meals, he borrows our kitchen to test new recipes and to exhibit his ill temper, which he does very well. He was once the galley cook aboard Barker's ship, the *Osprey*. As we left, Dummolard made some remark about mad Englishmen, but I am Welsh, so I didn't take it personally. At the foot of the steps, we met our butler, Jacob Maccabee, returning from Harm's morning constitutional. He was sympathetic to my plight, but Harm looked at me suspiciously. He followed after to chew my ankle, but his heart wasn't in it.

The Guv and I found a cab by the Baptist Tabernacle and rode silently to Russell Square. If I dozed, I wouldn't admit it. As anyone knows who has read *Sketches by Boz*, London wakes very early. Independent cabmen must already be about their business at half past five. Traffic was light in the West End, however, and soon we found ourselves in front of the back door to the museum that locked behind Phillip Addison and precipitated his death. Barker knocked and the door opened immediately.

"Come in," Flinders Petrie said, waving us forward. "If you

are seen, I will be sacked. Your names are persona non grata around here."

"Well, Mr. Petrie," I asked. "Is the mummy Cleopatra or not?"

Barker gave me a withering stare. This is what happens when one skips breakfast. The mind is slow off the mark.

"All in good time, sir," Petrie said. "Let me escort you through the halls. As quietly as you can, please."

He led us down the east stair, through the familiar hall, and into the mummy vault. The Queen of the Nile lay in state, as we had left her, composed and somehow alive. I wondered if Petrie, too, had fallen under her spell.

"You do not make my position any easier, Mr. Barker. Gentlemen, the identity of this mummy hangs on a knife's edge. There appear to be as many reasons why she must be Cleopatra as that she cannot. I suspect Hennings offered this assignment to me to ruin my reputation instead of his. Let me show you my findings."

We stood around the mummy. There had been an attempt to connect the unattached limbs to the torso, much in the manner of a hanging skeleton I saw once at the University of London. At the same time there were nicks and cuts that had not been there the last time I viewed her, and the abdomen had been opened and pulled back, revealing a cavity studded with ribs. It made me think of the postmortems I had attended at Scotland Yard, performed by the coroner, Vandeleur.

"Do you notice these flecks here?" he asked. "They are a homemade varnish. They are not the sort that is used for covering the wrappings on the exterior of the body. I can't determine when the ruby was placed inside. It could have happened at any time between 29 B.C. and yesterday. However, it was not inserted at her death. It might be possible the ruby was added later for a funeral that occurred after Emperor Augustus left Egypt, but I think some record would have been made. More likely, thieves sought to smuggle the ruby out of Egypt inside a random mummy."

Barker and I exchanged a glance.

"Look here!" Petrie continued, showing us a long strip of dirty papyrus. "This cloth from inside the mummy has the requisite number of threads, but it's dirtier than the outer wrappings. It should be cleaner, having not been exposed to the elements. Then there is this, which tops anything. Look!"

Petrie took the Nile Queen's hand and began unwrapping some of the bandages. When they were fully unwrapped, he pointed to symbols painted upon the wrappings.

"Writing," I said.

He nodded. "This is a ship's manifest. In the mummification process, even with someone as famous as Cleopatra, they reused papyrus."

"Is it dated?" I asked.

"It is. Unfortunately, it is two years after Cleopatra's reign."

"Oh," I said, disappointed. "Not Cleopatra, then."

"There is no sure way to tell. Not every event was recorded. There might have been a very good reason why she wasn't wrapped until later and it simply wasn't written down. Also, despite the poor mummification procedures during the Twelfth Dynasty, this process was quite advanced. There were spices in the wrappings, perfumes like frankincense and myrrh. She had her own perfume factory, you know. She was extremely educated and innovative. I won't say she was a genius. No, I will say it! She was a genius. Nine languages, raised in the Library of Alexandria, trained to lead a country, able to twist the hearts of Roman generals. Yes."

"She is Cleopatra, she isn't Cleopatra. She is, she isn't," I complained. "You must make up your mind."

"You see my dilemma?" Petrie replied. "What are the chances that some poor Egyptian tomb robbers would come across a fabulous jewel and stuff it inside a random mummy in order to smuggle it out of Egypt, and that mummy proves to be Cleopatra herself? The odds against it are staggering. The pathetic part is that the smugglers somehow lost both the mummy and her treasure, which have sat on a shelf lo these many years."

Barker nodded but did not speak. Petrie took the opportunity to plead.

"Mr. Barker, I don't know where you've put the stone, but I beg of you to return it to the museum. This is the best place for it."

"Mr. Petrie, the museum has one aged custodian and no guards," the Guv answered. "Had I given it to you it would be stolen within a week, and then what would the museum be? A laughingstock. You have too many scholars and not enough practical men."

"Guards can be hired," Petrie argued. "Methods can be improved."

"Aye, they could. But would they? It appears a good bit of the budget goes to acquisition, not facilities and security."

"I'll admit to that, Mr. Barker, but it isn't merely acquisition. It is preservation. This is the safest place in the world for important discoveries, save perhaps the Louvre. There is a fellow running about London claiming to be a member of the Cairo Museum—"

"Mahmoud," I supplied.

"Yes, that's the fellow. Personally, I wouldn't fully trust that he is connected with the institution without authoritative proof. I would not be against the idea of such a museum if the area were stable, but it isn't, despite Britain running the government. There are nationalists and Muslim reformers about. Our interference in their government was only supposed to be temporary. It will not last and what will happen then? I cannot help thinking of Napoleon's army, who used the sphinxes for target practice. It makes me shudder."

Barker cleared his throat. "May we return to your mummy, Mr. Petrie? Mr. Thompson might step in at any moment."

"Ye gods, so he might. Look at this, gentlemen."

He held up a small piece of what looked like very old ivory.

It was a cartouche. I knew who it belonged to, because it contained two hawks and a lion.

"Cleopatra!" I said.

"Correct, Mr. Llewelyn. This was attached to the abdomen of the mummy, and looks as ancient as the mummy itself, doesn't it? However, it isn't, I'm afraid. It's plaster, probably made in the last ten years or so."

"But it looks so real," I exclaimed. "So ancient."

"Yes, that's a wonderful trick," Petrie replied. "They carve or mold it, and then stuff it down a goose's throat. When it passes through the crop, it emerges as bleached and stained as Jonah of Nineveh. Canny people, those Egyptians."

"So, it's fake," I said.

"The mummy?" Petrie said, shaking his head. "No, Mr. Llewelyn, it's real. And the stone is authentic as well, isn't it?"

"It is," Barker stated. "We had it authenticated by a jewel expert."

"Did you? That's excellent."

"She's real, then," I insisted. "Cleopatra in the flesh."

"No, Mr. Llewelyn," he said, sounding like one of my professors at Oxford. "She's real, but I can't verify she is the last pharaoh. Let me put it this way. If part of it is fake, all of it is fake, even if it's real."

I scratched my head. "I'm afraid I don't understand."

"What he means, Mr. Llewelyn," the Guv said, "is that he cannot go to the board of directors and claim it is authentic when part is proven to be false. It would ruin his career."

'You've got it in one, Mr. Barker."

"Are you telling me this might actually be her, but it doesn't matter?" I said.

"Exactly."

I put my hands on my hips. "That's barking mad!"

"Welcome to the world of archeology," Petrie quipped, shrugging his shoulders.

We all looked down at the placid face of the mummy. It would be a crime if she did not receive her just due. However, I'm sure she was two millennia past caring.

"She really is extraordinary," he said. "I'm going to keep track of this mummy, wherever she goes. I hope at another time, if my career is assured enough to make a claim without sounding a fool, I'll see what can be done about proving her identity. Certainly, I shall get a proper photographer in, to get a view of her from every angle. I can do that much for the old girl, at least."

"Eventually, with Addison's persistence, the museum might have identified her, even without the stone," I said.

"Ah, lad, but he might not have noticed her without the weight of the ruby," Barker rumbled.

It seemed a miscarriage of justice, but it was none of my affair. If Egyptologists couldn't work out who Cleopatra was, the problem was theirs.

"Is there a way to prove she isn't Cleopatra, then?" I persisted.

Petrie pushed a lock of hair out of his eyes. "That's a shrewd question, but equally difficult. Look here."

He put a hand under her neck and lifted her head. Then with the other he peeled the hair off her head in one solid hank. It was a wig. Petrie lay the length of ruddy hair by her feet.

"Except for her lashes you won't find a single hair on this entire body. It was removed with a mixture of beeswax and pumice stone, what they call sugaring paste. Now examine her skull. Does it seem any differently shaped than any other woman's skull you have seen?"

"I wouldn't know," I said. "I've never seen any bald women."

"No," Barker said, trying to sound patient. "It looks the same."

"Exactly. The Egyptians practiced head binding at an early age. They found an elongated head to be more attractive. Neither this mummy nor Cleopatra has an elongated head because she was Macedonian Greek, not Egyptian. Also, this wig is red, which is an unusual color for an Egyptian. However, there are at least two contemporary paintings of her with red hair. There has been an argument for years that Cleopatra's mother was a slave girl, perhaps Gallic or Celtic. To my knowledge, and I've studied all week, she was the only red-haired woman walking about Alexandria. Now notice her lips. I know it's hard to see with the skin so darkened but look closely."

We leaned over the body. It was easier to look closer when one thought of it as a corpse. Still, I held my breath.

"The lips have been stained," Barker said. "They are purple."

"You are correct, sir. At the time of her burial, they would have been scarlet. As I said, Cleopatra owned a cosmetic factory. With all hair removed, the women of Egypt painted their eyelids and brows. Beauty was as important then as it is now, and Cleopatra knew every chemical available in the region. You've heard the legend of her being bitten by an asp?"

"Yes," I said. "Shakespeare."

"Horace said it first," Barker stated. He was on steady ground with ancient literature.

"Very good, gentlemen," Petrie answered. "And who was Horace? A Roman poet who never visited Egypt. The Romans considered her a degenerate and did all they could to blacken her name. As to the legend she was bitten by an asp, I examined the mummy thoroughly. There are no snakebites. An Egyptologist could study this one mummy for the rest of his life."

I was willing to keep an open mind. Petrie was spinning us one way and then another. I believe we were both growing dizzy.

"Now, I've examined the skin on the abdomen. There are marks there that show she gave birth. Cleopatra had four children, one by Julius Caesar. Yet this woman's figure was supple, though she was nearing middle age. She must have exercised often to keep her figure. Cleopatra was a seductress, but not out of wantonness. She was fighting for her kingdom against Rome,

and she needed allies. In the end, however, it made no difference. Caesar was murdered; Antony, as well. Rome conquered
Egypt and she lost everything, including her life."

"I assume she was in some kind of tomb or sarcophagus after
she died," I said.

"Yes," he agreed. "She was a pharaoh and entitled to a
proper burial. Her sarcophagus would be covered in gold, her
body studded with jewels. She'd be in a chamber full of treasure, and Marc Antony would have been buried beside her. The
chamber and her mummy have long ago been stripped of jewels,
wherever it was. I wonder what became of the Roman general
who betrayed his kingdom for her. If only we could determine
where the mummy came from."

"Wouldn't she have a pyramid or something?" I asked.

Petrie tried to keep the haughty look out of his eye, but I
saw it just the same. I'd committed a faux pas. Sometimes my
tongue outruns my brain.

"No, those were from an earlier time. A thousand years earlier,
in fact. I'd be looking for a secret chamber far underground, a
hundred feet or more, protected from tomb raiders. You know, a
family will choose a site and dig there for generations. It becomes
the family business, with possible untold riches at the end."

"The looters must have found her tomb, then," Barker said.

"Most definitely," Petrie replied. "They stripped her and the
chamber of anything valuable. They didn't care about the body.
They probably never heard of Cleopatra or Antony. They were
illiterate, but they knew how to find gold and melt it."

"Could it have happened recently?" I asked.

He gave a bark of a laugh. "Again, anytime between the birth
of Christ and now."

"Is there any way to determine where she has been the last
hundred years?"

"No, but she's had some ill treatment," he said. "The arm

and the legs, for example. The vandals tossed her aside like rubbish."

"What will become of this mummy if you decide it isn't Cleopatra?" Barker asked.

"She'll be sold, I should imagine. A lesser museum somewhere can make an exhibition around the possibility that she might be Cleopatra, even if I claim she isn't."

"If there is a chance that she might be Cleopatra, will the British Museum keep her?" I asked.

He shook his head. "It's doubtful. First of all, they already own a mummy of Cleopatra, an ancestor. Trying to attract interest in a second one without concrete proof won't attract revenue. Also, they could sell her for thousands of pounds more than what she originally cost them as part of a lot through Christie's."

"Did you speak to Christie's?"

"Of course I did. She was purchased from a reputable dealer in Alexandria, but there was nothing to indicate she was special in any way. Stripped of her jewels, there was little to recommend her unless viewed intently by a professional archeologist. We develop an eye, you see. I can look at her now and know exactly how she looked two thousand years ago. That's why I wanted to see the ruby. I want to picture what it looked like then."

"But it might not be ancient," Barker said. "It might have come from a mine in East Africa within the last ten years."

"That's why I'd like to see it, to authenticate it. I may be able to prove the ruby has been here all along, what tools were used to extract or alter it, and how the wound was recently made. The stone could prove it is Cleopatra, if I become certain it was buried with her. You must let me see it!"

"Had I met you a few days ago I may have been tempted," my partner said. "However, I am no longer in possession of it."

"Get it back," Flinders Petrie demanded. "Better yet, get the museum to offer them a price for it. Is it in London? Please don't tell me you've given it to the Louvre!"

The last he said with a kind of loathing. I suppose there is much competition among museums. Perhaps there was a bit of national pride as well.

"Alas," the Guv said, shrugging his wide shoulders. "I'm afraid I cannot help you."

"You understand, Mr. Barker, that Director Thompson is in the right, and so far he has been gracious to you. With each passing hour more pressure is being put upon him, by the board and by contributors. You are going to find yourselves in jail."

"That does not inspire the fear in us that it does in you, Mr. Petrie," the Guv replied. "We are professionals in our field, just as you are in yours."

"Yours is an actual field?" he asked. "I just assumed, no insult intended, that it was a situation one took when there was no other to be had."

"I am a major contributor to the museum, and Thomas here read at Oxford. Both the prime minister and the commissioner of Scotland Yard know me on sight."

"Not to mention the Prince of Wales," I added.

"Thank you, Mr. Llewelyn."

"My apologies, gentlemen. I had no idea."

"It isn't important," Barker dismissed.

"Let me level with you, Mr. Barker. I need this work. It could be the break I'm hoping for, a chance to work with the museum itself. I wouldn't do anything to jeopardize my future, and I'm already in an untenable situation. Last night I wondered if my name was put forward for this work so I could fall flat on my face in front of everybody."

"You seem a skillful kind of fellow, sir," Barker said. "I believe you will do well. Consider this an opportunity to see how the

British Museum works. Every calamity can be an opportunity, save perhaps your being seen in our company. We should go."

I assumed we would creep out the back door, but the Guv does not creep. We climbed the stairs and left the building a few minutes after it opened, lifting our hats to the director as he walked in the door. I'll always remember the look of astonishment he gave us.

"Blast," I said as we came down the front steps.

"You hoped it was her?" Barker asked.

"I confess, I did."

"It still could be," he rumbled. "Even Petrie is not certain. Any new factor could change the odds."

"You know I hate mysteries," I said. "I must know! Where is Cleopatra buried? Where are King Solomon's Mines? Who is Jack the Ripper?"

"You know who Jack the Ripper is, lad," Barker said, donning his gloves. "You handcuffed him yourself."

"Yes, but the public doesn't know that. It's still considered a mystery."

"Long-standing mysteries generally come to naught," he said. "If the mummy suddenly were able to come to life and answer our questions, we would probably be unimpressed by her answers."

I raised a brow. "I'd think you'd want to find a woman who was nearly a contemporary with Christ, you being a religious man."

"Having read about her in the Reading Room, I must say I am impressed," he remarked. "She did everything she could for her people, gathered and stored grain in good times and distributed it during famine. She made wise alliances, not only with Caesar and Antony, but with King Herod himself."

"She went to Jerusalem?" I asked. "I didn't know that."

Barker sniffed. "And you call yourself a scholar."

"I cannot be held responsible for everything I learned or did not learn at university."

He didn't answer. I assumed he thought I could.

"That was quite the demonstration Petrie gave us," I said as we stood at the curb. "He'd make a good detective."

"Private enquiry agent," Barker corrected, waving his stick for a cab.

CHAPTER 22

I t was too early for lunch. Barker settled into his outsized
chair while I stoked and refilled the grate. Down the street
the Shades public house would open soon, and I knew they
made a respectable cup of coffee, one that wasn't an outright
insult to the peasants picking beans on the side of a hill in far-
off Columbia or Peru. I was trying not to heed its siren call and
having a difficult time of it.

The telephone set on Barker's desk jangled. He snatched it
before I did and put the receiver to his ear.

"Ahoy," he said. "Yes, this is Barker. Good morning, Terry.
Why, of course. We'd be delighted. We'll be along directly. See
you then."

"Poole?" I asked.

"Yes, we are being arrested. He has been kind enough to allow us to come to 'A' Division of our own accord. I think that
very civil of him."

"The man's a saint," I said bitterly.

Barker spoke to the telephone operator and asked to be connected to a number. In a minute it went through.

"Yes, I wonder if you could get word to Mr. Cusp, please. Inform him that Cyrus Barker and Thomas Llewelyn are being arrested. Thank you very much."

My plans for coffee would have to be curtailed. If Cusp was pleading a case in court, there was no determining when bail might be posted for us. Cusp was a barrister, but out of some sense of obligation to Barker, he came to spring his old friend from the clutches of Scotland Yard in person in such circumstances. Perhaps it was to tweak their collective noses.

There was a hanging mirror in our lumber room. I washed my face, combed my hair, and straightened my tie. One wants to look one's best when presenting oneself for arrest. We donned coats, mufflers, and gloves and hefted our sticks. We would be the best-dressed prisoners in Scotland Yard that day.

"It is very decent of him," I admitted. "I don't like being dragged through the streets in handcuffs. However, now is the time, sir, if we are going to do a bunk."

"I gave him my word, lad."

"No, sir, you didn't," I said. "I distinctly remember that you didn't. I keep track of these things."

"It was implied, then."

"Drat. I hope we're out by noon."

We walked to New Scotland Yard, skirting frozen puddles and snowdrifts. A group of street Arabs were taking running leaps and sliding on the ice. I considered showing them my expertise in such matters, but we were expected elsewhere. When we arrived, I was glad to see Sergeant Kirkwood, my favorite copper, behind the front desk.

"Look here!" he announced to the lobby, his private court. "It's the Guv and his nibs, here to grace our cells with their presence. Detective Chief Inspector Poole is awaiting your arrival in his office with bated breath."

"Thank you, Sergeant," Barker rumbled.

The Guv and I climbed to the first floor to Poole's office. We knew it well.

"There's nothing for it, I'm afraid," I told my partner. "You'll have to tell them where it is now, no shilly-shallying."

"Nonsense," he replied. "I can shilly-shally with the best of them."

Thompson and Hennings were waiting in Poole's office when we arrived. One looked angry, the other concerned.

"What were you doing in the museum so early this morning?" Thompson demanded.

"We understood that Mr. Petrie would be making his pronouncement soon," the Guv said. "I hoped to speak to him."

"How did you get in before the museum was open?"

"A worker entered the building and we slipped through after," my partner said, which was true.

"Did Petrie speak to you?"

"I couldn't convince him to say anything," he replied, which was also true. Petrie had volunteered.

"I hope this is a lesson to you, gentlemen," Hennings said.

"I don't understand," Barker replied. "What have we done to earn such censure?"

"You know precisely what you have done," he demanded. "Give us the ruby!"

"Give it to us at once, gentlemen," Thompson ordered.

"I think there is a more pressing problem at the moment," the Guv said.

Thompson and Hennings looked at each other.

"What do you mean, sir?" Thompson asked.

"I'd like to discuss Liam Grant."

"Who is Liam Grant?" Poole asked, jotting in his notepad.

"He was a former volunteer at the museum," Thompson replied. "He was the one to whom Addison took the jewel when he first made the discovery."

"And what is the relevance of Mr. Grant to this conversation, Mr. Barker?" Poole asked.

"I am concerned about the possible unlawful detention of Mr. Liam Grant," Barker continued. "He was treated ill by your institution and banned for life."

"What business is it of yours, Barker?" Thompson asked. "We had every right to try to find out what happened that night."

"Perhaps I should talk with this Grant fellow, myself," Poole inserted.

"He lives in Russell Square, across from the museum," I supplied.

"I see no reason why a citizen should be banned from the museum who hasn't caused a disturbance," Barker said. "He in no way defrauded this institution or in fact, did anything but safeguard a piece of museum property."

"He is a thief!" Hennings insisted.

"Are you claiming he stole it, then?" Poole asked. "Walked right out the door with it?"

"No, but he had possession of it," Hennings said. "Addison stole it."

"We thought it best to sever our ties with Mr. Grant," Thompson explained. "Our relationship with him has been concerning. He believes himself to be a member of staff."

"A harmless eccentricity that benefits your patrons," Barker argued. "He is also a sponsor. Since you've banned him, you won't have the hundred pounds or more he gives to the museum every year. Now you are trying to have me arrested, shall you ban me as well?"

"Perhaps," Thompson said diplomatically, though Hennings seemed all for it.

"Then I am forced to stop the two-hundred-pound contribution I make each year. I also have several friends who shall hear about the matter."

"A letter to *The Times* might be in order, sir," I suggested. "Now, I don't have a private fortune. I'm just a workingman, but I do contribute now and again. But not now, and certainly not again."

Thompson was putting a brave face on it, though Hennings looked a little green. Would the museum continue his little party of earl's sons? Losing donors had not been in their plans this morning.

"Sir," Thompson said. "You are in possession of a very large stone that belongs to us. We demand it back."

"Sir," the Guv countered, "you were told this by a man you have banned and are considering having arrested. How can you believe his word? I tell you here and now that I am not in possession of the ruby."

"Did you have it, Cyrus?" Terence Poole asked. He is no fool.

"I did. It was given to me by Mr. Grant," Barker replied.

"Is it in your possession now, either with you presently, in your home or offices, or somewhere hidden?"

This was astute as well. I had to give Poole credit. He'd left him with no way to avoid answering the question.

"It is not, sir," the Guv said.

"Did you toss it somewhere, in the river, perhaps?"

"I did not."

"Where is it?" Thompson shouted.

"Let me ask the questions, please," Poole said levelly. If the director thought himself in charge here, Poole was disabusing him of the notion. He wasn't a patron of the museum, nor was he in awe of the director.

Poole turned to the Guv. "Mr. Barker, did you give over possession of the stone to someone else?"

"I did," Barker admitted.

"I see," Poole said. "Can you name this individual?"

"At present, no."

"You refuse to name him or her?"

Barker nodded. "Aye, sir. I do."

"Can you tell this person to return the ruby to its proper owner?" Inspector Poole asked.

"I can, but I will not."

Terence Poole nodded, as if it were the answer he expected. I assumed it was. He walked to the doorway.

"Kirkwood! Send Adams along." He looked at the Guv. "I'm sorry, Cyrus. You've ridden this horse as far as it can run."

"You're not to blame, Terry."

Terence Poole turned to me. "What have you to say, Mr. Llewelyn?"

"I don't believe that tie goes with your collar," I told him.

"A joker to the end. Adams, put these fellows in a cell."

It had been inevitable from the first. An old turnkey saluted and led us down a few flights of stairs and locked us in a cell without a word. Once we were alone, I turned to the Guv.

"I don't suppose you'd want to tell me where it is," I ventured. "If I know you it's probably simple and logical. Is it in your safe deposit box at Cox and Co.? In theory, the bank manager is the person you gave it to."

"It is not at the bank," he said.

"There are those nice lads in the Knights Templar also," I continued. "There's nothing like having a secret society about for hiding things. Munro's the head. Wouldn't it be ironic if Poole was hunting it while the entire time it was upstairs with the commissioner?"

"It is not there, either. Must you badger me as well?"

Barker removed his coat and lay on the cot, using it as a blanket. He yawned and stretched his arms.

"I'm taking a nap," he said, pulling the brim of his bowler down over his eyes. "Bram should be here in an hour or two. Feel free to speculate as you wish but do so quietly."

"This isn't fair," I protested. "I barely touched the bally thing. I don't know where it is any more than Hennings, but I'm locked in here with you."

"It is entirely fair," the Guv replied. "You are the one who introduced me to Liam Grant. We wouldn't have the ruby if it were not for you. You are culpable and fully deserve being where you are. You haven't been sleeping well, and you were up early. I suggest you take an hour's kip. Quietly."

"I'm hungry," I complained. "I didn't have any breakfast. Someone woke me betimes."

Barker was sound asleep. He can do so at the drop of a hat. I don't know whether it is something having to do with his time in Asia or that he sleeps the sleep of the just.

The next I knew, Cyrus Barker's hand was on my shoulder, shaking me awake. The turnkey was jingling the keys as he unlocked our cell. The Guv adjusted his bowler. Cusp must have convinced Poole to release us.

"What o'clock is it?" I asked, reaching for my watch.

"Nearly one," Barker said. "Terry convinced Mr. Thompson not to press charges, not yet, anyway. We are free to go."

I stood, clamped my bowler on my head, and staggered through the cell door, my legs full of pins. Barker looked down at me.

"You look pale. Let us have lunch at the Clarence. They serve a good joint, and you look like you need some blood in you."

We stepped out into Great Scotland Yard Street and sunshine. The gutters were gurgling and icicles dripping on our coats and hats as we walked under them. I didn't wait for the Clarence and its joint. I walked into the Rising Sun Public House, ordered a brandy, and downed it on the spot. Barker looked at me with possible disapproval.

"Medicinal, sir," I explained. I was definitely feeling under the weather. "Now I'm ready for the Clarence."

CHAPTER 23

I f there is any problem with Craig's Court, it is that there is no way of escape. At one time we could go down into the cellar and follow the telephone lines to the Embankment, but the company found the fault and bricked up the wall like a scene from "The Cask of Amontillado."

Despite the pint and good meal at the Clarence, I still had a sore head and jangled nerves. More than anything I wished the case were completed and I could worry about more commonplace things again, such as how my wife was getting along with my parents. I had reached a low ebb when that was a pleasurable topic to consider.

The front door opened, and someone entered and spoke to Jenkins in a low voice. The Guv was preoccupied, staring out the window at the building across the street, deep in thought about the case. He did not turn toward the outer office. A moment later

Jenkins entered in that formal manner he so enjoys, playing footman, tray in hand. He stopped at my desk.

"What?" I snapped.

As I said, I was unsettled. Trying to sleep in a jail cell will cause that. I believe jail cots were designed for that very purpose. The last thing Scotland Yard desires is for a suspect to get too comfortable. They'd use a bed of nails if they could.

Our clerk waved his salver in front of me as if offering me bonbons. Who would bother sending a message to me? I snatched a note off the salver, unfolded it, and read while our clerk glided off.

Have pity and put me out of my misery. Meet me at the Shades—ACD

"Davis," I growled. "He asked me to meet him at the Shades." Barker did not move a muscle to show he'd heard me.

"I'm off, then," I said.

I jammed my hands in my pockets and trotted out the door and past a few other pubs to the entrance. I stepped inside and looked about. There was no sign of the dratted fellow. I ordered a coffee and went upstairs. The Shades is a tall, narrow building shaped like a bottle. Davis was sitting at a table nursing a pint. I threw myself into the chair across from him.

"I'd gladly put you out of your misery, but I've already shot someone this week," I said. "You look like the morning after the night before."

He did, in fact. His eyes had dark circles, and he looked as haggard as a big strapping fellow can be. A waiter arrived a moment later, bringing my Black Apollo.

"I've seen her," Davis said.

"Whom?" I asked.

"Cleopatra, who'd you expect?" he replied. "I've been pretty much useless ever since. I can't stop thinking about her."

"She has that effect," I said. "But she's dead, you know. Has been for two millennia. Why did you send for me?"

"To warn you that the word is out," Davis replied. "There's a missing ruby, and the two of you are the only ones who know where it is. Reporters may soon be baying for blood."

"I cannot confirm your speculation," I said.

"Llewelyn, I don't care whether you can confirm or deny. I'm not a reporter or an inspector. I am a writer."

I clinked my cup as I set it in its saucer. "So do whatever it is writers do. Write something."

"I can't. Everything I write sounds complete rubbish. I've dried up like the sands, like the sands of . . . you see? I can't even summon a proper simile. I'm in a funk, and I have deadlines to meet. I absolutely must write an Egyptian tale or I won't be able to sleep. I promised my editor."

"You should speak to Flinders Petrie at the museum," I said. "He's a little pedantic, but he has some interesting things to say."

"I did speak to him for ten minutes," Davis said. "Oh, come. One story."

"We've already told you about the mummy and the ruby. What more do you want?"

"I don't know," Davis said. "Emotions. Opinions. Surely your partner has them."

"Mr. Barker is a very private person. I don't think he would approve."

The author took a pull from his pint and set it down again. "I've got a piece of information to trade, something that happened just this morning."

"What happened?" I asked automatically.

"Sorry," he replied, wiping the foam from his mustache. "No tale, no information."

"I don't . . . wait, what about a dream? I had a corking one the other night. Mummies, pharaohs, the whole thing."

Davis sat forward. "I like dreams. I believe in them. Tell it to me and if I can use it I'll make the trade."

"Fair enough," I answered.

I told him of Cleopatra's Needle and my wife turning into Cleopatra and the hideous kiss. Meanwhile, he took notes as quickly as I told him.

"Excellent!" he said when I was done. "I can use that."

"Good. What's the information?"

"While I was talking to Petrie, he was marched away."

"Marched away by whom?" I asked. "Thompson?"

"No, they were government johnnies," Davis replied. "At first, I thought they were Scotland Yarders, but they were obviously university lads. One can tell."

"Describe the one in charge," I said.

"Tall, slender, about thirty. Blond hair combed across his forehead. Sharp features, steel eyes."

"Hesketh Pierce, of the Home Office," I stated.

"He swooped in like a raptor and took Flinders Petrie away. He started an altercation, trying to protect his mummy."

"I must get back and tell Barker," I said.

I stood and left the Shades, hurrying to our chambers. As I drew nearer I noticed a closed cab parked in front of the Cox and Co. by our office. A citizen is not permitted to park in front of banks. I vaulted the front steps and jumped inside. A man was seated by Jenkins, as if our clerk was ready to commit a capital crime at any moment. Inside, three more men were seated, one of them in my chair. The man seated in our visitor's chair was Pierce.

"Excuse me," I said to the man seated in my chair. "Get your backside out of my chair."

One won't get anywhere in the enquiry business if one shows fear in front of a civil servant. Attack first and duck if the clout comes.

Barker and Pierce were talking, or rather, the Guv was explaining how he came to have possession of a ruby the size of a cricket ball. Pierce had a boot across his knee and looked relaxed. That was a good sign.

"Grant put it in my hand and seemed glad to be rid of it," Barker said. "He'd sequestered himself in his flat for several hours and was very nervous. I gather he had expected Addison to return in an hour or two. When he did not return, it was a sign to Grant that his life was in danger."

"You had it for two or three days, then," Pierce said. He's a cool fellow, calm when he wants to be, but dangerous when necessary. I always imagined he'd put me in a cell for an hour or two, then accidentally forget me until my beard curled around my ankles.

"Aye," Barker replied.

"Where did you keep it?" the Home Office man demanded.

Barker does not respond to threats or bullying. He is patient and polite enough, but he'll box the ear of anyone short of Her Majesty if he thinks he is not shown respect. Pierce is a canny fellow and knew this.

In response, my partner pulled open his bottom drawer. Pierce stood, came around the side of the desk and peered inside.

"Don't you own a safe?" he asked.

"Of course, I have a safe."

"You didn't think you'd need it for something as mundane as a giant ruby."

"I also needed to show it to people."

Hesketh Pierce tensed. Every muscle in his body was suddenly taut. "You showed it to people? What people?"

"A jeweler named Ira Moskowitz," the Guv replied. "I wanted to know how many grams it was. It was eighty or so, if that matters to you."

"Did you show it to Cargill?" the Home Office man asked. I don't know how he knew about our visit to the booking agent.

Cyrus Barker shook his head. "No, I know better than to show it to a bookmaker. I didn't even mention it. He didn't seem agitated about anything other than his wastrel son, whom I suspect was trying to go out on his own. He works for his father, collecting debts. He was last seen in Cubitt Town."

"Tweed caps?" Pierce asked.

"The very men. You are well informed."

"Always, but let's get back to the matter at hand," Pierce said. "At some point you grew tired of keeping the jewel in your desk drawer. You marched into Buckingham Palace and gave it to whom?"

"To Henry Ponsonby, Her Majesty's secretary, yes. We are acquainted."

"What?" I cried.

Hesketh Pierce ignored my interruption. "From what he said, the fellow despises you."

"But he remembers me," Barker answered. "I suspected it would eventually find its way among the Crown Jewels. It seemed the only sensible place to take it."

"It was entirely the wrong place to take it and the wrong person to give it to," Pierce insisted.

"And yet you gentlemen are here and it is safe."

"You knew it would take us a few days to track everything and decide what to do."

"I did," he admitted.

"And that the ruby would be safe until we did," Pierce continued.

"I did," the Guv rumbled again.

"You are a pain. Mr. Barker. A pain between the shoulder blades, or possibly lower."

Barker's immobile face broke into a grin. "So I've been told on more than one occasion."

"You did not think to tell Thompson?" Pierce asked.

"I neither know nor trust him," Barker stated. "At present, he is a cypher to me."

"Hennings, too?"

"No," Barker replied. "Hennings I understand well enough."

"You had every opportunity to keep the jewel," Hesketh Pierce said. "Why didn't you?"

"Are you encouraging me, Mr. Pierce?"

"No, merely questioning you."

Barker leaned back in his chair and pressed his fingertips together as he considered the question. They were fingers that had seen much ill-usage over the years, thick, gnarled and misshapen.

"I'd like to think myself an honest man," he said. "The idea did not occur to me. I suppose I could have asked Mr. Moskowitz to break it into pieces, but that would destroy the stone's strange beauty and its integrity. I could have kept it as it was, but I have enough such trinkets already. Then there is the danger that inevitably follows possessing such a large jewel. I guarantee you that Mr. Addison is not the only person who has died on account of that bauble. Where is it now, may I ask?"

"It's being looked after," the Home Office man said.

Barker nodded. "A proper answer, Mr. Pierce. The wise man is cautious. Let me ask a better question: What shall become of it? Shall it be returned to the British Museum?"

"Negotiations are under way," Hesketh replied. "A jewel has no place in a museum. Security is difficult. A man with a pistol and a hammer could steal it in five minutes. A vault would be necessary, guarded by shifts of men with rifles."

"What is being discussed?"

"I'm not privy to that," Pierce said, pulling a cigarette case from his pocket. "May I?"

He extracted a gold-tipped cigarette and then pulled out a thin brass tube as well, whose end ignited when he flicked it. I'd seen cigarette lighters before but had never observed one in use. He lit the fag, flipped the brass cap closed, and returned the lighter to his pocket. There was a stringent odor afterward, like hot metal.

"I've proved I have no desire for the stone and it is in your custody," my partner said. "What do you really think will become of the jewel?"

Pierce removed a bit of tobacco from the tip of his tongue and considered the matter. "The Crown could take it outright. It has the power and the right to do so. However, it is not the sort of thing Her Majesty's government does, taking other people's property. For one thing, it would be in the newspapers, and these days the monarchy works for the will of the people. Most of the time, anyway. It's very complicated. The British Museum is a nondepartmental public body. It isn't a part of the government, but I suspect it is still accountable to Parliament. Such a matter has not come up before. The Palace could purchase it, but that's another problem. Every pound spent is scrutinized by Socialists and other antimonarchists. This may become a fight in the Houses of Parliament. All thanks to you, Mr. Barker."

"Such a to-do over a piece of mineral," I said.

"I haven't seen it," Pierce admitted. "It is pretty?"

"In some ways, yes," I answered. "In others, no. It's rough and unfaceted, but still arresting to the eye. I'm sure much of that is the wonder of what it must be worth."

"I hope to get a gander in person before this matter is done."

"Did you get a view of the mummy?" I asked.

"I did," he said. "It nearly made me ill. What a hag she is. I assume she was a stunner at one time, but that was a very long time ago."

"There is something to be said for interring the mummy again," Barker vouched. "She has earned her rest like everyone else. It is a shame to have her displayed for lurid entertainment."

"She'd be buried again if I have any say in the matter," Pierce said. "Have they found your client? I heard about that. Bad luck, Barker."

"She is gone, washed out to sea," the Guv replied. "If not, the tide will change and she'll float back again. In either case, I cannot imagine her living through such a catastrophic event."

"Perhaps," I ventured, "she thought if she could not be buried with her husband, she could die as he did in the river. It was as close to her husband as she would ever get."

"That sounds fanciful," Pierce replied. "More likely, she was temporarily insane."

I could already tell he was losing interest. Cleopatra had tested her charms on him and failed.

"Are we free to continue our enquiry?" Barker asked.

"I assumed you were finished."

"Very nearly," my partner said. "We have no client, but I want to learn one or two things before I am prepared to put this case to rest."

"I shudder to think what further damage you may cause," Pierce said, arching a brow. "Stay out of trouble. Don't make me come back."

Hesketh Pierce stood, as did his silent comrades. We bowed. They shuffled out of the room, taking Jeremy's guard dog with him.

"Thomas," Barker said when we were alone again. "How accomplished are you at groveling?"

"Rebecca says I'm brilliant," I answered. "Why?"

"I want to repair our relationship with the museum and see if we cannot persuade Thompson to reinstate Liam Grant."

"That's good of you, sir," I commented. "Strictly speaking, Liam is not your responsibility."

"Both Grant and I did what we believed to be right, but Thompson won't see it that way. Also, I still have a few more outstanding questions for the director."

"Do you intend to dangle our contributions over the old man's head again?"

"Nay, I suspect that threat has outlived its usefulness." He stood and donned his coat. "Jeremy, we're going to the museum. If we aren't back in time, lock up and be on your way."

"Yes, sir."

The snow was gone from underfoot when we stepped out into Whitehall Street. We left our gloves and scarves behind. When we hailed a hansom, the mare was snorting as if she'd rather be frisking in a meadow somewhere.

At the British Museum nothing much had changed. The secretary in front of the director's office still deserved to be kicked and we were kept waiting for half an hour, though people flowed into and out of Thompson's office as if it were a stop on the Underground. Finally, we were led inside.

"Gentlemen," Edward Maund Thompson said from behind his outsized desk. He was neither pleasant nor cold, which I took to be a good sign. Pleasantry on the part of men in power is a harbinger of calamity.

"Mr. Thompson, I understand negotiations are under way for the ruby," Barker stated.

"Little thanks to you, sir."

"Aye," Barker rumbled. "I did not know your people and I felt a need to protect the Heart of the Nile."

"I hadn't heard that name," he admitted. "I confess, I rather like it."

"I give it to you, sir. Perhaps you have heard of the tragic fate of Mrs. Addison?"

"The Home Office told me," Thompson replied. "Has she been found?"

"Alas, no," the Guv said. "Were it spring, we might have found her, but this time of year it is next to impossible."

"We were going to make some sort of settlement for her,

though the amount hadn't been finalized. However, the credit for finding the ruby will be given to her late husband."

"That's very kind of you, sir."

"Mr. Barker, you should have given us the jewel," he chided.

"At that time, we had a fresh body and no obvious suspects," the Guv replied. "When given the stone, I felt safer passing it to a third party."

"But what a third party!" Thompson exclaimed. "I've had an intimidating afternoon. I've never spoken to the Home Office before."

"Aye, Mr. Thompson. It was a momentary decision and I regret the inconvenience."

Thompson waved the apology aside. "The Crown would have learned of it soon enough."

"I thank you for your good-natured forbearance," Barker replied. "Now I must bring up a similar matter: Mr. Grant. I would plead for forbearance there as well. In fact, forgive him instead of me if it must be one of us."

Thompson shook his head. "There is no need for that. Liam Grant is welcome here again. I was not aware what a favorite he was among my staff. There was something of a labor dispute yesterday, so we have hired him for ten hours a week so that he can consider himself a legitimate librarian. I am not as harsh as I seem, Mr. Barker. I understood what a predicament young Addison put him in. Let bygones be bygones. We'll say no more about the matter."

"Thank you, sir," Barker replied. "What was the decision made by Mr. Petrie?"

"He believes that the mummy from the vault is not Cleopatra VII. It was too good to be true that two priceless treasures should already be lying in our vaults."

"Perhaps Mr. Petrie can determine which member of the Ptolemaic line she was."

Thompson looked abashed. He combed his long beard with his fingers.

"I'm afraid that's impossible," he said. "First of all, Mr. Petrie is preparing to leave London for Cairo. He's found funding for a new dig. Naturally we shall be sad to see him go so soon. Also, Lord Grayle has offered us a generous endowment in exchange for the anonymous mummy."

"An endowment in exchange for a mummy you already have," the Guv said. "I must admit, sir, that you are an accomplished negotiator."

"The mummy was here," he answered. "But it was not the find we hoped. His Lordship made us an offer and terms were reached. That ends the matter satisfactorily."

CHAPTER 24

Two hours later, the telephone set clamored on Barker's desk. I made a long arm and snagged it first. I needn't have bothered.

"Barker and Llewelyn Agency," I said, in as authoritative a voice as I could muster.

"Put Cyrus on the line," an impatient voice crackled in my ear.

I held out the set to him. "The call is for you. It sounds like Poole."

Barker received the instrument with no special enthusiasm.

"Cyrus Barker," he said. "Yes? Why? Did he, the rascal? Very well. We'll be right along."

"Scotland Yard?" I asked when he had replaced the receiver.

"Aye. Apparently, Mr. Mahmoud has made a run at Director Thompson. He was stopped by the secretary."

"I'm not surprised. We had problem enough getting by him without an appointment ourselves."

"I shall suggest Terence have his officers dig into Mahmoud's records and whereabouts. It's what the Yard does best, collecting evidence."

We donned our coats again and stepped outside, but the day was practically balmy in comparison with the day before. We doffed them again, skirting melting puddles in Whitehall Street.

"It would be helpful if we had an occupation where we could accept a fellow's word at face value."

"What would be the fun in that, lad?"

"I'm beginning to feel that everyone in this enquiry is either lying to us or withholding something."

"You may count on it, but most people are not good at either," Barker stated, stepping to one side to avoid a puddle. He does not jump, and he most certainly does not hop. In fact, I'm surprised puddles don't jump out of his way.

"It's depressing," I stated.

"There are a half dozen reasons for lying, Thomas: to make one feel more important, to cover an insecurity, to embellish a tale, to conceal information, confuse someone, or put what someone else says into question. Those are used by relatively honest people. There's no telling what Mahmoud uses."

We reached Scotland Yard and worked our way through the bowels of that institution again until we found ourselves in an interrogation room. Mahmoud was sans jacket and fez and nursing a bloody nose with a handkerchief. Barker raised an eyebrow.

"It wasn't me, Cyrus," Poole informed him. "The secretary took offense at a man coming after his superior with a knife."

"I didn't," Mahmoud cried. "The knife was in my pocket, sheathed!"

"Wicked little thing it is, too," Poole said, dropping it on the table in front of us. It was perhaps seven inches long, with a curved blade in the Near Asian manner, the handle a stylized snake. It looked to be bronze. Barker took it up and examined it. He wiped something from the blade and rubbed it between his fingers.

"Blood?" Poole asked. Obviously, he wanted him for Addison's murder as well.

"Graphite," the Guv replied. "He uses it to sharpen pencils."

"According to what we have found so far, gents, this fellow is a confidence trickster, a smuggler, and a thief. He has no connection with the Cairo Museum at all."

"He stole my fez and mangled it!" Mahmoud complained.

"Serves you right for wearing it in the presence of a Detective Chief Inspector," Poole said. "I held off till you arrived, Cyrus. I wouldn't do that for anyone else."

"It is appreciated," Barker said.

"He slapped me on the back of the head as well!" Mahmoud complained.

I noticed the posh accent he'd affected in our presence was gone.

"Terence," Barker chided.

Poole grinned. "Boyish enthusiasm," he admitted.

"What's his story, then?" the Guv asked. "No, let me hear the Yard's information first, Mr. Mahmoud."

"First of all, his real name is Farid Ali," Terry replied. "He's led an interesting life, almost as interesting as yours, Cyrus. His father was the brother of the Khedive, Abbas Helmy Bey. I suppose you could call him a sort of prince, or he would be if we didn't run the government now. He's been peddling antiquities in Paris, Berlin, and the United States. Generally, he avoids institutions, preferring collectors who have more pounds than sense. Egyptomania, they call it."

"You sell your own country's antiquities after what you told us?" I demanded. He did not respond.

"Inspector, what is his modus operandi?" the Guv asked.

Poole shrugged. "It isn't complicated. He skulks into a museum, finds his mark, then takes them out to lunch with a story about his lost fortune."

"It's true!" Mahmoud said. "The British stole my fortune, leaving me no other way to make a living."

"When we went to his rooms at the Metropol, we found a key to a storage closet stuffed with jars, statues, and tablets. They looked like props to a play."

"I am being mischaracterized!" the Egyptian said, trying to look dignified.

"Not only that," the inspector continued, "he's been doctoring things to make them look older. We found paint and chemicals, and a box full of plaster scarabs still drying. And those funny crosses, too."

"Ankhs," I said.

"What's that?" Poole asked, as if I'd called him a name.

"Ankhs. The funny crosses are called ankhs."

"Thank you, O Educated One, for the history lesson."

Mahmoud attempted to defend his actions, but Poole pounded on the table in front of him.

"Don't speak until you're spoken to. I've got three officers out there who spent time in the Sudan. They'd like nothing better than five uninterrupted minutes with you."

"I think I will say nothing more," Mahmoud stated.

"Have any of his claims been substantiated?" I asked.

"There's been no word so far, but then many documents were destroyed when we stepped in to protect our interests in '82."

"It was an invasion," Mahmoud spat out.

"Thought you were going to shut your gob," Poole complained. "He's got another dodge. He joins occult societies full of rich people and claims to be some kind of high priest. Our friend here has them contributing to his upkeep. It's too bad for him there isn't an Egyptian embassy in London, or a solicitor. There's no one here to help His Highness."

"Is that all?" Barker asked.

"So far, that's the lot," Poole admitted. "More information will be coming in soon. I haven't found a connection between him and Addison so far, or the mummy."

"Mr. Mahmoud," Barker said. "You disappoint me. But then, I'm certain you disappoint a lot of people. Tell us about Mr. Addison and the mummy. And especially the ruby."

The man looked away after giving us a haughty look.

"So help me!" Poole growled, ready to strike him again.

"You'll say nothing?" the Guv pursued.

The man crossed his arms and refused to look at us. Barker turned to his friend.

"Terry, don't you think this gentleman would be more communicative downstairs?"

Poole frowned in puzzlement. Then he broke into a grin. "Downstairs, yes. We should give His Highness a tour. Come along. We've got a throne all ready for you. Shall I give him some bracelets?"

"It's your house, sir," Barker replied. "We are but visitors."

Poole put Mahmoud in darbies, then led him to the lobby and down a set of stairs. Mahmoud wrinkled his nose but was not prepared when we went up to a door marked Body Room. It was "A" Division's morgue. In fact, all the stations' bodies found their way here, including Phillip Addison and Coffee John.

"What's that odor?" Mahmoud asked, pinching his nose.

"Carbolic," I replied.

"It smells terrible!"

"Not compared to what it's masking."

We pushed through the door, our noses immediately assailed with the body-numbing combination of searing carbolic and decaying human flesh. I had been sick here myself during my first case, but after my fiftieth I could withstand the stench. Those who had not been here before could not. The poor fellow's first act was to be ill in a corner.

There were six corpses in the room, covered in sheets. There was another one uncovered with his skull opened. The coroner in charge of this room was Dr. Edward Vandeleur. We had spoken before him at many an inquest.

"Out!" he bellowed, his back to us. It was his customary response whenever the door opened. The man was charming at an opera, but a tarter in his sanctuary. He was recognizable by his mane of pale hair falling over his shoulders. I have compared him to a young Franz Liszt.

"Five minutes, doctor, if you please," Poole said. "We are taking a prisoner for a breath of fresh air."

"Good afternoon, Dr. Vandeleur," Barker greeted in his low rumble.

"Ah, Barker, Llewelyn," he replied. I leaned to one side to see what he was doing, then wished I hadn't. He was weighing a brain on a scale with gram weights.

"Mr. Mahmoud, the sooner you agree to answer our questions truthfully and with no exaggeration, the quicker you can leave this room," Barker said. "Otherwise, you can act as an assistant for the good doctor here for the rest of the day."

"He can begin by cleaning up that mess he made," Vandeleur said, scribbling in a notebook.

"I demand to be taken from this room," Mahmoud ordered. "This is duress!"

"The more you protest, the longer we will stay," Poole said. "We don't even notice the smell anymore."

"Doctor, is that a new cologne you're wearing?" I asked.

Vandeleur chuckled. I looked away as he began to cut the brain into slices like a loaf of bread.

The confidence man began to wobble, so I pulled a chair from the wall and sat him in it.

"Very well, I'll answer, but hurry!" Mahmoud moaned.

Excellent," Barker said, rubbing his hands. "What is your

connection to the lot of mummies purchased by the British Museum?"

"Not all of them, Mr. Barker," he said. "I have only an interest in one."

"Where did the mummy come from?"

"It was my father's," he replied. "He bought it in his youth from a farmer who found it in a wadi. The man was illiterate, but my father recognized the cartouche. He purchased it for ten pounds in your currency. The man ran off in case we decided to change our minds. My father swore to my brother Farouk and I that she was the famous pharaoh herself, and we must dedicate our lives to protecting her. More than anything he wanted to stop this, a display of our late queen in front of the English. It is too much like her being led into captivity in Rome as a spoil of war. Oh, take me out of here, please! I'll tell you everything!"

He gagged again. Barker and Poole dragged him out into the hall and sat him on the floor. He was perspiring heavily, his face pale. Barker gave Mahmoud a handkerchief to mop his brow. The three of us sat on the floor with him as the Egyptian leaned against the cool wall with relief.

At the time I thought the Guv was being brutal with Mahmoud, forcing him into a situation that made him violently ill. In hindsight, however, it seemed likely that Poole would have taken a few swings at him in the interrogation room, and the inspector had taken a course in the antagonistics school Barker runs. Mahmoud didn't seem the type who could defend himself or take a punch to the head. Even Thompson's secretary had bested him.

"Where was I?" he asked. "I've forgotten."

"Your father made you and your brother hide and protect the mummy," I prompted.

"Yes," he agreed. "Then the country was invaded. My father

lost his government position. Our house was sacked, our assets frozen. My father had undergone adversity before, however, and he had purchased some English stocks and securities. Also, a jewel of inestimable worth that it was not safe to show anyone at the time. It was our entire fortune. Father said no one must know of the mummy and the ruby. He also said we must leave Egypt for our own safety. Any relations to the Bey were a danger to the new government, and we would be imprisoned. France seemed the best choice. Father thought the ruby would be safest inside the mummy, since we were subject to searches at various borders."

"How did you escape?" Barker asked.

"We bribed a fisherman to sail to Greece by night, and a few months later we sent the mummy from Corfu to Marseilles by tramp steamer. We were supposed to meet it there, traveling overland, but my father had heart failure on the journey and died. By the time we arrived in Marseille, a week after the funeral, the mummy's crate was gone and everything in it. I beggared myself looking all over Europe for it. I never expected it would be in England, but eventually I found it here."

"No Balliol College, then?" I asked.

"I have two years at Al-Azher University, but Oxford would not accept any of my classes from Cairo. I was accepted but couldn't continue the tuition, with no steady income and my father's fortune nearly gone."

"What about your brother?" Barker asked, seated cross-legged on the floor.

"Farouk must be looked after. He has the mind of a six-year-old. We had servants to watch him before, but now the duty of tending to his needs has fallen to me. I'm not complaining, you understand. I love my brother."

"Is your brother at the Metropol?" Poole asked. "I won't believe your tale of woe until I meet him."

"Yes, he is, sir."

"So tell me, Mr. Mahmoud, how did you go from being a university student to a confidence trickster?"

"Inspector, I was intended from birth to follow in my father's footsteps and become an official. I wasn't taught to do anything but flatter, lie, and negotiate. No business in London wants to hire an Egyptian. However, it is an acceptable trade for a man with my background to sell antiquities, and I have also become respected among those with an interest in ancient religion and Theosophy."

Poole stabbed a finger at him. "And you sell fakes."

Mahmoud hung his head. "Yes, Inspector, I sell fakes. More properly, I doctor items that are without provenance when necessary. I love my country and its antiquities, but I need a roof over my head and have a brother I must look after."

"Mr. Mahmoud," Poole said. "Those are the same reasons every criminal gives for what he does: a roof and three meals, and maybe an orange for Christmas."

We were silent in that hallway then, each of us momentarily lost in our own thoughts.

"To your father's knowledge, then, the mummy really is Cleopatra?" I asked.

"Oh, yes, Mr. Llewelyn," he said, nodding. "I have no doubt. My father opened the abdomen and stuffed the jewel in its chest in front of me when I was thirteen. He swore upon it, and I don't recall him swearing on anything at any other time. I would have done a much better job matching the original bandages to the old. Natron, sodium carbonate, and bicarbonate would do it. A few drops of a stain I've made myself. It would have confounded Flinders Petrie."

"We should warn Director Thompson immediately," Poole said.

"That's what I was attempting to do when I was stopped,

to warn him," Mahmoud replied. "Whether he believed me or not. I didn't try to see the director to pass the time of day. I have acquaintances in the building so that I can stay informed."

Barker frowned at him. "Mr. Mahmoud, Lord Grayle has made an offer for the mummy. I fear Thompson has accepted. If I know Grayle it will be a generous offer, but still not worth what he will get for it if it were known to be the greatest archeological discovery of the age."

The Egyptian put his face in his hands and moaned.

"We must warn Thompson," I said, repeating Poole's opinion.

"Why?" the Guv asked. "We are under no obligation to do so, and he will not be pleased with the information. He put us in a cell for several hours. That was with your help, Terry."

"I rarely get to make my own decisions, Cyrus. You know that," Poole responded. "I follow orders and do my best to avoid my superiors. Sometimes I arrest people for no good reason, except to impress the brass. They like us arresting people. It makes it seem like we're doing our job."

"You do it well," I said. It wasn't intended as a compliment, but then he knew that. I turned to Mahmoud. "Here you are with no mummy and no jewel."

"I'm not the first Egyptian to be plundered by the English," he said. "At least I can say the same for the museum."

"It might be best if you left London, Mahmoud," the Detective Chief Inspector said. "You might try Edinburgh. There are wealthy lairds on every corner, and plenty of gullible people. I won't tell you to get an honest occupation. Just stay out of trouble on my watch. Now, I'm going to put you in a cell for an hour to make it seem like I'm doing my duty, then I'll let you go. Stay out of trouble and be gone when I stop at the Metropol tomorrow afternoon. You savvy, boy?"

"Yes, sir," Mahmoud said.

"We are square, then. If you could wipe that bloody handkerchief under your nose as you leave I'll be grateful. It impresses my superiors."

Barker suddenly reached into my jacket pocket and took out the agency's wallet. He removed twenty pounds and gave the notes to Mahmoud. Then he stuffed the wallet back into his pocket.

"You're an easy mark, Cyrus," the inspector said. "You've got too soft a heart."

"He needs traveling money," the Guv said. "London's loss is Edinburgh's gain. Unless you want him loitering about town for a few months more."

"I'm not impressed with the Edinburgh inspectors," Poole said. "They couldn't find their noses in the dark. Come on, Your Highness! Let's find you a nice cell to plan your next journey."

We helped Mahmoud to his feet. He was still pale and unsteady, especially when he reached the stairs. Poole led him to the visitors' cells, and we saw him locked in. He lay on the bunk, turned away, and fell asleep. It was the best thing for him, not that he would acknowledge it.

"I'll let him sleep for an hour then punt him out. That young fellow's got no luck," Poole said as we went to his office. I thought of Barker's little lecture on the matter. As we passed one of the desks an officer wrinkled his nose. It was the reek of carbolic on our suits. I wondered who did Dr. Vandeleur's laundry.

"Did you suspect the mummy and the ruby belonged to Mahmoud?" Poole asked.

"Not a whit," my partner admitted. "I assumed we'd never learn where they came from."

"Where was that famous Barker intuition?" Poole asked.

Barker looked slightly affronted. "It isn't intuition," he said. "It's mere common sense."

"'Common sense is not so common,'" I quipped, quoting Voltaire.

"Would you like a cell next to his?" Poole asked me.

When dealing with Scotland Yard, it's important to know when to speak and when to shut your gob.

CHAPTER 25

We were in a fish shop in the Strand. Barker and I had fried haddock and potatoes in front of us along with pale ale. The Guv was dousing his plate with malt vinegar like he was putting out a fire. He was eating mechanically, without speaking, thinking about the case.

The room smelled of hot oil and there were ropes and sailing gear hanging on the wall. A model of the HMS *Victory* stood over the fireplace and ensign flags hung overhead. I liked the restaurant, but the Strand was a landlocked place for such decorations.

"Forgive the question, sir," I dared ask. "Are we any closer to finding the truth than when we began? We don't have a clear suspect in Addison's death. I can't imagine what a group of street toughs and a mummy from the British Museum have in common. I suspect K'ing may be involved, but I don't see how.

Our client has been stabbed and drowned in the river, or frozen. The case is all tied in knots."

"I'm ahead of you, lad, but not far," he admitted. "I have several theories that I can test, but putting them all together and making sense of them is a challenge. As for the knots, be thankful for them. Knots can be untied one by one. That's what we must do, even if it means interviewing our suspects again."

"But there's more!" I complained. "There's the mummy to consider, whether she's actually Cleopatra. Who killed Addison and Coffee John? Is Davis merely after a story or is he after something else?"

Barker had cut his haddock to pieces, endangering the plate with his knife. He tucked a few bites into his mouth and chewed them with his square, white teeth, then doused his plate with more vinegar.

"I've got most of the knots untied, Thomas," he said at last. "Now I must weave the strings together to be able to understand the picture."

"We must do something," I said. "Didn't you vow to be done with this case by the New Year?"

"I did," he admitted. "Where do we begin?"

"Cargill's, without doubt," I replied. "We warned him and he may have sent his son away for a while, but we must try, nevertheless."

"Excellent," the Guv said. "I like your attitude."

I nodded. "I want to be done by New Year's Day, myself. Rebecca will be coming home soon. I demand a holiday. In fact, it is a holiday!"

"Very well," Barker said after swallowing the last of his fish. "You may have New Year's Day all to yourselves. Enjoy an entire day of domesticity."

He downed the last of his ale, wiped his mustache, and stood. I was slower off the mark. He was most of the way out the door as I called for the bill.

We headed north again on the Underground to the Alexandra Park in a particularly bone-rattling railway carriage. We arrived in Haringey and were soon entering the racecourse again. I wondered whether the booking office would even be open.

Barker was like a baying hound. I could not keep up with him without trotting. When we'd trod through the shavings for a few minutes, I could see Cargill's office ahead. A light shone from within the room. Barker seized the handle and entered just as I caught him up.

Cargill was seated in his chair again, but starting to spring from it. Most of the rest of the chairs, eight in all, were filled with men in tweed caps. We had run the gang to the ground.

There was what a musician would call a beat before everyone but Cargill pulled pistols. He hadn't given any orders; his men had done so on their own. Barker pulled both his Colts from the holsters under his arms while I drew the British bulldog from my back waistband. It was custom-made, small though accurate. We were at an impasse, but some of us were undermanned.

"Boys, put your guns down," Cargill ordered.

No one moved. The gang looked grim and determined. A couple seemed elated at finally doing something exciting and dangerous. Most of them were in their early twenties and life consisted of getting drunk, ogling young women, and picking fights. This was a novelty.

Barker had one pistol trained at the first four and the other trained on their peers. I didn't aim precisely. I'd wait to see what would happen before I fired.

"Mr. Llewelyn," the Guv said coolly. "Please train your Webley on Mr. Cargill. Whether you are shot once or eight times, I order you to put a bullet in his brainpan."

"Yes, sir."

This is it, I thought. *Goodbye, Rebecca. You warned me countless times that this work was dangerous.*

Another beat. We were getting up the nerve to shoot, all ten of us. The first shot and all the pistols would go off. The first would strike Barker and me. They wouldn't shoot once, either. They'd empty their pistols into us. The only thing I could do was to take their leader with me.

We locked eyes for the briefest second. He had paid no attention to me the first time we had entered his office. I was an appendage to the Guv, a satellite. Now I'd be the last thing he saw on this earth.

"Stop, you idiots!" Cargill bellowed. A stray bullet shot out one of the windows behind us. "I said stop! Put those guns down. You want us all on trial for murder? You want some of us dead? I'm sorry I ever bought those pistols for you!"

The men lowered the revolvers but didn't put them away.

"Who's in charge here?" Cargill demanded. "Put those guns back in your pockets or I'll take them away from you!"

Three of them turned their guns toward the betting agent, but there was no assurance in the act.

"Oh, that's it, is it?" he demanded. "I clothed you, fed you, and put a roof over your head and this is the thanks I get? Put them away immediately!"

The guns went back into their coat pockets. Barker returned his pistols to their holsters. I was the last man in the room with a gun in his hand, which was still pointed at Cargill's head. I could have shot him then and there. My brains would be splattered all over the wall behind me, but I could do it.

"Thomas," Barker said, coaxing me.

Reluctantly, I returned the pistol to my waistband. Everyone in the room gave a collective sigh.

"That's better," Cargill said, attempting to assert his authority. "My apologies, Mr. Barker."

"No need," the Guv replied. "Young men can be boisterous. I see they've returned to the nest."

"They have," the man answered. "Most chastened, although a few are still muleheaded. How can I help you?"

"I want to know what happened to Phillip Addison."

The room was silent, everyone reluctant to speak. One of them, a Cargill by the look of him, stepped forward.

"He was near his house," he said. "And Reggie run after him. Stabbed him once in the heart, quick as you can say knife. We bundled him into our hackney and took him to Cubitt Town."

"Why there?" Barker asked.

The young man shuffled his feet. Confession is difficult. Doing so in front of your mates is more difficult still.

"Reggie wanted us to form a gang there," he said. "Take it over. Make the merchants pay for security. Spark the girls, intimidate the boys, you know. Live like kings."

Barker nodded. They weren't the first to follow that plan. Generally speaking, it did not work, but occasionally it did if some blades were willing to try.

"Why Phillip Addison?" my partner asked.

The young man shrugged. He looked a little like his brother: taller and thinner, but still red-haired.

"Dunno," he replied. "Reggie said he was the one."

"The one to what?" Barker asked, crossing his arms. He looked threatening, but then he always did, due in part to the old scar that cut through his eyebrow and extends down his cheek.

"To use as an example," he said. "A warning. You don't go against the Tweed Boys or you'll end up like him."

"You have no idea why Addison was chosen?" Barker asked. "None at all?"

"No, sir," Cargill said. "I don't. Reggie said, 'Get him,' and so we did, but he ran. He weren't far from his own front door. Reggie thought he might get in, so he stabbed him."

"You think he intended to kill him all along?"

"No, sir, I don't think so. We was going to take him. Tie him up and question him. Reggie said he had some property, but I don't know what."

"I see."

"Reggie's not a killer, sir. He was trying to stop the fella."

"He stabbed a man in the heart, young man," Barker rumbled. "That makes him a killer whether he wanted to or not."

"Yes, sir," the boy replied.

He hung his head. They all did. I wondered what kind of father Cargill was, using his own sons to collect debts. With the money he made he could send his sons to Oxford or Cambridge. They could have been barristers or bank managers. They could make something of themselves. But no, Cargill brought them into the family business instead.

"Where is Reggie, sir?" Barker demanded.

Cargill looked stern. "Do not kill my son, sir. I've heard about your reputation."

"I don't intend to do so," the Guv replied. "But I can't make any promises. If he pulls a weapon I shall have no compunction."

"He is out there in the stables somewhere, I think," Cargill said. "Or in the Blandford Arms. Did he say where he was going, lads?"

The group shook their heads or shrugged their shoulders.

"Very well," my partner replied. "I have no further need of you, but I suspect Scotland Yard will want to speak to you. You should have gone to them yourselves after Mrs. Addison was shot. You should know his widow threw herself off Waterloo Bridge yesterday. You've got two deaths on your hands now."

The young men looked chastened. The eldest I recognized as the constable who tossed our room. He was the jockey we'd heard about in the Millwall public house.

Behind us, the door suddenly opened and Reggie Cargill stepped into the room. We weren't ten feet away from him. He roared an oath and ran, with Barker and me in hot pursuit. When we turned a corner, he was wriggling through a gap in a fence. In a moment, he was gone.

CHAPTER 26

We opened the paddock and went inside, but Reggie Cargill was nowhere in sight. Cautiously, we crossed to the far end, unlatched the gate, and stepped through. As we were trying to decide which direction to go, we heard the gate slam behind us and turned to find Reggie standing there with a pistol trained on us.

"'Ello, gents," he said. "Drop your weapons, won't you?"

Reluctantly, I tossed my pistol into the shavings. Barker considered the matter then dropped his as well. We were defenseless. Worse still, we were defenseless in an area far from anyone who might help us. The racetrack was gloomy and most sane people were either at home in front of a roaring fire or snug in the Blandford's stodgy rooms. The arena walls were too tall to climb and there were no witnesses. Our lives could be measured in minutes.

"Young Cargill," Barker said. "You're looking hale. Is your

foot healing well? Mr. Llewelyn was saying just the other day that he regretted shooting you."

"Not 'alf as much as he's gonna," Reggie replied. "I'm gonna shoot him in one foot, and then the other, and then between the eyes. You, Mr. Barker, I'm gonna blow your brains out. But first you're gonna tell me where you've stashed my bloody ruby."

"It is your ruby, then, is it?" Barker asked.

"Of course it is," Reggie spat out. "I'm waiting on a man I know who says he can split it into pieces. I can get two thousand pounds for it."

"A giant ruby for two thousand pounds?" Barker asked. "That's a miserable arrangement, sir."

"Isn't it, though?" the betting agent's son answered. "Once I find it, though, I'll be in clover. Cubitt Town will be mine and I'll be a wealthy man."

"You say the ruby belongs to you, but what about your father?"

"He has no idea about it," Reggie replied. "I'm going out on my own. The old man's holding me back. You see, he's not as ambitious as he was when he nobbled the London Cup. That was inspired, but now he ain't half become an also-ran. He just sits in his office and takes in bets and pays them off. He's tired and he's run out of ideas."

"And you're full of them, I take it?" Barker asked.

"S'right," Cargill replied. "Loads of them. My dad don't want them, so I'll take them myself. Just need a little of the ready, if you know what I mean. A bankroll to get me started. I'm not going to be his whipping boy any longer. So, where's my ruby, Mr. Barker?"

"I don't have it," my partner said. "I gave it away. I'm afraid I can't get it back."

Reggie's arm was getting tired. He changed to the other hand. "Just gave it away, did you? In exchange for cash?"

"No, Mr. Cargill. I gave it away as a duty."

"A duty?" he exclaimed. "What are you talking about? Tell

me where my ruby is right now or I'll blow your ruddy head off your shoulders!"

"I gave it to Her Majesty," he said. "That is, to her secretary, Lord Ponsonby. I didn't trust the British Museum at that time. People were getting killed. I needed a safe place and then I thought, 'Who's going to possess this jewel when all is said and done? It's a giant ruby, perhaps the largest in the world. What is its final destination?'"

"The Tower of London with the other Crown Jewels," I supplied.

"Precisely."

"My ruby?" shrieked Reggie Cargill. "You gave my ruby to the bloody Queen?"

"Here now," said a voice from the far side of the paddock. "Don't insult Her Majesty."

The three of us turned as one. Detective Chief Inspector Terence Poole stood in the open gate with at least five constables. Poole had his sidearm trained on Reggie and while the constables carried nothing but truncheons, no one in their right mind would believe he could shoot one and get away with it.

Reggie lunged then. He seized me by the wrist and yanked me toward him, clapping a pistol to my head.

"One more step and this 'un gets blood all over the sawdust. C'mon, Tommy Boy."

He dragged me backward. I tried to resist, but he clouted me on the temple. Blood trickled down my face. Poole couldn't get a clear enough shot to take him down.

Barker stood nearby, arms away from his sides. He wasn't tense or frightened. He was waiting. We looked at each other, as if it were the two of us alone.

Do I fight or do I go along peacefully, I wondered? I was trained to fight better than any soldier in London at that moment, but Cargill had a pistol to my head. *Do I scramble and probably die? Do I willingly give my life to save the others? Do I allow myself to be led along and see what happens?* I tried to work out what Barker would do in this situation. I decided to wait to try to find a more advantageous position for myself.

"Come along, I ain't got all day," he ordered, dragging me backward by my collar.

We came to the far end of the paddock and a gate. Reggie opened it and hauled me inside. It was another paddock, much smaller, with another door at the other end. There was a padlock on it. When we reached it, Reggie seized the lock with his free hand, found it secured, then reached into his pocket. He came up empty.

"Cursed!" he cried. "I'm cursed! Nothing ever comes off right 'n my entire life!"

"I've felt that way before, Reg," I muttered.

"Shut it!" he yelled. "This is your fault. Why did you have to shoot my foot?"

"You were coming at me with a knife," I told him. "You and all the others. What was I supposed to do? Stand there and let you stab me?"

"I wish I'd never seen your face!" he cried. "This is all your fault."

I wanted to say I felt the same, but I'd promised Barker I wouldn't let my tongue get me killed.

"What now?" I asked.

He turned away and ran to the padlock on the opposite gate, leading to the outer ring. He tried to shoot it with the pistol. It jumped twice but didn't open. Reggie screamed in anger. He was approaching some sort of breakdown.

"Reggie," I said. "You should give yourself up!"

"Shut it!" he cried. "No one asked you."

"Prison isn't so bad," I continued. "I did eight months and lived through it. At least you'd get away from your father."

"I said, shut it!"

I knew they were out there, Barker and Poole and the constables, probably no farther away than ten feet, on the other side of the wall. If I knew Poole, he was looking for something to act as a battering ram. I'm sure the two shots unnerved them.

Reggie put the gun to my forehead. I wanted to tell him it wouldn't help if he killed me. I wanted to tell him I had a wife and that I wanted to live. I liked my life. Against impossible odds, I'd become successful. When I'd gone home for Christmas, my mum was proud of me and what I had become. I'd had my moments, however, just as Reggie was having his just then.

"Reggie," I said. "I'm sorry I shot you."

The paddock was cold. The barrel against my forehead was hot. I was perspiring in my coat and shivering as well.

I didn't want the news of my death to come when Rebecca was with my parents. I didn't want her to find out when she returned to London. *In fact, if it's not too much trouble, Lord,* I thought, *I'd like her never to hear I was dead at all.*

"Are you well, Thomas?" Barker bellowed from the other side of the door.

"I've been better," I called.

"Cargill!" Poole shouted. "You're trapped like a mouse. Put down your weapon and come out."

I won't repeat Cargill's response, which was unprintable and demeaning to an officer of the law. Still, I'm certain Poole had heard worse. Those East Enders can get colorful with their verbs and adjectives.

We were still standing face-to-face. I could hear a buzz of conversation outside and orders being given in low voices, but I had no idea what was being said. I also had no idea of how much time had passed. It could have been three minutes or half an hour.

"Cargill!" Poole called again. "Come along, Reggie. No one will shoot you. We don't have all day. I have reports to write. Some of these men have shifts to go to."

Reggie pushed at my forehead with the pistol until my skull

pressed against the wood of the paddock. I still bled from where he'd struck me on the temple. Another new shirt ruined, as if I didn't have worse things to think about.

We stared at each other. I don't think he even saw me, off in some dark part of his mind debating what he should do. It was the most important discussion of his life.

"I can't do it," he finally said to me. He wasn't angry anymore. He looked frightened.

"Do what?" I asked.

"Go to jail," he replied. "Swing for it. Face my bleedin' father. Take your pick."

"Look," I said. "I'm sure—"

As I was in midsentence, Reggie put the gun to his forehead and fired. It wasn't the first time I'd been sprayed with a man's blood and brains, and I couldn't begin to number the bullets that have flown by my head. Cargill fell, disjointed and loose, his head a sodden mess.

"He's topped himself!" I called.

Slowly, the gate opened. Poole stepped inside cautiously.

"Crikey!" he said. "Are you all right, Thomas?"

I nodded. He turned and ordered a bucket of water and a towel from one of the constables.

"It's done," I said to Barker. "At least this part of it."

The bucket came and then the towels. I didn't care where they came from or what they were used for. As I wiped the blood from my face, I watched the water in the bucket turn redder and redder.

I kept remembering the shot, the momentary misshapen skull as the ball penetrated it before it returned to its original shape. I looked down. It had been a small pistol and inexpensive, the kind designed for only a limited number of shots before being thrown away. It must have been smuggled in from the Continent. A larger gun like Barker's would have done far more damage.

Poole questioned me over and over, though he'd been just on the other side of the door. I was becoming dazed.

I heard a scream then and nearly jumped out of my skin. It was Alfred Cargill, unaware of what had happened so close to his office. He'd followed the trail of constables to the paddock and the screaming that ensued was awful.

"Get me out of here, sir," I said to Barker. "I don't like the Ally Pally, and I don't like the north of London. Let's go back to Whitehall."

And so we did. We found a cabman who wasn't concerned that my hair was wet and my shirt tinged pink. My head was freezing and I put my tongue between my teeth to stop them chattering. It wasn't the cold, I knew. It was the shock.

Barker didn't speak. He wasn't solicitous. He let me deal with my own emotions. I stared at the scene in front of me, which ironically looked like a Christmas card. It had begun snowing again and there were still wreaths on some of the doors.

An hour later, I was in the bathhouse in the garden behind Barker's house, floating in the large bath, arms out, staring at the wooden rafters. I was floating in my mind as well. I considered asking Barker for the rest of the day off. I'd be perfectly justified to do so. But no. The case was unfinished. New Year's was coming in a day or two. Rebecca would be back and we'd spend it together at our house in Camomile Street. A whole day without a case to worry over. It seemed like heaven.

CHAPTER 27

And so that was that. The case was over. We had found Mr. Addison's murderer, and probably Coffee John's as well. We'd found the origin of the mummy and the ruby, and how both were connected. The British Museum now shared possession of the Heart of the Nile with the Crown, which was not a perfect arrangement but better than having Cyrus Barker shuffling it about forever.

Every *i* had been dotted, every *t* crossed, save one. It seemed to not worry Barker at all, but were I an oyster it was the grit that would eventually become a pearl: How had Reggie's gang descended so quickly upon Phillip Addison? It seemed as if they had taken him the moment he left the museum. One could not have a forgotten mummy languishing underground on one hand and a gang of professional bullyboys waiting to pounce on a fellow in the other. It was a mystery. I needed to know, but when I asked the Guv, he shrugged and gave me an aphorism

such as "everything shall be revealed in the fullness of time."
Someday I'm going to write a book called *The Analects of Barker*
so that I no longer need to carry his wisdom about in my head.

The case had taken us four days, four very crowded days
with no rest. We'd gone from one holiday to the next and were
about to start a new year. *What would 1894 bring us?* I wondered. *Would we still be alive by the end of it?* New Year's Eve was
tomorrow, and we were not safe yet.

I woke when Mac entered our room and drew the curtains,
allowing the morning sun to illuminate the chamber. I pulled
my wife's pillow over my head.

"What o'clock is it?" I demanded.

"A quarter past six, sir."

"And the date?" I asked.

"December thirty-first."

"No," I said. "It can't be. It feels like it turned 1893 just a
month ago."

"May I wish you a Happy New Year?" he asked.

"If you do, I'll brain you with a hat rack."

He lifted Rebecca's pillow from my head and returned it to its
proper place, ignoring the threat.

"Mr. Barker is exercising in the back garden," he informed
me. "Dummolard is making omelets."

"Say I'm ill," I told him. "Inform them that I've moved out of
the country, with no plans to return, while I slink out the front
door."

"I'm afraid I can't," he said. "We all have our duties to perform. You have yours, and this is mine. Happy Hogmanay!"

I threw Rebecca's pillow at his head. Hogmanay is a Scottish
holiday going back to both Norse and Gaelic history, which is
very like New Year's Day in England. The celebration starts on
the Eve at sunset, and the frivolities continue into the first of the
year, sometimes into the second. "Auld Lang Syne," written by
Robby Burns himself, is an anthem of the season, sung in all

English-speaking countries, even though we don't understand eighteenth-century Scots, or what the poem even means.

Aside from feasting and gift giving, the main activity of Hogmanay is drinking. Though in some laird's castle this might include wine, most often the chosen beverage is single malt whisky. Then there is what is known as first-footing. In the Scottish tradition, a tall, dark man must be the first to step into a family's home after midnight, carrying a gift, generally more single malt whisky. By so doing, he brings the family good fortune during the coming year and becomes a kind of patron saint of the house, or a benevolent uncle, if you prefer. He makes a toast, offers a blessing, and then presents are given and received a week after their neighbors to the south have opened and forgotten theirs.

Naturally, tall, dark men are in short supply, especially in a redheaded race, but Cyrus Barker is three things: he is Scottish to the core, he is tall, and he is dark. Though he does not mix often among his Scottish expatriates down among the Sassenachs, he is in great demand at this time of year. Often, he will visit ten or more houses between midnight and one in the morning. He considers it a duty to his people, but he does not particularly enjoy it. At each house he visits, a bottle of whisky is bestowed, a toast made for good fortune over the coming year, and a slap on the back is given, then he is out the door, while presents are passed around the table. That's all, really. But it's enough.

Barker's a good Christian man, give or take a few experiences in China. He's not teetotal but will drink a stout or beer at most. However, each speech he gives on Hogmanay is accompanied by a dram of whisky. Actually, it's more like twenty drams, because a dram is one-eighth of an ounce, barely enough to wet the sides of the glass. A tumbler of whisky neat holds two ounces. A bottle contains about twenty-four ounces. I believe that means that by one o'clock Barker will have poured most of a bottle of Scotch whisky down his throat. My duty was to get him from one house to another and then home again.

Whisky tends to make him sing, and Barker sings off-key at the best of times. It is hell. I hate Hogmanay, fortune and good cheer notwithstanding, and I think the Guv does as well, though he'd never admit it. It is a Tradition, and therefore one must do it. It is a Duty, and all those other words that must be capitalized.

When I came downstairs and was having my coffee and a truffle omelet, I watched Barker outside in his garden. A frost had come overnight, which is always beautiful, but especially so in an oriental garden. My partner was there, his jacket off, the smoke from his breath like a scarf around his throat as he performed the exercises he learned in far-off Canton. We'd tried everything over the years: exercise, priming his stomach with bread, filling bottles with clear cider, or developing a tolerance by drinking the night before. Nothing worked. Barker would be useless for days. It was a problem with no solution.

Our least favorite day of the year was ahead of us. The office was closed for the holiday, so we were at loose ends. Mac hates days off, which interfere with the natural rhythm of things. We kept trying to occupy the same space while he cleaned and polished, then apologizing, and then doing it again somewhere else. I returned to my room, found a copy of Stevenson's *New Arabian Nights,* and read until lunch. Dreading something requires time and energy. One must put one's heart and soul into it. If done properly it leaves little time for anything else.

Harm yawned in the hall and rested his chin on the floor, letting out a sigh. Gloom permeated everything.

We bestirred ourselves at seven that evening. The Guv and I dressed in conservative suits. We donned coats and bowlers and stepped outside. It was a few minutes' walk to the cab stand by the Elephant and Castle, where we took a hansom cab to the King James in Fitzroy Square.

The public house was no more than half full, but if the past was any indication, it would be overflowing by midnight. Tonight, the order that all public houses must close at that hour was winked at. The publican had the ten bottles Barker would distribute under the counter, though the Guv had already paid for them. I never asked, but I assume that being on the list of Barker's visitations was highly sought.

The room began to fill, and most gave us a greeting, albeit a formal one. He was reliably amiable, however, and spoke to those he knew. I understood he would have preferred to be at home in a chair by the fire, with a pipe and book. There is a veil between him and everyone, I think, including myself. He is and always will be a private person.

Someone started to play the bagpipes, which, strange to say for a Welshman, I rather like. It was loud in an enclosed room, however, and a little goes a long way. I was pleased when they switched to bodhrans and pennywhistles. Later they turned to singing ballads. Scottish songs are plaintive and melancholy for so jovial a people.

At eight the room was near full, at nine one could hardly move. The Scotch ale was flowing. Young women danced a fling and there were children underfoot. I was the sole Welshman in a sea of Scots, longing for some peace and quiet. A woman was at my elbow, and I vacated my seat for her and pushed my way to the street. There I stood under a gas lamp and thanked my stars this occurred only once a year. I was about to return when the door opened, and I heard concertinas playing inside. In fact, it seemed as if the entire building had become one large concertina wheezing in the night, squeezed by a celestial hand. I elected to stay outside for as long as I could stand the chill.

Ten o'clock came and I stepped inside. We had come to the speech portion of the evening. Figuratively, everyone patted each other on the back for having the good sense to be born Scottish. There was a kittenish swipe now and again at the Irish and the English. Fortunately, the Welsh were spared. After this there was communal singing, most of which was about a wish to return to their "haimland," as if it was either a faery land or a country so far away that one could never visit, when in fact one could be in Edinburgh in eight hours by the North Eastern Railway. The rest of the songs, a good many, were either about the Battle of Culloden or Bonnie Prince Charlie. History and historical grudges run deep in the North. One would think their countrymen didn't enjoy being an English possession.

Big Ben clanged eleven o'clock in the distance. I went outside again. A minute or two later, the Guv joined me.

"Have you memorized your toast?" I asked.

"Aye, a decade ago."

"What did you do to achieve this annual honor?"

"Very little," he admitted. "I stepped into this tavern for a half pint of stout around Christmas a dozen years ago and passed the time of day with the publican. Looking back, it was ill-advised. However, I can afford ten bottles of whisky, while others can't. Many of the ten families I shall visit are worthy and in need."

"I've always assumed you helped them now and again throughout the year."

He shrugged his wide shoulders. "A few of them ask. Most are too proud. So far, I have not been taken advantage of."

"That's good, then. What's going on in there?"

"They are serving food," Barker replied. "Are you hungry?"

I was dubious. "Haggis? Neeps and tatties?"

"I assume you've never tried them," he rumbled.

"Nor ever shall."

"Suit yourself," he said. "We'll be leaving within the hour."

He went inside the building. When the door opened, the aroma wafted past. I was a mite peckish, and it was cold in the square. I went inside, wondering if this had been a foregone conclusion. The haggis I would not try, but the neeps and tatties, mashed turnips and potatoes, were acceptable. As I raised a forkful, Barker dropped beside me out of nowhere.

"You see?" he asked.

"Why do people insist upon being proved right?" I asked. "So tell me, how far away is the first house you are to first-foot?"

"Not far. A half dozen streets away, perhaps."

"What's it to be this time? Stuff or starve?"

"I've decided it doesn't matter if I eat or starve. I shall be ill either way," he said with a grim look on his rough-hewn face.

"Without doubt," I agreed. "You understand they wouldn't hate you if you decide to stop carrying on with this tradition. They shall be disappointed, but they'll understand. It's too much for one man to take on."

"I'll nae be willing to disappoint my people."

"What people?" I asked. "You don't even see them the other three hundred and sixty-four days of the year."

Barker didn't answer but went to speak to the man who would be driving our carriage. I rose and went outside. As soon as I did a pair of hands seized my arm.

"Thomas!" a man said. He wore a dark overcoat with the collar turned up, a fedora on his head, and a scarf covering his face.

"Who are you?" I demanded.

"It's me," he replied, removing his hat.

"Mac?" I said. "What are you doing here?"

"I've come to relieve you. You've been doing this for ten years. I thought I'd give you a night off."

"Your conscience was bothering you, perhaps?"

"It was," he admitted.

"Mac, you don't have a conscience."

"I do!" he insisted. "I'll take good care of the Guv, I promise. I've left my cab. You'd better take it. You won't find another tonight. I'll tell him."

I didn't trust the man for a second. We'd been playing tricks on each other for years. There was an empty hansom, however, as rare as giant rubies. I ran for it, but as usual, it was already occupied.

"I'm sorry, ma'am," I said. "I thought this vehicle was empty."

"We can share if you lend me your coat," a voice said from within. "It's freezing out here!"

"Rebecca!" I exclaimed.

"In the flesh," she replied, smiling. "Cold flesh, that is. I wanted to show you some shoulder, silly me. Hand me your coat! I'm freezing!"

I climbed aboard. She was a dazzling sight. She wore a formal gown, black and deep scarlet. A dark veil was pinned to the back of her hair and an ostrich feather curled about it. I surrendered my coat without protest.

"How did you convince Mac to come?" I demanded.

"I didn't ask. I reached Lion Street around seven, and between us we planned this entire venture. Look here, he packed a hamper."

"Did he?" I asked. "I was almost forced to eat haggis. What have we got?"

My wife moved lifted the lid of the wicker basket. "Let's see. We've got potted shrimps, pâté de foie gras, a little caviar. The usual late New Year's Eve fare. Open the champagne like a good boy."

I'd have gone to France and trod the grapes for her myself if she had asked. I twisted the corkscrew and tugged for all I was worth. The cork shot from the bottle, leaving just a curl of condensation around the lip. I poured and we drank.

"Blast, it's cold!" I cried.

"Darling, there is a lady present," she said. "You've been among men too long."

"Scottish men, no less," I said. "Savages. I almost feel sorry for Mac among them."

"He'll survive," she said, patting my knee. She looked lovely, far better than I deserved.

"How are my parents?" I asked. "Why are you home early?"

"We'll talk about them later."

"This case has been maddening."

"We'll talk about that later, as well," she said. "Driver!"

"Yes, ma'am?" a muffled voice came from above.

"Just drive about. The choice is yours."

He clicked his tongue and his horse stirred and began to move.

"I've missed you terribly," I said.

She leaned forward and put her gloved arms about my neck. "That's probably the most sensible thing you've said all day."

CHAPTER 28

Almost a week went by. Cyrus Barker slowly recovered from his debauchery. Mac hadn't told me what happened that night, but he shook his head and rolled his eyes.

I handled a small case or two during that week, but nothing of any import occurred save one thing: we received an invitation from Lord Grayle. He got his wish and had purchased the mummy from the British Museum for what I assumed must be a fabulous sum. It was two invitations, in fact, and not the sort where one must fill a blank space. Mine read:

**This invitation requests the pleasure of
Mr. Thomas Llewelyn's
company at the Grayle Estate on 6 January 1894
for an inspection and examination of the mummy of the
Pharaoh and Queen, Cleopatra VII of Egypt.**

The event commences shortly after nine.
Drinks and light refreshment will be served.
Rooms are available at the inns in the
local village of Blessington.
Please RSVP

Those were the essentials, which were delivered in such an ornate script that I had to decipher it carefully. Barker agreed to go against his usual disapproval of His Lordship, so I sent along an acceptance for us both. I've never had the opportunity to send a letter somewhere using only the name of the house and its general location. There is only one Lord Grayle and one Grayle Castle.

"Are we going?" I asked Barker.

Barker grunted. "As contemptible as I find Lord Grayle, I have the feeling that our presence will be required."

On the eventful day, we traveled to Grayle Castle via the London and South Western Railway to Grayle's house in East Hampshire near Basingstoke. When we arrived at the station shortly after seven, there was a crowd of men in evening kit and overcoats, clambering to find a seat aboard one of a dozen hackney cabs His Lordship had hired for the evening. Everyone seemed to know each other, and I entertained myself with looking for famous men and trying to deduce a man's occupation by his manner. Lord Randolph Churchill was there, as well as Arthur Balfour. One could almost split the crowd by political party.

Barker nudged my elbow and nodded at a closed carriage nearby.

"Who is that?" I asked.

"The Prince of Wales, unless I miss my guess. His son is probably inside as well."

"Grayle must have a lot of friends," I remarked, looking at the knots of men in glossy top hats. "I'm sure many of them had to cancel their plans on short notice."

"I think it likely they came for the spectacle, rather than the host, as well as the opportunity to tell others about this event a decade from now."

It was near eight o'clock and dark as pitch. Stepping outside of direct light one was instantly plunged into profound darkness. We made our way into a closed cab. One of the other men inside was a man we knew, the crusader and spiritualist, W. T. Stead. He was animated and seemed pleased to have an invitation to the event, explaining that they had been doled judiciously to gentlemen of Grayle's acquaintance and could not be had for love nor money.

Soon, our carriage reached a set of old stone gates at the entrance to the estate. There were standing torches on either side of the road every ten feet, hundreds stretching on and on, higher and higher to a glittering castle at the top of a hill. Every window was lit and there was a carbon arc lamp of unusual size to illuminate the exterior. The stone was probably buff, but the lamp made it appear dazzlingly white. Something about the stone and the light reminded me of a pyramid, which I'm sure was not discernible in the clear light of day. As we neared the main entrance there were long banners draping the castle with hieroglyphics and a cartouche I was now able to recognize easily. Aside from the cost of the mummy itself, the exact price of which I never knew, our host was spending a fortune on the décor to set the mood. The guests grew more animated and self-congratulatory as they alighted from their carriages. There was something risqué about the whole affair, a group of men cut free from their wives for the evening, drinking and smoking expensive cigars, come to watch as Grayle sheared the wrappings from Cleopatra's mummy. It was prurient and in poor taste. It would have been far different if the mummy had been male. This was Cleopatra, however, who had already endured so many indignities throughout her life and reign. I suspected she had anticipated such an end and buried her crypt and that of her lover deep in the Egyptian desert. Not deep enough, apparently.

"Look at them," I complained to my partner. "I haven't seen this kind of irreverent chatter since I left university. They have no respect for the dead. There are MPs and judges and captains of industry here, possibly even members of the clergy."

"Is it the fact that they are doing this, or that it is in poor taste that offends you?" Barker asked.

"Both, I suppose."

"Does it feel as if she is calling out to you for protection?" he asked. "She's affected you, hasn't she? Or rather, you have affected yourself. She's bones and rags, you know, nothing more."

A butler greeted us at the door and examined our invitations. He seemed satisfied, but he kept an eye on us as we passed. When we stepped into the entrance hall, we were confronted by several exhibits, so that one felt as if one were in the British Museum again. We were swept along into the castle lobby. The walls were covered in ancient weapons, Viking helmets under glass, and Japanese armor flanking a staircase. It was some of the best each civilization had to offer.

"He's a ghoul," I muttered to the Guv. "A grave robber. Everything here was thieved from a corpse."

"You're a romantic, lad," Barker replied. "The corpses had no use for their possessions any longer, not even their own bodies. They went on to their reward or punishment long ago."

"Well, well," a man said behind us. "Hail fellows well met."

It was Terence Poole in a conservative black coat and matching bowler. He had a man behind him on each side. They were not constables but footmen, there to see that he did not impede the evening's activities.

"Terry," Barker greeted. "Are you ready?"

"You know I am," the inspector replied.

"Are you here to arrest Grayle as well?"

The inspector looked at me with scorn. "You think I want to throw away my career? I haven't come this far to step into the path of a peer of the bleedin' realm."

"Who is it, then?" I asked, not following the thread of the conversation.

"It's Clive Hennings," Barker stated. "I assume you examined Cargill's racing accounts, Terry?"

"I did," Poole replied. "Hennings owed him over five hundred quid. The only way for him to clear his debts was to call Cargill's son and tell him about the ruby."

"But they couldn't find it," I said, light beginning to dawn in the old Llewelyn noggin.

"And if they could, they wouldn't be able to turn it into pounds sterling," Barker explained. "Even the elder Mr. Addison's machines would have trouble breaking down an outsized ruby into smaller, salable ones."

I thought about the elder Mr. Addison. His house was grand, but it could be set in a corner of this castle and be lost. I could not begin to imagine how many rooms were in this place, and there must be dozens of outbuildings on the estate as well. Grayle's ancestors had probably owned the nearby town, which had sprung up hundreds of years ago to supply the needs of the castle. He might own it still, and the rent from his tenants paid for his treats from all over the world. Did he have a wife or children? If he were wise, he would sign papers to donate his collection to the British Museum when he was gone rather than see it broken up and sold by distant relations. I'm sure he was wise, and if he wasn't, he at least had the foresight to hire those who could be wise in his stead.

"Why wasn't Hennings arrested yet?" I asked.

"Lord Grayle has been keeping him close," Poole replied. "And until now, we haven't been allowed on the property. I had to get a court order."

I realized that during the week after Hogmanay, the Guv had been working with Poole to track Hennings's whereabouts. I turned back to the conversation.

"The two of you are not cut out for the Yard, I'm afraid," Poole said. "You dress too posh."

We were in evening kit. Barker had decided to wear his Astrakhan coat. I wore an elegant black-caped coat that went perfectly with my white tie and wing-tipped collar. I'd had it for a year but never had the opportunity to wear it. For some reason, at formal occasions Barker wears green-lensed spectacles, as deep and opaque as jade. I suspect he does not know he is eccentric, but no one has ever had the courage to tell him. To him, I'm sure, everything he does has a logical purpose.

We passed through a second room full of Roman antiquities, mostly busts missing noses or statuary with missing arms. There the queue came to a halt. People began to talk and complain, their comments echoing in the dome overhead. I stood on my toes and tried to peer through the crowd.

"What's going on?" I asked the duffer in front of me.

"There is a lift."

I looked at the Guv. "A lift, in a private residence. Imagine that. Have you ever been in one?"

"No," Barker stated.

"Nor I," I replied. "I've tried to avoid them. I have no wish to plummet to the basement. Is there a set of stairs available?"

"I don't see one," he said, which meant there probably wasn't.

One could have stuffed a dozen workmen into the lift, but the wealthy and important must have their formality and must submit to a pecking order. It was not first come, first served. One required a *Burke's Peerage* to work out the schedule. There was a manservant there as well, looking as much like the butler at the entrance as if they were kin. The lift held six. It seemed to take an eternity, especially since the Guv and I were neither fish nor fowl. Finally, we stepped in with four gentry. The lift was a kind of cage with doors that were drawn across to lock us in. I was in the belly of the beast. The floor began to fall out from under us and a few seconds later, the cage door opened.

We stepped into the chamber. My mouth fell open when I saw what was in the cellar. It was like a stage set for an Egyptian drama, only with an endless budget. The stone walls were carved with hieroglyphics stained with washes to look ancient. In the middle of the room was an open sarcophagus with its lid beside it. It was probably genuine and lined with white silk in preparation for the mummy's body after the event. There were gold thrones filled with gold-lined trunks, vases, and vessels. I did not believe everything was genuine, but if they were reproductions they were made of gold and not plate. Standing torches encircled the room. The floor had been covered in an inch-thick layer of sand.

In the middle of the room there was an altar of limestone. A form lay upon it that I recognized, though she was beneath a sheet. You may call it playacting, you may call it the whim of a spoiled aristocrat, but it seemed as proper a place to display the mummy as one would likely find on earth. Cleopatra lay in state under that sheet. She took the wind out of the guest's sails and the coarse remarks stopped. The room was magnificent, as was she, and I could not begin to imagine the budget necessary for such a production.

"Gentlemen!" a man called at the far end of the room. The hieroglyphics-covered wall opened to reveal a gentleman's club, with dark leather chairs and a bar lined with bottles. Some of the guests were in danger of becoming sober. The men rushed toward it. Meanwhile, Barker buttonholed me and led me behind a curtain where another drama was occurring. Hennings was being arrested.

"You can't take him away!" a red-faced Lord Grayle said,

trying not to shout. "He is necessary to this spectacle. He will be performing the operation! If you take him, I swear I'll have your badge and you'll be shoveling night soil by morning."

Hennings looked utterly miserable, darbies fastened on his wrists. Poole looked resolute, Barker satisfied. Another manservant stood nearby to do whatever Grayle ordered short of murder. Perhaps even that.

"Barker, I suspect this is your doing," Grayle complained. "You have thwarted me at every turn. I so wanted the ruby here, but the Palace refused. I had to make do with an imitation."

"My apologies," the Guv replied, although it was obvious he was being polite.

"Look, Inspector," Grayle continued. "I'll be responsible for him. The ceremony will take less than an hour. He cannot leave except by lift, and you may post constables there if you like. I have spent a fortune here, and I won't have my plans spoiled by an inspector from Scotland Yard. There are a number of important people here. One or two of them very important. You wouldn't want to displease the Prince of Wales, would you, Inspector?"

He nearly called Poole something unmentionable, but held his temper, not an easy thing for a peer of the realm.

"Money," Grayle said. "Do you want money? I could write a cheque. That woman, the widow, I'm sure she could use it."

"She's dead," Poole said between gritted teeth. "And don't you dare try to bribe me, or so help me, I'll put you in a cell."

"What can I do, Inspector?" he pleaded. "I'll take full responsibility. I'll even put it in writing. Mr. Hennings here will not escape. In fact, I believe this is a mistake. He wouldn't kill anyone. He's an employee of the British Museum, not a criminal."

"I'm not a judge, Your Lordship, just a public servant," Poole said with an attempt at patience. Not a fine attempt, but an attempt, at least.

"Your commissioner is a member of my club," Grayle continued. "I don't want to see you in trouble over this matter. You seem a stout fellow, with many years of experience. An hour, I ask. Just sixty minutes."

Terence Poole wavered. The commissioner was another matter entirely.

"Very well, sir," he agreed. "Against my better judgment, I'll allow you one hour, and not a minute longer. I shall stay close to the suspect, however. I would be much aggrieved if Mr. Hennings escapes. I believe he's as complicit in the murder as Reggie was."

Grayle's face was suddenly wreathed in a smile. "You won't regret it, Inspector Poole."

I gave Grayle ten house points for remembering the name. Poole unlocked Hennings's restraints and we made our way into the gentlemen's lounge. Maids in black dresses and starched white aprons were serving drinks and avoiding overtures from the men. The chairs were tufted leather, the tables oriental. The bar was mahogany, and every liquor I'd ever heard of was represented. The men had gotten over their somber mood and were becoming boisterous again. Then a gong sounded. It was time to get the festivities under way. At a word, everyone finished their drinks and crushed out their barely smoked Dunhills and we all returned to the chamber.

"Gentlemen!" Lord Grayle cried. "Tonight you will be part of an event that years from now you will tell your grandchildren about. It is a once-in-a-lifetime, no, it is a once-ever event. Tonight we shall examine in detail the mortal remains of Cleopatra herself, consort of Julius Caesar and Mark Antony. A temptress of ancient times, and we shall unwrap her. You will even have the opportunity to take home a piece of her wrappings."

There was a murmur from the audience. Gentlemen were smiling in anticipation, from the youngest blades to those with long, grizzled beards.

"Gentlemen, you may have heard of the so-called mummy parties of our fathers, which were little more than random unwrapping and merrymaking. Heads were removed and the bodies made to dance about. Tonight, we have the head of the Egyptology Department from the British Museum, Dr. Clive Hennings, who will be examining the mummy of Cleopatra and explaining his findings as he does so."

I glanced about the room. A few men looked disappointed. They'd have preferred the head removal and the carrying her about.

"See here, gentlemen," Hennings began. "The great seductress of her age, the beauty of all beauties, the female pharaoh! She died in 30 B.C. and she lies before us now. Most of her beauty is gone, but she is still an arresting sight. Some have even stated that she has a hypnotic control over men. I give you Cleopatra, Queen of the Nile!"

He pulled back the sheet. She lay as brown as a nut on the white fabric. Her wig had been splayed so that the russet plates encircled her head like a halo. She looked solemn and calm, even dignified. The crowd gave a gasp, a hundred men at once. A hundred and one if one counted Terence Poole.

At this point Grayle clapped his hands and a maid entered pushing a tray on wheels, the kind one finds in surgeries during an operation. A crisp linen cloth lay atop it, covered in instruments. From where I could see, there were both modern and ancient tools. We were behind the stage with Poole. The maid looped and tied a white surgical apron around Hennings. Then she helped him into white gloves. The archeologist moved beside the supine mummy, ready to begin the examination, with the maid as his assistant. He pointed to a crude knife with a handle wrapped in old leather in danger of crumbling to bits. The girl lifted it in the air for all to see.

"This is an actual Egyptian knife used in the process of mummification," Hennings continued. "The blade is obsidian, and the leather is believed to be water buffalo. It is over two thousand years old. We will now cut through the wrappings. Come closer, gentlemen. Let us begin."

The maid turned with the knife and suddenly jammed the blade into Hennings's ample stomach. She drew it out and over her head, spattering the men in the front with blood. Hennings was astonished, as was Grayle and all the rest of us. Poole put a hand over his mouth.

The maid screeched, her voice echoing loudly in the chamber. I knew that screech. I'd heard it before.

"My god!" I cried. "It's Mrs. Addison!"

She turned toward us. I was right. Her hair was pulled back into a bun under a pert white mobcap, but I recognized her just the same. She plunged the knife into him again and again as he let out a horrific scream. She tried to slash at Hennings's throat. She stabbed at his arms and shoulders. His face was covered in blood a second time, spraying from his arteries.

Poole knocked me aside and flew by. He tackled the young woman, but she stabbed him in the shoulder. Then Barker joined in, seizing her from behind. She gave another bloodcurdling scream and tried to turn and cut him as well, so I jumped in and gripped her right wrist, which held the ancient blade. She bellowed in frustration. I could not believe what strength she had in her limbs. It was powered by madness. God only knew what she had endured. She must have realized that Hennings was complicit in her husband's murder. He had given him up to Reggie Cargill in exchange for paying off his debt.

By then Poole, Barker, and I had her by the waist. She dropped her weapon, and the ancient blade was kicked across the chamber. She was unarmed but still immensely powerful. Now it was only a matter of letting her wear herself down. Meanwhile, Hennings had collapsed into Lord Grayle's arms, bleeding from no fewer than six wounds.

Grayle was pale and perspiring, his eyes starting from his head. His night, his plans, his life was spinning out of control. The crowd was yelling and everyone ran about in panic. The elevator had shut behind the fastest men. Now the rest would have to wait until it descended again, with a madwoman in the room, screaming for murder.

Elizabeth Addison turned suddenly and shook off all three of us. We had tackled men twice her size and they had not managed that feat. As she did so, her arm knocked into one of the standing torches that circled the room. It toppled toward the slab. Lord Grayle himself gave a scream as the torch fell onto the sheet and ignited it. The mummy underneath caught fire like a bale of straw. Grayle threw Hennings aside so that his head bounced upon the floor, where he lay dead. He tried to stop the fire but only flailed his arms around it. The body burned to ash in a minute or two. Cleopatra was gone in a puff of smoke.

I stepped away from the flames and glanced about. The men in the chamber, peers, MPs, even members of the Royal Family, were in a panic, each of them looking in a different direction for escape as the smoke rose to the ceiling. A madwoman was one thing, a fire in a sealed room another. Finally, they seemed to move as one toward the single elevator. The royal party disappeared, so I assumed there had been a secret staircase.

The elevator arrived, but the first few had to contend with five constables bursting into the chamber. They saw the woman in the sand, raving and thrashing with an inspector and two enquiry agents atop her, and came to give assistance. One slapped bracelets on her wrists, another on her thin ankles. After that the spirit went out of her, or at least became internal. She ceased to thrash and caterwaul and just lay on the floor with her cheek and hair covered in sand. Her starched apron was red with gore.

We sat on the floor, as we had outside the Body Room, our limbs crossed. We were breathing hard, even Cyrus Barker.

"Won't forget that for a while," Poole quipped.

Lord Grayle was bent over the altar, sifting blackened bits of bone and ash. He looked broken. He'd worked hard and spent a great amount to impress his friends, and all for naught. But then, he'd promised them a spectacle and had delivered spectacularly.

Poole issued orders to the constables. They lifted Elizabeth Addison and carried her out of the room, struggling and raving.

"Be careful!" Poole called after. "She may bite your ear off!"

The last few guests squeezed into the elevator after it returned. One could read the scene before us on the floor: footprints going in every direction, spattered blood, the sand churned from the thrashing, and sand mixed with black dust from a queen destroyed by the most ancient of scourges, fire.

"She was so meek!" the inspector said of Mrs. Addison. "Who would have thought she'd have it in her."

"Where are you taking her?" Barker asked.

"To Blessington Station," he replied. "We'll commandeer a guard van to take her back to London. It's Colney Hatch for her."

"I can't believe she survived a midwinter jump into the Thames," Barker rumbled.

We watched as some of Grayle's servants tended to him. His clothes were covered in ash.

Slowly, they guided him away, like an octogenarian. I looked about as the fire burned itself out. We watched as they lifted the body of Clive Hennings. His surgical coat was soaked with gouts of blood.

Meanwhile, Poole opened a small cigar case, and everyone took a cigarillo. I don't actually smoke, and Barker probably had a pipe and tobacco in his pocket, but we all lit, and sat, and smoked for a while, letting the ash from our cigars fall in the sand.

CHAPTER 29

We were on a late train bound for London once more. Terence Poole had commandeered a railway compartment. Mrs. Addison was in the guard van, guarded by the constables who had carried her off. Poole's wound was being dressed by one of them. We settled back into our seats and waited for the rhythmic movement of the train as it pulled away from the station.

"What a calamity," Poole remarked. "I may lose my rank over this."

"Did Grayle convince you to let Hennings participate in the ceremony?" Barker asked.

"You know he practically ordered me to let him go."

"There you are, then," the Guv said. "Lord Grayle, a member of Parliament, commanded you to not arrest Hennings yet. The commissioner should understand the difficulties of working with a peer of the realm. He's been in the same position before."

"Perhaps," Poole muttered, unconvinced.

"If it helps I can speak to Munro on your behalf, or I can write a letter."

"I was doing my best to keep your name out of it," Poole argued. "It would have to be you who wrestled her to the ground."

"How were you to know a maid would seize a knife and began stabbing people?" I asked. "It's not your fault. If your superiors expect you to be omniscient, you're in the wrong profession."

"I've thought that myself many a time," Terry replied, removing his bowler and unbuttoning his coat in the warmth of the carriage. "We've got a short ride, gentlemen. Soup to nuts, how did this entire thing happen?"

"Addison found the stone," I answered. "He planned to take it to Hennings but thought better of it and took it to his friend, Grant, instead. Addison went to Hennings's home and told him of the discovery, everything but the nature of the object he found."

Barker held up a finger.

"No," he said. "He told him exactly what he found, just not where it was. Hennings sent him on his way with a promise to meet him in the morning."

"Right," I said. "But Hennings owed Cargill over five hundred pounds and was being menaced by his son's gang. His life was in danger, but a jewel would square them, so he told Reggie where Phillip Addison lived and they took him in the street, not far from his home."

"So, Reggie killed Addison and tossed him into the Thames," Poole stated.

"No, he killed him and gave him to Coffee John, who dumped the body in Limehouse Reach."

"None of the gang has admitted it yet, so none have corroborated this information," Poole argued.

"Now's the time for you to question all of Reggie Cargill's men. I'm sure they'll confess."

Poole nodded. "The Thames Division suspects the body had to have been deposited by Millwall or Limehouse or it would have been seen earlier. People are out on the river at all hours, and Addison's white shirt was like a flag. It would definitely have been noticed if the body floated through the City and Whitechapel."

"The fact that it was found in Millwall was proof that the Tweed Cap Gang were a formidable gang, capable of doing anything," Barker said. "Reggie Cargill was hoping to get out from under his father's umbrella."

"So," Inspector Poole continued, "the body is found while they hide out for a few days in Millwall, and they get into a tussle with the local lads. Meanwhile, the missus hires you to look into her husband's death."

"Reggie must have had us followed," I said. "Because he knew who I was."

"I don't think Reggie Cargill was the greatest thinker in London," the inspector stated.

"Nor do I," I said. "I'm the one who shot him in the foot."

"No!" Poole said, breaking into a grin. "Wish I'd been there to see that. Did he pull out his knife?"

"They all did, and the only way I could stop him was to shoot him. I imagine he's more accustomed to giving pain than receiving it."

"Aye," Barker put in. "I doubt he'd have led the gang if his father hadn't financed it. He was impulsive and made poor decisions, while Cargill is a brilliant man in his own way and clawed his way to where he is today. The son had been spoiled his entire life and didn't acquire any of his father's skills."

"Who killed Coffee John, then?" Poole asked.

"Reggie Cargill killed him because Coffee John tried to extort him or turn him in for Addison's murder," Barker said. "It was easier to kill him than buy his silence. It's likely he was also responsible for my assistant's death ten years ago."

Poole scratched his head. "How did you work out that Hennings was responsible for Addison's death?"

"I heard him use the phrase 'long odds,'" the Guv said. "An archaeologist would not know that phrase, but a man who bet on the horses certainly would."

"Was Grayle involved?" I asked.

"Nay," Barker said. "I may have said in the past that he'd do anything to acquire a treasure, but I believe even he has limits. He spends lavishly but he doesn't cheat, and he doesn't murder."

"You two sound almost like mates, Cyrus." The Scotland Yard detective smiled.

"No thank you, Terry," Barker replied. "He's odious, but wealthy. Not the type I'd want to share an evening with, the current one notwithstanding, of course. That was business."

"I hate to tell you that your possession of the jewel will be a matter of public record," Poole said. "Grayle will find out that you could have laid your hands on the jewel at any time."

"Not at any time," Barker corrected. "The government had possession of it, and I had no idea where they took it."

"So you didn't lie when you said you didn't know where it was," I exclaimed.

"No," Barker said. "I went to Buckingham Palace and had it delivered to the Queen's secretary, Ponsonby. He was anxious to hear where it came from."

Poole laughed. "Clever, Cyrus. You should have been a solicitor."

"I prefer not to lie," Barker replied, as if expecting a challenge.

"What's to become of Elizabeth Addison?" I asked.

"She committed murder and stabbed an officer of the law," Poole answered. "She'll end her days in Bethlehem asylum or Burberry. The first, if she's lucky."

"Her sister must be told the news," the Guv said. "She assumed Elizabeth was dead."

"How do you suppose Mrs. Addison knew that Hennings killed her husband?" I asked.

"I imagine she's been trailing him since she jumped from the bridge," the Guv said. "She'd worked out who her husband's killer was and decided to get her revenge. She was more ruthless than I realized."

"Where'd she get the money?" Poole asked.

Barker removed his bowler and ran a hand over his hair.

"You're suggesting her sister may have helped her in some way?" he asked.

Poole shrugged. "I don't know that for certain, but Mrs. Porter may have given her sister the funds to do her own investigation."

"Perhaps," the Guv said, settling his hat again. "I would not charge her as an accessory."

"I might," Poole added.

"That is your prerogative, Terry."

"Yes, it is. We'll see how this matter ends and what Mrs. Addison has to say for herself."

Poole looked at the Guv. "All right, Cyrus. What are you thinking?"

"I was thinking that what we may take for a blessing can be a curse. Addison found a jewel, the making of his career, but was killed within a few hours because of it."

The train slowed with a squeal of brakes. We were in London again. It was nearing midnight. Barker and I were all in, but Poole had to collect a squad of constables and a vehicle to take Elizabeth Addison to a cell in Colney Hatch. My last view of her was a memorable one. Her hair wild, her eyes sunken, her beauty vanished. It occurred to me she might have preferred the scaffold.

EPILOGUE

With Elizabeth Addison's arrest, the matter was completed. At our request, Bram Cusp was the barrister, but there was little to be done for her. She was sentenced to three years in Bethlehem Hospital. It sounded quite harsh, but the facilities had improved since the infamous days of "Bedlam," enough that it was no better or worse than any other mental facility in London and far better than the infamous Burberry to the southwest. However, after being placed in Colney Hatch, she slipped into a state of catatonia from which she never recovered.

There was no public connection made between the death of Phillip Addison and Clive Hennings. London's most illustrious newspapers did not mention Mrs. Addison's name, or contain any explanation beyond the fact that a madwoman had killed Hennings, leaving that for the gutter press. Neither he nor Addison were given credit for one of the greatest archeological finds of the century, even if it was discovered in the center of London, rather than a tomb in Egypt.

An arrangement was made between the Crown and the British Museum regarding the Heart of the Nile. What it was precisely was not revealed to the public. The museum was allowed to exhibit the ruby in a glass case surrounded by numerous guards for a few weeks every few years. Otherwise, the stone was kept among the Crown Jewels in the Tower of London. The spinel was cut in an unfaceted heart shape, but not by my friend Ira Moskowitz's company. I saw it once as a visitor to the tower when I went to see a friend who was a Yeoman of the Guard. The stone did not sparkle, but on its small, black velvet pillow it seemed to glow from within. I found no pleasure in seeing it again. I believed Barker when he said that such a stone left death in its wake. It had already caused four deaths in a week.

As per usual, Lord Grayle landed on his feet like the proverbial cat. He took Cleopatra's ashes and put them in a cupric jar of finest alabaster, with a royal female's head atop it. The skull was buffed and polished until it gleamed white and was set on a stand in his ornate cellar, free from any protection. Once it was on display in his private museum, Grayle lost all interest in it and turned to his next acquisition, a map supposedly leading to King Solomon's Mines.

Inspector Poole somehow managed to receive both a citation and a reprimand for what occurred in the cellar of Grayle's estate. No one with a title in front of his name was injured, and many believed the matter was a stunt and jolly good fun. The event had been secret, which meant half of London knew by morning, though the news never reached the newspapers.

Edward Maund Thompson left the directorship of the British Museum within a few weeks. I suspected he was asked to resign by the board over the handling of matters that had involved us. However, he was knighted by Easter, so I didn't feel sorry for his predicament.

In my opinion, Flinders Petrie got it wrong, but the poor man's hands were tied. I believe the mummy was Cleopatra VII, lover of Mark Antony and Julius Caesar and murderess of her two brothers and sister. What's more, I think he believed it as well. She lost her ruby, but instead it was passed on to another female monarch, which I found fitting.

Flinders Petrie became a highly successful Egyptologist and revolutionized the field with his pioneering systematic methodology. Potsherds gained more respect and attention thanks to him. He was given a chair at the University of London, and his book, *Methods and Aims in Archeology*, sold well. I tried unsuccessfully to get through it.

With his access restored and a minor position offered him at the British Museum, Liam Grant was the happiest of men. He was so content, in fact, that he was able to leave Russell Square once in a great while, thereby falling into a trap set by my wife, who introduced him to her aunt Lydia, a spinster.

Lastly, the dream I told Andrew Cullen Davis was turned by him into a short story that was successful and well received. People stood in queues to purchase the magazine issue in which the story appeared, and I heard it was published successfully in Europe and America as well. That tore the plaster off, I can tell you. I vowed never again to give away a story to a writer. *Perhaps*, I thought, *I should set them down myself.*

As for Barker and I, we bowled into Whitehall Street the following Monday at a quarter to eight. Jenkins was waiting for us in front of the door, his arms full of the daily newspapers. We walked in, he distributing the papers while I made a fire in the grate. Afterward, I looked at the front page of *The Illustrated Police News* and saw there was no mention of the events that had occurred the previous Saturday night.

Opening my drawer, I placed a piece of stationery on my desk, pulled the inkwell closer, and began an account of the events at Lord Grayle's, including the attendees and all my impressions of what I had seen. When that was done, I lifted the Hammond onto my desk, slipped a sheet of paper into it, and began to type.

When I finished, I read over my account, satisfied. I put it in a folder along with my original notes and set it on the corner of Barker's desk. Then I stretched my arms while Big Ben tolled nine times in the distance. Barker was buried behind the morning edition of *The Times*. He suddenly harrumphed.

"Take one step in the direction of those Charing Cross book stalls and I'll sack you," he growled.

"We've been over this," I replied. "You can't sack me. I am a partner."

"Don't tempt me."

I returned to my chair and sat.

"Blast," I murmured.

ACKNOWLEDGMENTS

The book that you're holding in your hands right now is the product of a great deal of work and I am indebted to all those who help make it happen.

First, I'd like to thank my agent, Maria Carvainis. She and I have worked together through fourteen novels now, and I can't imagine doing this without her. Her advice and friendship over the years has been invaluable to me.

My editor, Keith Kahla, offers encouragement, inspiration, and critical feedback, which I greatly appreciate. In fact, the whole team at Minotaur is exceptional, with a special shout-out to Alice Pfeiffer and Hector DeJean. All of you make this process a great deal of fun.

My wife, Julia, has been my partner in crime from the beginning and takes Barker and Llewelyn as seriously as I do. She's my first reader and Barker's conscience, all in one. Thanks also to my daughters, Caitlin and Heather, who are the best cheer-leaders a writer could have.

And finally, many thanks to you, my readers, who invest your energy and enthusiasm into our daring duo. As always, your kind words make it all worthwhile.

WILL THOMAS is the author of the critically acclaimed Cyrus Barker and Thomas Llewellyn series, including *Some Danger Involved, Fatal Enquiry,* and, most recently, *Death and Glory.* He lives in Oklahoma.

"For fans of Victorian-era thrillers, who will find the rich aroma from Barker's meerschaum pipe

THOROUGHLY INTOXICATING."

—*Booklist*

AVAILABLE NOW (*Fatal Enquiry, Anatomy of Evil, Hell Bay, Old Scores, Blood Is Blood, Lethal Pursuit, Dance with Death, Fierce Poison, Heart of the Nile, Death and Glory*)